More Praise for

THE CITY OF DEVI

"Combines, in a magician's feat, the thrill of Bollywood with the pull of a thriller. Set in a city at the brink of the end, this is a fiercely imagined story of three souls haunted by a love that will change their most elemental ideas of identity. Manil Suri's bravest and most passionate book." —Kiran Desai

"*The City of Devi* is so exuberant and sexy, one may wish to purchase a prophylactic alongside it. When the world comes to an end, I will spend my last days in Mumbai clutching a copy of Manil Suri's dazzling epic." —Gary Shteyngart

"A pleasure to read. . . . Fascinating for its precision and detail." — *Daily Beast*

"Wild, kaleidoscopic . . . dazzling." —*Cleveland Plain Dealer*

"Suri's prose is reason enough to pick up the book, but what ultimately makes the reader turn the pages is the intertwined destinies of the three characters." —*Seattle Times*

"By daringly yoking erotic longing with terrorism in a trinitarian tale of amped-up mythology and end-of-world chaos, Suri forges an incendiary love story and provocative improvisation on India's monumental epics." —*Booklist*

"Stanley Kubrick's celebrated 1964 satire on the atomic bomb, *Dr Strangelove*, famously ends with the eponymous character stepping out of a wheelchair, thrilled that he can suddenly walk. As he does so, mushroom clouds erupt to the romantic strains of 'We'll Meet Again.' The Mumbai depicted in Manil Suri's third novel swells under the promise of nuclear attack with the same mixture of bombast, absurdity, and yearning. To this, add the melodrama of Bollywood, the vicious theatricality of organised religion, the carnality of a love that dare not speak its name, and you have a devilish, enjoyable carousel of a novel. . . . Consuming, passionate, and ultimately poignant."

—*Guardian* (UK)

"An extravagant and warm-hearted romantic comedy. . . . Suri's novel is written in vivid, cornucopian prose." —*Sunday Times* (UK)

"Clear and distinct, like the solo movements of a duet, Sarita and Jaz's individual tales of love and longing provide a multidimensional look at courtship and resolve, presenting how devotion persists even as the sky is falling." —Straight.com (Vancouver)

"We find in Suri a major novelist of rare accomplishment."

—*Baltimore City Paper*

"Imaginatively hypnotic . . . provocatively existential. . . . Suri's work is prophetic, foreboding, but remains equally hopeful. . . . This is a seminal undertaking—instructive, inspirational and timely; a tour de force that speaks volumes of mankind's imminent fate."

—*Kaieteur News* (Guyana)

"[Suri] creates flights of fiction that culminate finally in a gripping and impressive novel and prove him to be a master storyteller."

—*India Today*

ALSO BY

MANIL SURI

THE DEATH OF VISHNU

THE AGE OF SHIVA

W. W. NORTON & COMPANY | NEW YORK • LONDON

THE CITY OF DEVI

MANIL SURI

For information about permission to reproduce selections from this book,
write to Permissions, W. W. Norton & Company, Inc.,
500 Fifth Avenue, New York, NY 10110

For information about special discounts for bulk purchases, please contact
W. W. Norton Special Sales at specialsales@wwnorton.com or 800-233-4830

Manufacturing by Courier Westford
Book design by Barbara Bachman
Map by Adrian Kitzinger
Production manager: Devon Zahn

Library of Congress Cataloging-in-Publication Data

Suri, Manil.
The city of Devi / Manil Suri. — First edition.
pages cm
ISBN 978-0-393-08875-5 (hardcover)
1. Women statisticians—Fiction. 2. Triangles (Interpersonal relations)—
Fiction. 3. Ethnic conflict—South Asia—Fiction. 4. Nuclear warfare—
Fiction. 5. Bombay (India)—Fiction. I. Title.
PS3569.U725C58 2013
813'.54—dc23

2012041805

ISBN 978-0-393-34681-7 pbk.

W. W. Norton & Company, Inc., 500 Fifth Avenue, New York, N.Y. 10110
www.wwnorton.com

W. W. Norton & Company Ltd., Castle House, 75/76 Wells Street, London
W1T 3QT

1 2 3 4 5 6 7 8 9 0

for Larry

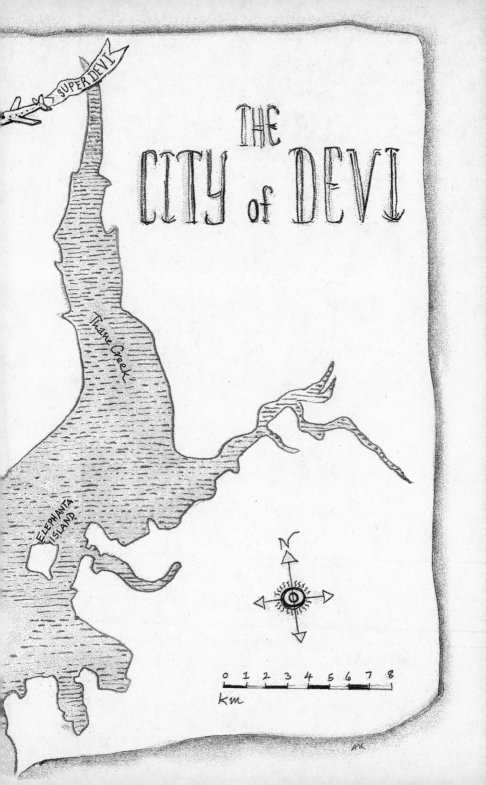

SARITA

1

FOUR DAYS BEFORE THE BOMB THAT IS SUPPOSED TO OBLIT-erate Bombay and kill us all, I stand in the ruins of Crawford Market, haggling with the lone remaining fruit seller over the price of the pomegranate in my hand.

"Is five hundred rupees not an outrageous price already? Why won't you sell it to me for five hundred?"

"Look at what's happening around you, memsahib. Do you think the orchards are overflowing with pomegranates? Do you think the lorries are driving into Mumbai every day and filling the markets with fruit? I'm only asking for a thousand because it's you, memsahib, but even three times that wouldn't be too much for this last piece. Which really was the best one in the pile to begin with."

I look at the sign for Crawford Market behind me, still smoldering from last night's air raid (or has it simply been another terrorist bomb?). All around are shops gutted in the fire. Remains of baskets lie scattered on the ground, pieces of fruit too charred for the scavengers to steal rest at my feet. I notice a tangerine that still has its characteristic knob at the top—it has been roasted to a black, perfectly whole crisp. Down the corridor, only one other stall stands intact—a spice merchant who has also somehow escaped the attack. He is using a stick to try and rouse the carcass of a dog that has died in front of his store.

The fruitwalla has a point. Supply and demand, he has me where he wants. This much I know: I must have the pomegranate before I begin my quest—some instinct deep inside insists it's my best shot. But what's tied into the folds of the silk dupatta around my neck is a few hundred less than the fruitwalla wants.

"Bhaiyya, listen," I try once more. "They're dropping the atom bomb this week. Atom bomb, you understand, not some firecracker that's demolished the market around you. On Bombay. Mumbai. Whatever you call it, the city's going to be finished. What would you do even if you *did* manage to squeeze out the extra money from someone? Take it to heaven with you? And what if nobody else came to your store?—most of the city has fled, you know. Is this what you want to happen to your fruit?" I nudge the tangerine with my foot, and it crumbles into ash.

But the fruitwalla is adamant, he won't sell for less. "It's all up to Devi ma's grace," he says. "She's the city's patron goddess, after all. Now that she's appeared in our midst, perhaps she'll save us, who knows? But even if she doesn't, even if she only lets me hold the money for ten minutes, at least I'll have it for that much time. At least I'll die with an offering for her in my hand."

Suddenly, the futility of what I am trying to do overwhelms me—how ridiculous to put such hopes in a pomegranate! I look at the smoke billowing out of the buildings in the distance and smell the soot that hangs everywhere. The garbage collecting for days, the stench of bodies rotting in the air. Ever since I started my vigil for Karun eighteen days ago, I've kept close to my building complex, sheltered from the mayhem. Trying not to obsess over where he might be now, why he left. With the internet dying out, together with phones, radio and television, even electricity, my only news about the outside has been through tidbits from our lone remaining watchman. Seeing the devastation all around today fills me with disbelief—the city, as I knew and loved it, is gone. Somewhere towards Metro, a gun fires three times—looters, probably, executed by the police. Or perhaps by vigilantes, the police force, according to our watchman, having also fled. I wonder what would happen if I bolted—wrapped the pomegranate in my dupatta and leapt over the rubble that used to be the entrance. Would the fruitwalla run after me? Would the vigilantes fire at me as well? Surely their code of conduct must frown upon the gunning down of women?

Perhaps the fruitwalla sees the calculation on my face, because he takes the pomegranate from my hand. He eyes me carefully, and I see him appraising the mangalsutra I wear. Has it been two years already since our marriage when Karun tied it around my neck?

I run the black beads of the necklace through my fingers, I feel the gold pendant. What difference does it make if I die with or without it?—at least this way I will feel I have a chance. I take off the mangalsutra and hand it to the fruitwalla. He drops the red and heavy orb, that is to give me Karun, back into my palm.

"Five hundred more, memsahib," he cries after me, remembering that I must have at least that much money. I do not turn around.

Now that I've accomplished this goal, I'm overwhelmed by the enormity of what remains. This morning when I informed the watchman that I, too, was leaving "for a while" like most of the other residents already had, the sole imperative in my mind was to find Karun, or risk everything trying. I couldn't bear to waste another day waiting for him, not with so little time left before the promised end. Except I didn't pause to formulate a strategy—I have no game plan on how to get to him. The last time we spoke, before the phones all jammed, he called from the conference center in Bandra, several miles north. Perhaps I can take a bus, I think to myself, before remembering the roads are bereft of traffic: anything with wheels and petrol driven off in the scramble to evacuate. Even the police station near the market lies deserted, stripped of all its jeeps. My only far-fetched hope is there might still be a stray train. I decide to head towards Metro Cinema and the railway station beyond.

The art deco "Metro" sign beckons as resplendently as ever from the edge of the building, but the adjoining wall and roof have been blown off. Banks of rubble-covered seats rise from the ruins like a multiplex of just-excavated coliseums. In the lobby of the theater, arranged faceup next to each other, lie three bodies with neat bullet holes in their foreheads. They are surrounded by a TV set, a car stereo, and several cell phones, with a sign above their heads that reads, "Thief does not pay." Some passer-by has deposited flowers at their feet. Why steal a TV when there hasn't been a broadcast for so long? I think of myself laid out next to them, the pomegranate positioned as a warning above my head.

I walk along the side of the building, past the broken windows and empty frames for coming attractions. An old poster of *Superdevi* lies among the glass shards, showing the girl goddess flying triumphantly over the city's skyscrapers. I remember the throngs when the film opened on all six screens, the advance booking lines stretching around the block. How innocuous everything seemed when it was released. Who would have ever thought a movie could lead us this far?

Karun and I went some weeks after its release—it was the first movie we saw together. Sitting by his side, I sensed his shyness thicken in the dark until it hung like a scrim between us. Would he reach through it for my hand? I wondered, did he share the attraction I felt? Would we ever be like a Bollywood couple, so joyously in love that we sang in gardens, danced around parks?

Before I can lose myself in such thoughts, the air raid siren goes off.

I SQUAT IN THE DARK in the bomb shelter basement of Bombay Hospital. Fingers of sunlight reach out through boarded windows, their tips tracing patterns across the floor. The air in the room is shared by so many people, I wonder if it has any oxygen left to give. The orderlies who guard the staircase door, their nostrils flaring with affected menace each time they exhale. The khaki-clad men standing in a knot, oblivious to the smoke their beedis create. (Who are they? Taxi drivers? Surely I didn't miss taxis still plying the streets above, willing to be hailed?) The doctors snoring in their cordoned-off chairs, the nurses giggling over old film star magazines, the patients (the ones

who have managed to drag themselves down from their rooms, anyway) cursing and groaning as they try to accommodate their bodies to
the unyielding cement. I listen to their hacks and wheezes and wonder
what they are suffering from, what pestilence they empty into my air.
Strangely, all I smell is fish.

It is not quite the clean fragrance of pomfret freshly caught, when
you first slice it, or prawns, cold and pink, when you pull their shells
off. No, this has a whiff of pungency, just this side of rot, the kind that
hovers over nameless denizens displayed in the sun too long. I think
back to the crush of people that materialized out of the empty streets as
if by a magician's trick. Was there a machiwalli in the crowd? Who
managed like me to squeeze in past the iron hospital gate and the gesticulating sentries somehow? I look around the room, wondering,
absurdly, if I might make a purchase. Small misshapen creatures left
over in the machiwalli's basket, best disinfected with spices and steril-
ized in hot oil. But none of the women carries a basket. They stare back
at me—housewives, maids, saffron-clad devotees, jewelry-laden
socialites. Have they smelled it as well? Are they thinking of crisp
machi-fry too?

Ever since Karun disappeared, the only way I can distract myself is
to think about food. I reminisce about the roasted corn vendors who
used to sit along Marine Drive, the shuttered dosa shop down the
street, even the McDonald's at Colaba that fell victim to the very first
bombing raid. Puris puff and crisp in my mind as I roll out my daily
quota of chappatis made with gritty black-market flour. Imaginary
chops sizzle in cumin-scented oil as I throw a stingily measured portion of lentils yet again into the pot. No matter how hard I try, though,
my thoughts keep returning to Karun. I would gladly forsake all the
food in the world, never let it stray past my lips again, if only I could be
assured of my reunion with him.

I unwrap the pomegranate from my dupatta. I picture its juice beading on Karun's lips. His tongue wiping it off, tasting the sweet and the
sour, leaving behind a thin trace of the red. Doubt clutches at me again.

To believe in folly like this, such desperation, such old wives' tales. And yet all I need, I remind myself, is for him to remember those nights we played this game. I squeeze the pomegranate for reassurance, feel the smoothness of its skin. What made him leave so abruptly, in such an agitated state? Was it me from whom he was trying to get away? Will I ever see him again—all the disasters that could have befallen him in the eighteen days since?

I calm myself by imagining the spell taking effect. He stretches in bed, his shirt pulls up, and I notice its shadow against his skin. I pull it up higher and kiss his navel, pull it to his neck and kiss his clavicle, then rest my chin on his chest and lose myself somewhere along the line that separates his lips.

IT WAS THIS LINE that first drew me in. Not the eyes or the nose or the actual lips themselves but rather the way they rested against each other. What did the darkness between them signify? A hint of mystery? A mark of shyness? I felt an invitation there to explore what lay beyond his face, a promise of empathy I had not sensed in the scores of photographs I had evaluated over the years.

Of course I expertly scanned the other parts of the photo as well. I made sure his ears were both the same size and examined his hair for flecks of gray. I searched for scars and blemishes and found one on his chin. (A fall from a swing, perhaps—was he a daredevil still?) His eyes were set a little close together, but I didn't find the effect unappealing. He looked like a boy posing in a childhood photograph, staring just past the camera at someone for reassurance—his mother, perhaps.

I kept being pulled back to the curve. The way it rose from the corner of his mouth to outline the innocence of each lip. The way it darkened intriguingly at its midpoint before continuing on its path, as graceful and symmetric as a mathematical plot. How did it change through the course of a day? Did it widen when he laughed, twist when he was angry, smudge when he was sad? What effect would desire have on it?

"Not bad, is he?" my sister Uma said, taking the photograph from my hand. "But let me warn you right away—he's a scientist just like Anoop and the rest of them, and you know how those people are." She rolled her eyes at me, though I knew she was fairly satisfied with my brother-in-law to whom she had been married three years. "Though you, with your statistics, should be able to better relate."

I took the photograph back from her. A scientist, I thought, and imagined Karun with test tubes and microscopes, with banks of computer lights blinking in the background. Only the sheen of filing cabinets glimmered behind him in the picture. "So, do we have a fourth person for the picnic?" Uma inquired.

"Why ask me?" I replied. She could tell I was intrigued. "He's Anoop's friend—let him be the one to decide."

Uma smiled meaningfully at my mother, who sighed. She believed in old-fashioned visits by the boy to the girl's house, not these sorts of informal meetings. She had objected in the beginning, when Uma started setting up picnics and restaurant outings and once even a movie with two male colleagues. But we had already tried more formal routes without any success. The networking, the astrologers, the classified ads, all these had failed. I had approved at least a half dozen boys and came close to matrimony on three separate occasions, but a last-minute problem always intervened. The most recent match was the worst, almost permanently killing my chances: the boy's grandfather passed away just before the wedding and his family declared me inauspicious, blaming the death on me. "Who knows how long our Bunty would have survived in her shadow?" they went around saying.

Last month I turned thirty-one (though prospective matches were told twenty-eight). In a few weeks I would complete my M.A. in statistics (my second master's—I already had one in management sciences). With this latest degree, I would be not only old but also over-educated, my prospects slimmer still. My mother knew she had no choice but to agree to events like this picnic—her fear was that I might embark on yet another degree, immure myself permanently in the nunnery of college. "Do you even know what kind of family he comes from?" she asked worriedly.

"We're just meeting him for a picnic, not digging up his ancestral tree," Uma replied. "He'll be here next Sunday—if you're so worried, you can ask him yourself."

I suspected that my sister had started arranging these meetings partly out of guilt. Being younger than me by three years made it all the more awkward that I remained unmarried. "Sarita's been so busy exercising her brain that she hasn't had time for her heart, the poor thing," my mother would offer embarrassedly, by way of explanation. Except I think she had it backwards, that I buried myself in books precisely because of my lack of popularity, of romantic success. Ever since childhood, I'd been burdened with the epithet of the brainy one—perhaps I would have gladly cast off this reputation had more opportunities for fun come my way. I sometimes wished I enjoyed schoolwork less—like Uma, for instance, whose circle of friends seemed to widen each time her class rank dipped. Even my mother and she bonded over their shared phobia of algebra in ways I never could.

By the time I finished my bachelor's in statistics, I had experienced the first inklings of how lonely a future might be lying in wait. "Numbers are her friends," everyone kept repeating, as if I shrank from the prospect of two-legged company. I applied for the management master's on a lark—with only twenty students selected nationwide, the scholarship offer caught me by surprise when it came. Could this be a solution? A way to break free of the shell I'd been pigeonholed in, to enter a field that depended on human interaction as its very basis? With the added remunerative promise of participating in the great Indian economic boom, surely this was an opportunity too good to miss?

It didn't work out. The classes were interesting enough, with various simulations and case studies and theoretical management games I excelled in. But putting these lessons into practice at my textile factory internship afterwards proved disastrous. Both the workers and their supervisors instantly pegged me as a pushover—a walking, breathing catalogue of weaknesses meant to be exploited, ruthlessly and at will. The labor union leaders kept threatening to strike, the personnel staff walked out regularly over claimed slights, and an income tax official closed the place down without notice (it turned out he hadn't been bribed). I fled at the end of my fourth week, never to use my degree again.

Statistics, when I returned for a master's, was as orderly as before, as tranquil and welcoming. But I kept yearning for something more— I could not be sustained just by my love of the discipline. I envied the most driven of my classmates, the ones whose eyes lit up with compulsive interest at the very mention of Bayesian theory, who launched into animated lunchtime discussions of unbiased estimators and Markov chains. Why wasn't I as possessed as they were? Why didn't I share their obsessive desire to blaze a fiery career path across the subject's firmament? Why did I keep mooning over such mundane distractions as falling in love or getting married?

Uma diagnosed my quandary as part of a larger problem. I was too content to let things flow, not resolute enough in any goal. "This is the twenty-first century—you have to know what you want, then set upon it with everything you've got." I suppose she meant to offer herself as example—the way she aggressively pursued Anoop at college, then flaunted him as her boyfriend for four long years before finally marrying him (much to the relief of our parents). We both knew, however, that this model simply didn't fit me. Despite the same underlying proportions to our facial features and body geometry (as far as I could determine), I felt neither as attractive as Uma nor as self-confident. Wasn't this the very reason why I'd tacitly entrusted to my parents the task of fixing me up, of curing the solitude that had started shadowing me?

My sister phoned me the night before the picnic. "You'll like Karun, I think. Just a hunch married people have."

He appeared at our house at ten a.m. He was wearing black sandals, khaki pants, and a shirt of blue cotton. I did not look at him as he said hello, despite Uma's call for assertiveness. Instead, I stared at the ground as I always did on such occasions, studying the guavas and parrots painted in green on the vestibule tiles around his feet.

I did let my gaze stray. Past the leather loop encircling his big toe, where I noticed the trimness of the nail and wondered if he had (like me) pared it the night before. Up the tiny hairs on the rise of his foot, ending just before the cloth of his trousers began. One cuff somehow caught high upon itself, so that the ankle (which I noticed was hairless) lay exposed. I did not let my eyes rise further, though Uma had teased me about his tireless legs and muscular thighs, about the strength that surely lay hidden in between.

It was his lips, the way they parted, that I wanted to examine. I looked once or twice towards his mouth but his face was averted each time. I saw the navy-colored emblem of a man riding a horse on his breast pocket. He was not well-built, not like the film heroes who bared their bodies in posters around town. But his chest rose and fell appealingly as he breathed, and I thought he looked healthy. The shirt, I decided, was American (though Uma claimed later it was a knockoff).

As we prepared to leave, my mother emerged from the bathroom, wearing her pink salwaar kameez with the white tennis shoes she reserved for special occasions. "I haven't been to the beach in so long. I thought I'd get some fresh air too, if you all don't mind." Clearly, she had decided that Anoop and Uma's chaperoning would not be adequate.

At Juhu, we walked past the stalls selling cold drinks and coconuts and dosas and bhel puri, past the games where one could win talcum or a bar of soap by tossing a ring, past the men hawking toys and jewelry from sheets spread out on the sand. For the last several years, this line of commerce seemed to encroach further along the beach each time we came. Most of the palm trees I remembered bordering the beach were gone, replaced by a string of hotels and buildings. A Ferris wheel had sprouted in the distance, and closer by, a giant inflated Mickey Mouse slide loomed above the sand. At the just-opened Indica Hotel, a large sandstone figure, looking remarkably like a sari-clad Statue of Liberty, toasted the Arabian Sea with its torch from atop a turret.

We walked quite far, all the way to the Sun 'n Sand, which my mother said was once the only five-star Juhu hotel. The umbrella man still stood in his usual spot, and Uma poked around through his collection to find something less frayed. He tried to rent us two umbrellas, pointing out that we were five, but my mother paid him his twenty rupees and told him we'd all fit under one just fine.

It was a very hot day, and muggy as well, the kind when the air hovers around skin, waiting to condense into droplets of sweat. Karun sat in the umbrella's shade with my mother, and Uma and Anoop and I on the edges, craning our heads to get out of the sun. My mother took off her shoes but not the peacock blue socks underneath (socks on a woman, she had always taught us, were a sign of superior breeding). She passed around glasses of orange squash from a thermos and took several sips herself. She let Karun talk a bit about the three years he'd spent in Bombay for college, the Ph.D. he'd completed in Delhi, the job at Anoop's institute for which he'd returned. Then her questioning began.

We had been through this several times before, but never on a beach. Sometimes I wondered if my mother wallowed in this part of the job so enthusiastically because with Uma gone, she knew I was her last chance. I shifted uncomfortably as she poked and pried into Karun's past—it was a picnic, not an interrogation, I wanted to remind her. But she was experienced, delicate, always indirect in her questioning. She found out quite quickly that he was an only child, that he was thirty years old, that both his parents were dead.

"Were the legal problems very difficult to resolve?" she asked, proceeding with a careful set of questions to determine what he had inherited (the flat in Karnal, near Delhi, where he grew up, but not much by way of family wealth).

I tuned my mother out and focused instead on Karun's lips. I imagined how the corners of his mouth might draw apart when he pronounced my name. "Sarita." The crease of his lips darkening first at one spot, then another, the different syllables causing it to expand and relax. "Sa-ri-ta." How would it sound on another beach somewhere, the sand spreading around just the two of us? Would it be pleasant to hear over and over again from his lips—the tenth time, the hundredth, for the span of an entire life?

The questioning stopped at noon. The sun saved us, by shrinking the shadow until it cowered underneath the umbrella next to us. Heat swirled into the area previously shaded and my mother began sweating so profusely that she lost her single-minded train of thought. "Karun must be hungry. Let's have lunch."

"Perhaps a swim first, to work up an appetite?" Anoop asked. He laughed when Karun wondered about the Mumbai seashore being polluted. "It won't kill you. Not like a dip in the Yamuna, my Delhi friend."

"You might as well go in while the girls and I lay the food out," my mother said. Not quite convinced, Karun nodded his head.

We all watched as Anoop got up and unbuttoned his shirt, preened a little, then unzipped his pants. His chest was dark and shiny with sweaty whorls, thick hair covered his legs. Uma had complained once that he perspired a lot, had made me blush with talk of his sweat rubbing off on her thighs in bed.

Karun was slow to follow. He felt shy, I could tell, taking his clothes off in front of us. We were embarrassed as well and looked away, my mother and Uma and I. From the corner of my eye I watched him begin to pull his shirt off, waiting for the instant it covered his face. This was my cue to inspect his body, appraise any muscle he might have on his ribs, follow the line of chest hair snaking down to his thin waist. He worked the shirt free from his head, and I quickly averted my gaze, but not before catching Uma do the same.

He hesitated so long over his pants that I thought he might wear them into the water. Finally, satisfied that none of our gazes were on him, he began to undo his belt, fumble with the buttons at his waist.

I'm not sure why I did what I did. "Are those eyes in your skull or motor headlights?" my mother reprimanded me later. Perhaps it was all the times I had been through this, the number of boys to whom I had been displayed. Always told to lower my head, to never let them see the whites of my eyes. Maybe it was the novels I read—the racier Mills & Boon romances of late, Danielle Steel instructing me on international sex and sin. Uma claimed it was her dogged exhortations finally having effect, her years of summons to my killer instinct. I felt it awaken deep inside me that day—the urge to rebel, determine destiny myself.

So I looked. I stared. I caught Karun with his pants midway down his groin and studied his embarrassment with interest. He lowered his eyes at once and tried to pull his pelvis free. The red of his swimsuit shorts spilled out violently from the sheath of his trousers. He colored, he panicked, he got a foot stuck, but I didn't turn away. I stared until my mother thrust the plates angrily at me, until his pants were fully shed.

Maybe that's why he stayed in the water so long, to wash my stare off his body. We waited on the shore, shooing away a stray dog that kept returning, holding down the napkin-covered sandwiches so the wind wouldn't blow them away. At last he emerged, the water dripping from his torso, his shorts a darker red and wrinkled against his skin. Anoop dried off, then slung the towel over Karun's shoulders for him to dry himself as well. Uma offered Karun a sandwich and a paratha on a plate, which he accepted with a thanks. He talked with Anoop as he ate, he looked at Uma and my mother, but he would not catch my eye.

IT IS GETTING SO DIFFICULT to breathe that I wonder if we are all going to be asphyxiated. Are these shelters safe anyway? Wouldn't the building collapse on us if bombed? Have we congregated in this basement simply for efficiency, because it would take only a single hit to bury us all?

Of course, it hardly matters where we hide if the Pakistanis have decided to jump the gun. If their promised schedule is a ruse as people claim, and this is the day they drop the Big One.

"They can't do anything—it's all a bluff," one of the khaki-clad men scoffs. "Forget the atom bombs, even the missiles to deliver them are probably fake. All tactics to scare us, all hoaxes." They nod their heads in agreement and I notice they wear matching saffron-colored threads around their necks. The effect is unintentionally dandy, as if they've taken pains to coordinate bow ties.

"Let's not forget they're Muslim—they don't have our shastras, our Vedic knowledge. To build an atom bomb, you need centuries of scientific skills."

"Besides, we have Devi ma to protect us. Let's see them harm even a single blade of grass on our sacred land."

Is he mad? Has he glanced outside on this singed sacred land of his, checked its current horticultural state? Or has his almighty Devi just been napping through the attacks? As if the daily terrorist explosions weren't enough (becoming just one more urban tribulation, like water shortages or corruption), for the past month and a half, we've had to contend with Pakistani air raids as well. The hollowness of his bluster must catch up, because he sobers. "It's October fifteenth today—the nineteenth is just four days away."

The rumors began soon after the war did, at the end of August. At first, they seemed like the usual saber rattling—hadn't Pakistan been sporadically ballyhooing its nuclear capabilities ever since the 2002 standoff? "It happens whenever they feel the need to bolster their own self-confidence—like now," my father said. For months, Pakistan had blustered about the unprecedented atrocities against Muslims in India, threatening military action but shying away from an actual strike. "Too bad they can't openly trumpet their achievements—all the terrorists they've sent in instead." Finally, with its prestige plummeting to humiliating depths, Pakistan was forced to ask China for help (a move the Pakistani president vigorously denied). In a flash invasion, Chinese troops poured in through the northeast frontier—just like during Nehru's tenure in 1962, my father pointed out. Their ostensible goal this time was to claim sovereignty over a border region so obscure that even our own prime minister had trouble pronouncing its name. The Indian government lost no time miring our military in this diversionary trap, then became too concerned with loss of image to pull out when Pakistan attacked from the northwest.

Ten days into the invasion, on September 4, the UN forced a bitterly resentful and chafing China to withdraw. That very night, Uma sent me the link for the communiqués that had surfaced on the web. The first was a report from the Pakistani chief of staff to their defense minister describing the planned piggyback of their attack in conjunction with the Chinese invasion. Even I could recognize its authenticity, what with its details of the number and type of weapons used, the exact positions of deployed troops, and operational and launch times down to the second. But it was the second communiqué that had left Uma so excited. It contained an analysis of the situation after the Chinese left: since India had stronger conventional forces, nuclear retaliation would be the only option if the war continued. The attached blueprint for an attack on eight Indian cities included a range of prospective launch dates.

My parents' next-door neighbors moved out right away, announcing an indefinite stay at their Lonavla cottage. But for the most part, despite their incendiary contents, the communiqués didn't cause the expected alarm. Pakistan's strenuous assertion of the documents being fakes had little to do with this, since nobody believed the claim. (Their foreign minister furnished a similar web folio detailing a purported mirror attack on Pakistan, which both *The Times of India* and *The Indian Express* dismissed as an obvious fabrication.) What kept the waters calm was the certainty that the West would simply not allow things to proceed so far. Uma even heard a rumor that the U.S. had intervened to shore up the Pakistanis after China's departure, that the pilots and planes and unmanned drones bombing us were now American. "They're supposed to be doing this for our own good, to even out the two sides and prevent things from getting *too nuclear*."

Then, on this year's September 11 anniversary, the unthinkable happened. Dirty bombs exploded in Zurich, followed by five other cities, including London and New York. Computer viruses began their voracious conquest of the world: blackouts stretching from Los Angeles to Moscow, thirty-seven airliners sent crashing into the Atlantic in a single hour, nuclear plant meltdowns from Texas to Canada to France. Soon, the entire West appeared to shudder and yaw—Uma texted me furiously about sieges in Turkey and Denmark, a brazen attempt to invade Spain through Morocco, retaliatory massacres all over North America and Europe. Except who could tell which reports were true, whether any of these events had really occurred? The cyber attacks had also been relentlessly knocking out news and communication sources—one afternoon, as I listened, even the BBC blinked off. Overrun by hackers and unchecked by any verification of its truthfulness, the internet went gleefully rogue ("American president assassinated," "Half of Europe perishes in nuclear attacks," "UN orders extermination of all Muslims"). Even these hoaxes started to fade, though, as power failures strangled off computers around the globe.

The only certainty to emerge was that we couldn't count on the West, so embroiled in its own cataclysms now, to protect us any longer. So when a new Pakistani communiqué surfaced the day after Karun left, settling definitively on a nuclear strike as a deterrent against defeat, the panic that had remained at bay so far started escalating. The proposal went into great detail about the order and logistics of the missile launches, picking the date based on how long the country's weaponry reserves could stave off collapse in the current conventional war.

By the next day, the message had mysteriously blanketed the web— all I could pull up on my computer screen was an image of the communiqué and nothing else. My watchman was also abuzz about it—a recorded version in Hindi had gone viral over phone networks. The same phantom voice called over and over again, inflaming the computerless (but mobile-equipped) masses with the inevitability of an October 19 attack.

Uma arranged for us all to flee in my father's car almost immediately after that. "The further south, the safer—the missiles will have a harder time reaching us in Kerala or Madras." She begged me to accompany them, as did both my parents—but without Karun, how could I leave? I waited on the balcony for him every night, wondering if he had got stuck somewhere, trying to return to me. Could he breathe the same air, see the same stars, which ever since the blackout shone so exuberantly?

Perhaps the others who've stayed have similar reasons. Or perhaps they just believe themselves invincible, having survived the terrorists and enemy planes so far. They say only ten percent of us remain (how they arrived at this statistic, I have no idea)—the city looks emptier by the day. Even with phones and the internet dead from lack of electricity, the nineteenth still fires Mumbai's synapses, powers its rumor mills. The date gives order to our lives through the chaos and confusion, blinks dependably through the haze. Europe and America could exist on a different planet: we're too mesmerized by our approaching doomsday to care about theirs.

My khaki friend articulates the question that throbs in all our brains. "It's not like the Pakistanis can be trusted—who knows when they really intend to launch? Why not finish them off first—why are we taking such a chance?"

OF COURSE, NO MATTER how terrifying the threat, one can't stay high on it for too long. We've learnt to distract ourselves, to flick through magazines while waiting for the bomb. I watch as people form clusters around the room, as the curds of a social order begin to thicken and clump. A group of businessmen stakes out the center by spreading a red blanket on the ground and surrounding it by a border of footwear. They sit on the blanket with their backs to the rest of the room, talking animatedly in Gujarati and massaging their bare feet. The Maharashtrians gravitate towards the right, forming a solid block next to the area cordoned off for the medical staff, while a south Indian language (Tamil? Malayalam?) emanates from the other side of the room. A circle of saffron-clad women hovers patiently near a man with high-caste marks on his forehead, as if waiting to see whom he will select as his bride. Even the far side of the room, which resembles an abandoned chemistry laboratory with its shelves of dusty flasks and beakers, gets colonized. I make out knots of people squatting in the dark between the stacks: servants, ayahs, laborers in shorts and torn white undershirts.

Should I try to be included in a group? I could ask about getting to Bandra, to Karun—perhaps someone might help. The congregation closest to me looks particularly affluent—men in safari suits and women in silk saris lounge like cocktail party guests. All that's missing are drinks in their hands. One of the women throws back her head and laughs splendidly from deep within her throat. I notice the heavy gold bangles she wears, the two necklaces, the earrings. Is this her idea of how to dress for war? Then I see the rip in her sari, the pleats spattered with mud, and feel guilty. Maybe she is fleeing from a bombed-out house, carrying all the valuables she can. Our eyes meet, and I nod at her in sympathy. She seems to reciprocate in a half-smile, as if a full one would be too reckless, would commit her too much. Encouraged, I get up from the floor, discreetly dust myself off, and go up to stand next to her.

"The bloody rascals," the man in the tan safari suit says. "Three years we gave them work, and they walked out, the whole lot of them, the day after the war started. Nobody's interested in service anymore." With his short hair and starched mustache, he looks like a colonel.

"Least of all cooks and gangas. And don't even mention drivers," a woman who might be his wife adds. Her sari is bright red with gold paisleys embossed on the border. Could she have been interrupted on her way to a wedding?

Another man, also in a safari suit, shakes his head in despair. "I thought at least our generation was safe, that it would be the next generation, our sons and daughters, who'd have to deal with this kind of disloyalty. But even if there was a smidgen of reliability left, this war will have killed it. God knows what we can look forward to—how much these bounders will ask for once they return."

"What about you? Have all your servants fled as well?" the woman with the jewelry asks. She is still only half-smiling, still erring on the side of caution.

"Oh, there's only two of us, so we've never really needed a servant." As soon as I blurt this out, I realize my blunder. The colonel coughs, the woman's expression turns to one of frightful regret. "Though the ganga who cleans the dishes did stop coming last week."

But it's too late, I've failed the test. A pall falls over the group, and the women dab themselves with their handkerchiefs. Their gold flashes at me in reproach for setting my sights too high. I throw out my question about the train to Bandra anyway, but am greeted with silence. "We don't have much occasion to go to the suburbs," one of them finally responds. "Certainly not by train." Conversation only normalizes after I meekly edge away.

I exile myself to the far side of the room—I will enjoy the unassuming company of the beakers and flasks. A man in sneakers and jeans sidles up. I ignore his throat-clearing, his fidgeting, the flurry of movements to attract my attention. In the midst of this air raid, could he possibly be trying to pick me up? "Hello," he says, in an accent that might be an attempt to affect a film star. Despite myself, I look up.

My fears are immediately confirmed. He is handsome, with lady-killer eyes and a very flattering haircut. His body, though compact, looks like it may have gone through hours at a gym to attain such definition. He probably sees me as fair game, now that my mangalsutra is gone. I give him a short and cauterizing glare, then turn away at once.

"I'm sorry, I don't mean to bother you. I was just wondering where you—"

I walk away mid-sentence. With all the problems I'm already juggling, a proposition is the last thing I need. I find a spot to sit on the floor, making sure a moat of ayahs surrounds me, to discourage my potential Romeo.

The woman closest to me sits cross-legged with a boy in her lap. She wears a coarse cotton sari with a red and green border, looped between the legs in the style followed by washerwomen. Perhaps I should befriend her for added insurance against my would-be suitor. How worthy I would feel for crossing the class barrier—a welcome distancing from the rich socialites' nastiness. The woman's son is clad in pants frayed to the calves, and a T-shirt so dirty that the picture on it is barely visible. I peer at his chest and make out a crudely done likeness of Donald Duck.

"Why are you staring at him like an owl?" the woman asks me in Marathi. She squirts a stream of betel juice out on the ground. Flecks of betel nut stain her lips orange—I notice a quarrelsome tilt to her jaw.

Would it be terribly elitist not to acquaint myself with this woman after all? As I try to negotiate this ethical conundrum, a loud banging at the door silences the room. The orderlies look nervously at each other, their menace evaporated. They proceed up the steps where one of them fumbles with the keys. Some of the khaki-clad men pick up chairs, ready to defend us against the Pakistani threat, apparently advanced to our very door.

The lock is turned, to reveal an ebullient group of doctors and nurses. They've risen to the call of duty, they proudly announce, by sticking with an operation even after the siren sounded in the middle. I look for a stretcher bearing the patient, but they've left him upstairs in his room. His appendix is out, so he won't succumb to it, but whether or not he weathers a bomb attack isn't in their purview.

The drama successfully concluded, the orderlies return to their scowling and the khaki-clad men to their strategies of defending the motherland. I can sense the woman still staring at me—I try not to look at her, but find my gaze pulled in. Her expression is no longer hostile but a mixture of amusement and craft. "Raju, say hello to Auntie," she says, not taking her eyes off me. "Auntie wants to know who that is on your shirt."

"Bimal Batak." Bimal the duck. I remember the new coalition government's edict to mollify their loony right fringe: all cartoon characters must now have traditional Hindu names. Bugs Bunny has become "Khatmal Khargosh." Superman was first dubbed "Maha Manush," but with *Superdevi*'s success, gets by as "Supermanush." Archie and his gang have been banned altogether for being too culturally subversive.

The boy starts complaining he is hungry, and his mother's gaze falls to my lap. Too late, I realize the reason for her sudden friendliness— she has spied the pomegranate. I quickly cover it with my dupatta. "I'm hungry, too," I tell the boy, and it's true. These days I am always hungry, we all are. For now, though, I have given up on fish. Suddenly, it's Marmite I crave.

THE MORNING OF THE PICNIC, I saw my mother rummage in the fridge for things to add to the chicken. We had eaten the bird the night before in a curry—just the skeleton really, since my mother had stripped the bones clean for the sandwiches. Not quite satisfied with her pile of shredded meat, she found some leftover coriander chutney to mix in, half an onion, chopped cabbage to pass off as lettuce, and the secret ingredient without which the taste would be incomplete: a generous dollop from the jar of Marmite in the corner of the vegetable bin.

Uma and I were raised on Marmite, we craved its saltiness, its aroma, its pungency, more than chocolate or ice cream. Even a trace mixed in stimulated us to eat foods we normally abhorred. Marmite could make us overlook the blandness of cauliflower, forgive the mealiness in chickpeas. My mother always dirtied two separate spoons while adding it to a dish, so that Uma and I didn't fight afterwards over who got to lick the tar-like residue clean. I remember the day after my ninth birthday, when we found the Marmite lying open on the dining table. We took turns spooning it into our mouths, in such voluptuous quantities that we were able to actually bite into each gob. Our mother found us lolling light-headed on the ground that evening, our faces all black and sticky and smeared, the jar between us licked clean. After that, she used elaborate hiding places to store her jars (including a half-full one she forgot about in the blanket chest, which Uma only found, and polished off, several years later). She continued to hide the Marmite in the vegetable bin out of force of habit, even after we grew up.

The first bite that day on the beach was perfection—the dark yeastiness of the Marmite rose into my nostrils and swirled into my mouth. Uma appeared entranced as well, taking small nibbles of her sandwich and rolling them around slowly with her tongue. Then I looked at Karun's face and saw his dismayed expression, noticed the way he tried to gulp down his bites without chewing. In the effort to impress him, my mother had added too much.

"Everyone loves these," my mother said, taking a bite of her own sandwich and nodding in agreement with herself. "It's the secret ingredient I add. Though I can't reveal it, since then it would no longer be secret." She tittered girlishly. Karun smiled at her, then bravely swallowed.

Afterwards, we played rummy. In an effort to make Karun win, my mother kept discarding cards she thought he might need. "Such good technique and yet such unfortunate hands," she clucked, as he ignored the latest offering she laid in front of him, the ten of spades. She frowned as Uma picked up a joker from the deck and declared once again. "My daughters seem to have sucked the air dry of luck today," she remarked, hoping to end our winning streak by throwing us the evil eye. But the cards (and Uma and I) refused to cooperate. "I'm getting bored of this," my mother finally announced, as Uma counted up the points in Karun's tenth losing hand. "Why don't we try something else?"

So we switched to sweep, which wasn't much better. We played flush and gambler, and Anoop even taught us poker at my mother's insistence. No matter what we tried, Karun continued to lose.

"You're not very good, are you?" Uma remarked.

"There's more important things in life than cards," my mother snapped.

"Perhaps he'll be lucky in love," Uma leaned towards me and whispered.

Worried about Karun's losses, my mother tried to distract him by asking about his work. "Anoop says you manufacture quartz," she ventured.

"Quarks," Anoop corrected. "And Karun doesn't go around manufacturing them, he studies them."

"It's all so fascinating," she said. "That man in the wheelchair—something Hawkings—not sure if he's still alive—he'd come to India once—did you ever meet him?" Karun shook his head.

"Poor bechara, though Mrs. Dugal says not to go by his upside-down face—that he'd make mincemeat of Einstein in a match of brains—is that true?"

Uma rescued Karun from my mother's question. "What exactly are quarks?" she asked.

So Karun started talking about the building blocks of matter, the fact that even protons and neutrons could be split, the six "flavors" of quarks with names like "up" and "charm" and "strange." His face took on an expression of wonder, like that of a child transported to a zoo, a circus, an amusement park. My mother's features began to relax as well, the drowsiness from her sandwiches and parathas rose in her eyes. She struggled briefly with it before succumbing in a corner of the remaining shade. "Don't mind me, it's the heat," she murmured, stretching out and covering her face with a handkerchief. "It's very interesting, all these flavored particles—like little sweets." Soon, she was snoring politely.

"Let's all go into the water," Anoop said.

THE WOMAN WITH the boy tries to attract my attention. I do my best to ignore her, but she is too determined. "Excuse me." She tugs at my shoulder. "He really is very hungry."

I cover the pomegranate with another fold of my dupatta and close my hand protectively over it. "It's always harshest on the children." I hope the compassion in my voice will be enough to appease her.

But the war has sharpened her senses too much. Her vision can slice right through cloth and flesh—she knows the position of my pomegranate, she can probably tell me its size, its weight, the number of seeds it contains. "It's always been his favorite fruit. If you could just share it with him."

"Share what?"

"The pomegranate. The one you have in your lap." She makes the assertion loudly enough for people around us to hear. Her voice is bold and righteous, even tinged with indignation.

What am I to tell her? That I need to offer Karun the entire fruit, not one with a segment rattling around in her boy's stomach? That I have searched all of Crawford Market for it, given up my mangalsutra for this chance? That I would have liked to help her—it is not due to heartlessness or greed I will not? "It's for my baby at home," I finally lie.

"All I'm asking for is a small piece, memsahib, as one mother to another." She appraises the bulge in my lap and I can see the primitive calculation in her eyes. "There's more than enough there for two—why just save your own child, when you can also save another?"

Emboldened by his mother's words, the boy advances his small brown fingers towards my lap. "Don't touch it," I hiss at him.

"How dare you," the woman cries. "How dare you talk to my son like that." She pulls his hand back, and he bursts into tears. "Do you think we're beggars, untouchables, that you can treat him like that?" She spits next to my foot, creating a fiery orange betel juice streak on the ground. "A curse on you and a curse on your pomegranate."

People turn to look at us. The woman lifts her hands into the air towards them and begins to wail. "Look how she has insulted me. Look what selfishness the war has raked in from the gutter." A maid sitting nearby gives me a dirty look before edging away.

The woman's son keeps crying. "Pomegranate," he repeats, between sobs.

For a moment, I waver. I almost give it away. What does it matter in the grand scheme of things? We're going to be annihilated by the end of the week anyway. But then I think of Karun, standing waist-deep in the sea. The water beading on his face and neck, foam sliding down his skin. The sun is so strong that I cannot make out the expression in his eyes. From the shore behind me come the sounds of crashing waves.

BY THE TIME I got to the water's edge, Uma had already entered the waves and was cavorting with Anoop some distance away. Unlike her, I hadn't brought a swimsuit, so I pulled my salwaar up my legs as high as the openings would allow, and wrapped my dupatta around my waist. Karun stood with his back to the sun, the red of his shorts flaring in the tide. "I can only come in up to my knees," I called out to him, but the wind blew my words away.

I raised my hand against the sky to shade my eyes, but the glare from the water was too strong to make out his face. Waves broke against him, their foam encircled his waist. He stood where he was, his darkened form emerging like the statue of a deity from the sea. Didn't they used to say a woman's husband was her god, her swami, didn't people still believe a spouse embodied divinity? Was I standing on the sands on the floor of Karun's temple, were those blessings that rippled across the water from him to me?

I waded in deeper. Coconuts bobbed and rolled on the water surface, their husks black from days at sea. A wave brought in a garland of brown marigold and wrapped it around my legs. I bent down to untangle it and watched it float away towards shore. Who had offered it to the sea, and why? Had someone been born, had someone expired, was it part of a marriage ceremony? A fisherman and his bride maybe, come to solicit a blessing from Mumbadevi? The goddess after whom the city was named, who some believed made her abode in this very sea?

I waved to Karun, but he still did not acknowledge me. I could see now that he'd folded his arms across his chest, holding them close to his body as if guarding against a chill. A chill which couldn't exist, the sea being as warm as bathwater. "Karun," I called, waving again, and this time, he waved back.

But he did not come to me. I stood there, wondering whether to venture in deeper. The water had already crept up my salwaar to my waist—any further, and it might begin the climb to my chest. I imagined the ride back home on the train, my clothes sticking to my skin, the outrage on my mother's face as men crowded around to leer. I turned, half expecting her to wade in after me, all thoughts of her own clothes getting wet lost in the attempt to rescue me from shame.

Nobody stopped me. A group of children paddled by on a raft, in pursuit of a boy holding a basketball high above his head. A fully dressed woman swam purposefully through the waves, the folds of her sari ballooning around her like the whorls of a jellyfish. On the shore, I could make out the red and white segments of the umbrella under which my mother slept. In the distance, the figure of a lone child emerged from the smiling mouth of Mickey Mouse and slid down his inflated tongue.

I took another step in. A large wave, its head irate and foamy, slammed into my groin. I staggered, and for an instant wondered if I should fall. Surely then Karun would have to run to me. I would be drenched, but the distance between us would be dissolved. Would he reach into the water and pull me up in his arms?

Before I could further evaluate this ploy, he came sloshing up to me. "Do you like to swim? It's something I've loved ever since my teens."

Could this be the criterion he'd set for a spouse—someone aquatically adept? I thought back to all those wasted swimming sessions at school, spent splashing around in the shallow end of the pool. "I never did learn." The confession brought with it that sinking feeling of having skipped over a topic, only to find it on the test.

Karun contemplated me silently. "I could teach you," he finally said, and I felt myself flush. Perhaps he didn't mean more than his offer stated. But how could he not see what an intimate invitation this was to extend to an unmarried woman my age? Fortunately, a wave thundered down upon us to hide the redness of my face. I fell over backwards, felt the sea squeeze into my ears and nose, tasted salt at the back of my throat. For an instant I was completely submerged—sand swept into my sleeves and packed itself in my hair. How would I face my mother now? I wondered, imagining the men on the train ogling me in my waterlogged clothes.

The water cleared to reveal Karun's face. The wave had knocked him over as well, his body covered mine. He tried to disentangle himself, but stumbled, and fell face forward into my chest. The tip of his nose plunged into my bosom, as if trying to sniff out some scent, dark and hidden, from deep between my breasts.

He sprang back up before I could react. "Sorry," he stammered, staring pointedly away.

A volley of small waves whitened the water around our knees. He looked so perturbed, I wanted to soothe his hand in mine. "It was the tide. It's too strong." He nodded but did not turn. "Have you taught many people before how to swim?"

He raised his head and regarded me without speaking. Was he having second thoughts—could our physical contact have made him change his mind?

Perhaps Mumbadevi herself sent in the next wave to set things right. She didn't topple me, not quite, just made me stagger and thrust my hand out blindly through the foam. She knew Karun would grab for it by instinct, hold on to it so I didn't fall. Prudently, she withdrew this time, without forcing an embrace like in her clumsy previous attempt.

"The tide's a lot less rough farther out," he said, as I tried to wipe the salt water off my eyes. "They're just ripples there—they only swell into waves as they near the shore."

"It must be very deep."

"The drop is quite gradual, actually. I can take you. You just have to hold on."

Somewhere from the beach came the call of a man selling shaved ice. "Gola, gola," he cried, "limbu, pineapple, ras-bhari." I pictured the two of us sharing a raspberry gola, taking turns to suck the syrup from the ice. The line between Karun's lips getting darker with each intake, the same intense crimson as mine. When the ice was gone and only the stick remained, I would press together our lips. Not to kiss, but to see how the curves fit, his crimson aligned against mine. For who was to say this wasn't the match that really mattered, more than horoscopes and birth charts and palm lines? That the compatibility between two souls couldn't be reduced to this question of geometry, of mathematics?

"We don't have to go if you're afraid."

In truth, I was a little nervous of water, had been since my school swimming pool days. But the iceman was far away on shore, my experiment there would have to wait. "As long as you think it's safe."

"It is," he said. Then he took my hand and started swimming backwards towards the horizon, pulling me along into the ocean, past the coconuts and the garlands, past the woman with the billowing sari and the children diving into the breakers, past the point I could hear the iceman's call or touch sand with my feet, until the waves were shorn of their foamy manes and the sea swelled silently against our chins.

2

A SCUFFLE BREAKS OUT IN A CORNER OF THE BASEMENT. THE Khakis have accused a man of being Muslim, they proceed to beat him. I see a doctor swing his stethoscope above his head like a whip, two women in nurse's uniforms wield umbrellas and try to elbow their way in. Even the woman next to me does her share, hurling insults at the victim across the room. "Son of a pig sisterfucker," she says, and aims a stream of spit in the direction of the commotion.

Although aware of the city's partition along religious lines, I've never witnessed the hatred fueled by this division firsthand. I now understand the advice my watchman tried to impress upon me so emphatically this morning: only the very brave or the very foolish venture into the wrong area of town anymore. Still, this is a hospital, I feel like shouting—even if it lies in a Hindu sector, does that mean the only treatment administered to Muslims is this kind of battering? Had we been at Masina hospital in Byculla, would I be the one meted out such violent medicine instead?

They claimed this could never happen. Bombay was too cosmopolitan, its population too diverse, its communities too interdependent to ever become another Beirut or Belfast. "Just think of the financial give-and-take alone," my father would say. "Without everyone's cooperation the economy would simply dry up." He'd point to the language riots of the fifties, the communal campaigns of the sixties and seventies, the waves of bomb blasts since the early nineties that blew up hundreds as they sat in trains or buses or offices. "Bring on whatever havoc you will—the city will remain united even if the rest of the country splits apart."

For a long time, he was right—even the Pakistani guerrilla attack in 2008 seemed to only increase the city's cohesive resolve. "See these people holding hands?" he asked, at the candlelight vigil outside the still-smoking Taj Hotel. "They're neither Hindus nor Muslims, but citizens of Bombay first."

I try to summon that spirit of unity now as I listen to the screams of the man being pummeled. How could we have fallen so far so quickly? Especially when Mumbai was on the verge of becoming such a world-class metropolis? The dazzle and architectural chic of the Bandra-Worli Sea Link, the City of Devi campaign that would fast-track us to international fame—who could have predicted that the seeds of our doom lay therein? I try not to loop once more through the arc of events that's led us to our ravaged state, try to tune out the muffled crunch of metal meeting bone through cloth and skin. I must become more hard-hearted for survival's sake, learn to channel my mind back to the memory of more pleasant days.

MY MOTHER'S REACTION to the swimming lessons from Karun disappointed me. I had hoped for tantrums, for drama, perhaps even a curfew, like my parents tried to enforce on Uma when she first started spending evenings late with Anoop. "It looks like a pillowcase," my mother declared upon seeing me in my high school swimsuit. "Can't you get something that better shows off your figure?" I realized then how old thirty-one was, how dire my prospects must seem to her.

So that weekend, Uma helped me pick something suitably revealing from a boutique in Colaba. Its blue and white stripes stretched over my breasts to remind me of yacht sails, of beach umbrellas. I imagined emerging from the showers like a Danielle Steel vixen, the water trickling down my neck and beading on my bosom as I walked seductively towards Karun. But at the pool, my courage evaporated as soon as I left the locker room. I covered myself with my arms as best as I could and scurried across to the shallow end.

Karun stood against the swimming pool wall, his knees bent, so that the water lapped against his throat. Sunlight set his body ablaze, the tiles burned blue and bright all around him, ripples spread glittering towards and away from his chin. "Come in," he said. "The temperature's nice." Although his gaze flickered over my swimsuit, he didn't comment on my new nautically themed breasts.

As usual, our bodies hardly touched. Each time I thought they would, he managed to skirt contact without making it look like a purposeful move. Today, we worked on the dreaded amphibian kick—he demonstrated the entire sequence without even grazing my leg. Was it just shyness that kept us so chastely separated, or lack of interest on his part? Where was Mumbadevi to transport me back into his arms?

"You worry too much about sinking," Karun announced. "Let's try it with a life ring around your waist."

For a while I paddled around like some hapless circus animal stuck into a prop for an aquatic trick. Finally, after slipping out for the fifth time, I voiced the obvious. "Don't you think it would be better if you kept me afloat with your arms?"

He touched me then, setting his palms against my stomach, sparking off all the right chemicals in my brain. I sensed a delicacy in the way he handled me, as if, made of china, I might drop to the bottom of the pool and break. This decorum worried me—how distressing if the only outcome of these lessons turned out to be my learning to swim.

We walked over to the beach at Chowpatty afterwards. I'd waited in vain each evening for Karun to take my hand—he didn't do so today, either. More than hand-holding, though, I felt the greatest longing towards the couples sharing snacks at the food stalls. Swimming left me ravenous, but it seemed too forward to suggest we split a bhel puri or dosa.

"Should we get something to eat?" Karun asked, and I almost swooned. I steered him to the vegetable sandwiches—the safest, I figured, given the staidness he projected. "I know from the picnic how much your family adores sandwiches," he said. "But would you mind if we tried something spicier, like dosas?"

The dosas tasted so good with their fiery coconut chutney that we ordered a second round. I boldly suggested we finish with kulfi, even deciding on the flavors—mango and saffron. The kulfiwalla rolled the frozen metal cones deftly between his palms to loosen the ice cream inside. He unmolded them on the same leaf for us to share, the intimacy of which prospect made us both blush.

We strolled along the beach, scooping up bites of the kulfi from the leaf with our plastic spoons. Karun ate more of the saffron, leaving the mango for me, since it tasted better. "I haven't had kulfi on the beach like this in ages, not since my college years in Bombay." He shook his head when I asked him if he'd kept in touch with his friends from then. "They've all moved away—things never remain the same."

Of course, I really wanted to ask him about *girlfriends*—here in Bombay, or back in Delhi, or even while growing up in Karnal. But I couldn't formulate a subtle enough way to pose the question. In three days, I'd ferreted out almost no useful information—Uma and my mother were appalled at my lack of data mining skills. We talked about such neutral topics like his research in particle astrophysics (studying quark densities to understand the origins of the universe) and the reason I chose statistics (all those exotic-sounding curves, from Gaussian to gamma to chi, I sheepishly confessed, drew me in).

As I tried yet again to think of some artfully camouflaged way of bringing up the girlfriend question, Karun stopped. "Look, it's the Trimurti." He pointed to a three-headed tableau in the sand. The sculptor had already completed two of the faces and was preparing to carve the third. "Vishnu the caretaker and Shiva the destroyer—my father had an interesting take on who should occupy the final spot in the trinity."

Wary that the evening's investigative opportunities might get sidetracked again, I didn't respond. But Karun pressed on. "Go ahead, take a guess—who do you think should rightfully be called the creator of the universe?' "

"Not Brahma? Isn't he the one who blows everything out in a single breath?"

"Ah, but creation comes from the womb, not the mouth—a simple matter of anatomy, as my baji would say. So logically, the true third should be the mother goddess, Devi."

"I think your baji was just pulling your leg. It's Vishnu, Shiva, Brahma, everyone agrees."

"Not everyone. Majumdar was one of the first to point out that Brahma's inclusion wasn't quite so successful, and other scholars have agreed. The fact is, few worship Brahma—not compared to the millions of Devi followers. Just think of all the temples she has in even the remotest spots of the country."

"So we should tell sculptors everywhere to forget about Brahma, to compose their Trimurtis based on a popularity contest?"

Karun laughed. "Absolutely. In a way, it's already happened. All those paintings and statues you've probably seen—it's always Shiva fused with Vishnu, or Devi fused with Shiva, or half Vishnu, half Devi. They're always trying to complete themselves, Baji said—find the attributes they're missing, the ones they crave. Brahma rarely gets invited to enjoy such intimate couplings."

Sensing the conversation veering away on a tangent, I tried to turn things to my advantage by squeezing out more information about Karun's family. "Was he quite religious, your baji?"

"By most standards, yes, but more than religion, I think he loved mythology. He'd relate a legend to me every night—the sea of milk that churned up jewels, the giant fish Matsya who saved mankind during the flood. It was such a magical way to understand the world."

"But not a very scientific one—not the best training for a physicist."

"Actually, he often added a scientific twist. Like relating the flood in Matsya's story to actual periods on earth when the oceans rose. Or using Vishnu's incarnations—first fish, then reptile, then mammal, then man, to tell me about evolution—I still remember that."

"So he was a scientist as well?"

"No, not really, though he probably would have made an excellent one if he'd received the opportunity. Family problems forced him to leave college after the first year—he ended up as a purchaser for a construction firm. But he never lost his interest in books, his curiosity—he dabbled in so many things. Gardening, for one—we actually had a pomegranate tree growing right there on our balcony. Mythology and science were his favorites, though—he found all sorts of colorful ways to combine them. For instance, he'd say that three was the magic number of the universe, its most intrinsic configuration—not just because of the triad of primary colors or our three space dimensions, but also because of all the trinities in different religions, especially the Trimurti. He was convinced that everything derives from the basic building blocks of Vishnu, Shiva, Devi. Pseudoscience you might say, or mystical nonsense, even—but it had a charming ambitiousness to it, sort of a layman's Grand Unified Theory. Perhaps that's why I went into physics—to get the training Baji never received."

Brahma had begun to emerge from the sand, and with him, a fundamental question arose in my mind. "And what about you—do you believe at all? The religion, the mythology—did you inherit any of that from your baji?"

Karun watched the sculptor pat one of Brahma's eyebrows in place. "When I was a child, I accompanied Baji in everything. The incense, the temples, the praying—it was such an essential part of my life. But things began to change soon after he died—I began to question more, notice contradictions I couldn't reconcile. Now it would be hard to feel the same, even if I tried. Take this carving. I know people might worship it as the Trimurti but I can't help think of the individual grains of sand of which it is made. Of the multitudes of molecules and atoms and electrons in each grain, the drama being performed invisibly at the levels we don't see. A trinity of gods emerging from the sand is one way of interpreting the universe's wonders, but perhaps other, more subtle ways can explain it all more usefully."

"So you're an atheist, then?"

"I suppose I fit that old physicist cliché of equating God with the laws of the universe—who said it first, Einstein? Baji's myths, I know, will never play out before my eyes, but as metaphor, they're still enchanting. Devi emerging resplendently from the sea, these sand carvings miraculously coming to life, even Baji's obsession with the number three. Which the universe seems to endorse, he'd be pleased to know—there are exactly three generations of fundamental particles that make up everything."

He asked about my family, so I related how my mother was the religious one, how Uma claimed to be an agnostic yet went to the temple regularly, how my father, at the opposite end of the spectrum, still ranted, all these years later, against replacing the secular "Bombay" (which he was only too eager to explain came from the Portuguese for "good bay") with the goddess-inspired name "Mumbai." "As for me, I'm somewhere in between—some days I call it Bombay, other days, Mumbai; some days I pray, other days, I don't believe."

"A probabilistic approach—how very apt. A statistician through and through, I see."

"Not quite. One day I'll tell you about my disastrous management degree."

The sun had begun to turn the waves orange by the time we left the beach. Perhaps it was the imminence of the 123 bus whisking me away, like it had every evening this week, leaving me again unfulfilled about Karun's romantic background. But as we walked to the bus stop, the question eating away at my mind abruptly broke free. "Did you leave behind a girlfriend back in Delhi, Karun?" I blurted out, then stared at the ground, mortified.

"No," he replied. I couldn't tell if he'd taken offense.

I should have stopped, but something about the lurid pinkness of the evening sky goaded me on. "I'm sure you must have had many girl-friends before, though." This time, I looked up to gauge his reaction.

His face fell, as if I'd exposed a hidden inadequacy. "No, not really." He looked away, blushing. "I've never had a girlfriend."

Was that it, then? A past so uncomplicated that it could be summa-rized so succinctly? And why not? The history of my own romantic life was just as concise, containing a single entry, that too uncertain: Karun.

Something opened inside me, much deeper than the girlish fanta-sies I had indulged in until now. I felt a swell of empathy towards him—at our shared lack of worldliness, at the inexperience that linked us, at the crushing mantle of studiousness he must have labored under as well. Sweat dampened his armpits, the hair at his temples looked inexpertly trimmed, a dark ring ran along the inside of his collar. I found each detail endearing, reassuring—the less perfect he was, the less I had to be. "I've never had anyone either," I said, taking the palm of his hand in mine without thinking. "I'm glad you moved here from Delhi."

He didn't say anything, but didn't withdraw his hand either. Behind us, the sun smeared and flattened at the horizon, losing all its fire as it sank. I didn't look at him when the bus came, not trusting my face to hide the closeness I felt. Instead, I quickly squeezed his palm and clambered up the steps to the top deck. As the bus pulled away, I looked through the rear window to watch him weave through the hawkers on the pavement, the bag with his swim things swinging by its sash at his side.

THE BEATING HAS stopped for the moment. The victim lies crum-pled in a corner of the basement—from his groans I know he is still alive. The Khakis stand around, discussing what more to do to him. There is not much else to occupy them in the basement, so I know they will come up with something. A few of the children, including the one interested in my pomegranate, advance cautiously to the victim. One of them spits at him, another bounces a rock off his back. "Beat the sisterfucker," the woman next to me urges.

A doctor tries to get through, but the Khakis block his path. Nobody touches him, they snarl. "Do you hear, nobody touches the sister-fucker," the woman next to me calls out. The doctor returns to his group. At least one of us tried, even if it wasn't me, I think guiltily to myself.

Someone finds a rope. I know what comes next, and feel sick that I'm going to just sit there and let it happen. I don't want to look, but my gaze remains transfixed. At the rope being knotted into a noose, at the other end being slung over a hook in the ceiling (so conveniently placed—was someone anticipating a hanging?). The man protests unintelligibly as the Khakis drag him from the corner by his hair. I catch a glimpse of his face, it seems to have caved in—only a mass of red remains where one might have seen a nose, a mouth.

He screams as they sling the noose around his head and begin to hoist him up. His feet leave the ground, and the screams turn to gur-gles. His hands claw at his throat, then find the rope and begin to draw his body up it, so he doesn't choke.

"You fool, you forgot to tie his hands," says one of the Khakis pull-ing on the rope. The body, released, hits the ground with a thud.

They look around for more rope. The woman next to me produces some cord from her bag, "for the sisterfucker," but it's too flimsy. "Use his belt," someone shouts, but he isn't wearing one. So they rip off his pants, and for good measure, his underwear as well.

As they tie his hands with his trousers, one of them starts cursing. Apparently, the victim's not Muslim—he isn't circumcised. They decide to carry him back to his corner, where they prop him up against the wall. The noose still dangles from his neck. A Khaki tries shaking him awake to offer him a cigarette.

—

BY THE END OF MAY, I knew I had learnt to swim as well as I ever would, at least in this lifetime. I could make it to the deep end of the pool, splashing along at Karun's side, using a medley of movements that bastardized both the breast stroke and the free style. Like someone learning a foreign language without concern for pronunciation or grammar, my swimming was free of grace or fluidity—I had found the crudest way of getting across without sinking.

We went to the beach after almost every lesson, eating our way through all the snacks (except the "cholera special" fruit plate). Sometimes, we sat on the sand to admire the sunset—every third day, we watched the sculptor embark on a new carving, tossing a five-rupee coin on the cloth he spread out on the sand. Karun would elaborate on his father's own unique interpretation of the Trimurti—how Vishnu, with his sunny disposition, represented the dynamism to make things work, while Shiva personified introspection, solitude, the tendency to withdraw from life. Which left the rest of nature's attributes for Devi to embody: since she received the power to create, she was the most versatile. "Baji said one of the three usually predominates in a person's personality. He'd see a child full of fun and frolic, or mischievous like Krishna, and tell its parents, 'You've got a lively little Vishnu there.' Or call someone very dreamy, lost in his or her own little world, 'a real Shiva.'" According to his baji, people went through the world searching for their complements. "A Shiva needs a Vishnu or Devi to pull him out of his shell so he can engage with the world, a Devi depends on a Shiva or Vishnu to provide her with seed, and poor Vishnu must constantly run after Shiva and Devi to ensure the universe keeps going. More than just pairing up, though, the universe needs the union of all three. When Shiva, Vishnu, and Devi find each other, when they all coalesce as one, then and only then is the circuit of the universe complete, its true power unleashed."

"So were you his little Vishnu?"

"No, I guess I was more Shiva—too much the loner, even when little. The Vishnu in our trinity was definitely Baji himself—always on the move, always keeping my mother and me going. We'd enact out my favorite myth, where Vishnu takes the form of an enchantress to seduce Shiva into the swing of things. I'd pretend to meditate, but then roll around laughing the minute Baji sashayed by, draped in a sari."

Despite these languorous evenings, our courtship didn't advance to anything more formal, like a restaurant meal or theater outing. Karun and I did return to Juhu with Uma and Anoop, to test my new aquatic skills in the sea (a "double date," Uma called it). We chose a Sunday, the most crowded time of the week, when a mass of humanity, dark and roiling, covered the beach. An ongoing battle raged against the sea, which churned at its most ferocious, the monsoon being only a week away.

We abandoned the idea of fighting the crowds and the thundering waves in favor of trying to sneak into the outdoor swimming pool at the Indica. Krishan Patel, a Silicon Valley–returned microchip entrepreneur, had announced the hotel as a grand celebration of India's triumph in the new world order, an "awe-inspiring homage" that would showcase the entire history and roster of accomplishments of his country of birth. The exterior reflected this—turrets and crenellated parapets evoked Mughal forts and palaces, balconies with lace-like Rajput carvings floated from the sides, and the futuristic glass and steel penthouse suites even sported a few intricately chiseled gopurams, rising above doorways in the Vijaynagar style. The idea of the sari-clad Statue of Liberty replica was to *beckon* to the West, Patel said, rather than look towards it, India being the new beacon of achievement, of opportunity.

Unfortunately, the opening did not go smoothly. Critics ripped into the fusion of architectural and décor styles ("a schizophrenic monstrosity," "Shah Jehan goes to the circus," "more gaudiness and less taste than at a Gujarati wedding"), the computers for the much-hyped laser tribute to desi IT advances kept catching on fire (literally bursting into flame), and a near-riot broke out at the "Stomach of India" restaurant when Jain tourists found a chicken bone in their vegetable biryani. To top it off, Patel had apparently gone bankrupt during construction—rumor had it that the Indica had been bought up and completed by the Chinese.

None of this turned out to matter. The hotel proved such a success that already, an annex was being built in the lot behind. A busy stream of people headed to the pool through the glass doors of the atrium today. Uma strode boldly along, taking Anoop on her arm as well, but the guard challenged Karun and me to produce our guest cards, and we all ended up in the Sensex Bar, drinking coffee.

Although the quotes scrolling along the walls in keeping with the stock market theme were distracting, the tinkle of teacups and pastry tongs helped soothe out the memory of the frenetic throngs on the beach. Anoop droned on about how marvelously his own investments were faring on the Sensex index, giving us a lowdown on the profile of each company he'd picked. How different Karun was from my brother-in-law, I thought—Karun didn't say much, but I couldn't bring to mind anyone else in whose presence silence could be so comforting. Afterwards, we stopped to admire the floor-to-ceiling Hussain mural in the lobby, commemorating the Indian invention of the decimal system. An enormous polished metal torus created by a sculptor named Anish Kapoor (who Uma informed us was Indian-born and very famous abroad) floated over us, casting shadows on the floor and walls that looked like skewed zeroes. The chairs, with wide circular rims in keeping with the theme, were also designed by the same sculptor—they reminded me more of wombs than zeroes, and were very uncomfortable (though I didn't say anything). Uma wanted to check out the Indus Valley theme at 3000 B.C., the disco downstairs, but I imagined standing around in the deafening music, holding five-hundred-rupee lemonades in faux Bronze Age mugs, and declined.

"You could have been brother and sister, the way you two behaved," Uma said later. "Even two rocks in a museum would generate more sparks. What have you been doing all these evenings after swimming—sitting and staring dumbly like statues at each other?"

"His tongue doesn't have to fly a mile a minute for me to like him. It's reassuring to know we enjoy each other's company enough that we don't need to stuff each second with inanities."

"Has he even tried to kiss you yet?"

"We've held hands. That's enough for me."

"Real hand-holding, or the brother-and-sister variety?"

I didn't answer. How to make Uma understand the bond I'd discovered with Karun? The matching of our temperaments, the similarity of our history? It was precisely his tentativeness that I found so attractive, the fact that he was as insecure, as uninitiated in romance as I.

"I thought as much," Uma said, shaking her head. "All this time you've spent together, and—*nothing?* There's something not quite right."

"It's supposed to be the fashion now, I realize, but not everyone can be as brazen as you with Anoop when you were first dating."

"Well, maybe you should tell that to Mummy. That you're even more old-fashioned than she is. Do you know she's been making wedding plans already?—just yesterday she asked if Karun had an uncle or aunt who could be approached with the proposal." Uma stared thoughtfully at me. "Why don't you take the initiative yourself, try to kiss him and see?"

"Don't be ridiculous."

Once articulated, though, Uma's suggestion persisted in my mind. Why hadn't Karun tried to kiss me? I had been the first to reach for his hand—could he be again waiting for me to take the lead?

The day it happened, we almost didn't go to the pool. The air had been turgid with the scent of the monsoon all day, and by evening, there were so many layers of clouds stacked above that the sky seemed to sag under their weight. And yet, no rain fell. As I emerged from the showers, a crack opened up between the crusty edges of two clouds and for an instant, buttery sunlight seeped out.

The pool was almost empty. A group of teenage boys floated about listlessly on the shallow side like bloated seals. The lifeguard ignored the swimmers even more fastidiously than usual—he shuffled around the spectator section, pulling tarpaulins over the wooden benches. "Let's sneak up the diving tower to catch the view," I suggested.

The tower had been kept cordoned off ever since a teenager struck his head against one of the platforms on the way down some years back. As we scurried up, our feet left smudged prints on the layers of salt and dirt on the steps. The clouds overhead looked even lower than from the ground, as if climbing a little more would allow us to reach up and poke holes to release the rain. More clouds, darker than the ones above, were massed near the horizon, like cars in a traffic jam, waiting to roll in.

The view from the top was spectacular, the pool having been built right next to the sea. The arms of the city stretched out on either side of us, reaching out to embrace the bay. The water looked neither blue nor gray but some strange and violent color in between, as if plotting to rear up at an opportune moment and swallow the entire shoreline. We leaned on the railing and looked out for the monsoon, a giant ocean liner scheduled to lumber in at any moment.

"I loved the monsoon so much as a child. Baji would take me up to the terrace of our building and we'd wave at the clouds. He said there were people in them watching us, emptying buckets of rain, waving back. When his heart failed, I couldn't wait for the next monsoon, because I knew he'd be one of the people in the clouds. Even though I was eleven at the time, old enough to realize otherwise. My mother sat there in the tiny terrace shelter and watched me go back and forth in the rain, waving and waving at the clouds. It rained a lot that season, because of all the extra buckets Baji emptied, I thought, to let me know he was all right. It might sound silly, but even now I sometimes feel like waving when I see a rain cloud."

"Why don't you?"

"I do, once in a while, when nobody's watching." A wave crashed below us, and I resisted the temptation to wipe off a tear of spray on

Karun's cheek. "But one has to let go. One has to grow up and not stay attached to things. That's what my mother said, especially once her cancer was diagnosed. She told me I could remember her for one year after she died, but then had to put her out of my mind. I think she saw the danger—the way I kept yearning, kept casting around even as an adult, to fill the void after Baji. Once she was gone, she knew the void would only double."

"Were you very close?"

"It's strange, but I remember little of her while Baji lived. I know she provided a loving presence, but his intensity overshadowed us all. She only really emerged for me when our perfect triangle collapsed, degenerated into a line. That's when I began to cloister myself, when I saw her strength, her determination to pull me out of my brooding. Every once in a while, a flash of grief would dart across her face and surprise me—although she absorbed my sorrow, she never shared her own with me. I always thought—hoped, even— that she might find another Baji to inject our lives once more with energy. But to search, you need time, which she didn't have. Eventually, she had to leave me to my own devices, simply to earn enough for us to eat. By then, I'd learnt to lose myself in my studies, use my reclusion more productively."

"She sounds like she was very strong."

"She became that way—fierce, even. I suppose she had to harden herself. She was ferociously determined I be happy in life. And quite ruthless with anyone she considered out to hurt me."

"Do you suppose she would have liked me?"

"Yes, I think so."

"My mother likes you too." It wasn't quite the symmetrical response, and the awkwardness of articulating it made me blush.

Karun stared silently at the clouds, and I wondered if I had been too forward. When he spoke, he did so haltingly. "I've always envied people who know exactly what they want. I sometimes wonder if I could ever be as sure as they seem. If I could experience the feelings I'm supposed to with the same intensity. My mother knew this doubt in me—that's why she kept urging me to search for a lasting anchor in life. I think she worried that after her, I'd simply drift around, vainly trying to re-create some past ideal."

My heart started racing. Did his words hold the hint of a hidden invitation? An allusion to the very topic I had been so apprehensive about broaching? I felt as if nearing the conclusion of some game of nerves, like threading the loop over the wire, I had just a short way left to go without making a mistake.

"It's been over three years since she died—two more than the year she gave me to mourn her. Every night, I can almost hear her whispering into my ear, 'Settle down now, forget the old. Marry, have a child, build a new trinity.' I thought it would be a simple matter, but in truth, I haven't been able to follow through. Even though I've been wanting, even though I've been lonely. Perhaps it's a matter of confidence, of being sure one can fulfill the expectations from the other side. Do you know what I mean?"

I didn't. Was he letting me know, gently, of his disinterest? Declining politely before I posed the question? "Don't you want to get married?" I found myself asking, more plainly than I would have liked. Then, when Karun didn't reply, I added, "I do."

"I know."

"But you don't want to," I murmured, completing the thought for him. A huge weight seemed to lift from me as I said this. The loop had touched the wire, the buzzer had gone off to announce I had lost. The suspense was over, I could breathe in the monsoon air freely.

"It's not that I don't. There's nothing I'd like better than to belong again, be part of my own family. I think I just worry too much about not knowing how things might turn out. Sometimes when you get close to someone, they end up caring for you differently. All the certainty people have—that you have—I wish I could feel the same."

Was he trying to caution me about something? I couldn't quite decipher his warning. "One is never completely sure, of course, but one has to try."

Here was my opportunity, I knew, to follow up on Uma's advice. I closed my eyes and brought my face to his, guided only by the thought of his lips. When I neared enough to sense his breath, I pressed my mouth quickly to his. Then I withdrew noiselessly, afraid of the bird-like sound my parents made on the rare occasions they kissed. I opened my eyes, but didn't allow my gaze to climb too high up Karun's face.

Did my adventurousness put the onus on him to reciprocate? Did he really want to kiss me back, or did he feel obliged, had I embarrassed him into it? I kept my attention focused on the line that first drew me in. It darkened in the middle, then separated in two, then blurred as his mouth drew closer. If there was drama in the universe, it should have started raining at that instant, but it didn't. There should have been thunder in the background to commemorate the event, lightning to illuminate the instant of contact. I felt the swell of his lips against mine, tasted the salt from the sea on their surface. The wetness behind them felt warm and strangely personal on my tongue. Something in my mind shrank from the idea of sharing saliva, but it was precisely this intimacy—so shocking, so electrifying—that left the muscles in my throat engorged and took away my breath.

We kissed again, and this time it did begin to rain. Slowly at first, then in a majestic sweep, and then, as the wind picked up, in large sheets that billowed in from over the sea and spun and whipped around the tower. The water seeped into my hair and pelted my face, but I didn't relinquish the contact my lips engaged in. Thunder started up, slowly at first, like a deep and distant drumbeat rolling in from somewhere near the horizon. It danced over the water, coming closer all the time, as if heralding the approach of the long-awaited ocean liner, which would surely be looming right behind us if I looked. But I kept my eyes closed, and my mouth upon his, until the thunder subsided, and bells began to ring.

Except they weren't bells, but whistles, and they came not from the sea, but from the guard below. He sprinted towards the tower, waving his hands, blowing his warning angrily. Round the pool stood the teenage swimmers, forced out by the rain, jabbering and pointing at us like excited monkeys.

"We should go down," Karun whispered.

I was about to follow when the realization came to me. We had kissed, it was true, but the compact between us had not yet been sealed. There was another step needed to affirm us as a couple—a ceremony to test his commitment to me. Standing up there on the tower, amidst the drama of the clouds and the whistles and the rain, I saw it. The chance to leave our old selves behind, make the break together to be free. "No, not that way," I said. Would he care enough to accompany me?

He didn't understand until I began to edge backwards along the platform. "You can't be serious, Sarita." He stared in bewilderment as I reached the diving board. "You hardly even know how to swim."

Some of the boys below guessed my intentions as well. "Jump, jump," they shouted, as the watchman began racing up the steps two at a time.

Karun advanced towards me. "Don't go any further, Sarita, or you might fall off. Here, take my hand."

"Only if you come with me." Gingerly, I put one foot on the diving board, then the other. The rain had made it slippery, but I balanced on it, testing its stiffness, gauging how it bent under my weight. The water looked agonizingly far, like something designed for a daredevil act— visions of the boy who had struck his head and drowned flashed through my brain. It would all be worth it, I told myself, as I tried to focus on the new life awaiting.

I reached the middle of the diving board. "Grab hold of me. I'll pull you back," Karun said, and this time he managed to clasp my hand. For a moment, I almost let him bring me in. But then the watchman, whistling and gesticulating, burst upon the platform. I took an instinctive step back, and the shift in weight made me lose my balance. In the split second before I fell, I released Karun's hand, but the momentum pulled him along as well.

I'd expected the jump to be exhilarating, like riding down a glass-enclosed elevator, with breathtaking vistas of the city flashing by. Instead, blinding rain obliterated the views, the sensation of falling was petrifying. The water packed a nasty wallop as I tore through its surface, knocking the wind from my chest and, it seemed, shooting up into my very cranium.

But it didn't really matter, because when I surfaced, Karun emerged right next to me. The boys around the rim hooted and clapped as he wrapped an arm around my body. As the thunder added its own applause and the engorged clouds lavished us with blessings, Karun towed me to safety.

3

SUPERDEVI RELEASED THAT SUMMER, DELUGING EVEN NON-MOVIE people like us with its hype. The most expensive Indian film ever made, thanks to the backing of *both* Hollywood *and* the Indian mafia! Lata M. teams up for her techno comeback with Lady Gaga (who Uma said was a famous pop star)—their title duet rockets to the top of charts worldwide! And up in the sky, a bird, a jet—no, Superdevi herself, zooming overhead behind a prop plane as we sat (and tried to ignore her) on the beach at Chowpatty. Supposedly, the script borrowed extensively from *Slumdog Millionaire* and *Superman* (films which neither of us had seen) in telling the story of a young girl from the Mumbai slums with the power to assume different avatars of Devi to fight crime. Uma kept herding us to McDonald's, which was giving away all nine incarnations from the movie as collectible action figures throughout India (and parts of England and New Jersey), free with food purchases (vegetarian only, so as not to upset Hindu sentiments). She collected eight of the figures, turning off the light at home to show us how they glowed in the dark just like Superdevi. Despite foisting dozens of McAloo Tikki sandwiches on us, however, she never managed to acquire the elusive Kali incarnation (toting her AK-47 from the final battle scene).

The movie managed to surpass even the most optimistic projections. I read breathless reports in magazines of kids dragging their families to see it three and four and even ten times, of the urban youth of India finding spiritual enlightenment in Superdevi's incarnation as call center worker to fight tele-fraud, of desis in New York and London and Sydney bringing such gaggles of white friends to screenings that the film quickly spilled over to mainstream international release. A Zee TV program documented how *Superdevi* wielded its greatest power over rural India, whose citizens experienced it not as movie but as religious odyssey (calling the heroine "Ooper-devi" which translated to "Upper-devi," in several Indian languages). The reporter followed scores of villagers making pilgrimages from miles around to get the Superdevi's blessing at a small theater in Ambala, where both fire exits had been converted into Devi shrines for patrons to leave flowers, coconuts, and monetary offerings. A guard stood on stage throughout to make sure audience members didn't try to touch the Superdevi for her blessing when she appeared on screen. Perhaps the most definitive evidence of the film's popularity appeared in the calendar art sold on city streets: all the goddesses from Laxmi to Saraswati to Parvati bore striking resemblance to *Superdevi's* child heroine Baby Rinky. Even our sand sculptor abandoned his trimurtis in favor of more profitable Devi carvings.

"This is for all the potato sandwiches at McDonald's," Uma said as she handed me two tickets for a Saturday matinee at the Metro. "I know neither of you much follows movies, but with Karun's thing for mythology, it should be interesting."

Bollywood had dramatically changed since I last looked, because *Superdevi* had slick production values and expensive special effects, unlike the tacky 1970s potboilers my mother liked to watch on DVDs. But the plot seemed just as hokey, as preposterous and formulaic, and I wondered what all the fuss was about. I had difficulty keeping Superdevi's more minor incarnations separate (Cyber Devi, X-ray Devi, and Antibiotic Devi, in particular), though with most of the story revolving around schemes to destroy Mumbai, she appeared for a good part as Mumbadevi.

To my surprise, Karun enjoyed the movie much more than I did— he seemed unperturbed by the frequent suspension of logic, the willful violation of every law of physics. "I wish Baji could have seen it. He always talked about Devi coming to life." Karun's one reservation related to the Vishnu and Shiva characters who popped up in the climax to form a terrorist-exterminating threesome with Superdevi. "They should have developed those roles more, seized the opportunity to delve deeper into the concept of the Trimurti."

As expected, sitting together in the theater brought back all of Karun's shyness. After the first half hour, though, he started to relax, as if the darkness had begun to dissolve through his inhibitions. We even held hands on the armrest between us following the intermission—in fact, I got the distinct sense that he relished the element of covertness. After that, we began going to the movies regularly—his favorite theater was the Regal, which, curiously, he said he'd frequented quite often in college. When I asked him to tell me something about the films, he oddly couldn't recall much of what he'd seen.

THE KHAKIS ARE on the warpath. Their commotion plucks me from my cinema reverie and deposits me back in the hospital basement. "Look at him," their leader shouts, pointing at the man they hoisted into the air minutes ago. "Look at the condition he's in." The man tries to sink in deeper behind the bandages plastering his face. Someone has finally removed the noose around his neck—it lies coiled on the ground, waiting for another victim.

"A complete outrage. These cowardly Muslims who've almost succeeded in getting one of our own Hindu brothers killed." He does not elaborate on how, exactly, the Muslims are to blame. "I've told my men to root out every last Muslim in this room so there's never a repetition of something like this. The HRM will find them and make this shelter safe for you again."

I should have guessed from the saffron threads: the Khakis are part of the right-wing HRM, the Hindu Rashtriya Manch organization, responsible for so much of the nation's bloodshed. They fan out through the crowded basement, peering at licenses and ID cards—when unavailable, they demand to see an intact foreskin. "My driver carries all the papers," the man in the tan safari suit sniffs. "When the all-clear sounds, you're free to ask him." He sputters in outrage as a Khaki roughly grabs his belt, then staggers to the floor bleeding after receiving a corrective punch in the face.

"No, please, stop," the woman with the gold paisley sari shrieks, throwing herself over his body, as if she's been watching Bollywood movies all her life precisely in rehearsal of this move. "He's my husband, he's Hindu—we're both Hindu—look, here's my mangalsutra." A Khaki bends over to take a closer look, then rips it from her neck and holds it laughing above his head.

A figure heads towards me and I stiffen upon recognizing my would-be Romeo. Is he going to try again to strike up a conversation? Then I realize he's actually threading his way away from the line of advancing Khakis. Our gazes meet, and something flickers in his eyes—I guess at once he must be Muslim. He's almost past me, headed towards the dark recesses with the bottles and flasks, when the woman with designs on my pomegranate spots him. "Look, that sisterfucker's trying to get away. Quick, catch him!"

Within seconds, two Khakis are upon him. "Let me go," he cries as they pin his hands behind his back. The muscles strain in his arms and neck. "I'm Hindu, I tell you. My name is Gaurav."

"Why were you trying to escape?"

"I wasn't—I just thought it was darker back there—I had to urinate."

One of the Khakis fishes around in Gaurav's pockets. He finds a sheet of paper which he unfolds and stares at myopically. It's clear he can't read. "It's just an old receipt," Gaurav says.

"Where's your ID?"

"At home. I left my wallet there to keep it safe."

The Khaki smiles. "Actually, you're always carrying your ID—

you're attached to it. My colleague will take you to the back and check while you use it to urinate."

They are guffawing and twisting his arms behind to lead him back when I find myself instinctively stepping forward. Perhaps the bashed-in face of their previous victim spurs me—I cannot stand by again, cannot stomach another body getting broken and hanged. A smidgen of guilt at having treated my Romeo shabbily is also mixed in—for all I know, his designs may have been completely honorable. "I know this man. You can let him go. His name is Gaurav Pradhan."

I'm not sure from where I get the surname. The Khakis are as startled at my intervention as I am. "How do you know him?"

"He lives in my building. He's Hindu. I've run into him at Mahalaxmi temple, many times."

As they wonder whether to untwist Gaurav's arms, my nemesis, the pomegranate harridan, pipes up. "She's lying. She has to be Muslim herself—that's why she's trying to save him. He must be her *boyfriend*." She uses the English word.

"Don't listen to her. You can see I'm a married Hindu woman—look at the bindi I'm wearing."

"Anyone can take some color and draw a dot on their forehead. If you're married, then where's your mangalsutra to go along with your bindi, Muslim bitch?" She spits in my direction.

The Khakis confer with each other. The woman summons up more betel juice to aim at me. "I saw them talking to each other not five minutes ago—the sisterfucker and his Muslim whore." She squirts, remnants dribble down her chin.

One of the Khakis turns to me. "Why don't you come with us to the back? We can sort it all out there." The gleaming new interest in his eyes unsettles me. He pretends to help me by the arm through the maze of people, but his grip is so tight I can feel his fingers dig into my flesh.

As I try to figure out how to extricate myself from the danger I've foolishly put myself in, the anti-aircraft guns start up. The sound of an explosion comes from outside, followed by another. The room seems to list to one side, as if the building is tipping over, as people run towards the slatted windows to peer through. A piercing whistle-like screech draws even more gawkers, and just as everyone crowds against the wall facing the street, it explodes.

A thrill passes through my body, a wild and terrified elation: I have been bombed. Then I hear the screams, see the arms and feet sticking through the rubble. The Khakis abandon their hunting game and rush to help the victims. I join in as well, in an effort to rescue two half-buried women—the white of their dresses identifies them as nurses.

I'm helping a doctor clear more fragments of wall when I feel a mouse-like movement in my salwaar. I look down to see grubby brown fingers easing out my pomegranate. It's the boy with the Bimal Batak T-shirt. I try to seize his wrist, but he wriggles free. He scampers over the rubble towards the hole in the side of the building and I scrabble up after him. Squeezing through the opening, I follow him into the bright sunshine.

He dashes down the road, but I easily outrun him. "Leave it," I order, catching him by the collar, but he does not obey. I grab his arm as he tries to bring the pomegranate to his mouth for a bite. "Little thug," I say, and twist so hard that he screams and lets go. He spits at me as I retrieve the fruit from the ground, then flings a fistful of gravel in my direction and runs away.

I stand on the road to clear my head. Anti-aircraft fire still echoes in the distance, but I know the planes with the bombs have already flown away. Behind me lie the smoking remains of the Liberty, and I wonder if this is the enemy's strategy—to destroy all the cinemas. An ancient building down the street lies in ruins as well—perhaps its tired bones have collapsed just from the trauma of witnessing the attack.

Still numb and euphoric over my bombing and escape, I head for the Marine Lines train station.

———

KARUN AND I got married that October at the Indica. We chose a hotel at Juhu in recognition of the picnic on the day we met. Our first choice had been the Sun 'n Sand, since it cost less, but we decided to splurge since they had no dates available until February. Uma tried to get us to have a funky ceremony on the beach itself, which I nixed. Although Karun would have preferred a court wedding, he went along with the entire priest-and-seven-circle spectacle for my mother's sake.

The guests were almost entirely from my family's side. When pressed to add his own invitees to the list, Karun put down the names of some of his research institute colleagues. I had been hoping to meet his long-term friends from Delhi and Karnal, but he explained it was too far to expect them to make the trip. He didn't even have any names from his three years of college in Bombay. "I got to know some people quite well, but I've lost contact since."

His only aunt took the train down from Delhi, accompanied by his two cousins. "We never thought our Karun was one to ever get married—to such a pretty bride, no less," they said in Punjabi-flecked Hindi. "There must have been something in your Bombay water, to have so quickly cured the bachelor in him."

Uma told me she'd tried to squeeze out information about Karun's past, but his relatives didn't seem that close. She was still trying to uncover evidence of a former romantic involvement—not as something to hold against him, but purely as reassurance that he was like everyone else. "All they talked about was his studiousness, how well he did in school. His aunt said he suffered from asthma after his father passed—to cure it, he took up swimming and practiced yoga every morning for an hour."

"He still does that. Is that the best you could dredge up?"

"I'm just trying to fill in the blank pages, Sarita. Everyone's so relieved at your marrying that they've checked neither background nor character—just this mad rush to get you wed. You've told us the story about how he accompanied you in the plunge from the diving board over and over, but have you really found out enough about him to spend your life together?"

"Of course I have. His background isn't so mysterious—it's not as if he comes from a long line of murderers. And we've talked about everything under the sun—from our favorite foods to our favorite theorems in calculus." The calculus bit, a lie, I threw in just to provoke her: I was closer to Karun in educational grounding and way of thinking than she, with her history B.A., could ever hope to be with Anoop.

"But are you two really in love?"

"I wouldn't be marrying him if we weren't."

In the four months since the diving tower, Karun and I had spent a good deal of time together. In addition to our newfound interest in cinema, we'd also started trying restaurants, especially several of the new ones that seemed to open every week in the mill area. On a day-long excursion to the amusement park at Essel World, we rode the Zyclone roller coaster four times in succession at Karun's insistence, followed by an equal number of rides on the new Super Drop, based on Superdevi's descent to earth after visiting the moon goddess. Our outings always felt a bit like playing hooky, as if being in each other's company freed us from obligations, gave us dispensation to have the fun we'd never had. Karun had become both more relaxed and more expressive—by my count, we'd exchanged five "I love you's" so far.

And yet, Uma had a point. Karun rarely put his innermost feelings on display. We hugged more than we kissed. I felt enkindled by his very presence, but the most passion he ever displayed arose while discussing physics.

"What's the matter with you two?" Uma scolded us one day for passing up an opportunity to neck as we sat on the couch watching television. "Don't you know the time before marriage is the best for romance?"

As I expressed mortification afterwards for my sister's pushiness,

Karun colored. "It's I who should apologize. I'm not very good at doing what's expected. Or even realizing what I should want. Sometimes I wonder if we're being too hasty, if you know me well enough."

I laughed off his words—the possibility that he might be having second thoughts alarmed me. Of course I knew him well enough— hadn't we discussed where we'd live (Colaba), what we'd eat (home-cooked food, with lots of restaurant nights off), even how many children we'd have (exactly one—we had to create our very own trinity, after all)? Besides, didn't millions of couples enter unions arranged by their parents, knowing each other even less? "We're still not married," I responded to each of Uma's jibes. "How refreshing, for a change, to encounter someone with an excess of propriety on his part."

To her credit, Uma ceased her doubt-raising once the day of the wedding dawned. She was the perfect sister, helping me with my jewelry and headdress, leading me to the ceremonial fire, ushering people away from the receiving line when they lingered too long. "Sarita, Sarita," she chided, when I said goodbye at two A.M. to take the hotel elevator up to the third-floor bridal suite where Karun had retired earlier. "Don't you know it's the bride who's supposed to go up first, sit waiting for the groom, blushing in bed?"

The door to the bedroom was ajar—Karun reclined on the crimson sheets draping the bed. White flowers, their petals creamy and luminous, lay scattered in a circle around his head. He must have dozed off waiting for me—he hadn't taken off his pants, and even his shirt was still all crisply tucked in. Only his feet were bare—I noticed again the hairless ankle I'd glimpsed the morning we first met. This was the moment I'd imagined all evening as we stood on the dais, shaking hands and accepting envelopes filled with cash. Should I awaken him by gathering up the petals and sprinkling them on his face?

But he was not asleep. When I sat on the bed, he laid his head on my thigh. "Sarita," he murmured, and opened his eyes. They were unclouded by drowsiness—instead, I noticed the sheen of anxiety in them.

"Is everything all right?"

"Yes. Of course. It's our wedding night, why wouldn't it be? I was just resting my eyes."

He slid along the bed to make room for me, and I reclined, also fully clothed, next to him. We kissed quickly. His jaw was tight, his lips stretched—I'd never seen the line between them communicate such nervousness. "It's hard to believe we're married now, just like my parents used to be," he said.

His tenseness had a curious effect on me—it focused my attention on trying to loosen him, making me forget my own diffidence. "Did you see the priest's stomach? Just his belly button looked the size of a one-rupee coin. And when he put the camphor into the fire—it was all I could do not to sneeze." I chattered on about the food and the gifts tally and the guests, and finally got him talking about his aunt.

Rather than tension, I felt a mounting anticipation. I couldn't wait for the montage running for weeks in my mind to commence. Shedding our clothes, pressing my face into his body, feeling his kisses on my breasts. As Karun described a holiday with his cousins, I gathered up my nerve and leaned forward to arch my bosom like a bridge over his chest.

He stopped mid-sentence and lay motionless, holding his breath. Only when I unfurled my sari did he think to unhook my blouse and bra to free my breasts. I shifted my weight so that they hung like fruit over his neck. He hesitated, then leaned up to plant a kiss on each of them.

They were more chaste than I would have liked, his kisses, but I sighed my appreciation. He responded with more, apportioning them equitably between my two breasts. When I moved higher, he kissed my stomach, then stopped to wait for approval. "These wedding garments are too hot," I said. "Let's take some of them off."

The cycle of cues on my part and responses on his continued after we disrobed—me to my petticoat and Karun to his underpants. I was struck by my enterprise—what had happened to my inhibition, my lack of experience? We rubbed our bodies together—he even took a breast in his mouth with my encouragement. There was something endearing about his willingness to please but also something tempering—the thought that he might not be aroused evened out the bursts of passion I felt.

Eventually, my initiatives faltered—I ran out of places to explore. I could not summon up the courage to venture uninvited below his waist. We lay side by side caressing each other. "Let's get some rest," I finally said, when it became clear no fire would be lit tonight.

"It's been a long day. I'm sorry I'm so exhausted." He buried his face in my chest to hide his embarrassment—or perhaps relief.

I turned out the light. Somehow, I didn't feel so dejected. Although I would have liked Karun to be more assertive, I had surprised, even exhilarated, myself by taking the lead to compensate. The gentle ebb and flow of the waves outside reassured me we had many days of married life ahead.

THE ALL-CLEAR SIGNAL still hasn't sounded, which worries me. Could the control tower for the sirens have been hit? Will people realize this and begin to eventually creep out of their holes? Or will they hunker in deeper to count out their days, convinced the silence outside heralds the end? The street lies completely empty—only an abandoned red double-decker bus looms ahead. Even the beggars who live under the bridge over Queen's Road have disappeared—I miss running the gauntlet of their badgering voices, their pawing hands.

I mount the steps to the station. The way to tell whether trains still run is to examine the evidence left by citizens who have performed their business on the rails. Something has come by to flatten deposits, but not today. Walking looks like the best alternative, since there's no electricity to feed the pantographs anyway. I pick my way over the tracks to the seaward side. The lawns of the line of gymkhana clubs are so unnervingly immaculate that I wonder if they still pay their gardeners to manicure each individual blade of grass. Perhaps this is the fabled sacred land the Khaki referred to, the one he dared the enemy to harm.

Further on, though, chunks of concrete litter the sidewalk—fragments from bolsters blown out of the seawall. One of these bolsters has sailed clear across the road to smash into a building—it sticks out like a missile fired into the ruined façade. In fact, every fourth structure along Marine Drive, the city's cherished "Queen's Necklace," seems to have been bombed. Markets, theaters, and now art deco buildings—is it incompetent planning, or simply bad aim on the Americans' part? Maybe it is the Pakistanis after all.

A gash in the land cuts off my path. Waves froth through the bolsters, up the gully, all the way to the ground floor of a building that still stands. Could a bomb attack have done this, or has the earth spontaneously split apart in protest? I remember the frustratingly impersonal chats with Karun after my early swimming lessons—didn't he say such fissures may be caused by rising sea levels? A woman appears at a balcony on the top floor and shakes a bed sheet open. It unwinds down the side of the building like a large white flag, as if she is signaling her personal surrender to any planes still lingering around. I wonder how she gets up there, how she negotiates the gully and crosses the moat that surrounds her teetering building. Will she go down with it when it collapses, determined to cling onto her flat until property prices recover?

I head the other way, towards Chowpatty. The uneasy sensation of being watched prickles my neck. Could someone be following me? I spin around, but no Khakis skulk behind the lampposts. The deserted curve of Marine Drive stretches emptily into the distance, terminating at Nariman Point in a tangle of blackened skyscraper shards.

I stand there, trying to comprehend the skyline without its iconic Air India tower, when the anti-aircraft guns start up again. Shells pop unseen in the sky. My first instinct is to dive into one of the vehicles abandoned mid-road—perhaps the police jeep with the missing wheels. But then I tell myself not to panic—I'm much too insignificant a target, enemy planes will hardly waste their bombs on me. Sure enough, the arrowhead formation of jets that zooms in from the sea streaks by overhead without slowing. A second later, I hear another drone, this one more gravelly, as if the engine has sucked in a pigeon it's trying to digest. This straggler flies on too, like the ones before, but then swoops around in a sharp arc to return. I watch in disbelief as he dives towards me, and run screaming down the road as fragments of asphalt kick up at my feet. He circles around for a third pass, chasing me all the way to the city aquarium nestling in its enclosure of palm trees.

I crouch in the vestibule, waiting for him to blow me up. It makes perfect sense: hospitals, art deco buildings, cinemas—surely aquariums come next. Only after several minutes elapse can I allow myself to breathe freely. The jet still executes its homicidal loop repeatedly in my mind, but I know I have escaped with a reprieve.

It's been several years since my visits here with my mother and Uma. The stone steps were smooth and polished then, the aquatic creatures carved on the walls didn't have heads or fins missing. Most wondrously, a family of seahorses glided in a window by the entrance like some mythical aquatic tribe. Their display tank is empty today, the entry doors chained and padlocked.

About to turn away, I remember the fish and chips café in the compound, where we gorged on crisp pomfret after each visit. Is that why fate has spurred me here today, to satisfy my seafood craving? Uma always commented on how macabre the location seemed, as if the whole point of the aquarium exhibits was to stimulate viewers' appetites. I tug at the handle and rattle at the chains, but the café remains securely locked. The door leading to the second-floor canteen, though, opens when I try it, and I scurry in.

Upstairs, the floor is covered with dust and broken glass. I walk into the kitchen and the pungency of fish assaults me almost at once. Am I imagining it?—has the machiwalli hallucination from the hospital returned? Or could years of frying have insinuated the odor into the walls? I begin to notice other things—the kerosene stove, the bottle of oil, and in the dark corner by the cupboard, the figure of a man lying curled up on a mat.

He awakens almost as soon as I spot him, and lifts himself groggily up on his hands. "How did you get in here? What do you want?"

He is barely twenty, but there is already a gauntness to him going beyond the war weariness I have seen in people's faces. He looks as if he has been fighting an enormous personal battle, with little success. "Are you the cook?" I ask.

"The cook?" He scrambles up to a sitting position, umbrage clearing the sleepiness from his face. "Do I look like the cook to you?"

For an instant, I wonder if I've stumbled upon a Khaki, given his rumpled khaki shirt with the epaulets flopping unbuttoned at his shoulders. Then I notice the aquarium logo stitched over his pocket and realize he's the watchman. He seems mollified by this. "I have a rifle downstairs, you know," he adds, as if to impress on me the powerfulness of his position. He takes out a large ring of keys from his back pocket to display as further proof, whisking them away as if afraid I will try to touch them. "Why are you here?" he demands.

"I came looking for fish."

A wary look springs to his eyes. "The display tanks are in the other building—"

"I meant to *eat*. Isn't this the canteen?"

"The canteen? Does it look open to you? Can't you hear the bombs falling outside? Where is the fish going to come from, fly into your lap from Chowpatty?" He shakes his head. "There's no fish. Now go away." He turns around and spreads himself out again on his mat.

I'm about to turn away when I spot a waste basket next to the cupboard. Sticking out from under its lid is a fish head, its eye dried open into a stare. "See?" I cry out, waving the lid in the air. "See, I could smell it. Someone *has* been eating fish."

The watchman springs back up. "Are you accusing me? Are you saying I ate that fish?"

I'm startled at his vehemence. "I'm not accusing you of anything."

"Anyone could have sneaked into the aquarium and pulled out a fish. How do I know who did it? Do I have ten heads that I can keep track of everything? And what am I supposed to eat—do you even know how long it has been since I've been paid?"

I wonder if he is asking for money. Perhaps I should offer him some of the notes tied in my dupatta. "Look, Bhaiyya. I haven't eaten either. If you can bring me a fish, even a small one, I'll give you two hundred rupees."

Instead of calming him, my words make him flare up. "How dare you insult me with such a bribe? You think I'm going to hand over the very creatures I'm supposed to protect? You think I have no self-respect? Why did you come here, memsahib, just to spit in my face?" He wraps his arms around his sides and hugs his body, rocking back and forth slowly on his heels, as if to comfort himself after my calumnies.

"I'm sorry," I say, backing away towards the kitchen door. "I didn't mean any harm."

I am almost at the door, ready to turn around and escape, when he looks up. "*Four* hundred," he says.

AN UNDERGROUND PASSAGEWAY connecting the two buildings leads us into the aquarium. Hrithik (not his real name, he confesses, but one he has decided to adopt after his favorite film star) tells me there might still be a few of my cherished seahorses around somewhere. "Though they're not very tasty."

The exhibits inside have no illumination, so Hrithik lights a candle. "These days, there's only enough generator oil to run the filters," he explains. "Not that there are too many tanks with anything left." He shows me a panel behind which tiny candy drop fish make small kissing gestures as if thanking him for the light. "I never tried these, I was always told the colorful ones are poisonous."

As we pass case after empty case, I realize just how many fish are missing. Could Hrithik have eaten them all? Perhaps he reads my mind, because he starts talking about how easy it is for fish to fall sick, the lack of food and supplies, the pressure to sell the best specimens to foreign aquariums. "For a while, we were getting live carp and pomfret for the restaurant and storing them temporarily in these tanks, just so that the visitors had something to look at."

We come to the central tank, illuminated by sunshine through a skylight above. A large ray floats by, exposing the various organs on its underside for me in a languorous display. Hrithik shakes his head subtly to indicate its lack of culinary quality. "Look, there," he says, pointing at a shadowy shape circling further back. "Very good to eat. Only one left."

"But it's a shark." I can tell by its triangular fin. A small shark, a baby perhaps, but a shark, nevertheless.

"It's the tastiest one left. I've been trying to catch it for weeks, but he always escapes. Look." He shows me a scar on his neck, and another one across his arm. "All over my body, especially on my chest. Once he even tried to bite off my leg." He stares at the water with animus on his face. "It's not possible to trap him—not by myself alone. But if there was another person—" He looks at me slyly.

"Something smaller would be better."

We settle on a fish with a blunt head and speckled skin that is swimming alone in one of the tanks further on. The fish seems quite dazed and lethargic, and doesn't flop around too much in the net when Hrithik scoops it out. "It would be dead in a day or two anyway," he reassures me.

In the kitchen, Hrithik uses only a few stingy drops of oil in the pan, with the result that the fish comes out more burnt than fried. The flesh is mushy and unpleasant, and there are no spices to camouflage the bitter aftertaste. It's nothing like the machi-fry I craved, but I eat as many of the pieces as I can stand. Hrithik wolfs down his share and whatever I leave of mine, acknowledging that the flavor is not good, and reminding me he recommended the shark.

The all-clear signal sounds as we finish. Pulling out the money for Hrithik, I notice the satiation on his face giving way to an inexperienced leer. "You don't have to pay me the full amount," he says. "Just stay awhile. It's not so safe outside, and I have an extra sheet here." He smirks.

I throw the notes at him. "I'll take my chances. Maybe you should ask your mother for permission first before you make such an invitation again."

His bravado crumbles immediately, and he doesn't meet my eye. I am at the door when he calls out. "Come back tomorrow and help me with the shark. You can eat as much as you want for free."

4

APSARAS FLITTED IN TO AWAKEN US WITH THE STRUMS OF THEIR celestial instruments the morning after our wedding. We had barely noticed the images from the Ajanta caves decking the walls of our bridal suite the night before: Bodhisattvas contemplating lotuses, maidens comforting their swooning princesses, even the Buddha gazing down (perhaps a bit too ascetically) on the newly betrothed every evening. In light of how things had played out between Karun and me, I felt relieved we hadn't booked the Khajuraho suite.

We breakfasted on the balcony. The décor took generous liberties with historical consistency: ornate Mughal chairs stationed around an Ashok chakra table from Mauryan times; railings, arches, and decorative flourishes that gleefully seesawed between north and south, old and new, Rajput and Dravidian. It hardly mattered—not with the sands sparkling up and down the coast, the waves rolling in with hushed booms, the sun falling on Karun as he selected fresh apricots from a platter and peeled them for me. Afterwards, we walked through the lobby, redolent with the fragrance of thousands of tuberoses this morning, to explore the exotic flowering plants in the outer courtyard, imported all the way from Hawaii.

We'd both brought our swimsuits, since this was our chance to finally experience the exclusive waters of the hotel swimming pool. The guard simply bowed us through without even checking the guest cards that now proved our legitimacy. The carved pillars and cascading steps cut into the long edge gave the pool a ceremonial air, like something one might come upon in an inner temple courtyard. How magical the water felt, how pure and vitalizing, like a baptism ushering us into married life. I wanted to reprise our first kiss, but felt too self-conscious and settled instead for a quick peck beneath the surface. We gave up on the idea of exploring the rest of the hotel, splashing and swimming almost until checkout.

UMA PICKED US UP at one and drove us to Karun's flat in Colaba. We had decided to defer our honeymoon by two months, when I would accompany Karun to a conference in Jaipur. "Carry her over the threshold," Uma said, "like they do in foreign countries." She giggled as Karun looked for a place to put me down, and helpfully suggested the bed.

I'd been to the apartment before, and instantly fallen in love with the view of the sea through the windows. Karun showed me the bedroom cupboard he'd emptied. "If you have more clothes, I can clear out some of my shirts as well." On the bed, under the covers, he'd spread the new sheets he'd purchased. "Uma said you liked roses, but this sunflower pattern was all I could find. They're still a bit stiff—I only had time to get them washed twice."

We spent the afternoon listening to his collection of classical CDs. "The sarod you hear is by the maestro himself, Ustad Ali Akbar Khan," Karun said, fitting me with headphones as he played one of his favorites. "It's the *Chandranandan* raga, his most famous composition." Afterwards, he talked about the first nanoseconds after the Big Bang when the primordial soup coalesced into protons and neutrons, then showed me a simulated film on his computer of gold ions colliding. "What this tracks is the condensation process in reverse—the particles blown apart into a plasma of gluons and quarks."

The flat came with Karun's job—in fact, the entire cluster of buildings was owned by his institute, an annex to the larger housing complex down the road where Uma and Anoop lived. "I didn't realize I'd be surrounded by scientists," I exclaimed.

He looked confused. "I didn't think you'd mind."

"I'm joking. My sister's married to a scientist—and now, so am I."

Just as we hugged each other, the doorbell rang. Mr. Iyer, a South Indian colleague from two floors below, stood at the door with his wife. They handed us a tiffin box filled with food: dinner thoughtfully packed for our first night. We spread out the containers on the small dining table in the kitchen after they left—in addition to dosas, sambhar, and idli, Mrs. Iyer had even cooked up some sweet upma with cashews and jaggery. Karun poured us each a glass of champagne from a wedding present bottle, then carefully stowed away the remainder in the rear of the fridge. "I usually don't drink, so I'm not good at knowing what one says."

"To us," I said, raising my glass. We each took a sip.

Kishmish, my guilty-pleasure television serial, came on at eight, so we dined in front of the living room set, the dosas and champagne balanced in our laps. "I started watching it when I was fourteen, and haven't been able to give it up since. I'd stay overnight with my friend Reena to study for our finals, and her mother would allow us this one break—she'd give us orange squash and potato chips."

As I stood in the bathroom, it struck me how much I felt back at Reena's. Karun and I had listened to music and talked about particle collisions instead of memorizing formulas and dates, but otherwise, it seemed the same. And yet, this was not some overnight visit. The doorbell would not ring tomorrow, my mother would not be standing there to take me back. I looked at my toothbrush leaning next to Karun's in the cup, the soap dish he had wiped out for my bar of Lux, the color-coded red towel he'd hung for me next to his blue one on the rack, and felt a surge of affection. I was here to stay.

We again got no further than the previous night's fondling. Perhaps the single glass of champagne really had incapacitated Karun, as he explained. He tucked us in amidst the sunflowers and went to sleep with my arm clasped against his chest.

All week, the aura of a sleepover lingered (especially once we took to wearing pajamas). Our lovemaking remained restricted to above the waist. Karun patted my thigh amiably each time I brushed it against his, kissed my hand whenever I let it stray. He offered frequent apologies (without specifying for what, exactly)—a fatiguing day at work, an unsolved equation rattling around in his head. "But you have no idea how much I'm enjoying sleeping together. It's the best part of the day."

One evening, on Uma's prescription, I greeted Karun in high heels and a short black Western-style dress she lent me. But this vixen incarnation left him baffled, not aroused. "Isn't it very uncomfortable to walk around in those shoes?" he asked, and I felt absurd enough to change.

"It can be difficult in the beginning," Uma consoled. "Especially with someone who has as slow a fuse as Karun. Anoop suffered from it a bit too—do you remember how hard I had to work to pull him in, play Shakuntala to his Valmiki? It's probably true of all these scientist types—always in need of polishing, always too distracted by their theories—they simply don't spend enough time around women. Have you tried just talking about it?"

"It's not exactly easy to bring up. Besides, he might freeze—I don't want to confront him."

"Then don't talk, just act. Touch where needed. You have to do something before he convinces himself that cuddling is all you require of him."

That night, as Karun lay shirtless by my side, I played with his trail of chest hair all the way down to his navel. I let my hand stray under the edge of the sheet across his waist. Slowly, I rolled back the sunflowers, then loosened his pajamas to uncover what nestled there. For a moment, I let him get accustomed to the sensation of being bare.

He kept his eyes closed, but shifted noticeably as my fingers began their exploration of his groin. His entire body tensed as I brushed against his manhood—the contact startled me as well. I waited a moment before trying a tentative stroke—this time, he emitted a truncated groan. I almost withdrew, but Uma's voice urged me to continue. "One of the partners has to take an active role," she said, "and in this relationship, it's you." Sliding my fingers around, I took Karun's penis in my hand.

"Sarita," he gasped, and I looked at him. His face was bloodless, his lips chalky, his eyes filled with panic. "Stop. I can't," he said, and instantly, I released him.

"I can't," he repeated, and pulling the sunflowers up to his neck, turned towards the edge of the bed.

EMERGING FROM THE canteen stairwell, I notice a man on the aquarium steps, trying to peer into the lobby. Hearing the door shut behind me, he turns around. "There you are, thank goodness." He comes down the steps towards me. "Are you all right?"

"I'm fine," I reply warily. He speaks with a slight accent, which I can't place. His features look keenly familiar—the short, impeccable hair, the hint of smolder in his eyes. I feel I should be able to recognize him—is he one of Karun's work friends?

"I lost you. When the guns started firing, you ran too fast. I walked all the way to the overhead bridge near Chowpatty, then thought you might have ducked in here and came back. I'm so glad." He pauses. "You don't recognize me, do you? I'm Gaurav, from the hospital. The one you saved? I know it was dark."

"Gaurav?"

"Yes, please call me that. I thought I'd repay you somehow."

"You've been following me?" The idea makes me feel vulnerable, exposed. Should I try to run back up the canteen steps? Which presents the greater danger: this man's stalking or Hrithik's adolescent fantasies?

"I just wanted to make sure you weren't attacked. All the hoodlums around in khaki—it's the least I could do, I said to myself. I tried to ask you before in the hospital where you were going, but you misunderstood, perhaps. I overheard you inquire about trains from those dressed-up people and just wanted to say I was headed to the suburbs as well."

His explanation sounds plausible enough—perhaps I've been overwrought in my assessment. He doesn't come across as a sexual predator, even if I can't be absolutely certain he's not lying. "You saved my life," he continues. "Let me do this to reciprocate. Ensure you get to your destination, accompany you for safety's sake."

I'm taken aback. War or no war, he's still a stranger, his offer plainly presumptuous. "I'm fine, thanks. I don't need an escort."

"I would consider it my privilege, my duty—"

"No, really. The duty was mine, to save you—you don't need to repay me. I've lived in Mumbai so long—believe me, I can take care of myself."

Before taking my leave, I make sure he understands he is not to follow. I look back a few times to check if he obeys, but cannot spot him through all the people around. I am struck by the throng—the all-clear sounded barely ten minutes ago, and already Marine Drive is swarming, as if the stadium at the other end has just let out after a cricket match. Wasn't the city supposed to have emptied out?—where have all these people been hiding? A multitude of heads stretches all the way to Chowpatty, like pixels packed in a photograph.

I immerse myself amidst these pixels, their flow carries me along. Smiles and laughs abound—people wave flags like on Independence Day, blow paper horns. Perhaps their jubilance marks the just-survived attack. In the distance, the footbridge Gaurav mentioned rises high above the road and adjoining tracks. THE NATION IS ON THE MOVE, a billboard across it for Nike footwear proclaims, in giant letters the colors of the national flag.

Ahead, the crowd bunches up to detour around another crack in the ground. Jets of water shoot spectacularly towards the sky as the sea tries to squeeze in. As I round the tip, a boy comes running up to hurl himself over the chasm. A wave crashes against him in midair, but his momentum carries him across. He lands and raises his wet arms in triumph—the onlookers applaud. A giggling young lady follows, her sari puffing up under her as she leaps through the air.

At the swim club, a crush of humanity forms a knot at the gate. I think of all the evenings spent there taking lessons from Karun. This is hardly the time for a swim—why are all these people trying to get in? Then I realize they're attracted by the vantage of the diving tower. Masses cluster precariously on the platforms, a thick line winds up the stairway. I watch to see if anyone will jump like Karun and me, but the clumps remain intact.

I near the footbridge, teeming with people as well. Hands and arms stick out through the gaps around the billboard and lob objects into the crowd below. A bottle explodes on the pavement nearby. A rock hits a woman who collapses to the ground, holding her bleeding head. I manage to pass under, unharmed.

Curiously, no projectiles fall on the other side of the bridge. A row of people crowds up high behind a second Nike billboard, faces craning towards the Chowpatty sands. I forge ahead through the crush on the ground, wondering what makes the aerial spectators so spellbound. I begin to see loudspeakers tied to lampposts—the sound of chanting fills the air.

A large cloth sign announces a yagna, a great holy fire ceremony. "Rise, O great Mumbadevi, to save your city," it proclaims. The list of sponsors underneath includes several temples and religious groups, but not the HRM. In fact, I can spot no Khakis in our midst. The men blowing whistles to direct the crowd wear no uniforms, no saffron bands adorn their necks.

And yet, saffron is everywhere: flags fluttering from poles, kiosks sprouting from the sand, a banner that has come loose and undulates in the wind—the beach has been inundated by a saffron wave. Behind the kiosks and a bank of generators lies the stage. It rises thirty feet into the air, supported by a cluster of bamboo legs, like a giant cricket hovering over the multitudes below. Stairways spiral up the legs—as I watch, men clad in loincloths ascend and seat themselves in orderly rows on the platform. The sun reflects off something—perhaps the white Brahmin's threads across their chests.

The scene reminds me of the Olympics—I wait for an athlete to go running up and light a flame. But the prayers commence and I realize the fire must already be consecrated. I have witnessed yagnas before, but on a much smaller scale. Mentally, I trace the actions of the priests as they consign camphor and ghee and saffron into the holy flame.

Musicians sit on either side of the platform, the tearful sighs of their shehnais rising to the heavens with the invisible smoke and the prayers. Will these offerings prevail upon Devi to take our side and vanquish the enemy planes? Or will she send in the sea to swallow the city— water exploding up through fissures like the ones already cracking the Marine Drive pavement?

"I come to you with a message of peace," the voice taking over from the priests on the loudspeaker announces. "We have gathered to end this war, to heal the differences between us, to appeal to you, O great Devi ma." A coalition of temples has organized this event, the speaker explains, to counteract all the divisive forces at play in the city and the country. "We are your true followers—come before us and reveal your wisdom, your mercy."

I have no time to stop and listen—my goal is to cross the street and be on my way. The Nike footbridge is too far behind, so I start inching towards the aerial overpass ahead. Sweat soaks through shirts and saris and rubs off on my skin. A child clutches at my hand, and I instinctively check to make sure the pomegranate is still in my pocket.

It takes me thirty minutes to reach the foot of the overpass, and another fifteen to push through the spectators and climb up halfway. How can the bridge withstand the weight of so many people? They listen raptly as the speaker exhorts them not to pay attention to rumors. "The real Devi ma has not yet descended. She is nothing like what you might have seen in the movies. She can only appear at a proper temple, not a godforsaken spot on a beach as some claim."

The first shouts over the loudspeakers are faint, and seem to emerge from just within range of the microphone. I notice the smoke is now visible—a thin black plume rising from the stage. For an instant, it strikes me that this could be part of the ceremony—perhaps the platform itself is to be burnt down in the finale. Then figures begin to leap off, while others try to scramble down the bamboo frame-work. The tarpaulin border hoisted over the edge starts smoking, then catches fire with a speaker-amplified pop. I spot flames—small bursts at first, leached of color by the sunlight, and then large sheets that roll around canvas and leap ambitiously into the air. Within sec-onds, the platform is engulfed. Bamboo, tarpaulin, steps, and priests all vanish behind a curtain of orange—the stage becomes a giant sea-side funeral pyre.

From where I stand, the ensuing horror unfolds like a carnage scene from a movie epic. The crowd surges away in waves as debris rains down flaming from the platform. Fueling the panic are the loudspeak-ers, which continue functioning longer than they should, broadcasting the grisly fate of those trapped on stage. By the time the fire finally cuts off their screams, an enormous stampede has been generated. I now hear the cries of people on the ground being trampled under the feet of the roiling mob. The surge is so strong that its edges push up the bridge. A few onlookers pitch over the sides, but I manage to hold on.

Finally, the panic abates. Mangled corpses litter the beach, a smok-ing hulk remains where the platform stood. People start dazedly mak-ing their way down. I almost stagger along with them before remembering I'm trying to cross over. More bodies lie twisted on the other side of the bridge—my knees feel weak as I pick my way across the sidewalk. I pass the New Yorker restaurant, where Karun and I sometimes had coffee after our swim. The Statue of Liberty cutout still stands intact, though blood spatters its ice cream cone torch.

I search for the alley leading to the railway corridor. After what I have witnessed, I'm too unnerved to continue on the roads—since the trains aren't running, it makes more sense to walk along the tracks. I turn at the Barista coffee shop and look for an entry along the line of buildings. At the very end, I find a narrow gap in the wall, through which I pull myself. The tracks are as deserted as before. I begin the long trek in the direction of the Mumbai suburbs.

THE NIGHT HE TURNED away from me, Karun's reaction left me so shocked that at first, I had trouble processing his words. "It's too soon," he may have said. "I need more time." I couldn't think of how to respond. Did he not find me attractive? If so, why had he married me?

"I was nervous even before the wedding. Not being used to any of this, not having had any experience. You can't realize how much pressure it's been."

"I haven't exactly been out practicing with other men either."

"No, please don't take me wrong—it's entirely my fault. I've always been very reticent about such things. I thought it was just shyness, but it's more than that—perhaps I need to know you better. Or perhaps you need to know me. I'm not explaining this very well—I'm sorry. If you could be patient, that's all I'm asking."

He wanted to continue sleeping together, continue cuddling. His contriteness seemed genuine, his proposal innocuous enough, so I agreed.

For the next several nights, we just slept. I had resolved to act stern and unaccommodating, but Karun was so solicitous, so apologetic, that I found my anger dissolving. I allowed him to wrap my arms around his body while going to sleep, to press his back into my bosom the way he liked. Sometimes he turned around to gaze at me, like an artist studying the fine points of a subject to paint it from memory. I reciprocated on these occasions, trying to absorb his essence through this shared experience of silent communing. Who was Karun? What did he feel? Beyond the atoms and molecules of which he was so knowledgeable, what constituted his being?

Once it ignited within me, I tried to subsume my physical longing in this curiosity. Each day when Karun left for work, I went through the flat, familiarizing myself intimately with his things. I buried my face in his shirts to see if I could discern a scent lingering from his body. I examined the pattern on each necktie to intuit what he found appealing. I noticed how he carefully folded each handkerchief, how he stored his socks rolled in pairs, how he stacked his underwear in orderly piles. Even the worn shoes he no longer used rested tidily in their original boxes.

I discovered Karun's past under the bed, just as neatly organized. An old suitcase held toys and games, including miniatures of racing cars and jumbo jets and three boxes containing Lego pieces. A small attaché, the type used by schoolchildren, contained report cards all the way from kindergarten, chronologically arranged. I felt a curious kinship well up within as I leafed through a stack of prize citations similar to mine—science, mathematics, geography, and the inevitable "moral instruction" (which I also unfailingly earned every year). At the very bottom lay a bound copy of his Ph.D. thesis, "Non-Abelian evolution of chromo-Weibel instabilities based on hadronic spectra observables." The fact that I found the title unintelligible (as he probably would my M.A. thesis on Fellegi-Holt models) made me smile.

In the last suitcase, behind two cartons of scientific books, a shock awaited me. I stared at the saris packed within, the dupattas and blouses, the salwaar kameez outfit. A small plastic container held earrings and bangles, inside another lay two necklaces and a ring. Had I just uncovered evidence of a past liaison? Did Karun have a romantic history he had failed to reveal?

Then I smelled the mothballs, noticed the men's suits with the old-fashioned lapels and the heavy brocaded saris. The clothes, I realized, had to be his parents'—Karun must have saved them in remembrance. Packed in under the outfits lay a photo album. The first picture, of his parents, was identical to the one above the dining table—his father looking out jauntily at the camera, his mother gazing dreamily past, as if in the distance, she could see the panorama of the rest of her life. Karun appeared as a newborn on the next page, then as a toddler with a shock of black hair. I followed him over the years—posing in a rabbit costume with a carrot in his mouth, accepting a trophy for best Cub Scout, sitting with his parents in a plywood Mercedes prop at a photographer's stall. I imagined myself in each photo, sharing each instant as he grew, insinuating myself into his life.

Abruptly, his father dropped out. The lines on his mother's face deepened, and Karun smiled more uncertainly now, if at all. Hair sprouted on his lip and chin, a mustache appeared, then disappeared. He still projected the same innocence, but the expression in his eyes became harder to read. The last photograph showed him holding up a framed degree, his mother standing proudly next to him.

My snooping didn't offend Karun—in fact, he found it amusing. Each day, I pulled out something different to ask about when he returned from work: which was his favorite board game? how old were his parents when they married? what prompted him to buy a pair of pants so parrot green? I took these opportunities to also tell him more about me. We pored over our albums together and compared his birthday photos with mine. One evening we forgot all about dinner, assembling the Lego into a giant structure resembling the Gateway of India (even though we had aimed for the Taj Mahal). I talked about my specialization in epidemiology, the drug tests I'd statistically analyze for Sandoz in the job starting next month. Karun tried explaining his dissertation—the gist (as far as I could tell) was the analysis of data from particle splitting to predict resulting instabilities.

The simplicity of Karun's past, its lack of surprises, comforted me. How endearing to discover a story so manageable that the boxes accommodating it fit under only half the bed. I imagined my own story rubbing containers with his, taking up the room left. "He's really like a child," I updated Uma. "We're only sleeping, so there's no pressure at night."

Except I always had an eye open towards advancing physical intimacy. By now, I'd learnt enough to be indirect, to tread delicately. Each night, I pulled Karun's waist to my pelvis with the subtlest of motions, cradled his buttocks, pressed in against the back of his thighs. Once I knew he felt comfortable, I reversed our positions as a gentle invitation for him to reciprocate. I made a game of everything—rolling across the bed in an embrace, snuggling at the abdomen so that our belly buttons "kissed," measuring distances on his body with my lips (six lip-lengths between his nipples, twelve from his Adam's apple to his waist). I convinced him to teach me yoga, for which it seemed natural to suggest undressing down to our underwear once the mornings turned humid.

It felt a bit like getting swimming lessons again, without the water this time. Each morning before breakfast, Karun coaxed out the correct arcs from my body, adjusted the lines of my limbs. I learnt quickly—my knack for yoga greatly exceeded my aptitude for aquatics. Warrior pose became my favorite—I tried to sneak a peek in the mirror each time we performed it. The two of us reaching towards the open window as if in a ballet, sunlight streaming in to warm our faces and splash down our necks.

Sometimes we went through an asana with our bodies touching, pretending we were one person. The shared intensity of holding the position together led to a heightened awareness of the points of contact between us. We started performing tree pose this way, so that Karun could support my upraised hands to correct my frequent bouts of imbalance. Standing flamingo-like necessitated pressing the heel of one foot high into the split between the legs. Every tiny adjustment translated into a movement we both felt at our groins—it was difficult to ignore the rub and push at this focal point.

Calming asanas like corpse pose could be even more provocative. With my body limp over Karun's, my consciousness kept returning to the contact below our waist. The stirrings I detected were not just my own, but I scrupulously resisted the urge to act on them. Instead, I let the asana work its magic, leaving Karun increasingly charged by my body pressed into his.

My patience paid off the evening Karun announced he'd found the wedding bottle of champagne hiding for months in our fridge. "Perhaps I'll experiment with something Italian for dinner to accompany it." The *cacciatore* sauce he served over spaghetti tasted suspiciously like his chicken curry, but went agreeably enough with the champagne (which, devoid of bubbles, still packed enough alcohol to dissolve away most of his inhibitions). As I snuggled up to him in bed that night, I noticed he wore neither pajamas nor underwear. "It feels nice—why don't you do the same?"

He was right—it *did* feel nice, especially when he allowed me to cradle his exposed self between my thighs without shrinking at the contact. He played with my breasts, taking the nipples into his mouth as I'd taught him, but with a curiosity I'd not sensed before (I now had an objective gauge of his enthusiasm against my leg). The next night, though we no longer had the benefit of champagne, he seemed even more engaged, kissing me in elaborate circular patterns across my nipples, my stomach, my waist; tonguing my belly button as if scooping honey from it. I found an old diary in which to start a tally, drawing a star next to the date of each such notable interaction.

By the end of a month, I had collected eight stars. Sometimes, our games brought us tantalizingly close to the act, and though Karun never followed through, I assigned an extra star for such occasions. The true breakthrough, when I finally conferred a third star, came in Jaipur.

Karun's conference there had been postponed due to a terrorist attack at tourist sites—we only had our Pink City honeymoon seven months into our marriage. The Hawa Mahal lay in ruins and the City Palace had been badly damaged, but Jantar Mantar still stood intact. We spent Karun's free day roaming the observatory—the ninety-foot sundial fascinated him, as did the giant sunken hemispheres for measuring astronomical coordinates. That night, a colleague from Princeton treated us to dinner at his hotel in a restored palace—despite the bombings, the restaurant portion remained unscathed. After several glasses of wine each, Professor Ashton dropped us off at our much more modest guesthouse.

I could tell from Karun's spirited state that the night would get a star, perhaps even two. Before I knew it, we were both naked, with Karun swiveling around over my body, pretending to be the shadow of the sundial. "This is my path in the morning," he said, bending over my head to kiss me in an arc across my breasts. "And this is where I reach at noon," he continued, leaning forward to plant kisses along my waist.

"And where do you fall after that?" I giggled as his hips pivoted above my face.

"Right into the hemisphere!" he declared, tilting forward to kiss me between my legs. I screamed, then burst out laughing as he kissed me again. His nudeness swung above me, and I almost grabbed it to retaliate. But then I remembered the injunction against touching, so I ensnared him with my mouth instead.

Fortunately, he found this uproarious, not distressing. We fell over on our sides, laughing so hard I had to release him. But he remained inches from my face, so with a cry of "Jantar Mantar," I seized him again. At some point, I realized he had stopped laughing, that I was more tangibly aware of him in my mouth, that the tenor of our play had changed. He made a small gasping sound as he withdrew halfway, then slid in again.

Although I did not manage to bring him to climax that first time, I could tell he enjoyed it. As did I, especially after he reciprocated in kind (which I allowed only because my self-consciousness had been neutralized by the restaurant libations). One of the first things to do upon returning home, I decided, would be to invest in a case of wine. Though we both seemed so amenable to this new diversion that perhaps we wouldn't need to be inebriated next time.

———

MAKING MY WAY ALONG the tracks under the bridge at Opera House, I feel it. It couldn't be, I think—there's no electricity in the overhead lines. But there it is, under my feet—the vibration, the rumble, that can mean only one thing. I force myself to keep walking without looking back. When the sound is loud enough to fill my ears, when I can smell the smoke and taste it in my mouth, I finally turn around. Puffing towards me is an old steam engine pulling two yellow and brown train compartments along the rails.

"Sister, come," I hear a female voice say as I jump aside onto the stones mounded against the tracks. A hand reaches out from the open door of the train—it is hennaed and bejeweled like that of a bride. "Come, I'll pull you in, don't be afraid." Without knowing why, I begin to run alongside. I run faster and faster, and manage to latch onto the steps hanging from the door, then reach up and grasp the proffered hand.

5

THE TERRORISM RESPONSIBLE FOR ABBREVIATING OUR SIGHT-seeing in Jaipur wasn't isolated. A series of attacks had continued ever since our wedding, with at least one set of bombs going off every two or three weeks in a different state. Other incidents of violence had increased as well—towns and villages all over India seemed afflicted by an epidemic of riots and rampages. Some explained this rising mayhem as a cycle of provocation and reaction engineered by the notorious Pakistani intelligence agency ISI, others pointed at Maoist insurgents or criminal syndicates. On the radio one day, I heard a news analyst trace the surge back to *Superdevi*, ascribing the blame to its climactic orgy of bloodshed.

As evidence, he enumerated several instances of theatergoers, inflamed after a show, running amok. In Ahmedabad, they broke into a nearby market and ransacked Muslim shops, in Jhansi, they beat up worshippers exiting a mosque, in Nagpur, they set an entire Muslim colony aflame. Right-wing politicians, recognizing the potential for a national conflagration, had joined forces to fan these sparks, he asserted—after all, hadn't the same type of religious chauvinism, engendered by the screening of the Ramayana on national television a few decades back, eventually swept them into power? A year after *Superdevi*'s release, free screenings (using bootlegged DVDs) were still being organized in thousands of rural venues, each followed by a fiery religious discourse on the film's supposed message of "purifying" the country's population. The Hindu Rashtriya Manch had recruited and armed a half million villagers, posting them in strategic outposts all over India for a promised battle against non-Hindus to uphold the Superdevi's will. "The entire country is a powder keg waiting to explode," the commentator declared. "People call *Superdevi* inclusive just because the producers contrived to give her a Muslim sidekick. But next time you see it, count the number of Islamic villains she kills. Every listener should demand an immediate ban on the film."

Bombay was the last place to call for such a ban. Not only were its audiences more sophisticated and harder to manipulate, but local entrepreneurs had dubbed Mumbai "City of Devi" to cash in on *Superdevi*'s success. By now I saw the name everywhere—on giant billboards, across the sides of buses and trains, even as a flaming pink neon spiral down the airport control tower when we returned from Jaipur. The moniker fit well—not just because *Superdevi* took place in the city (with the lead actress Baby Rinky a real-life discovery from the Dharavi slums) but also because Mumbai's patron deity Mumbadevi had the most screen time out of all nine incarnations. With both "Mumba" and "Ai" words for "mother" in the local language, which other metropolis in India could even come close to claiming (and capitalizing on) the mantle of the mother goddess's city?

The idea proved to be a marketing coup. "City of Devi" tours, combining locales from the film with religious destinations, became so popular that even temples with only a stray idol or two of Devi dusted them off to vie for inclusion. Some managed to install video screens in their prayer halls, even THX stereo, from the inflow of tourist rupees (not to mention dollars, pounds, euros). Literary festivals, dance events, school essay contests, and the Taj Hotel's "Best Avatar Costume" competition all bore the City of Devi logo: seven dabs of pigment (representing the seven original islands of Bombay) arranged into an artistically rendered image of Mumbadevi. The *Mumbai Mirror* published special pullout sections every Sunday on Mumbadevi myths—the demon giant vanquished by her, the devout Koli woman whose fisherman husband she saved, the time she brought fresh cotton to the city's embargoed mills (this last one newly invented, like several others—Mumbadevi never having enjoyed top-tier goddess status, like Laxmi or Kali, before this). Anxious to regain advertising ground lost to McDonald's, Pizza Hut came up with a computer mouse pad giveaway featuring the mother goddess smiling down benignly on various city sights. The promotion had to be hurriedly aborted when Muslims took umbrage at the image of Mumbadevi apparently blessing the entire Worli sea face, including the Haji Ali mosque clearly visible at one end.

In fact, several citizens' groups wanted to scrap the City of Devi designation entirely, on grounds that it violated Mumbai's secular spirit (my father was positively apoplectic). The organizers dismissed these qualms—the campaign had a cultural, not proselytizing, aim. It promoted commerce, the true religion of the city.

THE INTERIOR OF THE TRAIN compartment is unlike any I have ever seen. The walls are painted pink, with crimson banquettes and sofas lining the perimeter—light sconces bloom rosily from next to the curtained windows. A Kashmiri carpet stretches across the floor, all the way to a closed door leading to the rest of the compartment. Dressing tables flank this door, one on either side, with pink dupattas draped over their mirrors. I feel I have clambered into the boudoir of a traveling courtesan, the parlor of a mobile house of ill repute.

However, the three women inside are dressed as brides, not ladies of the night. They shimmer in red saris, dots of decorative white pigment glittering along the borders of their faces, diamond pins in their noses sparkling promises of virginity. "Welcome," the tallest one says. "I'm Madhu, and these are my fellow sisters, Guddi and Anupam."

"Madhu did said we're going to be Devi ma's new maidens from tonight," Guddi breathlessly announces. Her face is heart-shaped, her eyes spaced apart wide—she seems the youngest, no more than sixteen.

"Just see what they gave us," Anupam adds, pointing to her necklace, laughing in excitement as she jiggles her earrings. "And this sari—I know it's a secret, Madhu didi, but I have to tell her. It glows in the dark, just like Ooper-devi ma's sari!"

"Yes, just like Ooper-devi ma, in the final scenes," Guddi chimes in. "We're the first maidens to get them! Maybe we should show her—turn off all the lights and pull down the shutters. Can we, Madhu didi?"

Madhu tells them no. "Don't mind them. They're very naïve—Mura recruited them from their villages only last week. I've had barely three days to give them their city training. We had another one, too—Nalini—but she couldn't make it."

"Poor Nalini didi."

"She'd be so disappointed if she knew what she was missing."

"It was that time of the month for her," Madhu says. "It seems they don't keep such good track of these things in the villages, unfortunately. Mura's wondering what he's going to do, since he promised to deliver three of them this week. When I saw you walking along the tracks, it came to me that perhaps you could—"

"Oh, that would be so terrific, if she could take Nalini didi's place," Anupam exclaims.

"Yes, could she? Could we make her our sister as well? Please, Madhu didi, say yes." Guddi takes my hand in hers and presses it to her breast.

Madhu examines me closely, and frowns. "You seemed much younger on the tracks." She speaks in an injured tone, as if I've misrepresented myself. "It's hardly going to work if you look like their aunt instead of their sister—you must be already past thirty."

"But we could make her up, Didi," Anupam says. "All those powders and lipsticks you showed us. We could make her look young again by rubbing that magic cream into her skin—the one you said foreign memsahibs use when they're aging."

"And teach her to dance. Mura chacha wouldn't be able to turn her down, then, would he?" Guddi raises her joined hands above her head and starts sashaying on the carpet, alternating between classical Kathakali poses and moves from popular films. "We can perform together for Devi ma, all four of us."

Madhu is still dubious. "I suppose we might as well give it a try. At least she's not wearing a mangalsutra—if Mura saw she was married, that would be it." Before I can correct her, she hustles me towards the dressing table. "We better hurry—the train will be at Santa Cruz before we know it."

My ears prick up—Santa Cruz is only a couple of stations after my destination. "Actually, if you could have the train stop at Bandra, I could get off there—"

"Oh, but that won't be possible. The train driver's in the engine—the only way to get word to him is by pulling the emergency chain." Madhu says this with a regretful look, but can't quite conceal the trace of glee that brightens her face.

"Besides, we have to prepare you for Mura chacha, Didi," Guddi says. "This is not a chance you want to miss. He's resting back there, behind that door—he'll be getting up any minute." She sits me down while Anupam starts shaking a vial of white liquid. "It's good we still have Nalini didi's outfit—we can dress you in it."

Anupam starts to paint a series of white bridal dots along my brow, but I push her hand away. "I'm sorry. I really don't know what you're doing. Forgive me, but I don't want to be dressed up for your Mura chacha—I just need to get to Bandra."

Both Guddi and Anupam look at me in alarm. "Do you know what you're saying?" Madhu exclaims. "It's Devi ma we're dressing you up for, not just Mura. The real Devi ma, the one who's appeared at Juhu in person—not all these fakes people keep conjuring. That's why we're headed to Santa Cruz—haven't you heard anything? You're lucky to get this opportunity—only because Nalini can't join us. Devi ma herself, you understand?—to serve as her personal maiden. Though in your case, not to be impolite, it would be more matron than maiden."

"Please, Didi, you must agree," Guddi says. "Devi ma can be very quick to flare up if you show her any disrespect. There was a girl in our village who made a joke about the idol at the temple—said she was much fairer, that Devi ma had too black a complexion. Within a week she was dead—not only her skin but even her eyeballs turned black. We watched as the jackals ate her body—even her parents weren't brave enough to go near her after that."

My skepticism must show, because Anupam starts nodding and insisting it's all true. "Bhim kaka. Tell her about Bhim kaka," she says to Madhu, her voice squeaky with urgency.

"You probably haven't heard about Bhim, either, then? After all, he's only the most important man in the city." Madhu arches her eyebrows and stares at me until I nod—yes, I have heard of the leader of the HRM, almost mythically renowned for his bloodthirsty ways. "Think of this, then—Bhim himself, no less, has become a disciple of Devi ma. He challenged her at first, called her a pretender, but now falls at her feet at least once a week to beg her blessing. He's dedicated every last man in his army to her, declared that without her will, even a leaf won't drop in the city. In fact, who do you think arranges for this train, these maidens every week? It's Bhim—Mura just works for him. So forget about trying to get off at Bandra—if you don't fear Devi ma, at least worry about getting on the wrong side of Bhim."

The train engine toots, and I see we have already passed the Bombay Central bridge. I can always slip away at Santa Cruz and make my way south, I think. Yes, I will audition for Mura, I say.

Guddi and Anupam squeal in delight. Even Madhu seems to thaw a little—as the other two open jars of makeup and ooh over them, she starts curling my hair with a brush. "Guddi, find that memsahib wrinkle cream. Anupam, get some water from the thermos and wipe her arms clean." Her brush snags on grit, which she pulls out with a harsh tug. "Isn't it difficult enough as it is, that your hair had to be snarled like this? What did you do, rub in handfuls of dirt?"

The girls want to paint my fingernails with polish, but Madhu declares it will take too long to dry. "Just do the cheeks and lips, and let's hope for the best." She arranges a necklace that cascades in a series of filigreed chains down my neck and threads heavy gold earrings through my lobes. They all stand back to look at me—my face feels caked with makeup. "She'll look younger after you finish painting on the bridal dots."

Once I'm all decorated, Madhu insists I put on the "magic" sari. "It really does glow, believe me, but only if it's pitch-dark. In any case, your salwaar is filthy—do you really think Devi ma would tolerate anyone in such a rag?" I realize my mistake as soon as I change—neither the sari nor the petticoat underneath has a pocket, and I'm forced to wrap the pomegranate in the folds at my waist and hope for the best. As I sweat under the layers of heavy silk, Guddi and Anupam express delight at how bride-like the bright red color makes me look. Even Madhu grudgingly says that I no longer resemble their aunt. She draws the hem of the sari over my head and leads me to Mura's door, as if it is my wedding night. Just before turning the knob, she pauses. "I almost forgot to make sure. This month—have you already had your flow? We don't want to get Devi ma unclean."

THE TENOR OF THE CITY OF DEVI campaign changed abruptly. We awoke one morning to find that a phalanx of fifteen-foot Mumbadevi statues had invaded Mumbai. "It's a showcase for all the tourists coming to our city," the new campaign chairman, rumored to be an HRM man, explained. "So they can appreciate all the splendor and magnificence of Devi ma." The statues, however, projected more belligerence than beauty—ominous warrior figures with coarsely fashioned features, set identically in concrete. Many of them popped up next to crowded Muslim localities unfrequented by tourists, where their towering presence could cause the maximum provocation.

Soon after, the HRM-allied municipality banned the sale of meat on Fridays in deference to the mother goddess. The very next week, it issued an order directing all public establishments, including places of worship, to immediately start displaying the City of Devi logo. When churches and mosques protested that they found its image of Mumbadevi offensive, the HRM chairman, Shrikant Doshi, responded personally. "Devi ma only reveals herself to those who believe. Anyone who claims to see her in the logo can't then claim to be a true Christian or Muslim." His thugs issued ultimatums around the city, beating up non-compliant mullahs and priests, vandalizing their mosques and churches. In retaliation, mobs set upon Hindu temples, stabbing two priests at Babulnath and destroying some of the outer shrines at Mahalaxmi.

The riots that ensued permanently changed the character of the city. Even after they abated, an atmosphere of heightened animus, of extreme mistrust, lingered between communities.

I REMAINED ONLY passingly attentive to the City of Devi tensions, so immersed was I in my "Project Karun" diary. The milestone of our hundredth star was fast approaching. The day I logged it, I couldn't resist some calculations. Our performance had a weekly mean of 4.35 stars over the past five months or so, with a standard deviation of 2.72. If I ignored everything before Jaipur, the mean jumped to 6.67 stars per week, with $\sigma = 1.44$. I had no idea if these statistics were good, if they agreed with what might be normally expected.

"The average seems a bit low for newlyweds," Uma opined. "But why worry? You now know his machinery works, and that he's probably not a homo."

"Thanks for being so sensitive."

"Sorry. All I mean to say is that if you're having fun, then the numbers are right—it's the only thing that counts."

We *were* having fun. Karun still waited for me to initiate things, but I found, to my surprise, that I enjoyed taking the lead. Sarita the huntress, Sarita the tigress out to get her meat—surely there existed a goddess embodying these pursuits whom I was channeling?

More importantly, Karun had become an essential part of my life. I loved being woken up in the morning when he clambered back into bed to share his mug of cinnamon coffee. We read the newspaper over breakfast, trying to catch flaws in "scientific" polls and studies, marveling at the latest lapses in politicians' logic. I never knew what culinary experiment awaited me on evenings I worked late—once he even surprised me with Vietnamese. His Indo-Italian fusion had actually begun to taste rather wonderful, ever since Professor Ashton had mailed him packets of herb seeds from Princeton (we now had such European plants as sage and rosemary growing on our balcony). Sometimes, I discovered basil sprigs tucked into the folds of my towel—one day, I opened my cupboard to find sachets of lavender nestling between the saris. Each night, I liked to casually brush my toe against the hairless patch on his ankle for reassurance before closing my eyes. Our sunflower sheets grew softer, acquiring a silky smoothness over time.

The day my father suffered his heart attack, Karun held my hand all the way in the taxi to the hospital, his face as flushed, his knuckles as white as mine. "I've been through this when I was eleven," he whispered. "I know what it feels like." On the nights I kept watch, he insisted on staying behind with me—we sat till Uma relieved us at dawn, in adjoining chairs by my father's bedside. At home, he nursed me as if I were the patient, fortifying me with minestrone and vitamins, assuring me everything would be fine. Perhaps these ministrations did have some trans-curative effect, because my father was back to walking around at home in a fortnight.

I realized how much I'd come to depend upon Karun, to love him, to *know* him since we married. He was too reserved to reveal himself to everyone—one had to be chosen for this opportunity. Even then, I felt like a bee burrowing into a tightly closed flower bud, each whorl of petals yielding to reveal another nestling inside. Despite how deep I advanced, I could still sense some mystery enfolded at his core. A secret, a treasure, an inadvertent lure, waiting for me to discover in time.

Perhaps true consummation, the traditional way, was part of this promise, this enticement. The huntress would have to persevere longer to earn her four-star trophy. I was willing to wait, to proceed only when Karun signaled his readiness. Until then, our limited repertoire of "Jantar Mantar" (as we'd begun to call it) would be enough to sustain me.

Uma's pregnancy forced me to rethink my strategy. How would we ever form a trinity if Karun never got any closer to impregnating me? I reminded myself it wasn't a pressing issue—although we'd discussed the family question before our wedding, it hadn't arisen since (somewhat surprisingly). Once Uma delivered, though, the sight of my tiny new nephew at her bosom filled my own breast with longing. I had just crossed thirty-three—how close was the expiry date on my biological battery?

So I broached the topic unambiguously one night. "It's been a year and a half—perhaps we should try it differently? The usual way other couples do so—what do you think?"

Karun colored immediately. "So that we can be a family of three," I added to take away any sting.

Despite his unease, Karun agreed to my proposal of working towards it over the next few weeks. Each night, with his eyes closed, he embarked on this new exploratory mission. I tried not to make any movement that would startle him, even stifling the impulse to look down, much less stroke him or guide him. Instead, I mentally transmitted welcoming vibes his way—my encouragement, my appreciation, my empathy.

The barrier I needed to help Karun cross seemed mostly psychological. Sometimes he wilted too quickly, but on most nights he stopped even though physically still primed. Uma told me to try pomegranates. "It's the desi alternative to the oysters they prescribe in the West. The Kama Sutra says to boil the seeds in oil, but in my experience, a glass of juice right before works just as well." Karun seemed puzzled by all the freshly squeezed nightcaps I began serving, so I extolled their antioxidant benefits, telling him a bedtime dosage worked best. Hazy on the Kama Sutra instructions, I erred on the safe side by also downing a shot myself.

I shopped for pomegranates at the market near work—red ones rather than gold, because they clearly displayed the ardor I felt befit an aphrodisiac. I learnt to distinguish between the different varieties— the "Mridula" with its voluptuous crimson interior, the "Bhagwa" with its smooth and glossy skin (fruits from Satara were always the juiciest). I became an expert at separating the arils from the bitter white pith, at squeezing out every last drop of succulence. In a pinch, I brought home the bottled variety of juice one evening—it tasted flat and spiritless, nothing like the fresh.

We both got addicted to our bedtime tonic. Perhaps Karun guessed its purpose, even though I didn't confess. Each night, we tasted pomegranate on our first kiss—a few times, I noticed my nipple was tinged red. I wondered if the scent mixed with my own after Jantar Mantar, if I left telltale traces on Karun as well. Sometimes I saved a few kernels to sprinkle on our cornflakes the next morning, to carry over the spell.

Surely the same lovemaking associations must have evolved in Karun's mind as well. Perhaps this was the subliminal conditioning the Kama Sutra intended, because I did notice progress. Karun's explorations grew keen enough for me to cautiously anticipate success. I lay in bed under him every night waiting patiently for the next increment. Images from his past drifted through my mind—the photos and toy planes, the moral instruction citations, the fantastical Lego shapes. Soon the breakthrough would arrive to complete my assimilation of him. The planes taking off, the Lego flying through the air, like so many quarks and electrons, planets and Milky Ways. The two of us enveloped by the sweet smell of pomegranates as our very own supernova blossomed across time and space.

———

I SMOOTH OVER my sari to make the bulge of the pomegranate at my waist less conspicuous as Madhu leads me into Mura's section of the compartment. It is surprisingly shabby. Areas of fresh white paint compete with expanses of peeling railway-regulation green, as if someone abandoned a renovation project midway. One entire side still has sleeper berths stacked two high running along its length, and the floor shows gaping holes where walls and dividers have been yanked out. Could this really be the den of someone working for the great and mighty Bhim?

Mura sits in one of the lower berths, cracking open peanuts. He does so with the fingers of only his left hand, extracting the kernels and tossing them into his mouth in a single compulsive arc. He is small but bulbous, with a head larger than his body, as one might expect of someone employing a lot of brainpower—an accountant, perhaps. I notice an unhealthy sheen to him, an oiliness that oozes out of his skin and glistens on his scalp. Perhaps he has too many peanuts in his diet.

Madhu explains my presence and withdraws, closing the door behind her. The makeup must have worked, because Mura does not question me about my age. "Can you dance?" he asks instead.

"A little. Guddi said she could teach me."

"Ah, Guddi. She's so innocent, isn't she? Do you know, when I went to fetch her, she asked if she could bring her five-year-old brother along to meet Devi ma as well? These villagers—they're all so child-like. One can't even begin to explain the ways of the world to them." Mura takes off his thick accountant glasses and wipes his face with a handkerchief, and I wait to find out what he is getting at.

"Of course, you, being from the city, must know things work a little differently. For instance, despite whatever blemishes your layers of makeup might be trying to hide, suppose I choose you for Devi ma. The question then arises, what would be in it for me?" Mura's eyes bulge a little behind their lenses, like those of a child reminded of a favorite treat.

"I don't have much money, if that's what you want."

"Oh, no—I meant nothing so crass. But you do see my point, don't you? City people are different from villagers—more willing to be a little guileful if it gives them an advantage. With them—with *us*—there's no shame in asking for fair give-and-take." He pats the seat beside him. "Why don't you come here and sit with me on the berth? If nothing else, as a small reward in recognition of all I'm doing for our community?" He breaks open a peanut and holds out the kernels in his hand, as if I'm a bird he's trying to attract.

I ignore his offering. "If you don't mind, I prefer to stand." First the hospital Romeo, then Hrithik, now Mura—has my body pumped out some special pheromone today to provoke all these advances? Why am I suddenly so popular?

Mura shakes his head. "Unwilling to even sit by my side. Not even a little generosity of spirit." He looks at me reproachfully. "Perhaps then Mura will have to stand as well."

Just then, I hear the screeching sound of the engine brakes being applied. Peanuts sail through the air, Mura slides to the floor and I almost go flying as well, as the train slows, suddenly, violently. We come to a halt, and Mura gets up sputtering. "That driver, he must be mad to make a stop like this. You just wait here, I'll go investigate." He exits from the door to the girls' room, and I hear a bolt being drawn closed on the other side.

This is my chance to escape. I go to the door and call out the girls' names in a whisper. "Anupam? Guddi? Madhu?"

"Yes, Didi?"

"Guddi, can you open this door?"

I hear a giggle, and some muffled conversation. Then Anupam answers. "Didi? Mura chacha said not to let you out."

"It's just for a minute. I have to use the bathroom."

More discussion follows, and then Guddi speaks again. "We'd have to check with Madhu didi first. She's stepped out with Mura chacha. They won't be long." Anupam giggles in the background.

I decide to try a window. I pry apart two of the horizontal bars, but the widened space is barely big enough for a cat to squeeze through. Searching the compartment for something to use as a crowbar, I notice how much rustier the windows get towards the far end. The last window only has two bars still in place, one of which simply crumbles when I test it. Just as I knock out the remaining bar for an opening I can comfortably squeeze through, Mura returns.

"That stupid engineer. He wanted to return to Dadar, got cold feet going through Mahim. Some crazy idea of taking the Central Line to Ghatkopar, then switching over to the new metro rail. Never mind that those tracks are twenty meters up in the air. I told him there was absolutely no danger, that Bhim had personally arranged our passage."

I stand in front of the window as he talks, trying to cover the absence of the bars with my frame. Perhaps he won't notice the alternate plans I've made.

"It really wouldn't have done you any good even if you had managed to crawl through," Mura says softly as we start moving again. His voice sounds concerned, sympathetic. "Haven't you had a chance to see what's outside?" I look through the window at the pools of stagnant water by the tracks, at the line of shanty houses running alongside. Plots of spinach and salad leaves go by, just like anywhere along the suburban rail corridor.

"You don't realize, do you?—that fork at Dadar the engineer wanted to take? We're in Mahim now, the Muslim side he dreaded. It's the heart of their stronghold—when the killings began in force, the first area they barricaded themselves off in. But don't worry, we've paid them off to let us pass—they think we're just a harmless bunch of Christians headed back to Bandra over the railway bridge.

"Of course, you're welcome to go your own way. But there's no telling what they'll do to you the minute you step off the train. Especially when they see you in that pretty Hindu bridal outfit."

WHAT SENT BOMBAY careening most irrevocably towards its breakup into Hindu and Muslim sections was the Bandra-Worli sea link. Cutting across the sea to avoid crowded suburbs like Dadar and Mahim, the bypass connected the south to the north in ten minutes flat (seven with Uma driving). "Look at us," she'd say, zipping us over the structure that had taken sixteen billion rupees and a decade to build. "We're a top-tier international metropolis now—no less than San Francisco or Sydney."

Perhaps it was the acclaim lavished on the bridge as the crown jewel of Indian engineering that attracted the HRM's attention. The organization announced, out of the blue one day, that although operational since 2009, the structure had never been consecrated. For the next City of Devi project, massive religious processions would march all through Mumbai to converge at the bridge, where Hindu priests would confer their blessing and rename it the "Mumbadevi Sea Link." To further stoke this "new and incendiary mischief" (as *The Indian Express* called it), the HRM would fly in the top leaders of all the major right-wing organizations in the country to join in the ceremony.

By the time I turned on the television that morning, the toll booths had already been doused with vermilion and the swell of participants had reached the cantilevered section of the bridge. HRM's Doshi appeared in a close-up, trying to smile through the sweat pouring down his face. He struck a coconut on the concrete, breaking it open only after three attempts. Holding the two halves aloft as if he'd aced a magic trick, he ascended a small podium and began to speak.

"Many centuries ago, in the time of the Ramayana, our ancestors proved their engineering prowess. They built a bridge from India all the way south to Lanka so that Lord Ram could walk across the sea and bring back his Sita Devi. Today, Hindu engineers have repeated the feat of their forebears so that we can make a similar journey south, from Bandra to Worli." I switched the TV to another channel, but Doshi appeared on that one too, thanking Mumbadevi for showering her protection and blessings on the bridge.

Just as I readied to change the channel again, the camera drew back to an odd wide-angle aerial shot of the cable suspension spans soaring forty stories into the air. What caught my eye was how one of the central towers holding up the cables seemed to tilt out of the screen towards me. The giant fireball, accompanied by the sound of the explosion, came an instant later. Images flashed on the screen in jerky succession—people running about and leaping off, more blasts spewing debris and smoke, the two cable spans parting like the wings of a dying butterfly to collapse towards the water and sink. Each time I thought the mayhem had ended, a fresh explosion knocked out another segment. Eventually, as I stared aghast at the TV screen, only the smoking frame remained.

One hundred and eighty-two people perished that morning, including Shrikant Doshi and much of the leadership of the HRM and its allies. "Stay indoors," my father called to warn me, "there's going to be riots all over the city." Sure enough, rival factions plunged eagerly into a contest to see who could massacre the most Muslims—not just as reprisal (even though the explosions had all the hallmarks of sophisticated terrorists), but also to prove themselves the fiercest and most ruthless, and hence most deserving to fill the power vacuum. Our March for Unity failed to impress them, as did the anguished editorials composed by newspaper pundits.

The single bloodiest incident occurred that weekend at Haji Ali. A rampaging mob led by a previously unknown upstart charged down the walkway across the bay to the island on which the mosque stood. Bhim's army beheaded men as they prayed, dragged women out and raped them in the courtyard, impaled babies on sharpened sticks driven into the rocky beach. They also meticulously videotaped everything. Even censored for television, the clip broadcast that evening was so disturbing that both Karun and I had to look away.

Others, however, reveled in the images. The video propagated its savagery all across the country, its frames leaping from screen to screen through the population's billion-plus cell phones. (My father, to his horror, even received a digitally altered version casting the attackers as Muslims and their victims as hapless Hindu pilgrims.) After months of aimless venting, *Superdevi*-charged mobs in towns and villages finally found a focus for their hooliganism. The news turned so grim that Karun and I had to suspend our breakfast ritual of reading out to each other from the paper: twenty Muslim villages annihilated in western Gujarat, forty-one Hindu children in Lucknow circumcised with the same sharp stones used afterwards to bash in their skulls, Christians burnt alive in churches, Sikhs butchered on the street. Every group seemed to join in lustily, as if the national goal of religious integration had finally triumphed, and the bloodbath were a grand celebration of multiculturalism, of equal opportunity.

When Bhim wrested control of the HRM, we all heaved a sigh of relief. The competition for power had ended, the killing would finally stop. All through his ascendancy, we'd heard different myths about Bhim—a businessman kidnapped and tortured by Muslims, a professor whose family terrorists had wiped out. But nobody knew what he claimed to stand for—not until the rally at which he declared himself a fighter for peace. *"I pledge to set aside past bloodshed, extend minorities an olive branch,"* Karun recited from the newspaper the next morning. *"From now on, my goal is to promote harmony, to advance industry and science and art."* Supposedly, Bhim's model was to be Ashoka the Great, the ancient Mauryan emperor who united India with unrestrained savagery, but then ruled with great compassion and benevolence. In the following weeks, reports streamed in about his attempts to get city dwellers to join hands with rural followers, his dynamic success in connecting with the educated young. Even Uma toyed with the idea of subscribing (out of sheer curiosity, she told my enraged father) when Bhim inaugurated his TwitterXLP account.

He overlooked one detail: while the HRM may have crowned him their emperor, the country had different ideas. In the long-scheduled national elections that month, the HRM was soundly trounced. Enraged by this humiliation (which he blamed on the "cancerous seeds" sown by minorities) Bhim not only jettisoned Ashoka, but decided the HRM would bypass the political process altogether. The violence from the power struggle had never really died down—it still burned in the background, as self-sustaining as a nuclear reaction by now. Bhim stoked its fires, channeling its bloodthirst into a campaign to rid the country of Muslims once and for all.

He embarked on a "rath yatra" around the country—a chariot odyssey along which he evoked Hitler's call for a "final solution." Other leaders had undertaken rath yatras in the past, such as the famous crusade which led eventually to the destruction of the Ayodhya mosque. Bhim's was a high-tech version, employing giant video screens to incite spectators, sophisticated communication techniques to mobilize and manipulate mobs. Most successful was his use of the new TwitterSpeak service, which broadcast his messages to the cell phones of illiterate followers directly in speech form.

After that, the carnage surged to levels my father said had only occurred once before—during the 1947 Partition. It was self-perpetuating, he noted—as investors the world over fled from India's chaos, the resulting economic collapse made people even more ready to scapegoat their Muslim neighbors. "Our new central government leaders should be shot—so desperate to hold on to their coalition that they barely dare squeak out any criticism of Bhim." The BBC began using words like "ethnic cleansing" and "genocide" in its reports on India. Pakistan blustered a lot about intervening militarily to save its "Islamic brethren" but didn't as yet have Chinese support. It must have contented itself with an increase in terrorist financing, because soon after, a dozen landmark temples—from Badrinath to Meen-akshi—fell victim to bombs. Bhim used this as the perfect excuse to further ramp up the HRM pogrom.

The Times of India reported that several cities with enough of a minority population to put up resistance had split into Hindu and Muslim sections, with Christians and Sikhs slinking in wherever possible. Maps showing the imminent divisions for Mumbai began appearing on the internet. Although the boundaries changed wildly from day to day, our area of Colaba always fell in a Hindu enclave. The meatwalla, a Muslim, stopped coming to our door, as did the man who sold biscuits from the large iron trunk he carried on his head. The Ahmeds down the hall reluctantly traded their sea-facing flat with a Hindu family occupying a Dongri one-bedroom. The Mirandas, a Christian family on the floor below us, also disappeared, as did Dr. Kanchwalla, whose name could have been Muslim, but was actually Parsi.

Perhaps more people vanished as well, perhaps the upheavals around me were more dramatic. Caught up in the turmoil in my personal life, I failed to notice.

LOOKING BACK, I can pinpoint the exact night things changed with Karun. Pakistan had joined the Chinese invasion two days before, making a series of bombing sorties all the way to Delhi that morning. Rumors of an air raid on the rock carvings at Elephanta Island had left Mumbai on edge. Unable to find a cab, I had to walk back all the way from my mother's house. When I finally got home, Karun seemed rather keyed—from the rumors, I assumed. But it turned out he hadn't heard yet—something else must have happened to make him so tense. Before I could find out, he led me to bed, thrusting between my legs with such conviction that I thought we would at last achieve our fourth star. Abruptly, though, he lost his momentum, his expression slack-ened, his attention skittered somewhere else. He excused himself to get a glass of water, switching to kisses down my body when he came back.

The Jantar Mantar he performed, with a touch of delirium almost, rocketed me quickly to climax. When it came my turn, though, I didn't have much success. Eventually, he buried his head against my body and said he just wanted to be held.

He remained off-kilter all week, distracted to the point of feverishness (though his temperature was normal—I checked). Each night he came to bed seemingly determined to prove himself. Although he valiantly compensated afterwards, I saw him increasingly frustrated by his recurring lack of success. I scoured the nearby market daily for pomegranates but the war with Pakistan had taken them off the shelves.

I almost didn't make my weekly visit to my parents the following Tuesday, since Karun looked so unwell. But he insisted he felt fine—he seemed anxious I keep my appointment. I returned to find the flat empty—Karun came back only at eleven-thirty p.m. He looked disheveled, almost crazed—I could have sworn I smelled alcohol on his breath. "It's the astroparticle conference I've been organizing—we had an emergency meeting. First the riots, now this war—the preparations are not going well." He didn't look at me when he spoke, and I wondered if I should believe what he said. In the morning, I could tell he hadn't slept.

He grew increasingly jittery in the days that followed. Some nights, I awoke to find him sitting in the dark, his hands cradling his head. He refused to divulge what was wrong, insisting he'd be fine once the conference had been held. We stopped having sex—not even Jantar Mantar—the dates in my diary remained starless. The nightly air raids had thrown the city into complete turmoil—in fact, the entire world was teetering after the new September 11 attacks. I reasoned Karun must be wound up, like everyone else. He instructed me not to reveal his whereabouts to anyone who might ask—the hostilities seemed to have made him paranoid as well. Only later did the thought that somebody might be blackmailing him (about what? surely astroparticles weren't classified?) enter my head.

On our last night together, he clung to me with great tenderness. "I love you so much. When this is all over, we'll go and—" He didn't complete the sentence. I had the feeling he stared at me all night as I slept.

He left before I awoke, calling from Bandra that afternoon. "I'm at the institute annex—the center where they'll hold the conference. The attendees come in on Sunday, so with everything going on, I may as well just stay here till then." His cellphone seemed to be getting no signal, so he gave me the number for the front desk. By then, the idea of a conference in the midst of such global chaos was painfully absurd, but I could tell from his strangled voice how much he hated lying to me, so I kept up the pretense. Later, I realized he must have planned the trip—his duffel bag was missing, and even the classical CDs he listened to during yoga were gone.

Mr. and Mrs. Iyer came up to check on us after that evening's bombing attack. They mentioned in passing that the conference was cancelled three weeks ago—had Karun been planning his escape since then? I dialed the number he'd given me, but it kept returning a busy signal. The next morning, when the new communiqué about Pakistan's threatened nuclear attack appeared, I called again. I kept trying day after day without getting through, until the electricity failed and the phones went dead.

THE TRAIN PICKS UP SPEED. I keep my eyes averted out the window. Mura comes over and gazes with me at the houses going past. Only their tops are visible now, the rest obscured by a wall in between. "I remember when I was a child, we used to ride the train every Sunday to visit my uncle in Goregaon. There weren't so many houses then, or walls for that matter—at Santa Cruz, one could see all the way to the planes parked at the airport." He begins to caress the back of my neck. "Did you grow up in the suburbs or the city?"

I brush his hand off my body, but he manages to latch onto my fingers. He buries his face into my hair and inhales deeply. "Ah, that lovely fragrance convent school girls have. Is it the shampoo or the soap or just that wealthy South Mumbai scent?"

I turn around to try and squeeze away but he has me cornered against the wall. "Very educated, are you? College, probably. That's why you're not very impressed with our devi. Look at Guddi and Anupam, all bubbling with excitement. So completely convinced Devi ma's come to save her own city."

"You mean she hasn't? How devastating to hear that. This whole train and bridal charade you're putting us through, and you don't even have a devi?"

"Oh, we have her all right. Even better than in the movies, you'll see. The crowds worship her, even if convent girls like you don't believe."

"And you *do* believe? That she'll protect us from the Pakistanis? That she'll open her heavenly parasol to block their bombs on the nineteenth?"

Mura draws back. "Nothing's going to happen on the nineteenth— it's just a rumor the Pakistanis have been spreading to scare us. Who makes such an announcement if they really mean to attack?—they'd have simply launched by now, most assuredly. Or rather we'd have, even earlier, to beat them—if the threat seemed at all real to our military. Surely you could figure this out with your college degree?" He peers through his glasses to appraise me. "That's the whole beauty of Devi ma, don't you see? She gets to save Guddi and Anupam and the crowds flocking to her, keeps her promise to rescue Mumbai, without having to do anything."

"And what if you're wrong? What if the warnings are correct?"

"They're not, but we're prepared for any eventuality."

"Who? You and your devi?"

"Not the devi, Bhim. Do you really think he wouldn't have taken precautions—someone so visionary? I can't go into details, but if the Pakistanis do try any mischief, he'll make sure we're the most protected souls in the country. Which includes all of Devi ma's maidens, incidentally. So you're lucky I picked you—perhaps you could show some gratitude to me."

Mura comes closer again, and runs a hand through my hair. "So what do you say? In return for saving your life—surely you can agree to such a little thing?" He leans forward to kiss me.

I lay my palms on his chest as if in acquiescence, then push him hard. He topples over easily, tumbling across the floor like a plump and comical baby. He gropes for his glasses and locates them underneath his own body. One of the arms has snapped off. "How will I see with them now?" he asks mournfully, staring at the piece in his hand.

I am at the door, banging for the girls, when he is upon me. He rams his head into my back, knocking my breath out. I turn around, and he batters me again, like a fat and hornless goat, this time between my breasts. The impact of the blow sends me falling to the floor. The pomegranate rolls out of my sari, and the first thought that flashes through my mind is that if he tastes it, he'll be further crazed by its aphrodisiac properties.

But he pays it no attention. Instead, he squats over me as I lie there trying to suck air back into my lungs. "Such a small favor I ask." His face is red, he wipes tears from his eyes. "And instead, what do you do? You attack me." I try to sit up, but he pushes me back. "Convent girls—do they all have to be so haughty?" He holds me down and stretches out atop me. His body is soft and unnaturally yielding—even his lips on my neck feel spongy. "Please," he whispers, "it's not too much." I can still detect the peanuts on his breath.

I nod to buy time. "But not on the floor, not like this." Surprised, he peers at me to see if I'm lying. I give him a reassuring smile. "As you put it, for saving my life."

He helps me to my feet, and leads me to the berths. I stall by prodding the cushions on each, pretending to look for the softest. I'm running out of ploys and Mura out of patience when the undercarriage shudders—a sharp crack from below interrupts the steady rumble of wheels. Metal grinds noisily against metal, the compartment buckles and lifts, and to my disbelief, I see the wall outside the window closing in. I have just enough time to cover my face before we plow through, before a barrage of brick and mortar bursts in. The room tilts precariously around me, flinging me against a berth—then rights itself miraculously, the instant before tipping. A line of building façades whizzes by—I realize the train has left its tracks and is thundering down the center of a road.

Except that it's not quite the center, but an angle at which we hurtle—an angle that brings us closer and closer to the buildings streaming past. We mount something, the edge of the sidewalk perhaps, and the jolt dislodges the pomegranate from its hiding place. It lifts off the floor and sails by my face, serene as a flying saucer, as I vainly try to snare it. I imagine myself airborne as well, the walls around me weightless, the train a rocket launching into space. As the moment of contact arrives, gravity gives us a pass, and we rise above the buildings instead of crashing into them. The scrunching of metal, the splintering of wood—all the sickening sounds of impact surrounding me fade. We arc through the air, the compartments liberated from their earthly existence, our persons conveyed heavenward by the freed spirit of the train. I look down through the clouds at the long trail of Mumbai that stretches below us—from the string of suburbs unwinding north, to Colaba at the southernmost tip. For a moment, as we peak, everything is still. Then we begin our descent back to the city where Karun awaits.

JAZ

6

AS I WATCH THE WAR-POCKED LANDSCAPE GO PAST, I WONder again what my life would have been like had I never met Karun. Calmer, probably. Longer, too. To think that a single chance encounter has led to this wood and metal coffin in which I brace for my doom. Sweet, innocent Karun, as alluring as a blossom of the deadly datura and about as harmless. Samson had his Delilah, Adam his Eve, and the Jazter had you.

Already, I can see my epitaph. "Here lies Jaz, lover of his fellow men, done in royally by one of them." With a warning for others of my ilk (hunters—*shikaris*—I like to call them) inscribed on my tombstone. A list of cautionary signs to watch out for—the most flagrant being that even now, risking life and limb and that one other most imperiled appendage, all I do is search this benighted city for Karun.

I look at the scratches on my arms, smell the sulfur in my hair. Has the Jazter really been reduced to this? The mud on my designer hightops, the stains on my Diesel denims—what possessed me to subject my kickiest threads to such risk? Then I remember—Karun, whom I must find, whom I need to dazzle, whose rectitude I hope to penetrate.

Perhaps I'm too easy with the blame. With the impending bomb, the Jazter goose, not to mention his jeans and sneakers, are scheduled to be cooked anyway. I've rarely planned ahead, so no sense lamenting lost opportunities for escape. It might have been nice watching all this action from afar—say on the giant screen in Times Square. Except most of New York, for all I know, has been burnt to a crisp.

Since the future's so iffy, I'll turn my attention to the past. The underfoot clickety-clack marking out my remaining minutes begs to be drowned out with nostalgia anyway. I tune in to the sounds from twelve years ago. Children laugh and shout on the swings. Mango trees around me rustle in the wind. I sit in the park near Cooperage, waiting for the hunt to begin.

IT WAS DUSK when I first saw Karun. He looked much younger than all the parents milling around with their kids, which made him instantly suspect. He sat on a bench between the slides and the swings, an unopened book in his lap. He was trying very hard to be inconspicuous, I could tell.

I'd walked over after college to the park, to check out the evening's prospects. A teenager showing off his shiny new Reeboks. A bearded young Bohri promenading his burkha-clad bride. Day laborers out for a smoke, their arms dusted white with gypsum. I leered at them all with scrupulous impartiality. The couples, as usual, were clueless. The shikaris would know I was one of them.

My gaze kept returning to Karun. Such a fawn, he might even be younger than myself. His chin as smooth as his cheeks, his hair cut so short that his ears stuck out, his lips announcing a hint of succulence. Did he have enough meat on his bones, though, to warrant a shikari's interest?

He opened the book in his lap. His absorption in the pages seemed so immediate, it had to be faked. Was he performing for someone's sake? As I decided he'd do for this evening's prey, he looked up and engaged my gaze. He held it as long as he could, as if forcing himself to be brave.

Then the courage drained from his face. He arose abruptly and began to walk to the gate. By the time I made it through the turnstile, he had crossed the sidewalk onto the curb. Wait up, I felt like shouting. Don't you know the rules of the game? He was almost at the opposite shore of the road when I immersed myself into the river of traffic after him.

He started looking unflatteringly lanky on the other side, his ears protruding absurdly from his head. Had I really found him attractive, was he even in on the hunting game? But by now, all my carnivorous instincts had been aroused—I had to keep giving chase.

He unexpectedly veered right, through the entrance to the Oval grounds. Ahead, in the dying light, groups of boys wound down their soccer games. The path stretched out emptily, nobody using it to cross the field today. We soon discovered why—just before the road on the other side stood a locked metal gate. The way we had entered offered the only escape.

He stopped. Two boys in orange and black stockings ran between us, scrimmaging. One of them knocked chests with the other to get control of the ball. They engaged in the briefest of contact at their waists, then, laughing, sprinted away.

He took the opportunity to slip off the path. I followed the outline of his shoulders as he wafted into the dark. More soccer boys ran by, bare-chested this time, their shirts dangling out from behind their shorts. The sweat on their muscles glistened in the light from distant streetlamps.

Night seemed to be descending unusually fast. The center of the field was already a pool of black. Other denizens had begun to roam around in the playfield, seeking more nocturnal games. I heard the familiar signaling coughs I had heeded so often, caught a glimpse of a torso or head.

Tonight, I already had my quarry marked. I followed him all the way to the peripheral ring of palms. The lights of the city twinkled beyond the tree trunks, tall metal bars rose in between to cut us off. He wavered as he spotted them, then came to a stop. Had he really expected a way out?

It was time to move in for the kill. Time to prepare for the feel of skin against skin. Clumps of bushes rose chest high between some of the palms. Would he struggle very strenuously if I tried to drag him in? How loudly would he groan as I initiated him?

But he was new to the hunt, I reminded myself. Unversed as yet in the versatility of spit. I had to ply him with words first: what cricketers did he like, had he seen any films?

He turned around as I began my approach. Even in this light, I could make out the fear on his face. "Hello," I said soothingly. He stood frozen for an instant, then took off on a sprint.

I looked on dumbfounded. This wasn't literally a hunt—I'd never heard of anyone actually bolting like this. Then the adrenaline pumped motion into my limbs. He raced through the darkness, staying close to the border, and I ran after him. We could have been the last two soccer players on the field, still chasing each other after the end of the game.

It happened as he closed in on the entrance, as it occurred to me he might get away. He tripped over a tree root—his velocity so great that it launched him into the air. He flew through the night, like a daredevil player defying gravity to execute a flamboyant save. By the time I came up, he was lying on his back, grimacing in pain.

In nature documentaries, the predator, its work done, would sink its teeth about now into its injured prey. I felt the same stimulus from my own quarry's helplessness, but resisted the urge to pounce and have my way with him. "Are you OK?" I asked, but he didn't reply. Tears glistened in his eyes as he rocked on the ground, holding his left forearm at the wrist.

The need to touch him was overwhelming, so I took his wrist and examined it. He winced as my fingers brushed against the tender bone ridge. I held on longer than necessary to the unbruised part, fascinated by the soft hairs over the supple skin. Would offering to inspect the rest of his body as well seem too amiss?

"Why did you run?"

"Why were you following me?"

"Why do you think?" Immediately, I realized it was the wrong thing to say. "I just wanted to talk, that's all," I slipped in quickly, but my dare had silenced him.

His vulnerability—the dirt on his shirt, the rip in his jeans, the sneaker that had rolled off, made him achingly desirable. But the notorious Jazter carnality had been corrupted by guilt. "Here, let me dust you off," I said, feeling the full weight of responsibility for his fallen state.

He didn't protest as I brushed my hands across his shirt, then more liberally over his jeans. He winced when I eased his foot back into its sneaker. "Does it hurt?" I asked, but he shook his head.

When I stood him up, however, he winced again. "It's nothing, I'll just go home," he insisted when I suggested a doctor. Then he took a step and yelped.

Here was the opportunity to redeem myself, to rise like Mother Teresa above my lasciviousness. I bundled him, still protesting, into a taxi and took him to Bombay Hospital. The X-ray clearly showed the fracture—a thin dark line cutting into the outer metatarsal. "I really must go, I'll come back tomorrow," he started saying when the doctor ordered a cast. Red-faced, he whispered to me that he didn't have enough money on him.

It felt strange offering him a loan, but the ghost of Mother Teresa cheered me on from the wings. As expected, he refused, so I went and paid directly at the hospital desk. The cast was white and bulky—his toes peeped out like small caged pets. I felt myself succumbing again to his helplessness. Who knew the sight of hobbling prey could be such an aphrodisiac?

He did not want to disclose his address. "Just drop me off at Mumbai Central Station." But he was too wobbly on his crutches, so I accompanied him to his hostel, then up three floors to the room he shared. "My roommate's asleep, so I'll just say goodbye here. I'll have the money for you tomorrow at six."

I took the same cab home. My mother was waiting with dinner, but I had to go to the bathroom first, I said. The image of my fawn limping around in torn jeans swirled in my head. The Jazter had been stimulated a little too much—before he ate, he had to take care of himself.

BY THE TIME I knocked on Karun's door the following evening, I had fantasized so much that I felt ready to burst in, rip open his shirt, and throw him on the bed. Or perhaps on the floor, the reimbursement money from yesterday flying into the air as I plunged in to satisfy myself. Maybe Karun would be in the same state of ferment and join in the ripping and throwing as well. Though not in the plunging, an activity the Jazter refuses to permit on himself.

I didn't get a chance. Karun opened the door a crack, just enough to hand me an envelope. "Thanks for helping me last night. I've added in the taxi fare as well." The crack began to close, and he waved as if from a receding train.

I stood in front of the door, dumbfounded. Then I started hammering. "Who is it?" a different voice called out—its annoyance pleased me.

"Just a friend. I'll get it." The door opened, and Karun slid out. "Are you crazy?"

"Why are you whispering?" I demanded loudly.

He shut the door behind him. "My roommate's inside. What do you want?"

"I want to know what you were doing yesterday in the park."

"What do you mean?"

"Look, I just want to talk."

He began to say something, then decided against it. "Wait here." He went in and emerged a moment later with his crutches. "There's a Barista café around the corner—we can go there."

The crutches were useless on the stairs. He hopped awkwardly down the first flight, then gave in and took the arm I offered. Within seconds, the predator centers in my brain shot into high alert. I instinctively scanned the stairwell for cubbyholes suitable for a quick drag-and-plunge.

Relinquishing him to his crutches downstairs came with an unexpected consolation. Each time he bore down on the handles, his body tensed to reveal the location of underlying muscles. They were modest but endearing—a 6.8 on the Jazter scale. His buttocks arced through the air as he swiveled, inviting me to follow them. I felt a primeval satisfaction knowing he couldn't make a run for it.

"Ijaz," I said at the café. "That's my name, though everyone calls me Jaz. I thought I'd tell you since I saw yours at the hospital sign-in. Do you go to college?"

He nodded, then became studiously absorbed in his coffee when I asked him where. To put him at ease, I talked about my bachelor's in commerce at HR College. As I prattled on about the Sensex's stupendous rise on the Mumbai stock exchange, he stopped me. "What exactly do you want?"

"To get into international finance, I guess. To really understand how the world works."

"No, I mean what do you want from *me*? Why did you bring me here?" His eyes darted as he spoke, an agitated smile stretched over his lips.

That's where I muffed it. The Jazter code of conduct is quite explicit in such situations: Be direct. Don't risk being misunderstood with subtlety—bring out, so to speak, the ol' battering ram. Except my lust had been adulterated by an unaccustomed sense of responsibility, perhaps even tenderness. "I just thought we could be friends," I responded, aghast at my own sappiness.

His expression didn't relax. My usual fallbacks of cricket and the movies also fell flat. "Would you like to return?" I finally asked, and he said yes.

I followed him back to the building, my taste buds bitter with defeat. This time, his buttocks swung away not in invitation, but in declaration of their unavailability. The fact that I had failed to connect, that I wouldn't be able to have him, left me even more charged with desire. As he pitifully poked along, the tender thoughts grew stronger too, into an overwhelming feeling of protectiveness. I wanted to mother him as well as molest him.

Just as I prepared to wish him a final goodbye at his hostel, he turned around. "Jai Hind," he declared.

"What?" I had been given the brush-off before, but never with a patriotic slogan.

"Jai Hind College—didn't you want to know where I study? I'm free Friday evening—we could meet near there."

WE COME TO A HALT. The scenery outside remains desolate. What has happened to the people? Where has the war hidden them? It's good the Jazter has renounced his pastime of shikar, since park pickings must be exceedingly slim these days.

Then again, it's hard to tell. The population has taken to ebbing and flowing in waves. Perhaps it's the moon that drives them, exerting mass gravitational pulls on their brains. More plausibly, they're motivated by safety in numbers, given the unpredictability of each day. I feel the stares of wary eyes from distant buildings, imagine bodies carefully concealed behind drapes. Any moment now, they will realize their collective power and surge down upon us in an invincible spate. I've seen this firsthand through my days of surveillance—human tides pouring through neighborhoods, their abrupt rise, their unpredictable wane.

I hear people outside—only a few rather than a flood, but I draw back just the same. I cannot make out the argument they seem involved in. Have we arrived close enough to my prey? Is it time to stealthily slip away? I peep through the window, but do not see that one recognizable face. Which tells me we're not there yet, I need to hunker down again.

Footsteps near, doors slam shut, and we start to move once more. I check my watch—it's five p.m.—the day will start fading soon. There's nothing to do but brace for the return of the annoying clickety-clack. And lose myself in memories of my checkered courtship of Karun again.

ALL WEEK, I WAITED for Friday. Only one desire, surely, could have prompted Karun's suggestion of another meeting. I half expected him to chicken out, but he didn't. We had tea in the outdoor patio of Gaylord's—a venue I suspected was a tad expensive for him.

He came across as very different from our last meeting—so forthcoming he practically drowned me with information. How he loved science as a kid, how his widowed mother lived a few hours from Delhi, in Karnal, how his hostel roommate from the tiny state of Tripura had an unusual hobby (embroidery, I think). "It was difficult leaving my mother to come and study in Bombay, but we both agreed I needed to spread my wings a bit." He'd visited all the museums in town and attended two concerts of carnatic vocal music ("the wailing," as I called it—I tried not to grimace). He still practiced yoga every morning despite his cast, though he'd have to wait until it came off before he could go swimming again.

At first, he almost fooled me. I despaired he had taken me at my word about just wanting to be friends. Then I began to detect the cracks in his cover-up. The nervousness behind his chattering, the energy channeled into avoiding the one question he knew I would raise again. *Why had he gone to the park?* A question whose answer he must be intimately familiar with, no matter how hard he tried to suppress it. Had he come today hoping I would pry the issue free despite his fear of facing it?

Ordinarily, I would have lost no time obliging. But he worked his subterfuge so earnestly, it felt boorish not to play along. Besides, why not let him stew a bit—didn't even the most unyielding meat tenderize that way? So I talked about my parents—how they met at a Muslim student mixer in the U.S. "My father was in comparative religion, my mother in Asian studies—not only did they get married, but they even worked together. They returned to India some years later to have me, but when I was six, they went back to America." I told him I was a globalization victim, an international mutt, having grown up in so many different countries. "Singapore, Indonesia, Germany, in one year alone, followed by fourteen months in Switzerland." I showed off my French and my German: *"Tu as un beau cul," "Und ich hoffe, Sie erlauben mir es zu erforschen,"* after making sure he didn't understand either language (I refused to translate). Although our backgrounds differed so much, we were both only children—at twenty, we were even the same age! By the time we emptied our cups, it seemed plausible we could be friends.

About to deliver my coup—the question he both dreaded and craved—I saw I had a problem. Say I persuaded Karun into revisiting our unconsummated shikar—where, exactly, did I propose to take him? One needed two feet, both in good working order, to negotiate the bushes in the park or the lonelier stretches of Chowpatty beach. Karun's hostel came with a roommate infestation, our flat suffered similarly from a live-in servant. Would we have to wait until Karun walked before I could carnally inaugurate him?

So I didn't bring up the park—since I couldn't act on it, why scare him off? Instead I paid for tea, and when he protested, said we had to have a next time so he could reciprocate. That's how the Jazter (blushing even now at the smudge on his hard-boiled reputation) embarked on the unfamiliar custom of *dating*. We started meeting Tuesdays and Fridays, then Mondays as well, when classes ended early for both of us. Usually at a cheap place like Samrat, though sometimes for an ice cream splurge at the nearby Baskin-Robbins. (Watching the pink of his tongue shyly scoop up a taste of my Rocky Road made me hunger to share more than just dairy products with him.) Afterwards, I took a cab home so I could drop him off—a gesture he appreciated, since he had such difficulty battling the bus crowds on his crutches.

I called it my "February of Frustration." I came no closer to his butt despite cataloguing all the enchanting ways it turned and twisted (the half-swivel when he used only one crutch, the bump and grind when he tried climbing steps, the free swing when he used his body weight to go fast). The park glimmered in the background through all our conversations, endowing them with possibilities I did not articulate. I wondered if my efforts were worth it, if I stuck around only as expiation for his handicapped state. After all, the future did not guarantee gratification, March promised no plunge picnic.

Except a part of me *enjoyed* these vegetarian trysts. I rushed home for relief in the bathroom afterwards—the Right-Hand Express departed regularly by eight. (Sometimes I needed to catch multiple trains.) I wondered if Karun shared this torment—if to enhance it, he even exaggerated his helplessness. Dating, I realized, might have its merits—it wasn't just for suckers and sissies as the Jazter had always dismissed it.

Warning bells not only rang, they pealed, they pounded. Had guilt and sympathy combined unhealthily to form affection? What if this metastasized into something even more dangerous? The Jazter had always prided himself on steering rigorously clean of such marshlands. His dharma revolved around noodling and little else. No emotional ties, no lingering attachments—these were his bible's most basic tenets.

Yet here I sat starry-eyed, listening to Karun describe his afternoon chemistry experiments. Not a scintillating topic exactly, but I could imagine the mischief we could get into as partners in the lab. Especially after hearing of his past transgressions. "I used to take empty medicine bottles to high school to bring back samples from chemistry lab. Nitrates, chlorides, sulfates—I'm embarrassed to say I pilfered them all. I wanted my own mini-lab at home—I couldn't get enough of the colorful coppers and cobalts."

"So not so innocent as you look, eh? And are you still stealing?—perhaps setting up a lab in your hostel?"

Karun laughed. I realized I'd never actually got a good look before at his teeth—they sparkled, all sunlight and Colgate, like in a TV ad.

"Is that why your pockets look so full today?" I continued, hoping to catch another glimpse.

But he turned solemn, as if he'd allowed out too much mirth and needed to compensate. "My mother worked two jobs after my father died, so in the evenings, I'd perform experiments to entertain myself. I read a lot too, buried myself in books. I suppose I must have been lonely—though I didn't realize it back then."

I remembered returning from school to an empty flat myself on evenings when my parents lectured late. The long, stark weekends I spent left to my own devices, padding around at home, craving the company of a sibling or friend. "It's hard not to feel alone as an only child," I said.

That evening, I sat closer to Karun in the taxi than usual, our thighs touching even though the back seat had ample space. I wanted to hold hands the way working-class men, unspoiled by Western mores, did all over the city in innocent friendship. Instead I playfully kneaded Karun's neck, then eased my arm over his shoulder and let it rest there—he didn't draw away. At one point, I leaned across to lower his window, and our mouths came so close I could barely restrain myself from a kiss (he felt the pull too, I think). An outside observer might comment how the mighty Jazter had fallen if he'd been reduced to this for his quota of thrills. But I only wanted to be close, to express my fondness for Karun, to quietly bask in the camaraderie emanating from him.

7

PERHAPS IT'S A *FIN DU MONDE* THING, BUT I HAVE THIS SUDDEN
overwhelming urge to begin drafting my memoirs. The heartwarming
saga of little Jaz who came of age around the globe. Our story begins
way back in 1581, when the Mughal emperor Akbar simmered together
equal parts of Islam and Hinduism (with a pinch of Christianity thrown
in) to rustle up his own curry religion, "Din-i-Ilahi," or "Divine
Faith." The concoction didn't quite take—at least not until centuries
later, when my parents had the brainwave of updating the recipe for
modern tastes. They used Akbar's principles to formulate a version of
Islam that could peacefully co-exist with other religions (or so they
claimed). *An Emperor's Bequest to Islam*, their joint 1,300-page doorstop-
per, spent twenty weeks on the *New York Times* bestseller list in hardcover alone. The fact that they remained practicing Muslims (albeit the
liberal, wine-guzzling kind) put their message in high international
demand. Here was Yale luring them back to America with the promise of
dual professorships on my sixth birthday. Two years later, the king of Bah-
rain offering pots of money to come shore up his liberal credentials. An
instant appointment in the latest European country (Germany, Holland,
Switzerland) wanting to prove its open-mindedness after passing some
blatantly discriminatory law against Muslims. And after the Arab Spring,
even Qatar and Saudi Arabia stood in line to have their blemishes air-
brushed, their repressive images tamed.

Inflamed with the desire to change the world, my parents moved so
much that I felt I lived in a washing machine. Each time I tried to fit in

with a new culture or skin tone at school, the spin cycle came on. Human connections seemed pointless, lasting only as long as we remained in town. My sense of estrangement was the only constant, following me like a dependable pet across the years and continents. I felt so hopeless, so in thrall of a mushrooming interior darkness, that my company turned even the most misfit of my fellow students off.

At the time, I didn't realize that a deeper reason for my malaise lay hidden, something more incendiary than just our frequent relocation. My mother and father remained oblivious—beyond food, shelter, and clothing, they possessed only a hazy awareness of what other nurturing parenthood might involve. The fact that I found it impossible to get bad grades meant my school performance never cued them in on how little I worked or how despondent I became.

In Geneva, on my fourteenth birthday, I straightened out a paper clip and stuck it through my tongue. Then I tried to pierce the end back through again to form a ring, but couldn't, because of all the blood. I wiped my lips clean and returned to the dining table, where my parents waited, editing book proofs and sipping gamay. Mouth closed until the last instant so nothing dribbled out prematurely, I blew out the candles on my birthday cake.

That finally got their attention. The white of the whipped cream icing provided just the right foil to give the red I contributed a breezily decorative effect. Once we returned from the emergency room, my parents began to notice other things as well—the anti-Arab posters nailed to my wall, the swastika imprinted on my neck, the razor blade by my bed. I listened to them talk late into the night, their shock permeating through the wall. What an amazing notion that all that jetting around may have fucked me up!

Their solution was to move once more. To Mother India this time, which would unscramble my identity, fill my heart with pride in who I was, where I came from. That's how the young and still impressionable Jaz found himself sitting in the green-walled annex to the Byculla mosque in Bombay, fitted with a skullcap and equipped with a Koran.

Each evening, as the adults prayed upstairs, I stared at the paint peeling off the benches, trying to tune out the hadiths being explained by the imam. Could I escape again by piercing some other body part?

Fortunately, my cousin Rahim, who attended the same class, had alternative plans for my edification. My parents, ever pressed for time, arranged for me to spend the evenings at his home afterwards. At sixteen, Rahim not only exceeded me in age but also in girth—I experienced his weight firsthand, each time he sat on me at the end of our wrestling bouts. He insisted we strip down to our underwear like Sumo wrestlers—his sweat marked my body, smelling of whatever spice lingered most dominantly from lunch.

Rahim's mother had died a decade ago, and his father worked late, so we didn't have to worry about anyone supervising us. Soon we were undressing completely and wrestling in the buff. I'm not sure if my technique improved or if Rahim simply let me, but I started ending up on top more often than not. My thighs straddling his hips, my seat pressed into his crotch—even though I left his hands free, he never pushed me off. One evening, I had the bright idea of slapping him in the face with my penis as we horsed around. He looked at me strangely, then leaned forward and took me in his mouth.

For an instant, I hung there, suspended over him in alarm. Then I felt someone older, more experienced, take over. This person seemed conversant with the geography of Rahim's mouth, seemed to know just how fast and how deep to thrust, and how much to pull out. I found my neck arching back, my hands grabbing Rahim's head as he made soft grunting sounds. Perhaps the person was not as experienced as I thought—before I could stop myself, I had transacted my first orgasm, with my cousin's mouth.

Ladies and gentlemen, boys and girls, survivors of the coming October 19 holocaust or future alien voyagers: this is where my journey takes its most dramatic turn! The before and after, the B.C. and the C.E., the divine revelation that swept away all my baggage from the past. Suddenly I didn't feel hopeless, suddenly I found myself in control, suddenly the answers to all my questions popped and burst like fireworks. My identity flashed on, my confidence powered up, the path to my fulfillment in life blazed in the sun.

Over the next few weeks, Rahim and I poked and probed and plumbed. We matched appendages to orifices in every combination that sprang to our fevered minds. Dispensing with the wrestling, we dove directly each evening into racking up the notches on the bedpost (not to mention the sofa, the dining table, the kitchen stool, even the telephone stand, before it broke). The arduousness of some of our experiments eased appreciably when we discovered the lubrication properties of pantry ingredients. (Jam was too sticky, butter worked better than mayonnaise, but nothing rivaled the *glissance* of pure ghee.)

My parents couldn't stop beaming—how eagerly I trotted off to class every evening, how well their mosque experiment seemed to be working. (They even published a paper on this, "Therapeutic self-affirmative effects of religious instruction on troubled youth," soon after.) The fact that I'd begun paying attention to my physique was an added bonus. "Healthy mind, healthy body—just like the Book says," my father remarked, each morning he saw me performing calisthenics. In reality, roles had begun to emerge in my after-curricular activity—clearly, I was the boinker, Rahim the eternal boinkee. If I wanted to fit my emerging self-image, it behooved me to start pumping up.

A year and a half later, little remained of the boy from Geneva with the paper clip in his tongue—in his place stood the Jazter, virile, self-assured, buff (not yet, but working on it). Buoyed by my recovery, my parents again succumbed to wanderlust. Rahim had become too attached, boinking him too rote, so I felt ready to move on as well. What better place to complete my education than the great cruising expanses of America?

We ended up in Chicago. It didn't take long for me to notice the line of men lounging in their cars (all potential teachers) as I skateboarded past after school in Lincoln Park. Some of them took me along to the baths near the Loop, where I tried out threesomes and foursomes, to see how high I could go. The conspicuousness of my skin tone (which, while never debilitating, had often made me self-conscious in school) worked wonders for the trick count—I even switched *v*'s and *w*'s to accentuate my South Asian origins. Occasionally, high on Quaaludes, I spent a Sunday afternoon romping with the runaways at the bird sanctuary (even at my most stoned, though, I took care to protectively glove the Jaz-in-the-box). On a trip to San Francisco with my parents, I sneaked out to an all-night orgy in the Castro, making them wonder the next morning what had tired me so. As a side benefit to all these extracurricular opportunities, I felt easier and more relaxed around my classmates—in fact, I even initiated a few.

The two years I spent in the U.S. were like finishing school. I learnt etiquette and protocol, the right amount of sauna small-talk (both before and after), the polite way to guide a pelvis into the position I preferred. More importantly than picking up such lifetime skills, I liberated myself from doubt or shame. Sex was my true calling, my *raison d'être*—as guilt-free as yoghurt, as natural as rain. Such was the self-affirming sweetness of those days that looking back, even my most brazen exploits seem choreographed by Norman Rockwell himself. There I stand, above the mantle, in adorable congress with someone picked up at the baths, and on the wall of the dining room, the kitschy tableau, "Jaz gets blown in the park."

To my shock, my parents abruptly decided to return to India—to pursue the best opportunities for "true change," they vaguely explained. What about *my* opportunities? I felt like screaming—the fledgling recruits at school, the network of park contacts, the sauna niche I'd carved out for myself? Back in Mumbai, though, I found more shikar than I could have ever imagined—in gardens, on streets, aboard buses and trains. My training served me well—I now knew what signs to look for, which approach to take (the trick of affecting an accent, American instead of Indian now, worked once more to give me that foreign allure). The sheer diversity of fauna amazed me—closeted bania merchants in dhotis, hotshot executives on their cell phones, migrants teeming into the city from every state. Malayalis, Gujaratis, Bengalis, even an Assamese once!—the Jazter sampled them all to create his own desi melting-pot experience.

Ah, the stories I could relate. How unfortunate the bomb's made it too late to start a blog.

ONCE KARUN'S CAST came off, I sensed I had to act fast, or risk losing my prey. Before my seduction plans could unravel completely, my mother's ninety-year-old Habib uncle gave them an unexpected fillip by peacefully passing away. As soon as my parents left for the funeral in Lucknow, I assured our servant Nazir that my lips would be sealed in case he wanted to slip off himself to secretly visit his village. This resulted in an empty flat, a phenomenon rarer than a lunar eclipse.

My dinner invitation seemed to catch Karun off guard: "Your liberation from the cast—we have to celebrate." We lived at one of the fancier addresses in Worli, in a fourteen-floor building rising by the sea. Karun looked flustered when he glanced around the flat upon entering, so I hastened to ascribe the poshness to my parents, not myself. "They're those rare people who've figured out how to spin philosophy into money, scholarship into wealth."

But his discomfort stemmed from something else. "I thought we'd be eating with your parents—I didn't realize even your cook was away."

Sitting on the couch, his entire body, from fidgeting hands to restless feet, thrummed with nervousness. He declined the Scotch I'd figured on plying him with, so I suggested we eat. "I managed to cajole Nazir into making his famous chicken biryani before he left."

It helped—ballasted by the food, Karun became a bit more placid. I knew I had to lure him into my room before the sluggishness wore off and he bolted. "Would you like to hear some of my qawwali disco?" I asked, and proceeded to explain the synthesis of Sufi religious music and old dance hits I'd been experimenting with. "The new fusion wave—it'll storm the music world once I set it loose on the internet."

He followed me unsurely into the Jazter sanctum, where, truth be told, no shikar had ever entered before. I immediately closed the door and tethered him to the computer with a pair of headphones. I proceeded to play excerpts from several of my concoctions—Fareed Ayaz and the Bee Gees, Donna Summer and Mubarak Ali Khan, finally arriving at my pièce de résistance. "Ready for some 'Dancing Queen' like you've never heard it before?"

"I'm sure it's very nice. It's just that I'm not so familiar with these songs."

We lapsed into silence. I wanted to rub Karun's back or slide my hand around his shoulder, but couldn't think of a way to feign the right spontaneity. But then he gave me an opening. "I thought you didn't swim." He pointed to the picture of a group of men in bathing suits on my wall (the one right next to my vintage posters of Ricky Martin and RuPaul, neither of which apparently had lit any lightbulbs).

"I don't. That's the U.S. Olympic diving team." Seeing his confusion, I clarified. "Not that I can dive, either. I just enjoy looking at them."

He showed no reaction, as if my last sentence had magically dissipated on its journey through the air. So I pressed in a bit. "Who would you say is the most handsome? If you had one to pick?"

This made him redden. "I wouldn't know." He looked pointedly away from the picture.

"Come, come, surely that's not such a hard question to answer. I like the dark one on the left myself. His chest, especially—the way the water beads on his skin." I decided to go ahead and rub Karun between the shoulder blades—playfully, I thought, though perhaps it appeared manifestly suggestive. "It's OK, there's no need to be so uptight about it. Believe me, Karun, I know you better than you think." I placed my other palm on his thigh—for some reason, I felt the need to punctuate.

In the postmortem, my behavior amazed me. How could the Jazter have plugged through months of painstaking pursuit, then risked it all in a moment of such indelicacy? For an instant, Karun simply stared at my hand, as if calculating whether he could possibly ignore it. Then he sprang up from the bed. "I have to leave," he said.

I caught up with him as he fumbled with the door at the entryway to the flat. "It's locked. I have the key."

"I really have to go."

"I'll open it, and you can go, but first you have to answer one question. Tell me, truthfully, why you came."

"What? You're the one who invited me. For dinner. Have you forgotten?"

"Not today. Why you came to the *park*. What you were searching for. All these weeks, the question you've evaded."

He glared at me. "The children. I came to watch them play. Someday I hope to have my own. Satisfied?" His voice had a defiant tone. "Not for this, not for what you were thinking, what you were trying. It's outrageous."

"OK, fair enough. You've obviously had enough time to cook up a response. But you must be crazy if you expect me to believe it. Even crazier if you believe it yourself."

"You're the one who's crazy—"

"I know the way you were staring at the park. The way you've been carrying on with me. Tea and ice cream, what crap. Why don't you just be honest and admit it?"

"Open this door." He began pounding on it. "Open this door at once. Somebody help."

"No need for such drama. Here's the key." I threw it at him. "There are taxis around the corner—I hope this time you have enough money in your wallet to pay the fare yourself."

HE CALLED ABOUT an hour later on his cell. "I have to tell you something." I didn't answer. "About your question." Again, I kept silent. "Are you there?"

"Go on, I'm listening."

"Not like that. I'm downstairs."

He had found the path that circled around to the small strip of beach behind the building. As I approached, he rose from the fallen palm trunk on which he sat. "Jaz?"

"Yes, it's me." I stepped carefully toward him across the debris-littered sand. The moon shone down through the palm fronds, covering him in a delicate crisscross of light. He looked insubstantial, lace-like, like a spirit that had lost its way and been captured in this lunar mesh.

For a few minutes we stood in silence, watching the bay. The tide was the furthest I'd ever seen, the waves streaks of silver that appeared almost stationary. "I'd read about the park," he finally said. "On the internet, while still in Karnal."

It all came tumbling out—how after junior college in Karnal, he knew he had to spend his three senior years somewhere else, how he'd found postings for similar parks in Delhi, but it still seemed too close to his mother and his family. "I felt dreadful applying for the scholarship, but I knew I had to go far away to survive. It still took me a year and a half in Bombay before I got together the courage to do anything."

He began telling me more—about grappling with his inner feelings, the doubts he had. Too much information smothers passion every time, I wanted to warn him. Before the moment could drift away in a flow of words, I leaned forward and locked his lips in a kiss.

His mouth felt small, perhaps because his tongue didn't know how to respond. I held his head and pressed my body into his. He sighed—a sound that emanated from deep within his throat and didn't fully escape. The moon's filigree covered my person as well, its rays now engulfed us both in their net.

Upstairs, I led him by the hand to my room. His skin tasted salty but fresh. He cried out when I took him in my mouth, grabbing my head and finishing before I could slow him down. Afterwards, he buried his head in my chest and shyly asked if he could reciprocate.

We slept curled up together. I offered to get us a second pillow, but Karun said no. "I want to be as close as we can—I've never spent the night with someone else." It occurred to me that this was the first time for me as well. For all these years, I'd been used to shikar, in which one doesn't need a bed.

THE SUN HAS SUNK LOWER, but dusk hasn't arrived yet. It looks like we're passing through one of the shabbier tracts of Matunga or Mahim, but I can't be sure. It's easier to tell at night, when the poor areas are the only ones without light. The rich have their own generators, prompted by the past year's power cuts.

What will I do once the sun sets? The bulbs and switches in my compartment surely don't work. Boxes of incense and candles lie stacked next to a pile of saris in a corner, but the Jazter, a non-smoker, is matchless. I pull the tarpaulin off a row of crates running along a wall and discover a weapons cache. Gingerly, I sort through the rifles, the ammunition, the hand grenades, wary of triggering off my own private October 19. I find nothing to illuminate my surroundings—at least not without a bit of a blast.

Wrapped in a cloth is a handgun. It looks as cute and compact as a toy—surely it fires nothing more potent than caps. I've never handled a gun before—I'm startled by how much it weighs. I look for the safety catch, such a frequent hiccup in the novels I've read, but cannot locate it. Dare I squeeze the trigger to see if it's loaded? I place it back atop the pile, then pick it up again. Ever since the war started, I've felt unsafe—all the people out to get me, as in this morning's close shave. So I stash the gun in my side trouser pocket. Immediately, I worry about accidental discharges. I try to corral the Jazter jewels out of harm's way but they keep swinging back.

This all seems so unreal that I feel like laughing. To think I need a gun to protect against those who'd kill me for being Muslim. The joke is on them—the last time I prayed was with Rahim, in the mosque annex. It's too bad they don't know about my true religion of noodling—a reason to really get their nuts in a snit.

THE NEXT DAY, Karun seemed to slip rapidly into morning-after regret. "What time is it? My roommate must be wondering where I went."

"It's only ten, and it's a Saturday, so just relax. I'll freshen up a bit and then whip us up some omelets." He looked at me wide-eyed, as if stricken at the thought of eggs. "Of course, if you like, I could make you something else—"

"No, it's not that. I just have to go." He fished out his shirt from the jumble on the floor and put it on, then hopped around on one foot as he tried to get the other through a trouser leg. "I'm sorry—I just need to be by myself."

My shikari reflexes kicked in with full force, juices astir at my prey's escape attempt. "Wait," I said, struck by *déjà vu* as he scuttled to the entryway, shoes in hand. "I won't let you leave just like that."

The locked door stopped him as before. "Could you give me the key, please. Please?"

"Or what? You'll threaten to cry for help again? Go ahead, scream all you want, be my guest. I'm not opening the door until after breakfast."

"I'll come back, I promise. Some other time, believe me. Right now, just let me go." Tears sprang to his eyes, panic to his face.

"No, Karun. It's always scary in the beginning. You can't just keep running away like that."

He let me take his shoes and set them down, then lead him back to my room. I tried to steer him to the bed again, but he slumped in a chair instead. Minutes ticked by without him speaking. Finally, I prompted him. "Why don't you finish telling me what you started last night on the beach? What made you go looking in the first place on the web."

He must have been waiting for encouragement, because he opened up at once. It began with an innocent question at a family gathering—his cousin Sheila asked him why he didn't have a girlfriend. "Everyone stopped talking just then, and in the silence, I turned absolutely red. I mumbled something about waiting to finish my studies, that not all my college mates were paired. 'Yes, but you don't ever even talk about women,' Sheila said. 'Not to you, he doesn't,' my mother shot back in my defense. People laughed, and the conversation went on, but Sheila's remark stayed with me. One of those thoughts that keeps burrowing deeper, once it gains entry into your head.

"Why *didn't* I take any interest in the opposite sex? My mother, I knew, kept waiting for me to say something about a girlfriend. The boys in junior college, just like the ones in high school, talked about nothing else—it was all I could do to tune them out. I wondered if I might be different—could I prefer men? A purely intellectual hypothesis, mind you, like one might make in physics or mathematics—I'd never detected any actual such feelings in myself. But it quickly became an obsession—I started reading everything I could find about it on the internet. The only scientific way to answer the question, I realized, was to put it to an experimental test."

"But you'd never even tried it with a woman."

"I thought about it. Going to a brothel or something sordid like that. I couldn't get up the courage. Just like I circled the park so many times, too scared to go in, before the evening we met."

"The evening you ran away."

"I panicked, as I did each time I thought about explaining myself at tea afterwards. It's hard to bridge the gap between theory and experiment. As you can see, even sitting here talking to you now takes an effort."

"I'm honored, I guess. To be your science experiment." The Jazter had been called many other things after sex, but never that. "And what have you discovered from this experiment?"

"I'm not sure yet."

I was. After last night, I knew which band he played in—down to the exact instrument. But who was I to argue if he felt he needed to research an encore concert? "I'll be glad to help any way I can."

We had breakfast, and then I prepared the bathtub, using a bubble solution my mother had got from France. At first, Karun wouldn't get in with me, despite my promise of only vegetarian fun. But then curiosity got the better of him. "Nobody I've known has ever owned a bathtub—I suppose you must see them all the time in the West." He put a foot in tentatively, as if mindful of popping the bubbles, then lowered himself to face me in the water. "I always imagined from the photos that they would feel like small personal swimming pools. But actually, this is so much tinier."

He dodged his body out of the way when I tried to soap him up. So I splashed him, and tickled him with my toes, to which he did respond. Before long, other parts of our anatomy inescapably got involved. And yet, the Jazter scrupulously restrained himself—not so much to honor his gentlemanly word as to preserve Karun's stamina for afternoon research.

Back in my room, Karun noticed the stack of games I had as a kid. "A model train set! Does it still work?"

"Yes, but it takes forever to set up." I tried to steer him to something snappier, like Boggle or Mikado, but his mind was set. So I took down the toy village accessories from the top of my cupboard, and the box of extra rails from under my bed. Karun dove right in, spreading out the components, coupling the bogeys, installing the village, down to the tiny plastic men and women. As he stretched out over the tracks to peer at how they aligned through a tunnel, I had visions of the train choo-chooing (*chew-chewing?*) through the valley of his ass.

Between my lecherous fantasies, I helped Karun with the setup. "This was always my favorite," I said, demonstrating how two sections of track could cross with the help of an elevated bridge. "A great spot for nifty accidents—one train derailing atop another, even a bomb attack once that set the bridge aflame."

The talk of havoc got Karun all excited—he couldn't wait to set up a collision once we finished laying the rails. We rammed engines into each other, made cars fly off the tracks, and in one particularly tragic accident, watched as a runaway train mowed down an entire village. "It's even better with fire," I said, and a pyromaniacal gleam immediately sprang to Karun's eyes. We drew the curtains and turned off the lights, then sent two trains to their mutually assured doom by stuffing them with matches and lit birthday candles.

Later, as we lay amid the ruins (in the finale, an enemy air raid had blown apart the tracks), I took one of the engines and ran it down Karun's back. "Does it tickle?" I asked.

"No," he said.

I skimmed it lazily over his buttocks. "And now?" He didn't answer, so I rolled it down his leg, teased his ankle with it, then rolled it back. "This little engine thinks it's time for another experiment." I worked off his pants and underwear, then pressed the engine playfully into his cleft.

Karun still didn't speak, but stretched out more fully, crossing his forearms to rest his head. He sighed as I retraced the engine's path with my lips, kissing him all over, using my tongue to tease out ingress. I moved to position myself in place, the condom already discreetly slipped on, my mouth still planting kisses to keep him relaxed. "Shh," I whispered, as I began to enter and he tensed, "it'll feel better in a second." I wrapped myself over his body as completely as I could, to convey my tenderness, to let him feel our oneness.

That night, I awoke around three a.m. Karun lay beside me, his mouth open, the air flowing in and out in regular breaths. He looked innocent, untroubled—I wondered what dreams unfolded in his head. Could I be in them, could his scientist mind be tabulating the results of his tests? We still had tomorrow morning—I'd have to think up some more games, some other experiments. Right now, though, I just wanted to gaze at him, feel the warmth of his body next to mine, absorb the pleasure of sharing my bed.

8

THE FIRST THING THAT STRIKES ME WHEN THE TRAIN CRASHES
through the wall and barrels down the road is the collisions Karun and
I used to engineer. The candles, the matches, the smoke billowing out
from the windows, the flames burning paint off the cars. Surely when
the weapons in my compartment detonate, they will surpass any of our
extravaganzas. Too bad I'll be seated right in the middle. The Jazter
would have preferred being a spectator of the conflagration to come,
rather than an ingredient.

The compartment twists and grinds around me like a giant pepper
mill, and I am rendered airborne along with everything else inside, but
only for the instant before we land on our side, skid along the ground,
and come to a crashing halt. Three separate miracles occur in those
milliseconds—I am unhurt except for a bruised arm, the weapons
decide not to go off, and most magically, the door at the rear of the
compartment bursts open. Perhaps Allah does have a soft spot for sod-
omites after all.

I climb out and see the engine lying on its side like a downed beast,
smoke still heaving out in dying spurts. Behind it, the first compartment has somehow remained upright, though the roof has caved in and
the walls have dramatically scrunched up. It all looks very cool—
something we never could have done with the toy set. Two women are
trying to pry loose a third—her upper half gesticulates animatedly out
a window while the rest disappears inside, as if she is being eaten alive
by the car. For an instant, I fear it is Sarita, who will no longer be able

to lead me to Karun, but then I spot her sitting dazed on the road next to a wheel that has rolled off. Standing beyond are the engine driver and his assistant, contemplating the wreckage with identical small wrenches in their hands, as if with this single tool, they will get the train back on its tracks.

I run up to Sarita. For some reason, she's changed into a bridal costume since I last saw her—the lead of her sari unfurls in a flaming red swathe around her feet. "Come, we have to get out of here." She just stares at me when I offer her my hand—I notice the line of white dots decorating her forehead. "We don't have any time." Something flickers in her eyes, and I wonder if she's placed me. "It's Gaurav. From the hospital. And the aquarium. Remember?"

"Gaurav? What happened?"

"The train derailed. Probably an ambush. We have to run."

"But how did you find me?"

"I'll explain everything. Just come with me." I can see the confusion on her face begin to harden into suspicion, so I squat down beside her. "I know you told me not to follow, but I did—I jumped into the rear compartment when I saw you get on. I still want to save your life, do the same thing you did for me. But we have to leave immediately, since whoever made the train derail will show up any minute."

"I . . . I don't think. The girls. I can't leave them here."

So we try to get the girls to come with us, but they're reluctant. "Mura chacha's still inside," the one half stuck in the train says. Her name is Madhu, and despite her sandwiched state, she seems in charge. "Can you go in and free him? Then we can all go visit Devi ma."

Sarita declares she wants to search the wreckage as well—not for this Mura character, but for a pomegranate. I think I have not heard her correctly, but she starts babbling about how it's the last pomegranate in all of Bombay and her very fate depends on it. I wonder if she has a concussion—is there a way to unobtrusively check her scalp? Madhu, meanwhile, barks orders at the other girls from her horizontal position. "Guddi, leave me alone and go fetch the train driver. Anupam, get this man here to help you lift the sleeper berth that fell on Mura chacha. You there. Go and help."

She gets very irate when I reply there's no time. "Mura chacha's much more important than a few of your precious minutes. How can anyone be so selfish?"

I'm trying to drag Sarita away from the train as Madhu continues to hector me when there is a retort. "I've been shot," Madhu screams, and holds up her hand. She has, indeed, been shot—blood streams down her arm and drips from her shoulder. More shots ring out, and she slumps forward, dangling limply from the waist. As the other girls scream, I grab Sarita's hand and pull her behind the bogey to take cover. She stops jabbering about her pomegranate.

We scramble down a side street, Sarita's sari blazing as conspicuously as a flag. The sounds of gunshots ricochet between the walls on either side. A few times, I think I hear someone running behind us. I lead Sarita in a zigzag through the labyrinth of an abandoned slum, finally stopping at a curbside bus shelter to catch my breath. For a moment, neither of us speaks as we gulp in air.

"Are they going to come looking for us?"

I shake my head. "My compartment was full of weapons. That's probably what they were after." As if to endorse my words, the rat-a-tat of a machine gun starts up. The sound is uncomfortably close, a little beyond the buildings we face—we must have circled around inadvertently.

Someone laughs, a man screams, and I hear more gunfire. The screaming resumes—its cadence is pitiful, pleading. "That sounds like Mura," Sarita says. "Those shots—I wonder if Guddi and Anupam—" She looks at me, her lip bloodless.

Before I can offer her any reassurance, a motorcycle revs up. We hear it circle behind the buildings, then begin to get closer. "It's coming down the street," I say, grabbing Sarita's hand and pulling her down behind the shelter wall. I peer cautiously over the edge after the motorcycle has passed, then duck again, as another motorcycle, then a van, come rumbling up behind. The cries are now coming from the van.

"It's the Limbus," I whisper. "They're just like the hoodlums in khaki, only Muslim. We couldn't have done anything." I've read about the group appropriating the word for "lemons" as their badge of honor—the same epithet used for years by the HRM to denounce Muslims who supposedly curdle the country's milk-and-cream Hindu population.

The street lapses back into silence. The sun just manages to clear the empty buildings that run down its trash-strewn length. From the direction of the rays, it seems the Limbus are headed west. Is that the direction in which Karun awaits? Sarita is unresponsive when I ask her destination. "Bandra," she finally reveals. "My husband is there, at a guesthouse."

I'm tempted to press her for the exact address, but I know she's still mistrustful of my helpfulness. "I actually need to make it further north to Jogeshwari to see my mother, so Bandra is on the way," I say to assuage any suspicions. "Is your husband east of the railway line or west?"

"West. Near the water." I try to get more details by engaging her in conversation but she rebuffs me with monosyllabic replies. Perhaps she's still shell-shocked.

I wonder how to proceed. In addition to the Limbu-infested areas in between, we're also cut off from Bandra by the expanse of Mahim creek. Rising sea levels and repeated monsoon floods have extended this breach all along the Mithi river, which at one point was little more than a canal emptying sludge into the creek, but now has widened into a chasm. The most direct way across the water is to go back and follow the train tracks, but the Limbus probably have that staked out. The alternative is to aim for the Mahim causeway bridge ahead—perhaps there will be a crowd of people crossing, and we'll stick out less. Except I can't quite imagine blending in with Sarita all decked up like a lollipop. "They wanted me to be one of Devi's maidens," she explains apologetically when I ask about her outfit. "It's even supposed to glow when it gets dark, just like Superdevi."

"Well, we're in Mahim now. If you don't look Muslim, we're both dead."

"But there's nobody around."

"Not here, not in this no-man's-zone—the Limbus probably cleared it out as a safety buffer. But ahead, there'll be people everywhere. When the rioting started, Mahim is where thousands of Muslims fled." I hand her my handkerchief. "We'll figure out the sari later, but let's start by wiping off your forehead."

Sarita smears off her bindi and bridal dots and returns my handkerchief—the stain on the cloth looks a dark and clotted red. She runs her fingers nervously through her hair. "Won't they still suspect?"

"Not if we say you're my wife. Mrs. Hassan. That's my name. Ijaz Hassan, not Gaurav. You must have guessed back at the hospital that I'm Muslim."

Sarita looks startled, and I realize I may have committed a terrible blunder. What if Karun has mentioned me to her and she's recognized my name? To my relief, it's the thought of playing the begum to my nawab that flusters her. I remember how she fled when I first tried to talk to her in the hospital basement—who knew the Jazter came across as such a predator of female flesh? "Couldn't I be your sister instead?" she asks.

That would certainly ease her worry. Except, even with her features half obscured by shadows, one can tell there's no resemblance. About to be paralyzed once again by the conundrum of what Karun could have seen in her, I remember her looks won't actually matter. The rules in this new Mahim decree that women remain properly veiled, so it's fine to play my sister.

She's not pleased when I explain this to her. "You mean I have to keep my face covered?"

"Actually, your whole body. We'll look for some cloth to use as a burkha—to conceal your sari as well. The Limbus call the shots—I hear they go around punishing infractions with whips."

We decide that she'll be Rehana Hassan, my virginal and impeccably virtuous younger sister. Maybe not too virginal, since the story is I'm escorting her to rescue her ailing husband, who's stranded in Bandra. "Where will we spend the night?" Rehana inquires.

"At the best boutique hotel in Mahim. We'll pay my dear cousin Rahim a visit."

ONCE MY PARENTS' return shut down our research lab, I tried to find other venues to facilitate Karun's experimentation. He quickly dismissed my usual haunts: the beach at Chowpatty was too exposed, the alley near the Taj too seedy (I didn't even bother suggesting the Bandra station facilities). I tried reasoning with him, pointing out that the city didn't offer anything more hospitable. Hadn't he come to Bombay after reading about park activities on the internet? What, exactly, did he now expect? Surely his training had taught him to take risks, to show some spunk, if not for his own fulfillment, then at least for the cause of scientific research?

But he remained unmoved. The tale of the Jazter and the physicist might have ended there, had not the Mumbai University library come to the rescue. Although I had often looked up to see the gothic structure indulgently witnessing my plunge fests at the Oval, I had never before stepped into its august halls. The place was cool and silent when we entered that afternoon, stained glass windows soared towards the cathedral-like ceiling. The books looked appropriately old and solemn, dusty tomes with cracked binding locked away in glass-paned wooden prisons. We stumbled upon the door behind a cupboard in a deserted reading room. It blended in so perfectly with the dark wood of the walls that only the presence of two small bolts, also painted brown, gave any indication it wasn't just another panel. Opening it and stepping over the knee-high base led to a tiny balcony which time (and the staff) seemed to have forgotten. The floor was filthy with bird droppings—in fact, several pigeons burst into energetic flight as we emerged (though a few continued cooing in the eaves, unconcerned). Two stories below us stretched the verdant greens of the Oval, to our right rose the university clock tower, Mumbai's own Big Ben. "The heart of the city, and no one knows we're up here. This is perfect," I said.

Karun was scandalized when he understood what I meant. One by one, I addressed all his concerns. Yes, it was dirty, but nothing a blanket or dhurrie couldn't cover. True, it was outdoors, but lying down, we'd be completely shielded from view by the balcony enclosure. No, I didn't believe other patrons would find it or try to enter, but had he noticed the door had bolts on this side as well? Even as I ticked off these answers, I knew I'd never be able to lure Karun back.

So there remained only one option. "Did you get today's *Times of India*?" Bewildered by my question, Karun took the paper he bought every morning out of his rucksack. "It's good they've bulked it up with all these tabloid supplements," I said, as I opened up the sheets and spread them over the grunge at our feet. Before Karun could recover from his disbelief, I bolted the door. "Don't worry—we're just going to lie here for a minute so you can see for yourself."

Despite his resistance, I managed to pull Karun down—he was too nervous of attracting attention to protest out loud. I lost no time unzipping his pants—once sprung free, he could no longer deny his arousal. He gasped each time my tongue found something else to probe, struggling briefly, unconvincingly, when I tried to turn him around. The paper rustled noisily beneath us, but only the pigeons heard. At the end, as he climaxed, Karun remembered to whisper out his moans.

After that, I had much more success in overcoming Karun's decorum, his squeamishness. The dove nest became our love nest, but I pushed his boundaries to include other venues as well. During an uncrowded matinee at the Regal, we treated the empty last balcony row to action it probably had never before witnessed, either on screen or otherwise. At a secluded spot in Versova, north of Juhu, we attempted it while waist-deep in the sea—the waves kept ruining our rhythm, so we had to find a spot under the palms to finish. I even got Karun to give me a hand job while barreling down Marine Drive on the top deck of an empty 123 bus late one evening. The experience proved so memorable that it moved the Jazter to poetry: "Salt air flew as the Jazter blew," "Sea breezes rushed as the Jazter gushed," "Scenery whizzed as the Jazter jizzed"—there's a haiku in there somewhere, if he can get the number of syllables right.

Karun's amenability to these escapades surprised me. I could tell he enjoyed sex, but I didn't get the impression he *hungered* for it—it would never be the all-consuming force that fueled the Jazter. Rather, it occupied a single drawer in the orderly portfolio of his needs, one whose replenishment he could control and monitor. Perhaps he viewed our trysts as experiments, contributions to a broader ethnographical study on the congregational patterns and mating behavior of homosexuals. More likely, what attracted him was the chance to set responsibility aside and regress to a reckless adolescence. "I feel like a kid again," he said each time we assembled the train set or rode the roller coasters at Essel Park, and I think our undercover adventures generated a similar thrill.

I enjoyed these naughty bits as well, despite once having been enough with every other conquest in the park. What puzzled me was all the extra time I still expended on dates with Karun, given that I'd already prevailed in my shikari motives. We journeyed to far-off food stalls and Udupi restaurants to unearth the best vada-pav and idli-sambhar (he only had money for holes-in-the-wall). Some evenings, we strolled along Marine Drive, perhaps sharing an ear of roasted corn. On weekends, I lugged my books over to his hostel, so that we could sit together in his study hall and prepare for our upcoming exams.

Perhaps what attracted me to all these extracurricular activities was the way Karun's preoccupations seemed to dissolve in my company. I loved watching his seriousness lift and a more carefree personality emerge, like a face behind purdah only a spouse could unveil. My favorite game was to see how often I could provoke his smile. Each time I scored, a jolt of realization ran through me—this was something only I could accomplish, a privilege extended only to me. He liked to tell me about his parents, to compare childhood notes about fending for ourselves. I made sure we fucked whenever the conversations got too emotional or too long—we weren't lesbians, after all.

His smartness pleased me, even though I found his atoms and galaxies only mildly interesting. (Perhaps his own family's erudition biases the Jazter more deeply than he cares to admit.) One morning, Karun called to excitedly announce a link between our two fields— he'd come across an article on pricing financial derivatives using quantum techniques.

I took him home for dinner with my parents—something unthinkable with any of my former liaisons. "It's so nice to meet Ijaz's friends," my mother declared, and joined us for Scrabble on the dining table afterwards. My father beamed benignly and commended me for taking such an interest in physics. (A *physicist*, I wanted to correct—I was taking such an interest in a *physicist*.)

The only person not so oblivious was Nazir. "I could make some tea," he offered, "if sahib will be retiring to his room later with his friend." But I felt too self-conscious taking Karun to my room, so we contented ourselves with some footsie under the table instead.

Nazir put his perceptiveness to good use. The next time my parents left on a trip, he demurred when I offered him some time off as well. "It's so expensive to go to my village. If only I had the two hundred rupees for train fare." It took some bargaining before he settled for a hundred, with an extra twenty to cook the biryani.

THE THREATENED BOMB has done what a thousand traffic engineers couldn't—made walking through even the most congested areas in the suburbs a breeze. Although baskets and crates and handcarts lie discarded everywhere, the cars that normally choke the streets are gone—driven far off by owners in search of safety. The menacing specter of the Limbus has scared away the pedestrians. Even the rag-pickers have vanished, with the result that an unclaimed bonanza of paper swirls luxuriantly at our feet.

An imposing figure stands guard in the center of the traffic island up ahead. Sarita and I both freeze at the same instant, as though motionlessness will magically confer camouflage, even though we are in the middle of the street. Then I note the apparition's abnormal height—it rises even taller than the traffic lights. "Nothing human can be that size," I whisper, and we cautiously resume our advance.

Sarita recognizes it first. "It's one of those Mumbadevi statues. The warriors the HRM installed during their 'City of Devi' days."

Except someone has chopped off all six arms. The neck has been hacked through and the head turned upside down. Dirt fills the eye sockets; lips, nose, ears have been chiseled away. Hatchet marks and paint splotches cover the whole body in an angry patchwork. With her vandalized torso and rearranged parts, Mumbadevi looks like a sculpture composed by one of the more misogynist cubists—Picasso, perhaps. And yet she still stands, too heavy to topple over from her pedestal, gazing with her desecrated eyes at the destruction of her city, managing a mute dignity in the dying sun. "We're definitely getting closer to the Limbus," I say.

Behind Mumbadevi stretches a boulevard lined with shuttered storefronts. Every third or fourth shop is charred—in one, I think I spot the remains of an arm sticking out of the debris. Mahim has not been spared by the bombing, Sarita remarks, but I tell her it looks like Limbu handiwork. "They probably targeted the Hindus to drive them out of business when the war first started." I position myself between her and the shops so she doesn't glimpse any hiding body parts.

My partner in extreme tourism has become much more inquisitive, I've noticed—asking me several questions about my background and job. I answer truthfully as far as possible, confident she won't figure me out. When it comes to explaining why my mother's in Jogeshwari, though, I get carried away—spinning a heartrending tale about early widowhood and property-snatching relatives. "Why aren't you married?" she throws in, as if trying to trip me up after getting my defenses down. I give my standard reply of not having found the right person yet. *But I'm hoping you will lead me to him.*

Sarita is quite forthcoming when I ask her questions in return, except when I try to learn what her husband might be doing at a Bandra guesthouse. Then she responds in monosyllables, and I wonder if she's stonewalling. It occurs to me that she simply might not know, that Karun may not have confided in her. Might this bode well for the Jazter's chances?

The silence of the boulevard makes the cacophony of billboards covering the building façades even louder than usual—there are exhortations on the behalf of Suzuki cars, television serials, skin-lightening creams. "New Singapore Masala Chicken Pizza!" a sign screams outside an abandoned Pizza Hut, reminding me I haven't eaten since breakfast. The door is missing, and though I'm wary of grisly discoveries lurking in the interior, we enter. Inside, the place has been meticulously looted—even the countertops in the kitchen have been ripped out. Only the wall posters remain—a fading explanation of the ill-fated "City of Devi" computer mouse promotion flanked by announcements for more new flavors: "Cauliflower Manchurian," "Texas Tandoori," even the improbable "Swedish Ginger-Garlic."

I'm getting increasingly faint imagining all these pizzas, when we hear the bells. I pull Sarita deeper inside, but then see through the window that the sounds come from children on bicycles. They circle outside the door, perhaps a dozen boys in scruffy shorts and undershirts, some so young their feet barely touch the pedals. "You won't find anything in there," one of them shouts. "To eat, you have to go to the mosque—at eight p.m., they feed anyone who shows up."

I wave them away as we emerge, but they follow us down the street, ringing their bells and crisscrossing our path. "What a lovely wife you have," they hoot. "So sexy in that red sari without her burkha—too bad the Limbus will beat her up to teach her a lesson."

The oldest in the group, a boy of about twelve with long scabs on his cheeks, stops his bicycle right in front of us. "Come this way." He gestures towards a narrow alleyway trailing off. "The guards on the main road have rifles. They'll only let you through if you pay a lot."

Although I'm confident I can prove I'm Muslim (if reciting all the Koran verses I know by heart doesn't do it, there's always the anatomi-cal identity card), I lose my nerve. Sarita would present a problem even if less flamboyantly dressed, plus what if they find my gun? I take her hand and follow the boy down the alley, wondering if he's leading us into a trap. The feeling intensifies as he ushers us through a large wooden doorway into an empty compound, then chains his bicycle to a post and disappears up some steps. I'm looking for rifles to start blaz-ing at us from the windows circling the compound when the boy returns. "Here," he says, handing Sarita a length of brown fabric. "Put this on."

"What is it?" she asks, holding up the sturdy cotton material. "It looks like a tablecloth."

The boy shrugs. "It used to be. But now it's a burkha. My mother cut out the eyeholes and sewed together the ends—she used to cover my sister with it while shopping before we had a proper one made. I'll let you have it cheap—just fifty rupees."

Sarita declares she's not about to wear a tablecloth, but I take it from her and give the boy a twenty, who smiles and says his name is Yusuf. He scampers to a door on the other side of the compound. "See?" he says, throwing it open. "You're now past the guards."

We step into a market lane—so thronged with humanity that it almost makes up for the desolation of the neighborhoods we've trudged through. Unlike my last time in Mahim, every last woman is now enveloped in a bulky burkha and most of the men sport skullcaps and beards. (Did they begin growing them the minute war was declared?) Flaming torches affixed to the energy-sapped lampposts give the scene a festive, medieval air. Sarita stumbles along beside me, looking like a child playing "ghost" under her tablecloth. "I can't believe it," she suddenly exclaims, pointing at a man sitting by the road selling pomegranates. She buys a large red specimen for fifty rupees to replace the one lost in the train. "How that swine in Crawford Market cheated me!"

"This one cheated you too," Yusuf says. "I could have got it for fifteen."

Both the quality and variety of wares being hawked from the pavements amaze me. The pomegranates, like the glistening apples and pears and oranges, nestle in individual foam compartments—packing usually reserved for only the choicest imported fruits. Tins of meat and fish, practically never spotted outside of tony South Bombay boutiques, lie stacked in bountiful, artistically spiraling pyramids. One vendor sells nothing but five different kinds of toothpaste—upon closer examination, the brands are all unfamiliar ("Denticon," "Protect," "Kingcol") with writing in English and Arabic, even Chinese! Where does all this come from? I ask Yusuf. The question stumps him initially, but then he brightens. "We must manufacture it all here in Mahim," he proudly declares.

We haggle over how much he will charge to lead us to the Hotel Rahim. His first bid is a new pair of Adidas, being sold by one of the hawkers for three thousand rupees, but he soon capitulates when I hold fast to my offer of another twenty. "That's the way to the one restaurant still open," he says, pointing down a narrow lane as we pass a row of old buildings. "People claim they've started chopping up dogs to use in their kebabs, but my mother says that's just the way tinned meat tastes. And if you go further, you'll come to the main road with the mosque—you can join the line if you want to eat for free."

Yusuf tells us his father died when he was three, that in addition to his sister, he has a sixteen-year-old brother who's with the Limbus. "Not by choice—they came to our door one day, and my mother didn't have anything to pay them off. When my brother resisted, they caught me by the hair and started beating me with a whip." He points at the scabs on his face. "Luckily, I'd seen them do it before in the market, so I had enough sense to cover my eyes with my fists."

Sarita is so distressed that she hugs him to herself and kisses the scars that extend to his forehead. He looks up craftily at her face. "Why don't you get me the Adidas? That way, I can outrun them if they try to catch me again."

Just past a shuttered post office, the crowd peters out and the buildings give way to a large swathe of blackened ruins. Except for the odd intact wall or doorway, everything for a few blocks seems to have been consumed in some terrible conflagration. "Did the Pakistanis bomb the area?" I ask, as we pick our way through the rubble and charred timbers.

"The Pakistanis? No, they never bother us. They just fly past above. Though once I saw a big fight in the air, with rockets and everything. One of the planes exploded—I'm not sure whose it was. The whole city shook when it landed. You could see the smoke from everywhere, just like when the bridge blew up. We tried to find it on our bikes, but it was too far away—we rode all the way to the devi standing on her head before turning back."

"So this wasn't caused by another plane crash?"

"A plane crash?" Yusuf laughs. "No, it's the Limbus who did this. See that arch still standing there? That was the entrance to the new Ad Labs Cineplex. The Limbus said movies are against the Koran, so they set the theater on fire. But the flames spread and all the buildings around burned down with it. Including their own headquarters." He chuckles, then gets wistful. "I used to love watching movies there. The seats were so good you could see every part of the screen. Now the Limbus will beat you if you even hum a film song." He starts singing softly—a snatch from the theme of *Superdevi*, then looks around to make sure nobody is listening.

The ruins give rise to an area of town that shimmers through the dusk with a familiar yet unexpected luminosity. I realize it is the light from electric bulbs. "Most people here have their own generators," Yusuf explains. "It's where the rich live." He points to a building with tastefully lit awnings over each window. "That's the Hotel Rahim—I've never been inside. They say Shahrukh Khan himself once stayed in it."

As we part, he high-fives me. "That's the way they do it in America—I've seen it on TV." He starts running down the lane, then turns around. "If you need help, just ask for Yusuf—everyone in Mahim knows me."

THE MONSOONS ARRIVED, putting a serious crimp in our sex life. The beaches turned stormy, the library balcony wet and sludgy—so many pigeons sheltered in its eaves that droppings fell as profusely as rain. Even the Regal, perversely, got packed, showing hit after sold-out hit. One evening, we snuck into the deserted racecourse at Mahalaxmi but couldn't get into the covered stands—we ended up so drenched and muddy trekking across the turf that no taxi would take us back.

June went by, and then July, each week getting wetter (but more parched in terms of sex). The fact that I spent so much of my leisure time within striking distance of Karun made this forced abstinence even harder to bear. "It's the eternal tragedy of being gay in Bombay," I lamented. "Never a place to yourself." With city rents so high, most sons (the Jazter included) lived with their parents until marriage (the Jazter excluded)—and usually well after as well.

Rahim escaped this fate. His widower father passed away just as my cousin turned of legal age, leaving him the sprawling turn-of-the-century flat near Chowpatty where the two of them lived. I'd barely seen him since returning from the States, so I was surprised to get the invitation from him in the mail.

"He says it's a wedding celebration. All men, lasting all night. Knowing Rahim, it's probably going to get quite wild." I slid Karun the card across the tea things on the table. "But we don't have to worry about anyone—the important thing is we can do what we want, spend the night together."

"You mean there'll be other people around?"

"Who cares? We'll wrap ourselves in a blanket and hide in a nook so that nobody can even see us."

"I'm not ready for such openness."

I'd been through this before with Karun—his extreme trepidation at the slightest hint of exposure. He'd used the same reason to veto disco nights organized sporadically at different clubs around the city by the local Gay Bombay group. "Don't you think it's time to loosen up a bit? Or are you still waiting for your report card from the experiments to come exonerate you in the mail?"

"It's hardly like that. I just don't want to blare out such a private matter to strangers at a party."

"What you really don't want to do is admit you're just like them."

"That's ridiculous."

"Which part? That your report card is stamped *H* for Homo or that it's a label you just can't accept?"

"If you feel that way, maybe you should go to Rahim's yourself. I'm sure you'll find someone more to your standards amongst all those other men."

I stalked out of the tea shop, incredulous Karun would pass up such an opportunity in the middle of a drought. What was he, a camel, that he had used his hump to store up the sex we'd had? Why couldn't he have a normal libido, be a slave to unseemly urges like everyone else? The Jazter jewels had turned so blue that they'd be a pair of twisted ice bonbons soon. I needed massive quantities of immediate action to restore them to their natural state.

Walking to the bus stop, I realized I'd become too fixated on Karun in the past few months. Release was release, with whomever one found it—that's what the Jazter had always said. Hadn't another wise man, the Buddha himself, warned about the evils of attachment?

So I spent the next few days frequenting old haunts again—the alleys near the Gateway, the facilities at Bandra, even the Oval in the rain. I rode the "gandu car," the notorious last compartment named after all the backdoor action it saw, on late-night suburban trains. I got lucky with a cashier wearing a McDonald's uniform in the sparkling tiled toilet of a newly opened shopping mall. But as I entered him, as my body heaved and strained, I found myself conjuring up Karun's face. Guilt flooded in—as if I'd been unfaithful, as if I'd strayed.

It became an aversion therapy program, the way this guilt tainted every encounter. My favorite pastime lost its luster—the chase no longer thrilling, the prey too coarse, too anonymous, too un-Karun-like. How could this have happened? I felt like railing. Such crippling fallout from just a few innocent months of dating?

"You look completely lovelorn," Rahim declared at his party, after admonishing me for not having kept in better touch. "Will I have to torture it out of you or will you tell me who he is?" He had developed a sashay to his walk—more matronly than nubile, and discovered mascara to somewhat alarming results. "Mum's the word, I see—but that's OK since I have a number of people here who'll make my little Jazmine forget him."

The "wedding" involved Rahim's friend Akbar, who appeared in ceremonial drag—a red sari complete with ankle bracelets adorned with tiny bells. "She believes in married life, just to a different husband each month," Rahim explained. "She's tired of repeating the nikah, so tonight we're going Hindu for a change." Sure enough, the bride and groom (wearing the traditional headgear of jasmine buds) did their seven circles around a floor lamp representing the fire, after which Akbar swirled a platter with flowers and a lit oil lamp in ritual circles in front of his betrothed's face. "Now kneel down and repeat them around the part that really counts," Rahim instructed, and to hoots and claps, Akbar obeyed.

Afterwards, the crowd gave a collective yank on Akbar's sari, unwinding it in a long swirl of fabric that sent him spinning across the room like a top. Watching Akbar prance around in his bikini briefs, I felt glad I hadn't brought Karun—who by now would have probably stalked out. The game of musical laps that followed took forever to play because of all the poking it prompted, after which Rahim herded us into the study he had converted into a pitch-black back room. "This is the way to fight back the respectability drowning our poor deluded sisters in the West. Long live masti, long live mischievousness."

Wisps of sunlight seeping around the papering on the windows woke me in the morning. I extricated myself from under the arm across my chest and got up from the floor—it took me a half hour to find my clothes. By the time I reached home, my mind pounded with the thought of Karun. I had not talked to him for days—what if I had let him slip away? I longed to coax out his smile again, yearned for his steadfastness—even his scientific prattle seemed so charming in retrospect. I had to see him despite the absence of fleshly prospects. Would I have to finally yield ground to his pontifications about life being more than sex?

Gathering up my courage, I dialed his number. "Where have you been? I've missed you," he said.

BY SEPTEMBER, WITH THE RAIN still keeping us chaste, I wondered if the monsoons would ever end. Just as I prepared to splurge on a hotel room in desperation, my luck turned. My parents announced their departure for a week-long conference in Jakarta. I declined their invitation to come along, which puzzled them. "I suppose it should be OK with Nazir here to look after you." I had to pay him the entire five hundred saved up for the hotel room to coax him into taking a vacation of his own.

I got down to the first order of business with Karun right away. I fucked him in every room of the flat, in my parents' bed and on the kitchen floor. When he tired, I revived him with a bubble bath, then fucked him some more. He locked himself in the toilet, not emerging until I promised to stop. I made a good-faith effort to keep my hands (and other parts) off, but lasted only an hour. By the third day, though, even I was too sore.

Fortunately, we had college to attend. I came back at five, worried he might not return, wishing I hadn't wielded my wicket to such excess. At six, the bell rang. Karun must have recovered as well, because when I herded him through my bedroom door, he didn't protest.

Eventually, there arose the pesky problem of food. Nazir had demanded too much money for biryani this time, and we'd already devoured the refrigerator scraps down to the stalks of coriander. "I used to cook while my mother worked evenings," Karun said, so we went shopping in the nearby outdoor market.

Except neither of us knew how to haggle. Vegetable hawkers saw us treading carefully through the monsoon muck in our sneakers and raised their prices two- and threefold. "I know your mother," a fisher-woman purred. "She always buys pomfret here because she knows I never cheat." Chicken sellers, egg grocers, even a samosa-vending tout, all smiled widely in welcome with the glint of rupee coins in their eyes.

"They can smell our inexperience. We need a strategy," Karun said. "How about if I act willing to buy, and you pretend to pull me away because the price isn't right?"

So I tried to channel my inner diva to play the shrewish wife. I accused the cauliflower seller of eating the good parts and trying to palm off the leaves, ordered Karun to return a bag of plums because they'd be all pit inside. I overplayed my role with the fish, voicing so many suspicions about its freshness that I provoked the fisherwoman into a fight. We fled to the chicken shop, trailed by a hail of curses in Marathi.

Unfortunately, the hen we bought remained tough even after three hours of cooking. Karun made various attempts to tenderize it—add-ing vinegar and yoghurt and pungent powders he found in the cabi-nets, even stabbing at the pieces in frustration with a knife. At midnight, I suggested we just dip bread into the gravy. Karun's eyes widened as he tasted it. "I think I added too many chilies."

"It's nice," I told him, trying not to choke. I discreetly got up and brought us some water. By the end of the meal, we were using chunks of raw cauliflower to buffer each bite.

"I can wash off the chilies and try again tomorrow," Karun said. "I guess it's been a while since I cooked."

He looked so dejected that I pulled him to myself, nestling him between my thighs. I buried my nose into his hair to identify the different curry spices, like one might the bouquet components of a fine wine. His fingers smelled mostly of garlic and ginger—kissing them, I noticed the tips stained yellow with turmeric. "It's fine. I enjoyed our little chemistry experiment. Plus it was fun going shopping." I put my arms around his chest and rocked him from side to side.

Sitting there, with Karun in my lap, I caught a glimpse of a future I could never have imagined. Karun and the Jazter, snug and domesticated like this, rocking gently through life. I almost burst out laughing, but then stopped. Was the picture so corny, so absurd, so completely removed from the realm of possibility? What future did the Jazter see for himself, exactly? Would his days of shikar continue indefinitely, or did he dare look beyond the beaches and the train stations and the alleys? Could he, in some part buried deep within, secretly crave conventionality? (Or was that too much of a heresy?)

I kissed Karun's neck. The future, as always, felt too abstract to worry about, too nebulous, too otherworldly. What mattered was the here and now. The feel of Karun's body as he reclined against me, the spices perfuming his hair and resting in their jars in the kitchen, the defiant chicken on the counter waiting to be subdued some more in the morning. I felt grateful for each magical moment we'd spent playing house together, grateful for the four days we still had left.

9

AS YUSUF SLIPS INTO THE DARKNESS OF MAHIM, I TRY TO PRE-
pare Sarita for meeting my cousin. "He owned an enormous flat at
Chowpatty which he sold to buy this hotel. You might find him a
bit—um—*unusual*."

Rahim opens the door himself, and shrieks upon recognizing me.
"My sweetie. My little Jazmine. What a surprise. After all this time,
you've finally remembered your Auntie Rahim." I'm unprepared for
how rotund he's become in the decade or so since I last laid eyes on
him. His cheeks have acquired an unworldly ruddiness, his lips an
ethereal gloss; his mascara addiction, so startling at the party at his
house all those years ago, seems decidedly out of control. Could this
have really been my first heartthrob, the one who presided over the
Jazter's mizuage ceremony, plucked the virginity diamond from his
nose? Although thinking back, it really was more the other way round.

"Well don't just stand there, come to me." He wears so much attar
that fumes rise from my shirt after we hug. I finesse my lips out of the
way as he tries to kiss me. "Oh, you're shy because we're not alone."

Sarita watches transfixed—somewhat worrisome, since this is
hardly the place to pick up her sorely needed makeup tips. "And what
gorgeous creature do we have here? All dressed up as a bride for the
Pandvas, no less." Rahim theatrically undrapes the sari edge from her
head and sharply intakes his breath. "Naughty, naughty! The leopard's
a bit full-grown, isn't he, to be changing from spots to stripes? Or
should I say from meat to fish?" He cackles noisily.

"This is my friend Rehana." I try to muster my most formal tone. I can sense Sarita abuzz with questions about Rahim and me, but I avoid looking at her. "Her husband is sick in Bandra so we're going there to bring him back to Mahim. The Hindu getup is a disguise, to get her past Bhim's goons."

"Ah, a damsel in distress. You're reuniting her with her true love and all that. Our little Jazmine has grown up to become a humanitarian. Forgive your Auntie Rahim her dirty mind if she wonders where your interest lies in all of this." He notices the tablecloth Sarita clutches to her chest. "Don't tell me that's supposed to be her burkha."

"It's the best we could do on such short notice—we bought it on the street off an urchin."

"Oooh—it's ghastly. Auntie can't bear to look at it. Wait here." He disappears up the stairs and returns a moment later carrying a purple number with a delicately embroidered face flap. "Sometimes Auntie likes to dress up as a *real* auntie," he says to Sarita. "I just *love* your sari—remind Auntie to tell you when she was a bride herself."

The hotel is over-the-top—marble from Italy, carpets from Afghanistan, even commodes from England, or so Rahim claims. "The same brand used by the Queen—truly a royal throne for a royal shit." Every room is decorated in its own distinctive style—the one thing they have in common is they're all unoccupied. This fact does not seem to perturb Rahim—he leads us merrily from floor to floor, leaving a trail of lights blazing behind. "More fabulous than the Taj and the Oberoi combined, don't you agree?"

Coming down the stairs, he asks how "Auntie and Uncle" are doing. I say they're fine, hoping Sarita either hasn't heard or doesn't realize he's talking about my parents. "And that boy you refused to tell me anything about the last time I saw you? The one you followed all the way to Delhi, or so I heard from the grapevine?"

"That was a long time ago. We haven't been in touch for years." I want to pull him aside and warn him not to ask me anything personal, but Sarita's right behind me. Fortunately, he doesn't blurt out anything else incriminating.

We enter the dining room, set with an enormous buffet. Platters of salads vie with a cornucopia of cakes and pastries. "Shabbir! Parvez!" Rahim calls, but no one appears. "I must apologize—this war's made the staff situation quite appalling." He goes around whisking domed lids off serving bowls to reveal curries and stir fries, kormas and cutlets. "You must try the foie gras—we have a whole case imported from France," he says, cutting off a generous wedge from a tray of cheeses and pâtés. Sarita gasps when she discovers a jar of Marmite among the condiments.

As we eat alone at the long, empty table, I can tell Sarita is as mystified as I am by all this lavishness. "We're ready even for the Chinese guests who visit once in a while. Though try finding a chef who can cook a decent lo mein." Noticing our expressions, Rahim stops. "You're probably wondering where all this food comes from, correct?"

I nod. "Not only here, but also in the markets."

"All the pomegranates they're selling," Sarita adds. "In most places, you'd be hard-pressed to find a carrot." She takes a timid bite of the foie gras, grimaces, then smears it with Marmite.

"It's quite simple, really—let's see if you can guess. Who do you think would want to set up an outpost here in the heart of the city? A Mecca for Muslims to give them a taste of their promised land?" Rahim looks expectantly from Sarita to me, waiting for us to answer, tapping at his plate impatiently at our dullness. "Oh, come on. Who'd benefit most by getting a foothold in India? Who's been wooing the Muslims ever since Independence? Who's been trying to instigate Hindus to massacre Muslims all along—so they can step in as benefactor to the victims?"

"Pakistan?" I ask unsurely.

"No, the Republic of Finland. *Of course*, Pakistan. Who else? What they didn't manage for decades in Kashmir, they accomplished overnight in Mahim. With some help from their Dubai friends, of course. The beauty of it is that all the channels were already in place—the old Arab sea routes from the sixties and seventies to smuggle in cigarettes and electronics, the new ones that the Pakistani ISI has been using for some years now to sneak in their terrorists. They're still sending in the same boats, but filled with apples and onions instead of whiskey and televisions. OK, perhaps a few jihadis too—God knows nothing gets accomplished in the world these days without terrorism. But the primary effort is to have everything freely available in Mahim—meat and delicacies to pamper the elite, cheap tins for the rest, even Marmite for your friend here, who's welcome to keep the jar, incidentally. They haven't gotten to the point of revealing themselves yet—still all very hush-hush—only a handful of residents know, like myself. Still, this has to be the land of plenty, not just for prestige, but so that refugees pour in and the area grows. That's why they've not slacked off—it's much harder since the war started, but they still manage to slip in enough boats under the nose of the Indian navy."

Rahim's explanation is preposterous. "Are you seriously suggesting that Pakistan is setting up a colony in India? Here, in the middle of Bombay, in Mahim?"

"I know. It sounds completely insane, doesn't it? But that's precisely the point. Who would ever even imagine such a thing? Suspect the ISI of quietly engineering this for years? Why do you suppose every bomb blast in Bombay has led to at least one or two suspects with a flat in Mahim?"

"But this isn't even the most densely populated in terms of Muslims," Sarita points out. "Why not Mazgaon or Byculla or Dongri?"

"Because, quite simply, the sea route is essential. You'd have to go way far north to Mira Road before finding a suburb with as many Muslims living right on the coast. Of course, the goal is to eventually link all the Muslim pockets from here—expand south to the areas you mentioned and perhaps also to the north and east."

Which sounds even more kooky. Could lead from his mascara be leaching into my poor cousin's head? "Why stop there—why not take over the whole city?" I ask. "Rename it South Karachi and drive all the Hindus into the sea? I'm sure the ISI could find somewhere to resettle Bhim."

Rahim laughs. "Yes, it's all quite fantastic, I agree. They need to bring their plans back to reality. And you're right, they're severely underestimating the HRM and Bhim. Remember, though, that this was all a sleeper plot, something to dabble in on the side—they never expected to actually activate their scheme. This 'South Karachi' as you call it only came into being thanks to the HRM—the 'City of Devi' campaign was a true godsend. All the ISI had to do was keep the bloodshed going, provoke some more attacks using a few well-placed jihadis. But my Jazmine's not quite convinced, I see—so let Auntie show you something interesting on the map." He pulls out a place mat on which the boundary of Mumbai is outlined around the "Hotel Rahim" logo. "See how nicely one can isolate Mahim?—the railway tracks along here, the creek to the north, the bay to the west. Once the stage was set, they only needed to blow up the sea link bypass. That poor bridge—doomed from the start—some rumors have it that ISI agents actually managed to plant explosives during construction in the cement itself."

"Terrorism with a vision."

"Not terrorism. Strategy. With the sea link gone, they used the air raids to bomb the remaining bridges to our east. Leaving the connection between north and south nicely squeezed. Now every truck, every convoy, every goods train must make the long detour around or come through Mahim. Not only can they control who gets through, but they've set the stage to collect some hefty fees."

"And the Limbus? Are they ISI agents as well?"

Rahim's face darkens. "They're a bunch of juvenile savages, that's what. Buffoons who couldn't care less about the religion they profess— they'll drive us all off the face of the earth. We needed an army in a hurry to keep us safe, which is why there was no choice but to ask for their help. Except they'd been watching too many Taliban videos or smoking too much hashish, I don't know which. Within days, they started banning music and film and TV and going on burning sprees. A new target every night for weeks—temples, video stores, fast food restaurants to show they're anti-American. Even the Hinduja hospital, because they declared the 'Hindu' in the name blasphemous. The crowds flocked in of course—who can resist a good bonfire, especially if every other type of entertainment is gone? But then their hijinks started turning entire blocks into ash—you saw the one next door. So now—get this—they've declared that burning is too *Hindu*—that it derives from cremation, that it's against the Koran. Muslims, they've announced, are only allowed to *demolish* the un-Islamic, never burn. Not that they've left anything un-Islamic still standing—half of Mahim is gone. To keep the masses entertained, they started performing stonings in front of the mosque. Except with stones so hard to come by in Bombay they rapidly ran out—so now they behead their victims. Genuine Hindus, guaranteed—to prove it, they slice off the foreskins first and toss them as souvenirs into the audience."

Noticing our aghast expressions, Rahim hastens to assure us that most Mahim residents share his aversion to the Limbus, but are too scared to speak out. "Even the refugees, those who've lost everything in the riots—even they don't condone the Limbus' antics. I suppose they're a necessary evil to keep us safe—perhaps in time, they can be trained."

The question I can't bring myself to confront Rahim with is where he fits in all of this. Is he a stooge, a Pakistani lackey? I take a bite of the pineapple pastry I've selected from the buffet—the custard cream filling slides smoothly down my throat. Do I thank the ISI for this treat?

It turns out my cousin has an even more sinister patron. "It happened while he was here on a clandestine visit—a VIP who loved my hospitality so much that he took over all my loans for me. The loans that were threatening to wipe out your poor Auntie Rahim. Can't tell you the name, because you'll recognize it—all I'll say is he lives in Dubai and Karachi now, but still controls most of Mahim."

"You mean a gangster? Like Dawood or Shakeel?"

Rahim titters. "Whoever it is, the ISI has full faith in him—they've entrusted their entire operation to his men. He still makes it personally to Bombay more often than people might imagine—always comes in by sea with a large entourage. As do his associates, some of whose names you would also recognize—we're actually quite full most nights. That's why I keep dinner ready—I never know who might show up, and when."

"So what you're telling me, basically, is that you work for the mafia underworld. Maybe one of the same dons who fled to Dubai after slaughtering hundreds in bomb blasts all over the city?"

Rahim stiffens. "Perhaps you need to look around before you point any fingers. Check to see who's being slaughtered and who's doing the slaughtering. Just the massacres in the past year alone—have you been keeping track? Gaza to Germany, Houston to Haji Ali, not to mention all the internment camps. We're being annihilated, Jaz—if we don't take help from whoever offers it, there might soon be no Muslims left. Besides, this isn't some cheap two-rupee street hooligan we're talking about—my patron is someone cultured, someone sophisticated, some-one who appreciates foie gras with every meal."

"Someone who'd still have no compunction in blowing up all of India. Or perhaps that's too passé—thinking you owe your homeland anything."

"How sweet—the little pup calling Auntie's patriotism into ques-tion. After spending half its life abroad, no less. Well let me tell you, my flag-waving Jazmine, while you were swilling beer and chocolate with the Americans and Swiss, I was being bottle-fed the Indian dream. Nehru and Gandhi, *Saare Jahan Se Achcha*, the whole secular ideal. So what if our government perpetrated years of carnage against its own citizens in Kashmir? Or systematically filtered Muslims out from its armed forces and police regiments? Or turned a blind eye each time the

Hindus decided to here and there roast a few minorities alive? None of it really affected me. I was content to keep singing patriotic songs, brand Pakistan the enemy, march against terrorism with all my fellow brainwashed Muslims hand in hand through the streets.

"Then the HRM started its Devi rampaging. Beatings, rapes, murders—they all happened to people I knew, people alarmingly close to me. On Linking Road, I personally saw the corpses in their shops: blackened mummies still sitting at the till, waiting to give change back from a twenty. Entire families wiped out and nobody did anything—not the government, not police, and certainly not our *fellow* Hindu citizenry."

"But that's exactly how they want you to think—Hindu versus Muslim instead of just Indian."

"It doesn't matter what one thinks. You can scream you're Indian, you can disavow your religion, you can even be the next incarnation of Krishna for all your Hindu countrymen will care. Their HRM will pull down your pants and check your foreskin and slaughter you just the same."

Rahim takes a deep breath. "Listen, Jaz, you've known me for years. Just look at me, just look at my fabulousness—I simply can't conceal who I am. You can never imagine what a hard time I've had all my life fitting in. But all the insults and abuse I've endured have taught me one thing: how to protect my own skin. Before being an Indian, before being a Muslim, I'm a survivor—prepared to do whatever's needed to stay alive. If you and your friend want to come through this war, I'd suggest you start doing the same."

AS WE SIP OUR after-dinner coffee, I remark on the fact that none of Rahim's big-shot gangster sponsors seems to have checked in. "It's still early," he says. "They find it hard to give me notice, now that mobile phones don't work."

"So it's nothing to do with the nuclear firecracker that Pakistan might be lighting this week?"

"You mean those rumors? The phones and the internet?" Rahim waves his hand dismissively. "That's not Pakistan, that's Bhim, trying to empty out the city."

"Why would he want to do that?"

"Who knows? Perhaps he figures it'll be easier to take over. Or perhaps he's just hoping to scare the Indian army into a preemptive strike. God-willing even our military isn't so stupid. The important thing is that Pakistan would hardly sink so much into their colony here if they intended to blow up the entire city."

"So it's just a coincidence that your hotel is empty. Did you at least have a lot of guests yesterday?"

Rahim ignores my question. "They'll be here soon, believe me. I'm sure they're already on their way."

By nine, he's plainly worried. He tries his cell phone repeatedly, as if it might have miraculously started working. He sends some of his servants to the Limbus to check if they've heard anything. He reiterates his bomb theory several times, coming up with even more far-fetched motives that might explain Bhim's ploy (to scare up more followers, to feed his own vanity). At nine-thirty, the doorbell rings. "They're here," Rahim announces, both triumphant and relieved. He rushes down the stairs to personally usher in his guests.

He returns after a while. "We need to clear out from here—my clients prefer to dine privately. Let me show you to your rooms." Sarita is alarmed at being ushered into her own separate suite, but he assures her I'll be just down the hall. "The sheets are Egyptian cotton—you'll sleep so soundly you'll forget all your worries."

We bid Sarita good night and Rahim walks me to a room down the corridor. The minute we're inside, his expression changes. "That was the Limbus. They're on to you. They ambushed a train today and took a Hindu prisoner or two—they're looking for the ones who escaped. A kid named Yusuf says he led you here—they roughed him up a bit after a friend ratted on him. I told them I hadn't let anyone in, but they still wanted to search the hotel. It's only when I reminded them who the owner is and how angry he'd get that they relented—they're milling about outside now, waiting for permission from their higher-ups." He pauses, then looks at me gravely. "She's Hindu, isn't she? I should have guessed—that way of sliding her sari over her hair."

My mind races. "Do they have the rear covered as well? I saw an alley between the buildings—there must be a back entrance, correct?"

Rahim looks at me sadly. "There is, right through the kitchen, and it would make a perfect escape. Except I can't allow it—my boss would kill me if the Limbus didn't. But fortunately, there's a simple solution to all this. We'll tell them the truth—that you're Muslim, that we're related—you can swear you didn't know she was Hindu when we turn her in." He brushes the back of his fingers against my cheek and smiles. "It wouldn't be so bad to stay here with me now, would it? Just like old times, my little Jazmine."

I swipe off his hand. "Don't be absurd, Rahim—I'm not turning her in. Plus, there's no danger to you—even your servants haven't seen us. Just show us the back entrance, and the Limbus will never even know we came."

Rahim shakes his head. "You don't get it, do you? She's Hindu. *Hindu*, don't you see? All the things I've talked about, all the information she now has stored in her brain. A few words from her and the HRM will be targeting my hotel by the end of the day. You know I've never had a prejudiced bone in my body, but times are different now, there's too much at stake." He shakes his head again. "What in the world possessed you to bring her here? I would never have thought you would endanger me like this."

"Listen, Rahim—"

"No, *you* listen. I want you to come with me to her room and act as if nothing's happened. We'll go downstairs nice and easy, and you can hand her over yourself to the Limbus to get in their good graces."

That's when I pull out the gun. It seems cartoonish, but also quite appropriate, given that the whole situation—the train, the hotel, the nuclear threat—feels like something from a movie script. Rahim senses it too. "What are you now, Jaz Bond? Double-oh-Six, the *chhakka* secret agent? Shouldn't you at least butch yourself up a bit?"

"Let's go get Sarita. Quietly." I try to sound authoritative, project all my conviction and ruthlessness right through the muzzle of my weapon. But it doesn't quite work—the gun feels so alien and uncomfortable in my hand I have trouble keeping it level.

"Oh, please. You shouldn't play with such toys. You know you have no intention of using it. The Limbus will be up in a second if they hear it—even my servants might stop their gossiping for once and come investigate." Rahim casually pushes my hand away, as if correcting a child. "But I *am* impressed. You would actually resort to this, just to protect her. What hold does she have? It must be something to do with love, isn't it?"

I'm loath to reveal anything, unsure I can trust Rahim. On the other hand, there seems little choice but to take the gamble. "That boy you mentioned—the one who went to Delhi. She's married to him."

Rahim whistles. "Tell me."

So the Jazter relates his tale. Rahim is misty-eyed afterwards. "All my life, I've waited to care like that for someone. And have him care as much for me." He smiles ruefully. "I suppose you didn't know your auntie was so sentimental, such a helpless romantic at heart."

He tells me the best option might be to take Cadell Road, the main street past the mosque. "They're going to be on the lookout for you, no matter how I try to throw them off. But it's bound to be an entertainment night if they've captured prisoners from the train—so you might be able to slip through amidst the crowds surging towards the mosque." He folds my fingers around a roll of money. "The causeway to Bandra is probably too dangerous—you might have to find a boat across. Either way, it's going to cost."

"And you won't get into trouble?"

"With the Limbus? They're too stupid to figure anything out. And my boss isn't here, so he'll never know."

We hug, and I glimpse an expression of guileless affection on Rahim's face which takes me back many years. Or perhaps it's just the light from the table lamp, catching him in such a way to make him look very young. "I hope you find him," he says.

As I step into the corridor to go get Sarita, he calls after me. "Actually, I did come close to caring a lot for somebody once. But I was only sixteen, and thought it was just a crush."

INCREDIBLY, MY VISION did come true—Karun and the Jazter ended up living together in our own private flat. Not in Bombay, but Delhi. That's where Karun returned when he graduated with his bachelor's, to be closer to his mother, and also pursue a post-graduate degree. Since I received my bachelor of commerce at the same time, I said goodbye to my befuddled parents ("But Mumbai is the financial capital!") and took up a job at an investment center in Connaught Place.

Our joint apartment almost didn't come to pass, simply because nobody would rent us one. To head off any reservations, we'd prepared an explanation of wanting to share expenses to save money for when we married. But the sticking factor turned out to be religion rather than two men cohabiting. I'd heard of landlords in Bombay refusing to lease flats to Muslims, but they were ten times more bigoted in Delhi. ("All that terrorism, you know," one explained rather kindly.) The question of Karun renting a place in his name didn't arise, students being a category possibly even less welcome than Muslims.

For a while, we lived in a "barsati" in a Muslim section of Old Delhi. Coming from Bombay, I was not familiar with these single-room structures, built as servants' quarters on house terraces. Ours came with a tiny toilet, a cubicle for bathing, and a hot plate (for which the landlord, Mr. Suleiman, charged us fifty rupees a month for the extra electricity). The place (our "penthouse," as we called it) had the advantage of complete privacy—only the most determined intruders would climb four floors to barge in on a terrace that baked all day in the heat.

Still, for the two months we spent there, Karun (or rather Kasim, the Muslim name we made up to give Mr. Suleiman) and I were able to relax into the tranquillity of quotidian life for the first time. We made tea on the hot plate each morning and shared a packet of Gluco biscuits for breakfast (seven biscuits each, with an extra one sometimes, which we split in half). We left at around eight and returned only after sunset, trying out all the oily but inexpensive dhabbas in nearby markets. Sometimes, we went for a movie, but usually just watched television on the small portable set we'd smuggled up (so that Mr. Suleiman didn't charge us even more for electricity). Once it cooled down enough, we had sex in the room, then dragged the charpoys outside to wherever the breeze seemed strongest that night. Karun liked bedtime stories, so I usually narrated a fairy tale we'd both heard as children. By the time I got to the middle, he fell asleep.

On very hot nights, I tried to cool us down by talking about all the snow I'd seen while growing up. The great blizzard of Chicago when we shivered without electricity for an entire week, the white-daubed houses and carpeted streets that turned Geneva into a postcard. The trees aglitter with ice under which I lay, the snow chairs I built to cozy up in, the frozen lakes across which I danced and skimmed. Karun, who had never experienced snow, snuggled closer, as if he could actually feel its chill. That's when I told him the nearby Yamuna had frozen solid against its banks, that the roads downstairs were hushed and white, that the gleam of our rooftop came from snow, not moonlight. Once, I even taught him how to skate, as if the terrace outside our barsati had been converted into a giant ice rink.

I awoke every dawn when the birds just started chirping. I rolled into Karun's bed—I enjoyed cuddling with him in the cool. Sometimes, I pressed and poked with my erection, or stroked his groin, or nibbled at his foreskin. I loved bothering him like that while he lay half asleep—he either groaned and turned away, or succumbed to my advances. Afterwards, he tried to catch a few more winks. I held him in my arms and waited for the sun to rise from behind the rooftops, to brush his skin with its first delicate strokes of golden light.

Perhaps our abode wasn't as private as we imagined. Perhaps other residents stirred at the same time of dawn in their barsatis. One day, as I played with a still-drowsy Karun, a rock came hurtling onto our terrace from an adjacent rooftop. When I returned that evening, a knot of women who lived in the lower floors stood gossiping on the steps by the entrance. The way they went silent and stared as I passed made it clear they were talking about us. The next day, Mr. Suleiman braved the four floors to our barsati to order us to leave.

I HAD NOT WANTED to enlist my parents' help in getting a flat, since I didn't want them to know about Karun and me living together. But I needn't have worried. When, after two weeks of filthy hotel rooms, I finally gave in, my father readily swallowed the story I'd concocted about wanting to save money. "That physics student—I remember him. It's good to have friends with such diverse interests."

He put me in touch with Mrs. Singh, a widowed friend of a colleague, who asked Karun and me to come directly to the Green Park flat she had for rent. She looked much younger than I'd expected—about fifty, perhaps. Although dressed in the observant white of a widow, I noticed her feet peeking out from under the cuffs of her salwaar astride exuberantly pink sandals. "I live right below, but you have your own private entrance. Mr. Singh had that installed just before he passed." Her scrutiny alternated between Karun and me, as if trying to figure us out. "It's only a one-bedroom, but it does have two beds." She pointed them out—they looked as modest as the cots in Karun's

Bombay hostel. "I normally rent only to husband-and-wife couples—I had the mai pull them apart for you this morning and put the night-stand in between." She locked gazes with me. "This is the way they should look when the mai comes in at ten every morning to clean."

"I'm not sure I understand."

"Look, Mr. Hassan. You're telling me you and your friend want to save money. Fine. I didn't ask, and I don't care. You won't find another Punjabi woman in all of Delhi who's less inquisitive than Mrs. Singh. But I draw the line at gossip. I like my tenants to be quiet and clean. All I ask is you not give the mai any reason to start her tongue wagging." She stared at each one of us in turn. "I can show you the kitchen if we're agreed."

The flat rented for half my salary, so it didn't look like we'd be saving much money for our purported weddings. "Plus, I'll need a year's rent in advance as deposit," Mrs. Singh said. "Which is pretty standard for Delhi." I had to SOS my father for help again—fortunately, he agreed to wire me the money.

The next two years were the happiest in my life. I felt like the hero (sometimes the heroine) of one of the fairy tales I related to Karun every night. Swirling through flower-laden fields, galloping across magical plains—who cared if it was only Delhi's congested lanes, as long as I had Karun by my side? We perfected the art of haggling, and learnt to tenderize even the toughest Delhi hen by marinating it in yoghurt overnight. We bought half the board games on the market, and several new accessories for my train set, indulging every whim our childhoods had denied. Rearranging the furniture for the mai each morning became a drag, so we learnt to squeeze together in the same bed. At night, we made love with barely a gasp or creak so as not to disturb Mrs. Singh.

Her demeanor softened soon after we moved in. She helped us fill out the application for a phone line and figure out the electricity bill. She gave us cucumbers from her vines on the terrace, and remembered to wish us well on both Muslim and Hindu holidays. Two months after we moved in, she sent up a large pot of chicken lentil soup when we both got the flu. Most endearing of all, she treated us as a couple—long before the shopkeepers downstairs fell into the habit from seeing us together so often. The bania advised us to start buying detergent in the family size to save money, the vegetable woman remembered I liked okra and Karun peas, the meatwalla saved us just enough chops for two persons to eat.

The only thorn in our side was Mrs. Singh's eighteen-year-old son Harjeet. He scowled each time he encountered us on the steps, positioning his hefty frame to make it awkward to pass. He made raucously loud homophobic comments from the verandah when he got together with his Sikh friends. We stopped hanging out our clothes to dry on the terrace when gobs of dirt started mysteriously landing on them (underwear seemed especially vulnerable). He lifted weights in his turban and shorts on the landing outside our door on Sundays, so that he could mutter obscenities in case we accidentally glanced his way.

Fortunately, we spent most of our time on weekends exploring the city. On one such expedition, we chanced upon an expansive shrubbery-filled park that bordered an enclave of foreign embassies. I instantly realized its potential as a shikari's paradise. Sure enough, men loitered all around, standing near the gate, reclining on benches, leaning against trees. A central pathway over a suspended red and white rope bridge had the most action, with shikaris and their prey working the circuit as if modeling their wares on a fashion runway.

On a whim, I took Karun by the arm and joined the men parading up the path to the bridge. A space immediately cleared all around us, as if in deference to our coupled state. I felt people's curiosity, noticed them peering to catch a glimpse. Was there a measure of jealousy mixed in, resentment that we promenaded like royalty through their midst? Had I risked attracting their malediction, their evil eye, their nazar, by flaunting our good fortune in their face? Karun didn't seem to notice the reactions—he blithely pointed to the trees, the gardens, the red and orange flowers.

That evening, I finally uttered the phrase whirling around in my mind. I could no longer remember when the inkling had first arisen, when it had fledged and strengthened, when it had parsed together the words for its own articulation. An idea, an expression, antithetical to Jazter philosophy, one that blasphemed his Gita, his Koran, his Bible. Our stroll in the park had given it that final energy to break free, when I realized how lucky I felt to no longer be a shikari. I raised myself up on my arms when I felt it coming, so that I hovered over Karun, looking directly into his face. "I love you"—the words felt unfamiliar yet silky as they slid from the Jazter's lips.

For a moment, Karun didn't respond, and I wondered if I'd overreached, overplayed my hand. Then he leaned up to kiss me. "I love you too," he replied.

THE ALLEY BEHIND the hotel is deserted, except for rats enjoying a moonlit supper of discarded kitchen waste. We race past the rear of several buildings, Rahim's large purple burkha billowing and flapping around Sarita's slender frame. Cadell Road, when we get to it, is thronged with men, though thankfully a few burkhas dot the crowd as well. I try to keep us hidden from the Limbus glowering menacingly from the edges. Every so often, they gesture, with their rifles or the stiff plastic tubing they wield as whips, to pull people out for checks.

The skyscraper tower of Hinduja Hospital rises to our left. The Limbus have only managed to blacken it, not burn it down—even the charred shell of the aerial tunnel connecting the east and west wings still hangs above the road. Broken medical consoles, mangled hospital beds, smashed operating tables lie scattered around, like bodies dragged out of the building and clubbed to death. An MRI scanner seems to have been the object of particular wrath—its pallet twisted and burnt, its cylindrical tube hacked open in half, electronic entrails spilling out colorfully over the pavement.

Ahead, the air is thick with the smell of generator fuel. Loudspeakers blare religious sermons, the torches give way to floodlights beaming down from poles. Every once in a while a roar of approval erupts from somewhere up ahead. I'm uneasy about the crush—so strong that it's impossible not to be carried along. We're headed in the direction of the causeway, it's true, but what if that's precisely where they hope to scoop us up?

The road narrows, and more Limbus appear, blocking every side street and alleyway. It already appears impossible to make a break for the water, to choose the boat alternative Rahim had suggested. A few hundred meters away, a mound rises from the ground, splitting the crowd into two streams that slowly circle past. A pair of rifle-toting Limbus stands on this platform, flanking a smaller figure between them. Even from afar, I realize it must be Yusuf—they're funneling us through so that he can scan all our faces.

Sarita sees him as well, and immediately slows down—I nudge her on to maintain her pace. There's no way to turn around—the Limbus will get very excited if anyone attempts an about-face. Instead, I veer us through the flow at an angle, so that we gradually shift towards the edge. The doorway to a building stands unguarded ahead—if we can make it through, we might escape.

Barely have we stepped onto the sidewalk, though, when a whistle sounds, followed by a whole cacophony of them. We've been spotted from above—a Limbu gestures with his rifle from his balcony perch for us to stay clear of the building. I hastily pull Sarita back into the anonymity of the crowd before the terrestrial guards can pinpoint whom they've been whistling at.

We near Yusuf, and I notice his face is swollen. Blood runs down from his ear and mouth, several of his scabs have ruptured again. I try not to look at him—to be cautious, I tell myself, though it's really due to guilt. But he catches my eye when we're still several feet away. Recognition floods in—he opens his mouth and raises his hand to point me out. I brace myself for exposure—the accusing finger, the triumphant shout—can I really blame him after the injuries I've caused? One second extrudes slowly into the next—is it even worth fumbling for my weapon, should I simply let the Limbus gun us down? But at the last instant, Yusuf redirects his raised hand to wipe his chin—he licks the blood off his lips and closes his mouth. As we pass, he flashes the tiniest of smirks, while keeping his gaze trained resolutely at the crowd.

Sarita is so distraught at his condition that she tugs on my arm to go back—I'm thankful the burkha keeps her agitation masked. "His brother's a Limbu, so he'll be OK," I whisper, and pull her along.

The road runs past the mosque turnoff to the causeway bridge, but the throng pressing in from the opposite direction makes it impossible to continue. Limbus push through, trying to bring order to the whirlpool of people, flailing their rubber tubes to herd everyone in through the entrance lane. We have little choice but to follow, towards the ornate green arch with white Urdu lettering that frames the mosque. The four minarets and star and crescent flag rising from the top of the gate are just as I remember. I've been here twice with my father—once to observe the ailing supplicants who come to seek a cure on Thursdays, once just to soak in the tranquillity of the inner sanctum housing the graves of a Sufi saint and his mother.

Now, the Limbus have erected a tall stage with loudspeakers in the tiled plaza. "These infidels, these kafirs, who tried to kill our innocent children with their terrorist train—" one of them recites, standing next to a slaughtering frame, the kind found in a halal abattoir. Ropes tether two blindfolded figures in bloodstained clothes to a pole. The man on the left pulls and strains to free himself, but the other simply sits slumped on the ground, his head lolling limply on his chest. A rock from the crowd bounces off his body and elicits a weak groan, but he makes no move to protect himself.

"I think that's Mura," Sarita says in a strangled voice. "What if they've got Guddi and Anupam as well?" She wants to stick around to make sure her train companions aren't led on stage, but the queasiness is rapidly spreading in my stomach, and I pull her away before the "entertainment" Rahim warned us about can begin.

On our last visit, my father led me down a long flight of steps to show me the strip of beach at the rear of the mosque. Looking for a way to distance us from the stage, I spot the passage that leads to these steps—miraculously, they are unguarded. We climb down to the sand and have barely walked a few paces before we bump into the missing sentry zipping up his pants by a urine-stained wall. He tries to unsling his rifle, but to my surprise, I have faster reflexes. The gun magically appears in my hand, I am transformed to Jaz Bond in an instant.

Except I haven't quite mastered the art of 006 dialogue yet, I can't summon the lines I'm supposed to spout. After an awkwardly silent moment, Sarita has the presence of mind to order the Limbu to drop his rifle and raise his hands. She even waves him along through her burkha as if packing her own pistol under her chador.

We walk in a procession along the wall of the old Mahim fort. The sentry stretches his arms high into the air as if accomplishing this smartly is a point of pride for him. He's almost my height, and about my age as well—doing an automatic shikari appraisal of his shoulders and back, even our builds appear the same. The thought flashes through my mind that our positions might have been reversed had our birth circumstances been exchanged. I try to imagine myself barefoot in a raggedy salwaar kameez like him, trading in the comfort of my Italian sneakers, the snugness of my designer jeans. What would it have been like to grow up in his place? Perhaps surrounded by religious zealots, perhaps hungry, perhaps illiterate? Would the Jazter have turned into a Jihadster? Might free will have prevailed, or was it solely a function of fate?

"A function of opportunity," I hear my father say. He always maintained that the difference between the tolerant and the extremist was not so great. "Looking into the Other, we can always find something of ourselves within." By which logic I, too, should have the power to reach out to this Limbu: plant a notion, sow a seed, that might influence him. Who knew what native intelligence lay under that scruffy exterior, what sensitive personality, what endearing face? I decide to share the fact that I'm Muslim—this will be the stepping stone towards establishing a connection.

"Lying dog!" He turns around and spits in my face. "I know you're one of the Hindus who got away from the train. We're all around— you'll never escape."

So I try to establish my Islamic credentials by reciting the opening of the Koran, not only in Urdu, but also in Arabic. This only enrages him further. "You'll rot in hell for passing such holy words through your infidel lips!" He spits at me again, but this time I dodge out of the way.

Not only does my bridge-building experiment crash, it provokes the Limbu to get louder and more abusive. "Just try crossing the cause- way—our guards will cut your pig-fucking bodies to bits." Sarita pulls back her veil to register her alarm at his ranting—will I have to kill him to ensure we're not found out? Except I know I can't—the only gun this Bond has ever discharged is his own. What I do instead, as our captive brazenly starts calling for help, is to step forward and tap him on the back of the head with the butt of the gun. "Ow," he says, turn- ing around to look at me angrily, so I tap him again, a bit harder. This time, he staggers to the ground. Reluctantly, I tap him a third time, and to my horror, my hand comes up covered in blood.

We break into a run, clearing the ramparts of the fort, sprinting around a row of sheds whose corrugated roofs reflect the moonlight in strips. Thousands of bamboo poles lie stacked in front, more burst forth from wooden pens, like toothpicks rising from giant holders. Trucks loaded with bamboo stand abandoned all around, parked right on the sand. Looming ahead, I make out a pair of ghostly white cylin- drical structures that remind me of the tanks of a petrol refinery. The sea to our left is calm—in the light of the moon, its surface looks oily. The tide is low, but the smell is worse—a blend of putrefying fish and sewage.

I slow down, then come to a stop. Sarita draws up beside me. The causeway is just visible beyond the cylinders—a shadow shooting off over the water towards the fabled shores of Bandra. From this angle, it seems a lot lower than I imagined, something one could almost leap up to grab and swing across by the rafters. Beyond such acrobatics, though, the only practical alternative seems to be to run the gauntlet of surface guards the Limbu has boasted about. "It's not going to work, is it?" Sarita says. "We'll have to find a way by sea like Rahim warned."

So we start searching the sands for a boat. But other than some tarpaulin-covered vessels too enormous to move, our quest only yields two upturned scuppers, with visibly rotten wooden bases.

"I LOVE YOU." Perhaps I shouldn't have pushed my luck with those three fateful words. Or perhaps the evil eye from the shikaris at Nehru Park did stick. Although we lived together for three more years, things between Karun and me began unraveling soon after that walk. It started when I accompanied him on a Sunday visit to Karnal to meet his mother.

All during the train ride, Karun kept rhapsodizing about her sweetness, her empathy, her gracious fortitude through the years of hardship she had endured. With the stories he'd related already, I expected someone with a halo over her head—a combination of Mother India and the holy Mary, who could whip up a killer curry to boot. She did, in fact, look ethereal when I first glimpsed her at the door—sunlight shining off her white sari and sluicing down her cascade of silver hair—a queen mother from a fairy tale.

Except she turned out to be more witch than fairy. "Karun's told me so much about you—this spell you've cast on him. One day I'll have to come and see for myself why you're so special as a roommate."

"It's the flat that's special, not me—since we're so close to Karun's college."

"Surely not closer than the campus hostel? But I suppose if he moved you'd have to pay the full rent yourself."

She had prepared the garlic mutton Karun always mentioned so reverentially. To me, it tasted quite acrid, with alarming chunks of gristle left in, to stretch the meat, perhaps. "Karun tells me you're hoping to save money for your wedding. Who's the lucky girl?"

"I haven't found one yet, not exactly."

"No girl? Aren't your parents looking for one?"

"I'm just not in any hurry."

"Why not? You've already got a job, so this is the time to settle down. Don't wait too long—you know how people can talk. I keep telling Karun even he should marry, but perhaps he's too taken by your example. Who better than a wife to look after him while he's slaving over his physics? All the time he wastes on shopping and cleaning, not to mention these kitchen experiments with you every night. Besides, I'm fifty-five already—it's time to give me a grandchild."

She asked the obligatory questions about job and parents, being careful to display only polite surprise at my being Muslim. ("I didn't realize Jaz stood for *Ijaz*—Karun's never used your full name.") Instead, she used her inquiries to peck away at the central riddle of why I was in Delhi, living with her son. "Didn't your mother try to stop you when you chose to move so far away? Surely there are better jobs for you in Bombay with all the financial centers there?"

"I needed the change."

"That's the same thing Karun said when he applied for his Bombay scholarship. I'm not sure why everyone wants change so much—each time my life has changed, it's been for the worse."

After lunch, she carefully unfolded two ten-rupee notes from a tiny purse. "Why don't you go get some jalebis from the sweet monger? It's three, so they should be really fresh." I rose to accompany Karun, but she waved me back to the sofa. "Not you, you're the guest."

Unsure what Kali incarnation she planned to metamorphose into once Karun left, I scrambled to turn on the Jazter charm before she could produce a phalanx of extra arms or a garland of severed heads. "He's very smart, your son. You must be so proud of him." A bit lame, but I couldn't muster any other compliment.

It was enough. The smile frozen on her lips since my arrival finally broke through to her eyes and lit up her face. "He topped his class every year in school right from the eighth standard. Studying so hard every night that I'd have to insist he put away his books and go to bed. I have all his report cards saved in his old attaché case."

She told me how they collected one-rupee coins in empty jam jars for him to spend. "Except he always bought books, so one day, I decided to empty all the bottles and get him something fun—a game, perhaps. You should have seen his face when I told him what I'd done—I don't think I ever saw him so furious." She laughed. "But he ended up loving my purchase—a small telescope, not much more than a toy really, since that's all the money I had. He would set it up by that window and study the stars through it every night." She gazed towards the corner of the room as if Karun still stood there peering through his telescope, and for an instant, I could picture him as well.

"Did you know his father passed when he was eleven?"

"Yes, Karun told me how much you've done for him ever since."

"No more than any other mother would have. But with just the two of us left instead of three, I had to keep every fiber in my body attuned towards his success. I'd always known he was a bit of a dreamer, prone to get lost in thought, unsure of what he wanted for himself. Channeling him into science was easy—his father had already laid the groundwork for that. The books, too, he'd always liked—I taught him to bury all his grief in them. It tore my heart to see him so lonely, but I told myself it would pay off in future happiness. Even that day in the toy store, when I went to buy something purely for fun—the telescope, I couldn't help thinking, might be more profitable, lead to a possible career interest."

"You were just doing what was best for him."

"That's what I thought. Except if I'd encouraged him to make some friends, to go to movies or play cricket, he'd have suffered from his father's absence less. He'd be less inclined to take the wrong path to cure his aloneness. Less vulnerable to having his head turned, to fall under anyone's spell."

"I don't think I know what you mean."

She fixed me in her stare, the clarity in her eyes breathtaking. "What I'm trying to say is that Karun is my son, the focal point in my life—I understand him better than he understands himself. He'd find it difficult to hide even a sneeze from me—anything going on in his life, I can tell. I know exactly what will make him fulfilled, who will bring him misery and nothing else. I can look into people's faces and recognize their natures much better than he can—I'm prepared to do anything in my power to keep him safe from harmful influences. His happiness is sacred to me—I've worked too long and hard to let him just throw it away like that."

Whole minutes seemed to elapse before she released me from her gaze. "I'll make some teas for the jalebis," she finally said.

"I THINK SHE KNOWS about us," I told Karun on the train back. "I think that's why she probably doesn't like me very much."

"That's absurd. If she did know, she'd like you more, not less. I'm thinking of telling her anyway." Seeing my stunned expression, he retreated. "It's only a thought."

But he did disclose things to her, on a visit some months later. I could tell by his disheveled hair, his wild-eyed look, when he returned. "She didn't take it as well as I thought. She wants me to marry—she reminded me of everything she's done and said it's the only thing she asks in return. She thinks you're a bad influence, not so much because of your community or religion, but the foreign ideas you've brought back from living abroad. Ideas against our culture, she says—she demands I move out at once."

That night, Karun didn't want to have sex, but I insisted. I wanted to remind him why he stayed with me, to head off any notion he might form of leaving. At first, he simply spread his legs and stared into his pillow as I explored him with my tongue. He offered no resistance or reaction when I wrapped him in my arms and began to enter him. As my thrusts increased, he tried to shake loose, but I held him in place. He arched his neck back, crying out and curling his fingers into fists as we simultaneously came.

Cuddling him to my neck the way he liked afterwards, I asked him if he'd do what his mother wanted. "Don't worry. I just have to make her understand that this is the way it is." He said it defiantly, as if affirming it more to himself. "Besides, I'm no longer eligible for the hostel, and it's not like I can afford my own place."

He underestimated her. She developed cancer, the witch. The timing couldn't have been more perfect—one Sunday, he bravely recited for her the speech he had rehearsed; the next, she calmly countered with her announcement. "She'd gone for a checkup last week. The results came this Thursday. It's quite bad, since it might have spread to her spine. She says I shouldn't worry, that she's resigned to her fate. I know it's crazy, but I can't help thinking that if I hadn't told her—"

"You're right, that is completely crazy. You know there's no connection."

"Still, I can't help but feel responsible. After all she did for me. And now she's not even asking for anything."

Of course she's not, I felt like saying—was it so difficult to understand her strategy? Didn't he realize the power of guilt? For all I knew, she might have fabricated the whole three-hankie drama to wean him away from me. Would it be too untoward to ask if I could take a good, hard look at the X-rays myself?

Then I felt sorry for him—even bad, a little bit, for the witch. "If you ever need to bring your mother to Delhi for tests or treatment, she can stay with us."

But she refused to come to Delhi, even though it offered hospitals much better than any in Karnal. She claimed it was too far, though Karun and I both recognized this as a protest against my continuing presence. She began playing the matrimonial market for Karun, soliciting matches and responding to newspaper ads. Each Sunday, he returned with a new packet of notes and photographs. "All she keeps begging me for is a grandchild in the time she has left."

As her health declined, Karun spent Saturdays in Karnal, then Fridays as well. More months went by, and he changed his status to part-time, then suspended his university work altogether a year and a half into her illness. He spent two months nursing her through chemotherapy, and when she was better, began returning to Delhi on Sundays. I wanted to go to Karnal to see him, but he stopped me each time, saying he wouldn't be able to get away from her bedside.

About a year after Karun's mother received her diagnosis, an unrelated problem had cropped up. Mrs. Singh fell in love with a Sikh gentleman living in Noida and started spending a lot of her time there. We'd had an inkling something was up ever since encountering her in a bright orange salwaar kameez one evening, trailing clouds of perfume down the steps. With her daughter recently married off, this left Harjeet as the only day-to-day occupant of the flat below.

At first, we tried to ignore his increased harassment. Instead of just blocking our way on the steps, he now started bumping into us, causing groceries to be knocked out of our hands on more than one occasion. Our mail disappeared from the common receptacle downstairs, forcing us to rent a post office box. The unemployed Sikh youths he hung out with became a permanent fixture downstairs—each night, they got drunk and sang Bollywood songs with crudely altered lyrics ("Homo Shanti Homo," "Love Mera Shit Shit"). One day, we found a puddle of urine outside our door—another time, a pair of underwear stiff with semen on our balcony.

Mrs. Singh, when we finally tracked her down, dismissed our complaints—her Harjeet was a good boy incapable of anything like that. If we had a problem, we could always find another place. Except we couldn't, and we all knew that. In addition to the problem of finding a landlord open to both Hindus and Muslims, rents had shot up dramatically in keeping with the overheated economy.

Although I learnt to brush off Harjeet's bullying attempts (swaggering past when he blocked my way, responding in kind when he muttered insults), Karun got more cowed. He peered down before descending the steps to make sure Harjeet wasn't lying in wait, and came up with only the most anemic rejoinders when verbally taunted. "I hate it," he said. "Is this what we have to look forward to our whole lives—dealing with people like him?" I sometimes wondered if he spent more time in Karnal just to escape Harjeet.

WITH KARUN GONE so much of the time, the Jazter's urges often remained unrelieved—he no longer got regularly milked. The palm, the sock, the fruit, the fowl—their creative use helped, but only in a limited way. For a while he fought the good battle, thinking about the park he'd stumbled upon with Karun, but not venturing near. Riding a bus to the stop one day, but turning back at the gate. Darting in just for a little peek at the flowers after that, but trying not to notice the fauna frolic. Joining them for a quick modeling jaunt down the runway the next time, but the self-control still commendably in place.

And then it happened. A glance exchanged, a path into the trees, a bed of grass with the familiar blue ceiling. A quick game of cobra and burrow, mongoose and den, and relief came surging in (or out, technically). Shirts tucked, zippers zipped, no need for pleasantries to be exchanged. The bus waiting to take me back—such a convenient one-stop shopping trip.

I got home congratulating myself on the solution I'd found—why hadn't I thought of it before? The answer lay in wait—guilt broke upon me in an overwhelming wave as soon as I stepped through the door. The cupboard we shared, the bed we slept in, the table at which we ate—everything reminded me of my betrayal. Hadn't I professed my devotion to Karun each time he clung tightly to me during his brief home visits? How could I have done this to him, especially with his mother so sick?

But logically speaking, what difference did it make? Since I didn't intend to tell him, the question of hurt didn't arise. Besides, I always used protection, so I wasn't exposing him to any risk. In fact, my actions promoted a positive outlook, an upbeat disposition, which helped me be more supportive. *Wer rastet, rostet*—what rests, rusts. Surely it behooved the Jazter to remain prepared, to keep his parts well-lubricated?

So I went back to the park. I reacquainted myself with sweat and spit, how different men smelled, how they felt, how they tasted. I explored all the cruisy new internet sites, learnt the mores of shikar in virtual spaces. Each time Karun returned home, I suspended these efforts and concentrated solely on him. He had grown thinner and looked gaunt—in his hair, I even found a few strands of grey. He spent a lot of time lying in bed, with no appetite for sex and little resistance when I initiated it. I wondered if he suspected my transgressions, somehow sensed the other men my body had been intimate with. He spoke very little of his mother except to say she was steadily deteriorating—the doctors had given her a few more months to live. He didn't mention the matrimonial ads any more. Sometimes he leafed silently through his abandoned Ph.D. thesis.

I tried to rally my affection for him, to remind myself of the joys of our relationship. But his listlessness was so draining, his gloom so contagious, that I felt relief at the end of each visit. Sighing away the guilt, I continued in the same taxi to the park after dropping him off at the train station.

WALKING ALONG MAHIM BEACH, still on the lookout for something seaworthy to Bandra, Sarita and I stumble onto a group of people huddling against a shed. At first I start, my hand instinctively dipping into my pocket to close around my gun. But then I notice they're not

Limbus—everyone's much too clean-cut and well-dressed. "Hello," one of them calls out, her voice friendly, breezy. She seems in her late twenties, as do the others. "Are you here for Sequeira's? The ferry should stop by any minute."

"Sequeira's?"

"It's the End-of-the-World Party tonight, haven't you heard? They've even promised us electricity!"

Like the other two women, she carries a burkha folded loosely over her arm instead of being robed in it. She accepts a cigarette from one of her male companions—its end burns bright orange as she takes a drag. "Aren't you afraid they'll spot you smoking?" Sarita asks, staring.

"Who, the Limbus?" The woman laughs. "Don't worry, they never bother us here." She takes another drag of the cigarette. "Are you hiding from them?—is that why you ask?"

Sarita begins to stammer a denial, but the woman interrupts her with another laugh. "I'm just teasing. And it's OK even if you are. We won't tell—no Limbus among us." She offers Sarita the cigarette. "Here, would you like a puff?"

Sequeira's turns out to be a nightclub on the Bandra side. "How strange you haven't heard of it. I thought for sure that's where you were headed when I saw the jeans and the sneakers. That's what all the men wear—it's practically a uniform. Not that I mean to pry into your destination, but you might as well have a look if you're trying to get across."

Just then, a bell chimes softly behind us. A dark shape has materialized from the sea—as we watch, a small boat detaches itself from the ferry and approaches through the ripples. An ark borne by fairies through the heavens couldn't warm the Jazter cockles more, I think to myself, as our means of escape from Mahim draws up.

"This is the part I hate," the woman, whose name is Zara, says, taking off her shoes. "You have to wade into the water to get to the boat. Which means that afterwards, on the dance floor, your feet remain sticky all night with salt."

THE INCIDENT WITH Harjeet occurred when Karun came back for a short visit before they took his mother's new tumors out. The convalescence period would last well into the winter, so he wanted to get his sweaters and coat. He had purchased a medical garter his mother would need after the operation and was just opening the metal gate downstairs when the motorcycles pulled up. "Home, Sweetie?" Harjeet called out, and his three friends laughed and whistled.

We'd agreed Karun should simply not react when taunted, so leaving the gate open, he hurried up the path towards the house. The motorcycles vroomed in behind, right through the gate. "A present for your hubby?" Harjeet said, and still astride his bike, yanked the box out from Karun's hands.

He couldn't help but reply, he told me, even though he probably shouldn't have. "Give that back."

Harjeet pulled the garter out of the box and held it up, dangling by a strap. "Look! It's some sort of women's underwear. Does Sweetie get to wear it, or does Hubby?" He took a deep sniff of the material. "Mmmmm—smells good—must be Sweetie."

"It's for my mother."

"Look, everyone—not just a sweetie, but a motherfucker too! And Hubby must join in—who does he fuck first—the sweetie or the mother?" Harjeet wrapped the garter over his head and, getting off his bike, started prancing and singing, "I'm a gandu and a ma-ka-chod too."

Karun managed to get into the house, but Harjeet and his friends followed and cornered him in the stairwell. Harjeet started snapping the garter at his crotch—one of the shots hit home, making him double up in pain. "Perhaps the sweetie would like a taste of uncut Sikh instead of the same old hubby-mian every day?"

They began to grab at his clothes, but he broke free and ran up the steps. For a while, they banged on the door, even ramming it a few times, but the bolts held. I found him huddled in bed, his shirt torn, scratches on his arms and face. "We have to go to the police," I said, unsure, even as I made the suggestion, as to what reception we could expect.

"I can't. I have to return tonight. The operation is tomorrow."

I kissed his face and held him close. "Don't worry. I'll think of something while you're away."

"The things he said about my mother. I don't think I want to stay here any longer."

We had sex before he left. It was more comforting than passionate, and I held him in my arms afterwards as long as I could. "I love you," I said, and he whispered the words back to me. I imagined the two of us living in a new flat somewhere, perhaps even back in Bombay. His mother, Harjeet, my indiscretions, left floating behind in a different universe far away. "I love you," I said again, and not knowing it then, kissed him for the final time in the home we'd built. Then I took him to the station to catch his train.

SATURDAY MORNING, I knocked on Harjeet's door. No other option remained but to talk to him, since Mrs. Singh wouldn't help and I didn't have any evidence to file a police report. (I could have threatened him with physical violence, but the thirty kilos he had on me gave me pause.)

He answered the door in his undershirt, with a handkerchief over his knot of hair. "What do you want?" He looked more surprised to see me than irked.

"I want your harassment to stop. What you did to my friend last evening—stop bothering us. Just stop."

He stretched lazily. "Or else you'll do what?"

"I'll go to the police."

"And you think they'll listen to a gandu like you?" He laughed. "To you and your sweetie friend? Where is he anyway? We must have really scared him if he didn't even have the courage to come down."

"His mother has cancer, so he's in Karnal for a few months."

Something shifted in Harjeet's eyes, but it wasn't the remorse I hoped to elicit. "Well, tell Sweetie we're very, very sorry. We'll all be waiting on the steps to greet him when he returns." He slammed the door in my face.

That evening, the motorcycle friends burst into one of their sessions even before getting fully drunk. They sang all sorts of Bollywood numbers about separation and longing. They even performed "My sweetie lies over Karnal, my sweetie lies over the sea"—given their deep Punjabi vernacular, I hadn't expected them to be conversant with English ditties. They finally stopped when neighbors from the adjoining house threatened to call the police.

At two a.m., someone knocked loudly on the door. For an instant, I had the irrational thought it might be Karun—I'd been trying to reach him all day to ask about the second operation they'd performed on his mother. Instead, I found Harjeet, so drunk that he held on to the doorjamb for support. "I just thought—" he said, and stumbled into the room.

For the next few minutes, he stared at the walls, trying to condense a coherent thought. "I sleep right beneath you now, in my mother's room," he finally said. "I can hear you go to the toilet."

He planted himself on a chair, then slid off over the side. He mumbled vague apologies (or perhaps they were threats?) while sprawled out on the floor. At one point, he caught my leg and tried to pull me down next to him. It took me the better part of an hour to drag him out the door. I left him on the landing softly singing one of his homo songs to himself.

The Jazter had sometimes wondered about the reason behind Harjeet's belligerence—the ensuing week left no doubt. It was like watching a fairy-tale battle, a personal jihad—the entire gamut of reactions compressed and played out. One day he tried to push me aside on the steps, the next, he stared lasciviously as he let me pass; in the evenings he sang insulting songs with his friends, then staggered up to my door drunk. Most bizarrely, he resumed his exercises on my landing, wearing a thong (and matching head knot) so electric yellow it made even the Jazter blush.

At first, I simply ignored him—when he knocked, I kept my door shut. Then—purely in an abstract sense—I started wondering how he would be to fuck. I peeped through my window as he strained at his barbells—the muscles on his chest bulged and popped. In body type, he would have to get an A-minus in terms of what the Jazter usually looked for. There was the added bonus of doing it for the first time with a Sikh—another species of prey checked off. The bottom-line question: What would be the harm? After all, the Jazter had already cheated so many times in the park.

So I decided I'd forge ahead. Give the Sikh my very own seekh kebab. With home delivery an option, why go foraging in the park? I slipped a note in his mailbox. Lose your friends for an evening and come up as soon as it gets dark.

He was very nervous, so I made him go back downstairs and get some rum. We didn't talk much as we sat on the sofa and passed the bottle between us. I took the liquor away to the kitchen before he got too drunk. The bed I shared with Karun seemed too much of a betrayal, so I spread a mat on the floor. "Why don't you take your clothes off?"

His body looked even bigger naked. The way he arranged himself on the mat with a pillow under his stomach made it clear what he'd come for. So dispensing with the niceties I put on a condom. All this economy pleased me, made me feel back in the park.

He cursed in Punjabi as he contorted and bucked under me. It felt like riding a whale, like harpooning a sea monster. He wanted it again after we'd rested, so I summoned up the energy to lift his massive legs and do him faceup. When he asked for a third helping, I passed.

At the door, he hugged me awkwardly, but we didn't kiss. The next evening, we dispensed with the embrace as well. He began coming up regularly, with an extra afternoon visit on the weekend. He still got boisterous when his motorcycle buddies were around, but the homo songs had long ceased to offend.

For a while, I felt quite happy with the arrangement—Harjeet's body nicely fit the bill, plus it was so readily available. Then I realized the problem I'd created for myself. How would I extricate myself once I tired of Harjeet, or even more pressingly, once Karun came back? I racked my brain, but couldn't come up with a solution, other than moving out. Hadn't Karun said he didn't want to live in the same building as Harjeet when he returned? Should I be looking for another landlord who would rent to us?

I needn't have worried. The door opened one evening as I fucked Harjeet on the mat. With Harjeet's usual noisiness, neither of us heard, and I continued all the way to climax. As I slumped forward, my gaze alit on Karun's figure, standing with a bag still in his hand. Even in my fuzzy state, his shock came through clearly, I felt his horrified stare. "My mother died last night. I cremated her this morning," he said.

10

KARUN RETURNED AFTER I LEFT FOR WORK THE NEXT DAY AND moved his belongings out. I tried calling him on his cell phone, but he didn't answer—the number got disconnected soon. I sat down to write him a letter of apology but quickly found myself bogged down—my behavior with Harjeet looked even more outrageous on paper, especially when juxtaposed against the loss of his mother. Besides, I didn't have his mailing address in Karnal even though I'd been in person to the flat. One day, I took the train there, but a padlocked door greeted me. The shopkeeper downstairs who gave me the street number told me nobody had stayed in the flat since the death. I even tried Karun's university, but they had no idea of his whereabouts.

His leaving proved unlucky for me. When I told Harjeet I couldn't imagine having sex with him again, he flew into a rage and punched me in the face, then kicked me several times as I writhed on the ground. It took six stitches to sew up my lip and several visits to the dentist to have a knocked-out tooth fixed. Just as the pain in my ribs subsided, I found my office locked when I arrived at work—the company had gone belly-up. I couldn't find another job—the market dried up overnight due to the sudden economic downturn. My pocket got picked and someone (Harjeet, I suspect) broke into my apartment and stole my computer and television.

I moved back in with my parents in Bombay. I missed Karun intensely, feeling so depressed I couldn't get up some days. Now that I had squandered my relationship, I wanted nothing more than to recapture it. Despite almost seven years together, something profoundly unfulfilled remained between us—as if I was on the cusp of absorbing a deep and personal message Karun had been trying to convey. I sent several letters to the Karnal flat, but received no reply. The prospect of frequenting my old haunts looking for release again felt sordid, pathetic. I didn't quite understand this—hadn't I been cruising the Delhi parks quite breezily just some weeks back? Karun's memory rose like a pillar of light, emitting a radiant integrity I felt compelled to emulate.

I forced myself to go to gay events to find someone else. I met Sonal at a Gay Bombay disco night—he had his own tiny place at Andheri. For the four months we dated, I kept comparing him to Karun and coming up short. His body felt all wrong, his aroma didn't intoxicate. He had no ambition beyond being a sales clerk, and talked incessantly about Bollywood films. Within a week, I felt I knew everything I needed to know about him—no reserve remaining to intrigue me, like the smile I gradually learned to tease out on Karun's lips. I went out with other people as well, but none of them lasted as long.

After almost a year of unemployment, a financial advisory firm in Hyderabad offered me a position. I took it, determined to use the new surroundings to pull me out of my malaise. Indeed, the huge central lake soon set my dormant shikari radar abuzz again. I spent several agreeable evenings there, strolling the periphery to ferret out the activity spots, observing the intriguing new species of local prey. The vivid mix of the North and the South in their features, the Muslim and the Hindu, the fair and the dark—all packaged with a small-town innocence, an old-fashioned politeness, which I found particularly restorative. I never knew what language they'd lapse into when fucked—Urdu or Telugu or a mix of both (only the techies came in English). It occurred to me that such local delicacies, such *spécialités du terroir*, must exist in every state. Perhaps I needed to go on a therapeutic national pilgrimage (my very own Haj, my personal rath yatra) to sample them all in their natural locales. What better way to feel the pulse of the nation, to connect with the poor and the rich, to track all the shining progress new India had made?

But the only trips I took were to Bombay and Delhi for business, and these invariably plunged me into a melancholic state. I felt strangled by the nostalgia, by the memories of my days with Karun. I tried not to look up while walking the streets of the capital so as not to catch glimpse of a barsati. In Bombay, I took various detours to avoid the Oval, the university library, the Regal, all the landmarks across which our history had played. Each time I returned home, it seemed to take weeks before the hangover of my past life lifted. I threw away the photos I had of Karun and ceased my letter-writing campaign.

Work provided a welcome distraction. Recent political reforms had injected considerable excitement into the China-related investments I tracked (along with a majority of analysts at the office). The newly sanctioned Youth Democratic League, initially dismissed as a propaganda tool to voice aggressive, ultranationalist positions unofficially, had tapped into a country-wide generational vein that made its popularity surge well beyond the Chinese government's control. Its rabid calls to pull the plug on the U.S. debt, teach Europe a lesson for censuring China over human rights in the UN, invade not only Taiwan but also Korea and Japan, had resulted in wild swings in the yuan, especially once the League demonstrated its clout by calling a successful one-day nationwide shutdown to protest their country's kowtowing to the West. To my fascination, Indian stocks didn't tank along with their Chinese counterparts as they historically had (along with much of the developing market). Rather, they went up: investors took shelter in India's relative stability with each new alarming power gambit by the League. I also started noticing the converse: a bump in the Shanghai exchange each time a terrorist attack caused a drop in the Sensex, as if India and China had been locked into a zero-sum game. (Had I been a professor like my parents, perhaps I could have written a paper to christen this coupling the Jazter Phenomenon.)

By the end of my fourth year in Hyderabad, despite the bombings now seemingly endemic to major cities, the balance had still tilted dramatically in India's favor. The Sensex almost doubled in that period, while Shanghai and Hong Kong showed respective losses of twenty-five and forty-five percent. The unsuccessful efforts of the old-guard loyalists to rein in the increasingly brazen initiatives by League hotheads made it difficult to say who really controlled China anymore—our office trade reports all forecast further upheavals as the country flailed its way towards a new political order. Before we could take much comfort in the future, though, the Mumbai bridge explosion came along to upend all the pundits' predictions.

Much worse than the series of jolts to the market were the shock-waves that seemed to physically rip through the country. Hyderabad, in particular, dove eagerly into mayhem—perhaps due to historical grievances, or a population comparably split between Hindu and Muslim, or perhaps even because the Telangana separatists had found it beneficial to fan the flames. I stood in my balcony and tracked the plumes of smoke advancing every day—first the Old City in the distance, then the enormous emporiums along Raj Bhavan Road, and then the restaurants and bars around the lake. The city remained shut for six days, then several more when explosive-laden trucks demolished both the Birla temple and Mecca Mosque over the same weekend.

As Bhim's forces embarked on their nationwide crusade, things started looking particularly grim for Muslims. My father announced he'd accepted a position in Geneva, and we were all moving to Europe. I quit my job (most financial companies like mine were on the verge of folding anyway) and flew back to Bombay for my visa interview, wondering how I'd fare living among the Swiss again (would they succumb to my new shikari skills?). As our plans progressed, we faced the question of what to do with the flat. The HRM had already begun clamoring for Hindu areas to be cleared of Muslims as a precaution against sabotage and ambushes. With the Siddhi Vinayak temple so nearby, our building had little chance of escaping inclusion in such a

Hindu enclave. Some Muslim families set up exchanges with Hindus who owned flats in predominantly Muslim localities, but my father didn't think it worth the trouble with us emigrating.

I decided to write one final farewell letter to Karun. With the envelope all sealed and stamped, I found I'd misplaced his Karnal address. In desperation, I wrote to his Delhi university to ask if they still might have it in their records. To my surprise, the physics department secretary wrote back. Karun, she informed me, had returned to finish his Ph.D., then moved on to Mumbai. I stared at his neatly typed Colaba address.

ZARA TELLS US THE ferry comes from Worli, close to where the sea link used to begin. "Sequeira's offered the service for years, ever since he opened his club. We worked at the call center then, and went dancing late at night after our shift ended—he always had samosas and chutney sandwiches waiting for us. Quite a character, as you'll see—I've actually come to know him quite well. Now that we're grown up and past our call-center fun, my friends have spread out from Worli all the way to Versova. But luckily, there's a ferry stop near each one of us, so even with this war and everything, we can still get together at Sequeira's."

"And the Limbus simply let you come and go as you please?"

Zara laughs. "Sequeira pays everyone off—especially the gangsters who control the waterways—the same ones who control most of Mahim, incidentally. The Limbus can't afford to antagonize the gangsters, so they keep their distance from the upper beach. They quietly take Sequeira's money and pretend they don't see the ferries. This is India, after all—accommodation above everything. Besides, these Limbus don't have quite the power they'd like you to think. Over the workers and refugees, yes—but not if you have connections or wealth."

"Still, a nightclub? Isn't that exactly what they're supposed to be against?"

"Ha! See those floating lights further up the creek? They're smaller boats, operated by the low-caste Dalits who live along the Mithi river. They'll take you anywhere across for a fee. You know who they'll always have as customers? Limbus crossing over secretly. Ever since the ban on alcohol, every Christian in Bandra seems to have opened up a speakeasy across the creek. Go to any of the cheaper ones and you'll see Limbus pawing at the women and lolling around in their drink."

Zara tells Sarita that if she wants to take her burkha off, the boatman will keep it until it's time to return. "It's not so difficult a compromise, I suppose. If the Limbus insist I keep myself covered in return for keeping me safe, then fine, I'll oblige. As a Muslim, I'd be too scared to live anywhere else. Even Bandra, where they supposedly welcome all religions, where some of my younger friends, both Christian and Muslim, fled. They'll be the first in line when the Hindus decide to expand—there's little to separate them from Bhim's men."

We pass between two pylons of the sea link that still stand, like pillars of a massive nautical gate, a memorial to the ground zero where destruction began. I look up to see a section of bridge dangling directly overhead, strands of metal cable sprouting from its edges. To think the city had succeeded in this herculean battle with the sea to connect its north and south halves—will it ever be able to replicate this triumph? A light breeze from the open bay beyond ripples the water, which appears surprisingly high for low tide. Does the rise in level stem from global warming, a consequence of the cataclysmic monsoons we've been having? Or has the sea sensed the city's vulnerability, flowing as it does each day around the ruptured link? Is it reconnoitering the shores of its old enemy, building for a secret assault? The final surge that will rise up to conquer Mumbai?

The night unexpectedly fills with disco music playing from speakers on either end of the ferry. "The captain figures that once we cross under the sea link, we're out of Mahim," Zara says. A few of the passengers even begin to dance on the deck. Zara tugs at the burkha Sarita still has on. "When will you take this off?"

So Sarita works her body out of its purple cocoon. She emerges radiant, like a butterfly. More accurate, a *radioactive* butterfly: her sari glows a startling red as if steeped in uranium-spiked dye. She looks at herself in horror and amazement, smoothing down the folds, brushing at the electrified pleats with the back of her hand as if she can somehow calm the fabric. "The glowing sari," she whispers. "This must be what Guddi meant."

"That's so cool!" Zara exclaims. "It reminds me of my friend Rashida. Her wedding headdress had a thousand tiny bulbs flashing on and off during the whole ceremony. But tell me, how does it work?— do you have batteries hidden somewhere in the petticoat?" Zara feels the material, then examines her fingertips as if to check whether the fluorescence has rubbed off. "I promised not to pry, so I won't even ask why you're dressed in this particular red."

But she can't quite shake off her curiosity. She keeps alternating her gaze between the two of us, commenting on what a "cosmopolitan" couple we make, how bride-like Sarita appears, in a "temple" sort of way. Finally she blurts it out. "You're Hindu, aren't you? And he's Muslim! That's why the Limbus were chasing you—they caught you in the middle of your elopement!"

Sarita starts to dispel this notion, but I smoothly cut her off. "It's correct, more or less, what you've guessed. But promise not to tell anyone—we have to keep it a secret to be safe."

Zara actually squeals in delight. "I knew it! And the sari? Don't tell me you went and actually got married?"

"We did. Just this morning." It's too tempting an opportunity, too wicked a prospect—the Jazter and his lover's wife, linked together in matrimony. Besides, it seems the perfect way to explain away Sarita's flamboyant getup, not to mention our presence in Mahim. I proceed to weave such a rousing tale of childhood sweethearts yearning to unite across the religious divide that stars light up Zara's face, tears tremble at the corners of her eyes. Sarita looks on in consternation as I describe risking life and limb to venture into the Hindu area where she lived. "If the bomb killed us, I wanted to at least die married. Even her mother melted when she saw our resolve—she found a last-minute priest to marry us in the temple downstairs." My mistake, I said, was to sneak back into Mahim for my father's blessing. "He was so outraged he set the local Limbus on our tail—we've been on the run ever since." Our only hope now was to make it to Bandra, where Sarita's brother might take us in.

"All we have is the clothes on our back. That, a little money, and a love no longer afraid to speak its name." I take my sweetheart's startled hand in mine and kiss it.

Zara wants to call her friends around so I can relate my story to them, but I remind her again about the need for discretion, for safety's sake. "You'll have to tell Sequeira, though," she says. "He'll be absolutely thrilled. He's always trying to get different religions together—says it's the very spirit of Bandra. Just ask him, and I'm sure he'll personally take you to your brother's in the morning."

Once Zara shimmies away to the dance music, I apologize to Sarita. "I hope that didn't upset you. It seemed the best way not to get her suspicious about your outfit."

"It's OK," Sarita says, though the chagrin hasn't quite cleared her face. "I wouldn't have thought all those stories were necessary, but what difference does it make? We'll all be going our separate ways soon enough anyway."

The ferry docks beside a floating gangplank. The boatman collects the fares as we exit—a whopping two thousand per person, which includes entry to Sequeira's. As I count out the money, I mentally give thanks to Auntie Rahim for the financial help.

Although we can hear the nightclub, feel the pulsing throb of its music through the air, we can't see it. A man with a flashlight leads us along a path marked out with white rope. Sarita glides along at my side, casting a soft red radiance on the rocks, like a luminescent creature from the deep taking its first magical steps on land.

The club materializes from the darkness, a large, faceless structure with the looming air of a warehouse. "Sequeira used to have his disco right next to the water," Zara explains. "But then Mehboob Studios down the road sold him this place. It might not look like much, but they filmed parts of *Superdevi* in it." The cavernous space inside is broken up into a series of recycled movie sets. People sip drinks in the seats of an Air India plane, they climb the sweeping staircase of a palatial mansion, lounge around the gardens of a Mughal palace. In the center, I even see what looks like the surface of the moon. "Remember the famous scene from the movie? When Baby Rinky voyages to the moon to get the magic crystal from the goddess there and attain the powers of a devi?"

The lunar surface is actually a dance floor—about two hundred people, in their twenties and thirties, gyrate to the tune of a remixed disco version of "I am Superdevi." As we watch, a woman takes off her top and dances in bra and shorts among a group of shirtless men. "It's a rebellion against the burkha," Zara says, as another woman, also down to her bra, joins in. "A few months ago, nobody would have dreamt of something like this. But now people just want to thumb their noses at the Limbus. And Bhim as well. If the younger set doesn't do it, who will?"

The Air India bar has a price list—Zara notices me wince at the thousand-rupee beers, the fifteen-hundred-rupee martinis. "Sequeira's been jacking up the tab every week. He thinks everyone our age must have made so much money in the boom years that he's doing us a favor by giving us a chance to enjoy it before it gets too late."

Just then, Sequeira himself appears in a spotlight on the balcony above the Mughal garden. He's dressed in vintage Bollywood—silver suit and top hat, white gloves and a bejeweled cane—something Amitabh Bachchan might have worn in one of his potboiler films, circa the seventies. "Welcome to the end of the world," Sequeira says, swinging and wheeling jauntily, like old people do to show they're still spry. He raises his cane to acknowledge the catcalls and cheers that rise from the dance floor. "You're the brave ones, the ones who haven't abandoned Bombay despite the rumors, despite all the efforts to tear us apart. This evening, Sequeira's is going to be your reward. Whether or not the bomb falls, the most important thing tonight, like every night this week, is to dance as if tomorrow will never dawn!"

The crowd roars, the spotlight goes off, and Sarita gets even brighter at my side as the club is plunged into darkness. A siren starts up and a rocket-shaped missile descends from the ceiling. Inscribed along the sides are the words A T O M B O M B, blinking red lights outline its tail and fins. As it touches down, the darkness erupts with blinding flashes and thunderous explosions. "Superdevi" starts up again, and a horde of onlookers swarm to the dance floor. Zara insists we accompany her. "Your duty as newlyweds. Plus you need to burn up the floor in that sexy sari!" She goes on without us only after extracting a promise that we'll join in for a future song.

The dancing makes me morose, bringing up memories of the one time I managed to drag Karun to a Gay Bombay disco. It took a good deal of further cajoling to actually lure him onto the floor, where he remained stilted and self-conscious. And yet, I found the awkward little twists I was able to coax out, the unsure waggles and bobs, completely endearing. I never did fulfill my new year's pledge that winter to teach him the moves.

Sarita seems lost in nostalgia as well—could she have had better luck? At teaching Karun something more staid, like the waltz or foxtrot? I imagine them swirling down a polished ballroom floor, smoldering in each other's arms. A burst of jealousy lances me at the thought.

She glances up at me, suddenly alert to my presence. Does she suspect something amiss, now that she's had a chance to slow down and cogitate? I brace myself for more questions about the newlywed charade I pulled on the ferry, but she's honed in on a more perilous slip. "When Rahim asked you about his uncle and auntie—I thought you mentioned your father died early?"

So she *did* catch Rahim's inconvenient little revelation back at the hotel. "You misunderstood. He was asking about my father's sister and her husband, not my parents. They're auntie and uncle to both of us—my poor cousin, stuck in that hotel, doesn't get to see them as much."

She narrows her eyes and knits her brow, but lapses into silence. Just when I think I might slide by with my response, she springs the question I've anticipated all along. "Were you and Rahim—*together?*"

Normally, the Jazter is militantly up-front in such matters, but this is hardly the shrewdest moment to promote gay visibility, to wave the rainbow flag in her face. "It happened a long time ago. Kids try out all sorts of things, you know."

I think that should do the trick, convince her to drop it, but I'm wrong. "And now? Is that what—? Has that become your—*preference?*" She has trouble enunciating the word.

"You mean men? You're asking if I sleep with men? Not that it's any of your business, but no." Twenty questions is the last game I want to play, so I vent the words with all the offended self-righteousness I can muster.

She colors immediately. "I'm sorry. It's just what Rahim was saying about a boy you followed—"

"Forget what Rahim says—he looks at everything through a lavender lens. That was just a colleague who brought me to Delhi for a job, not even a friend. The fact is, I'm not like Rahim—never have been." The Jazter deserves to rot in hell for uttering such self-denying blasphemy. All in the interest of regaining his true love, he swears silently, to Allah or Jesus or Krishna or anyone else up there listening.

We go back to gazing at the crowd, Sarita's forehead furrowed again. Perhaps I should ask her to dance—throw her off by flaunting my newly proclaimed hetero state. An ancient ABBA song comes on, the perfect opportunity, since it's a tune even she must surely be familiar with. But she interrupts me as I try to summon up the right amount of swagger to make my bid. "Delhi's such an interesting city. When did you live there?"

Her matter-of-factness makes me instantly vigilant—is she trying to figure whether Karun and I overlapped? Fortunately, Zara rescues me from having to respond, by bringing over Sequeira for an introduction. He looks even older up close than he did on the balcony, his face a palimpsest of deep-set wrinkles under powdery makeup. "My goodness," he exclaims. "When Zara said you were a glowing bride, I didn't think she meant it literally."

"I told Uncle about your elopement. He said he'd help you find your brother in the morning."

"Of course I will. But the morning's a long way away. The night, as they say, is young—we have a lot to celebrate."

The champagne a waiter brings over is nice and chilled, and most importantly, free. Though the Jazter can't help feel a twinge if this is to be his last taste, and it hails from Nasik, not Reims. Sequeira makes several expansive toasts to us, barely sipping from his glass, but generous with the refills each time I knock back mine. "See, we must have known you were coming. Not only do we have disco lights instead of candles tonight, in honor of your wedding, but—you must have felt it already—air-conditioning!"

"Blowing your entire stock of generator fuel already?" Zara laughs. "Not to mention the champagne reserves. What if they don't drop the bomb after all?"

"Actually, my dear, it's all thanks to our intrepid merchant class—the Gujus, the Banias, the Marwaris, the whole lot. They're so crazed by the idea of showing a loss in case their warehouses blow up that these last few days they've been coming door to door and practically giving away their stocks. In fact, have you looked in the cave? It's the first time in months I've had the power to hook it all up."

"Not the cave!" Zara grabs Sarita's hand in excitement. "It's amazing—you won't believe it!" She leads us all past the dance floor, through a door in the backdrop of the mansion set. We find ourselves in a large chamber whose blue walls give way to the emptiness of the warehouse above. In the center two women zap and dart and fly through the air as they engage in a laser fight.

It takes a moment to spot the machinery whirring above, the wires holding them up, the straps and harnesses and levitating foot stands. The "lasers" consist of tubes that emit a green fluorescence—showers of sparks fly each time they touch a surface.

"The fights in *Superdevi*," Sequeira says. "This is what they used. It's quite a neat mechanism, actually. There's a control lever they each have which raises and lowers them through the air, but the rest depends on how they thrust their bodies."

"But where have you hidden the other machine, the one with the flying platform?" Zara asks. "That's what I want to ride—it's my favorite."

"Ah, don't remind me. It's all too sad—I had to give it away. I'm not allowed to tell anyone what they're using it for now—let's just say it's the price one pays. Even here in Bandra, to remain open, to remain safe."

Zara tries to pry out more information about the missing machine's whereabouts, which she says gives the illusion of floating in the air without wires or harnesses, but Sequeira remains secretive. Instead, he leads us to the head of a line of people waiting to take the place of the battling devis. "You're newlyweds, so you get to jump the queue. Uncle Sequeira's wedding present: the first fight of your marriage, for good luck's sake."

The idea is so absurd that I laugh. Zara chimes in that it's a lot of fun and we have to try it, that it will look especially spectacular with Sarita already dressed in her devi sari. I am startled when Sarita nods yes. "Unless, that is, my darling husband is too scared." She looks at me defiantly and I'm forced to take up the challenge.

"For the movie, they hid the harness under Baby Rinky's clothes," Sequeira explains as he straps us in. "That's why you couldn't see it. And the foot pedestals, being blue like the background screens, are invisible." He shows us how to operate the motion lever and puts a laser in each of our hands. "May the best superhero win."

It takes a while to get the hang of the contraption—for the first few minutes, we just dangle around, with little control. Then Sarita zaps me with her laser, and although it doesn't hurt, the buzz and sparks make for a startling effect. I swing away, then turn around to attack, but she has compensated, and hovers out of reach. A determination, a fierceness, burns in her eyes, as if she's assumed not only the luminous uniform but also the fiery mantle of the avenging, all-knowing Super-devi. It's impossible, I think, my mind racing through our entire inter-action to see if she could have perchance figured out I'm her rival from clues she's received. She lunges again, her laser aiming for my throat like a sword, and it's all I can do to twist away my body. Could some intuition, some sixth sense, have shown her the picture, like one of those game show contestants guessing an entire word correctly based on just a single letter?

Sarita lands another score, zapping me on the cheek. This time I strike back, and she yelps in surprise as a shower of sparks cascades down her body. She recovers quickly, and flies back at me, the end of her sari coming loose and swirling behind her like an incandescent cape. I dive towards her as well, swinging myself just out of the way in the last instant before we collide. Our lasers connect, creating a tre-mendous outburst of light and energy—the effect is dazzling, even if our choreography falls short of the finesse in swashbuckler movie swordfights. A crowd of onlookers below eggs us on, hoots and hol-lers, begins to take sides. Immersed as we are in our aerial duel over the one we both seek, Sarita and I barely notice their cries.

I HAD EXPECTED our goodbye meeting to resemble one of those sad old Hollywood romance endings—music swelling in the background, sepia cinematography, a wistful sense of drama. But seeing Karun ignited me—I felt five and a half years of buried emotion, of stifled pas-sion, burst forth from deep within. "Karun," I said, wanting to kiss and crush and engulf him with my body. Only my guilt restrained me.

He stood at the door and gaped. I noticed, through my euphoria, that he looked different—not exactly older, but more cognizant, as if he'd experienced more of the world. The weight he'd put on had helped fill out some of his most conspicuously skinny parts. Even his ears no longer stuck out as flagrantly. "I thought you were in Hyderabad," he responded finally.

So he'd received my letters to Karnal. But not written back. "I returned to Bombay just a little while ago. Perhaps we were meant to meet again—our destiny."

My comment flustered him. "How did you find me?"

"From your university. Can I come in?" He didn't move, so I asked again. Still he didn't respond, remaining there silently. "Karun?"

"Things have changed." He looked down at the floor, then back up at me. "I'm married now."

To my credit, I didn't do anything outrageous. I didn't call him a fool and storm away, or remind him of his predilections and guffaw in his face. In fact, I may have even congratulated him. "Are you going to call her out and introduce us, or do you keep her hidden behind a veil?"

Karun shifted uncomfortably, and I realized he hadn't told his wife anything about us. "She's visiting her mother until late this evening."

I decided I'd set his mind at ease. "You don't have to worry—I just came by to say goodbye. I'm moving with my parents to Switzerland in a bit."

All through the elevator ride down, I kept playing the scene through my mind. The pat on his shoulder I'd contented myself with, the awkward way he had reciprocated. The disingenuous promise he'd made to keep in touch by email. I felt a sense of *déjà vu* as behind the door swinging shut, I saw him wave goodbye. Hadn't he tried to pull the same escape at his hostel room the day after we'd met? I'd hammered at his door and spoken loud enough to force him to accompany me downstairs.

So I pressed the seventh-floor button again. I banged on Karun's door, and when he opened it, pushed him aside and strode right in. He came running up behind me and I turned around and grabbed his shoulders. Summoning up Cary Grant and Clark Gable, I pulled him to me and kissed him.

Perhaps he hadn't seen those black-and-white classics, because instead of melting, he broke free and staggered away. I caught up and kissed him again. This time when he struggled, I pulled him down to the floor and pinned him under my body. "What do you think you're doing? Are you crazy?" He turned his mouth away.

I wanted to rip his clothes off and take him despite his protests. Perhaps a part of him wanted the same. But I could see the determination in his mouth, the stiff set of his neck. He got up as soon as I rolled off.

We sat across from each other, the dining table between us presumably buffering him against further attacks. He waited for me to exhaust my apologies, then told me he'd already seen them all before in my letters. "I don't think you ever understood, Jaz. All through my mother's illness—whether I was mopping up her vomit or her blood or her feces, I'd take my mind off her misery and my own by thinking of you back in Delhi, waiting for me."

He talked about how he lit his mother's pyre and sorted through the ashes afterwards for intact bone shards. "I remember thinking that the flames had not only consumed her body but the very link that connected me to the world. I felt as if I'd just been released into a vacuum to spend the rest of my life in solitude. Except I wasn't alone, I had you to moor me. All through the journey back, I contemplated our future together—not the easiest choice, but one I was ready to commit to. Imagine my shock when—"

He'd thought about writing back to me a few times, but one simple fact stopped him. "If you'd sunk so low as to do it with Harjeet, it stood to reason that you'd done it with others as well. Who knew what a future with you would hold? The only remedy was to look for someone else."

I began to apologize again, but he held up his hand. "An even more chilling thought struck me—how could I ensure this 'someone else' wouldn't be just as unreliable? For all I knew, this might be business as usual for you and your friends. That's when everything my mother had been pushing for over the past months began to make sense. She knew, of course—she could see right through me. She recognized the risk, which is why she wanted me to try the other sex."

The Jazter listened to it all in stoic silence—how Karun met his wife three years after we broke up, how they dated and fell in love. Cruel and unusual punishment—being subjected to a list of the ten million angelic qualities this Sarita had. "I see now the gift my mother bequeathed me—a chance at fulfillment, at tranquillity. The opportunity to be a father, to give someone the childhood I never had. I've discovered myself, Jaz; I've discovered who I'm meant to be. More than that, I've found the one person who's perfect for me. I can only wish you get as lucky, Jaz—that you find someone as right for you in Switzerland." Not quite satisfied with his speech, Karun thrust a wedding album into my hands.

Let's just settle the most burning question right away—in the looks department, the Other Woman simply did not make it to the Jazter's league. (And we won't even mention fashion sense—whom did she take along to help select that wedding sari, her cleaning lady?) Perhaps I'm being too prejudiced, perhaps she had some plain and mousy kind of appeal—hadn't Karun mentioned, after all, that she was an analyst or librarian or something? Snarkiness aside, I noticed something quite intriguing—Karun's strained expression in several of the photographs. I knew him well enough to recognize the forced cheer, the eyes that didn't smile—in a flash, everything he claimed about his discovered utopia seemed suspect.

But how to confront him? I could probe into his sex life, but that would be too intrusive. Asking point-blank if he'd mentioned me to his wife might simply make him hunker down in defense. Threatening to tell her if he didn't comply with my wishes would be blackmail. And then a perfectly devious strategy struck me. "Let's have a final dinner together. That way I can meet Sarita before I leave."

He hemmed and hawed about schedules and availability, but I suggested we call Sarita right away to see when she was free. We agreed tentatively to meet at my flat in a week—with Pakistan recently joining the war, not to mention the continuing terrorist attacks, a restaurant seemed unnecessarily risky. The fact that my parents would be there reassured him. We exchanged phone numbers—as expected, he gave me his personal cell number, not the one for his home landline.

THE RE-SEDUCTION OF Karun Anand commenced at seven p.m., when he arrived alone at our flat (Sarita had to go again to her mother's, he lamely explained). His nervousness pleased me—hadn't Casanova himself attested to the ease of conquest once the fear of being seduced is already present? "How many years has it been, my physicist friend?" my father boomed as if on cue, dissipating some of Karun's skittishness. My parents left soon after on their goodbye rounds, leaving us alone in the flat.

At first, we simply talked about how China had been forced to withdraw four days ago to avoid a massive embargo. "Did you hear them rage against the UN? The Youth League must be gnashing its teeth—I'm sure the entire invasion was at its behest." The Pakistani communiqué threatening nuclear attack had surfaced within hours, but we both thought the war would end well before their announced D-day. I nodded when Karun wondered if my parents would be safe going around in the blackout. "They know how to take care of themselves."

One should never really risk Phase Two in the bedroom, but that's where I led Karun. His apprehensions all melted (as per plan) upon seeing the train set assembled on the floor. "Do you still have the boxcars with the candles?"

"Of course. I packed every piece myself in Delhi when I moved."

We sat amidst the tracks and set up our first collision in years. Not only did the candles ignite the paper we crumpled under the bridge, they also launched the wave of nostalgia I'd counted on (Phase Three). Once I figured he'd been sufficiently softened, I pulled him in a friendly hug to myself.

"No," he said, stiffening and moving away.

"Don't worry. I'll be gone soon. I'm not after anything, so just relax."

Except I *was* after him, which meant it was time to move to Phase Three Alternative (nostalgia aborted, try alcohol instead). I took him into the kitchen. "I bought us some samosas—there's a shop down the street which still manages to find all the ingredients. Plus my parents have been getting rid of all their wine before the move to Switzerland, so we can help ourselves."

He sipped warily from his glass as we sat on the couch. "This one's a Merlot. I'll open a Cabernet so you can compare the two." Later, I had him try a Pinot as well, wondering just how amused my father would be to see all the half-drunk bottles from his collection. "Which one do you like best?"

My man preferred the Cabernet, the most conducive choice (alcohol percentage 14.3 as opposed to the Pinot's paltry 11.4), so that's what I refilled his glass with. He rebuffed neither the arm that presently snaked around his shoulder nor the hand that casually patted his thigh. I tried again to kiss him, and this time he didn't resist. The feel of his mouth transported me—through beaches and balconies, bedrooms and barsatis, all the spots I'd ever been with him. In an instant, this was no longer a farewell romp I was trying to engineer, but a replay of our entire relationship. A Broadway tribute, a Bollywood spectacular—the nights we'd spent, the years we'd shared. Karun's face glittered from a giant screen which rose and stretched in all directions—I wanted to unhook it from its moorings and wrap it around myself.

The Fourth and Final Phase called. "Let's go back into my bed-room," I whispered, taking his arm to lead him from the sofa. He freed himself from my grasp, and remained seated. I tried again, saying we'd be more comfortable, it would be cozier, but to no avail. "I can tell you want to, Karun. Besides, I'll be out of your life for good soon."

For a while, he just sat there, breathing hard. Then he spoke in a quiet voice. "I shouldn't have come. Even this, even what we've been doing—I feel so ashamed, every minute I stay."

"So I see you haven't forgiven me yet. Do you want me to apologize again?"

He gave a short, humorless laugh. "That part I actually get, Jaz. You are who you are—there's little more to say. I can't claim any sur-prise coming here today, only a little disappointment that after all this time you still can't think beyond sex."

The words stung, they felt uninformed, unfair. How to get across the years of yearning I'd endured, not to mention the flood of emotion unleashed today just by kissing him? The sense of incompleteness that had dogged me, the day-to-day contentment I'd failed to regain? "So all the letters I wrote, all the efforts I made don't count? You think they were just to get you back in bed?"

"Isn't that where you were just trying to lead me?"

"Perhaps I only wanted to hold you. To remind myself of how your body felt. Anything further would still have been an expression of my love—it's what completes the two of us. You have to forgive me, Karun, for missing you so much. For thinking ahead to Switzerland or wherever I end up. Perhaps you could give me something to cling on. If we're never going to see each other again perhaps it wouldn't be so hard."

He hesitated, but not enough to give me hope. "I'm sorry, Jaz. I can't do it. Not to Sarita, I can't. Thanks to you, I know exactly how it feels to be in her place."

"But why would she ever know?"

"No, Jaz, that's the way *you* think, not I."

"Really? And I suppose you've been completely honest with her, have you? Told her everything about us?"

"That whole part of my life is done for—I left it behind when I met her. Marriage is about the future, not the past—I didn't ask her about herself either."

"How perfectly convenient. I didn't know it worked that way. You complain I'm still the same, but in my eyes, you've grown immeasurably, Karun—as a hypocrite. My great shining example. At least back then you only lied to yourself, instead of trying to delude your wife as well. Is that why you came here without her today—to work on your marriage?"

"You're right. It was a mistake." He shot up from the couch and headed to the door. This time, I'd left the key in the lock, and he was able to open it.

"Be sure to give Sarita my best," I yelled, as he slammed the door behind himself.

THE ZURICH DIRTY BOMB attacks occurred on September 11, four days before my family's departure to Switzerland. Explosions along the Bahnhofstrasse and at the university hospital left large swathes of the city uninhabitable. Similar strikes followed later that day in New York, London, Rome, Toronto, and Frankfurt. As if the choice of date weren't incriminating enough, jihadi literature turned up near two of the bomb sites, and a video claiming responsibility, by a new Al Qaeda-like group, appeared on the internet.

Those anticipating the next big terrorist incident for the past several years may have sighed with relief that it had finally occurred. They might have pointed out that despite widespread panic and disruption, the damage didn't approach that caused by a single thermonuclear explosion. But the real destruction in this case, illustrating just how much this September 11 heir had evolved over its parent, came with the ensuing cyber attacks. The dirty bombs were merely the gunshot starting the race, signaling hackers with fingers poised over keyboards to launch their malware.

Five weeks later, the Jazter still marvels at how quick and easy it was to unravel the order of the entire world. First came the news hoaxes, saturating the internet, whipping up the panic already frothing in place. A fake suicide truck attack on the hastily called NATO summit in Brussels was so convincingly reported that even CNN listed the names of heads of state supposedly felled. Warnings of an imminent electromagnetic pulse over the U.S. touched off hysterical runs on banks all the way down to Mexico and Belize. Meanwhile, the armies of cyber bugs on the loose found crevices to crawl through even the most impregnable firewalls. They invaded enough strategic nodes and sources to wrest control of the entire global news network.

Perhaps this was the greatest genius of the cyber jihadis: the monopoly they clinched on information. They realized how helplessly addicted the population had become to *knowing* in this information age. So what if news was tainted or unreliable?—people needed their daily fix. They would gladly swallow the most improbable rumors, the most outlandish fabrications, to quell the ravenousness within. Even the Jazter, always a voracious consumer of news, succumbed to this junk food urge.

Not that some of these inconceivable scenarios didn't turn out to be true. The viruses had gained cunning by now, learned to down bigger game. They sabotaged power stations and exploded gas lines, bewitched airliners over the Atlantic into executing suicide dives. People could no longer separate reality from fabrication, trust the ground they walked on, the world they lived in. Did Morocco actually invade Spain? Did a string of reactors really blow up in France? The actual answers mattered less and less, as panic (and despondency) increased.

But harking back to the early days right after September 11, the one irrefutable fact was that Switzerland immediately rescinded my family's visas. Their government pushed through an emergency law overnight, banning all Muslim visitors. My father scrambled to find another country that would accept us, but similar bills popped all over, effectively shuttering the West. The only options that remained were Islamic states, particularly those in the Gulf.

My parents already had tourist visas for Dubai, so that seemed the most promising choice. Unfortunately, well-heeled Muslims trying to escape India mobbed every consulate in Bombay (even the one for Pakistan, essentially manned only by the watchman ever since the ambassador fled). My father pulled every string he could to get my passport stamped, but the Dubai embassy informed him there would be a six-month wait.

With time of the essence, and Dubai only a temporary destination, we realized the only practical solution was for my parents to go ahead without me. From there, they could more effectively lobby other Arab states for a permanent haven, and get me a visa directly to that country. The UAE itself seemed promising, since my parents had lectured in several of the emirates after the democracy rumblings generated by the Tunisian revolution. The Saudis might also be interested, having recently offered them both university positions. (Akbar's underlying tenet of a divine right to power had appeared particularly attractive ever since the Arab Spring.)

All of this looked quite bleak for the Jazter. Beggars can't be choosers, but surely some alternative to the rampant repression against his ilk practiced in these places had to exist? Even if shikar was popular among Arabs as reports claimed, Riyadh or Sharjah weren't exactly high on my list. I tried to find consolation in the reports that, compared to Iran, the Saudis had probably beheaded fewer gays.

Since I would be staying behind, I needed a safer place. Fortunately, we managed to exchange apartments just two days before my parents left. The new residence was located in the Muslim quarter behind Crawford Market—a shabby flat, old and crumbling, with a shared pair of toilets at the end of the outside corridor. But the place was secure—or at least relatively so, compared to our previous address.

The day before I accompanied them to Ballard Pier to catch their ship, I found my father sitting on the floor of one of the musty rooms, his books and prayer scroll collection spread out around him. I recognized the well-worn Koran by Nafi that he still pored over for hours. "See this?" he asked, holding up a copy of *An Emperor's Bequest to Islam.* "It's from the first edition—they only published five hundred of them—that's all they expected to sell. Your mother and I worked on it for eight years—this is the original copy the publisher sent us in the mail from New York." He opened it to the dedication page, to the inscription I'd read many times before—"May the light always shine on our son, Ijaz." "The only thing more thrilling to hold in my hands for the first time was your tiny body, just after you were born."

He closed the book and laid it down on the floor. "We always hoped you'd accept our gift to you, Ijaz. When you spurned it, when you showed such disdain for religion, we understood, of course. What child hasn't experienced the need to rebel? But we felt so sad. Not because we'd lost a follower, but because you'd never see the beauty we had. All the wisdom contained in these texts, the answers to so many problems ripping us apart now." He caressed the cover of an old text-book on comparative religions, then ran his fingers over the ornate Urdu letters on one of the scrolls. The dusty light shone around his head like rays from God.

When he looked up, though, his face was haggard. "They've won, Ijaz. I don't know what we'll do. They've finally taken over Islam—hijacked it completely with their threats and bombs. All our work, all our effort, all our credibility—all lost. We have to go on trying, of course, but with everything that's happened, who'll believe us now?" I shifted uncomfortably, unable to think of words of comfort.

"You know what makes me the most ashamed? Having to leave you in this state. Not knowing if we'll ever see you again. I never thought I'd be the type to abandon my own son."

"I'll be fine. No need to worry, it's probably only a matter of a month."

He shook his head. "That's been the problem, all along. We've never worried about you enough. Right from Switzerland, we've always left you to find your own path. You might have thought us disinterested, but our fault has been to trust you too much. Not interfering in your life, not asking what you liked, what you loved—we simply took it too far." He held out his hand, and I put my palm in his. Had we enjoyed a different relationship, we might have hugged.

"Take the physicist, for instance. We could have done so much more to encourage you on. Such a sincere boy, so smart, such a relief to see you bring him home again after all these years. I told your mother we had to give you your privacy. We thought we'd stroll around while the two of you were in the apartment, but the blackout made it impossible. We ended up drinking six cups of tea at that tiny café near Lotus."

"I had no idea—"

"I hope you'll see more of him once we leave. Tell the neighbors he's your cousin—it'll be much safer with two people living here rather than just one. Plus, your mother and I will feel much better knowing you're with someone so close."

"But how did you know?"

My father seemed genuinely confused. "How did I know what?"

CHAOS REIGNED at the docks, the multitudes clamoring to get on the old freighter of such biblical proportions that they might have just learnt of the Great Flood. My father's contacts had managed to procure two of the last tickets out for him, and moreover, avoid the trap of air travel which had essentially ground to a halt. Right up to the moment my parents entered the processing booth, people were offering them lakhs of rupees to buy their slots. I waited around afterwards, but couldn't spot them in the crowd surging up the gangplank.

Watching the ship launch into the churning grey sea, I realized my odds of ever seeing my parents again were small. The Jazter would probably never succeed in migrating, never have to test Arabia's tolerance for shikar. Back at the apartment, I could still hear my father's words ring in my ears—get Karun to move in, live with someone I loved (I'd decided that's what he meant after all). We could always find somewhere in the countryside to take cover, should the city situation deteriorate too much.

I called Karun—the first time since he'd left the flat in a huff eleven days ago. My news, that I would be staying behind longer in Bombay, dismayed him. "Why should you be so upset when you don't care?" I asked, and he hung up. After that, he clicked off on all my calls.

So I decided to confront him at his institute. Nobody challenged me at the entrance—in fact, the watchman pointed the way to the correct office when I said I had an appointment. Karun stared in disbelief as I shut the door behind me. "How dare you come here?"

"I want you back, Karun. I want us to give it another shot. My parents have left for good, so we'd have the place to ourselves."

"Are you crazy?"

"I'm not saying to move in right away. Just spend the night with me. In the morning, you can decide what you want."

"You *are* mad."

"Could you just listen? I saw it in your eyes the last time, Karun, and I can see it again standing here right now, so it would be nice if you dropped the pretense."

I tried to kiss him, but he ran behind his desk and picked up the phone—either to call for help, or to use as a club in fending me off. "Get out of here at once."

I began following him, both on his way to work and back. Usually, I stood at the bus stop facing his building or the phone stall right opposite the institute, but sometimes I had to conceal myself before he ventured out. A few times I accosted him along the way—springing out of the abandoned police kiosk near the church, or the ruins of the bombed-out McDonald's, to remind him of my proposed one-night experiment. He neither slowed nor spoke, and I resisted the urge to physically restrain him. Twice, I tailed him when he emerged from the building with Sarita, but at a more measured distance. (The Jazter had to grudgingly admit she carried herself presentably enough in person. At least for a librarian.)

I ratcheted up the pressure by telephoning her at home later that week, and leaving a message for Karun to contact "Mr. Masood." (After racking my brains on how to unearth Karun's residential number, I had finally found it listed in the phonebook!) He called back that very evening. "Don't you dare do that again," he shouted, then began pleading for me to leave him alone.

"You know what I want, Karun."

"I just can't," he said, and I could tell he was crying. "It's not fair. I've worked so hard."

"A single night, that's all I'm asking."

"Just let me go. You're pushing me too far. You've had your chance."

Although I felt Karun's anguish, and found it more than a little loathsome playing the stalker, I knew I couldn't ease up. I left more messages with Sarita, and surprised Karun again at his institute. One evening, I walked right up as he waited to cross Wodehouse Road, and put an arm around his shoulder. Another time, I followed him into his building elevator, and forced my lips onto his after the other passengers got off at a lower floor. I even tried his doorbell while Sarita was away, but he refused to respond.

And then, one morning, Karun didn't emerge from his building. I thought he may have slipped by earlier than usual, but he didn't show up at the institute gate that evening, either. Two days later, I glimpsed Sarita making a brief foray to the corner grocer and heaved a sigh of relief—they hadn't packed up and left. She seemed distraught when I called later with my usual "Mr. Masood" alias. "He's not here. I'll let him know when he returns."

That night, a series of explosions awoke me at about one. The walls in my bedroom radiated orange, and I jumped out of bed, thinking the building was on fire. But the conflagration, I saw from my window, raged further down the road, in the direction of Metro cinema. For hours, the sky flashed and popped with bursts of anti-aircraft fire.

The next morning, the air itself seemed different, as if a new and insalubrious season had swept in overnight to lay siege on the city. As I walked the deserted route towards Karun's place, my instincts screamed for me to return to the safety of the flat with every step. Swathes of charred cotton and linen hung from the trees outside St. Xavier's School—an explosion at the cloth merchant premises opposite had sent bolts flying everywhere. A band of people milled around the still-smoking ruins of Metro cinema. "Don't go any further," they warned. "The roads to the south are crawling with HRM snipers." Trains had also stopped running, they informed me, making it impossible to detour around.

More bombing raids followed, severely curtailing my surveillance trips to Colaba. By now, the threats of nuclear annihilation had emptied the city. The fact that I never actually *saw* the exodus puzzled me—when had everyone slinked off? My neighborhood remained desolate, its streets free of departing hordes each time I ventured out.

There seemed little choice but to leave myself. The HRM had become increasingly brazen in their attempts to take over the area, and my store of rice had almost run out. The few times I'd managed to reach Colaba, I had seen no sign of Sarita, cutting off my last link to Karun. I'd gambled by staying and lost—pushed too hard and scared Karun off. It was time to give in to my self-preservation instincts and head to safety.

But as I left the flat this morning, an overwhelming wave of nostalgia carried me south. I felt I had to make one final sentimental pilgrimage to Karun's building, an homage of sorts. I stood there for an hour, looking up at his floor, trying to imagine the two of us ensconced safely behind the empty windows. How would our life have played out? What unreachable part of myself had I lost when I lost him? Just as I bid my last maudlin farewell, Sarita emerged.

———

WE RECLINE SIDE by side in our bridal suite. Despite my vigorous protests that Sarita and I would be fine camping out on the dance floor with the other stragglers (the ones who didn't leave on the ferry back to Mahim, like Zara), Sequeira has insisted we spend a few hours alone in this room. "It's your wedding night, your suhaag raat. You're going to need every bit of privacy we can muster. Not the best setup for what you'll be up to, but I'm sure you'll find a way." I can still feel Sarita glare a hole through me as he laughs. "Sleep well. Though I suppose that's hardly the point, is it?"

The "suite" is little more than a storeroom behind the Air India set. Our bridal bed consists of two surplus airplane seats that Sequeira informed us didn't quite fit in with the rest. "They're first-class, so I couldn't use them—too much of a recline." He's right—I've never been so comfortable in any plane flown in my life. Sarita seems equally at ease—fluorescing serenely, snoring softly.

As I marvel at the absurdity of the situation (the Jazter and his slumbering *liebling*, on the night of their eternal union), a sudden thought sobers me. Unlike me, Sarita *has* been through a suhaag raat before. With Karun. Who must have lain by her side and gazed at her face with the same proximity as I do now. And then? They had kissed and caressed, most certainly. What had her lips felt like? Had he been aroused by the fragrance of her body?

I lean forward to take a good sniff, but don't smell anything. Try as I might, I cannot see Sarita through Karun's eyes. I cannot picture him consummating their wedding night. Perhaps it's my personal prejudices, the innate Jazter skepticism for Kinsey one through five. What if Karun's the fabled perfect three? If through all our years together, he's harbored a closeted ambidexterity?

Except that wouldn't explain his agitation at my reappearance, his attempt to flee from me. Or rather from his own cravings. The Jazter remains confident he could beat Sarita any day in desirability. Sadly, though, for the Karuns of the world, sex isn't everything. What if he's developed feelings for this glow-in-the-dark woman next to me? In addition to her wifely loyalty, chances are she has a pleasing personality. And then there's the whole unfair issue of reproductive capability. Can the Jazter really be so cocksure of victory?

It occurs to me that I have no strategy for tomorrow. What will I say to conquer Karun when we confront him side by side? How will I explain away all my lies to Sarita? What if Karun pretends not to know me?—will I unmask him in front of his wife? Not that she's necessarily so unsuspecting. After our little laser joust, I have no idea how much she knows, what she herself might be plotting. I drift off to sleep watching her luminous breasts fall and rise.

Sequeira wakes us at noon with a breakfast tray laden with eggs and tea, toast and biscuits. "For the newlyweds, the special Sequeira breakfast—believe it or not, fresh eggs from real hens." He beams happily when I say protein is exactly what the missus and I need to replenish what we expended overnight. *Frau* Hassan scowls again—chalk one up for the Jazter, who at least has a sense of humor (though perhaps Karun isn't the best one to appreciate it, given his own deficiency in that department). We fill up on the food, and pack away as many biscuit rolls as we can carry, since we don't know when we'll eat next. Sarita gives me the jar of Marmite for safekeeping, so that she doesn't finish it all at once.

Sequeira has a house at the northern edge of Bandra, and offers to drop us off in his car at Sarita's "brother's" place. I can see her itching to get away from me and go her own way, but of course she can hardly desert her new husband so brazenly. "He lives on Carter Road, near Otters Club," she reveals reluctantly.

The day has a whitewashed, almost Mediterranean look to it. Waves lap at the rocks shoring up the wall next to the road; the sea is refreshed, rejuvenated, since last evening's low tide. "You really should settle down here if we ever get past the nineteenth," Sequeira says. "A mixed couple like you won't find any other place so welcoming." He gives us a short history of Bandra (*Bandora*, as he says the island was called) from the time the Portuguese first built their church of Santa Ana. "With all the Christians we have, nobody cares if you're Hindu or Muslim. It's truly the queen of suburbs, the only one with such a cosmopolitan feel."

"But aren't you afraid the Limbus will take over? Or, more probably, Bhim?"

"They haven't, so far. I have a hunch they might actually like us as a buffer in between. Not that we take any chances. War or no war, this is Bombay—money still rules everything. We pay them off—their men make the rounds of all the businesses every week."

We sit squeezed together in an implausibly tiny Nano, which Sequeira deftly maneuvers around abandoned cars and large chunks of debris on the road. An impassable pile of rubble from a bombing raid forces him to detour east. He points to a tall building on a corner, with sleek elliptical balconies that seem to float in the air, like a real estate agent might. "Nobody lives there, can you believe it?—all the people who've fled the city. You could walk right in and have your pick of empty flats for free. Think of when the war is over—these places worth millions of rupees."

"*If* they're still standing. There's a reason they're so empty."

Sequeira nods. "True. The bomb. But nothing's happened yet, and chances are nothing will on the nineteenth. That's what I tell myself, in any case—that neither side will be so foolhardy. Just three more days of uncertainty.

"Afsan, the ferry captain, thinks I'm crazy. He's quitting on the eighteenth—making one final trip to Madh Island, then continuing on to some faraway place for safety. He keeps asking me to join him—he's even offered to make Diu his destination. That's where the Sequeiras are from, where my brothers and sister live. I might take him up on his offer—he certainly knows how to tempt me. Except my children here would be so dismayed, the ones at the club who've come to depend on me. I have this superstition that I can keep them safe as long as I keep the party going every night." He kisses a small locket around his neck, then touches it to his heart.

The lanes leading down to Carter Road all seem blocked—one by a fallen building, another by an overturned truck. Sequeira stops the Nano a few blocks away to let us out. "Who knows what's the best course of action—to stay or to flee? You're a very inspiring couple. God be with you, whatever you decide."

Sarita turns to me the minute Sequeira has driven off. "I have no idea how to thank you for all your help. But now that it's safe, I can really make it from here by myself."

"Nonsense. It'll only take a minute. After all this time, I'd at least like to say hello to your husband."

After a few more attempts to shake me off, she reluctantly lets me follow her down the lane. We squeeze by the truck, which lies on its back with its wheels in the air, and find a flight of steps to clamber down towards the sea. I'm thinking some more of how Karun will react upon seeing the two of us when Sarita gives a cry and starts running. For an instant, I stand there dumfounded—does she really believe she can give me the slip this late in the game? Then I see the shambles of the waterfront—the twisted benches and utility poles, the charred, frondless palm trunks that line the yawning bomb craters. Otters Club seems to have vaporized; all that remains are a pair of tall metal gates secured with a profusion of chains and locks—a final attempt, perhaps, to keep the unwashed hordes out.

We run past the ruins of a park whose jogging track, still marked into neat lanes with white paint, cants into the water like the deck of a sinking ocean liner. Sarita veers into the road, then comes to a stop beside a space-pod balcony that seems to have alighted fully intact from the jumble of ravaged buildings around. "Karun," she shouts, pausing after each call to see if he will emerge waving at her from one of the listing windows or doors.

But the wreckage remains silent. A wave crashes behind us, the water churning up a furrow in the land almost to the point where we stand. "It's gone. It should have been right around here," Sarita says, and in an instant, I feel harrowingly close to her, or at least to the panic rising in her face. She wanders down the road, still calling, and I follow.

Her memory turns out to be off by a block. "I've only come here once before—Karun says they use it mainly for conferences." The two-story structure sits squatly next to the bombed remains of a formerly elegant apartment house. Perhaps the guesthouse's government-bureau ugliness (complete with dingy, pigeon-splattered "Indian Institute for Nuclear Physics" sign) has spared it the fate of its neighbor. A folding metal grate, the type found on old-style elevators, is drawn across the entrance. The locking mechanism looks punctured, as if by a gunshot—a length of stiff wire, twisted tightly into a loop, serves as the jerry-rigged replacement.

Sarita rattles at the bars, then undoes the wire, and slides the grate open. We ease past the splintered remains of the front door, still hanging on by a single hinge. The lobby is dark and gloomy. An ancient framed poster that shows a welter of electrons swarming around a hive-like nucleus announces a particle physics congress held in April 1999. A sofa and two folding chairs sit next to an unmanned desk, but otherwise, the room is empty.

"Hello," Sarita calls out, but nobody answers. "I wonder if they have a ledger." I try not to look too interested as she rummages around in the drawers of the desk, even though I have a sudden, desperate desire to find Karun's signature before she can. But the search doesn't turn up anything. "All the guestrooms are upstairs, if I remember."

Halfway up the steps, I start feeling very anxious. I'm totally unprepared for the coming confrontation, I need more time. If I could only steal a few minutes alone with Karun, perhaps things might work out fine. Sarita knocks on the first door, then turns the knob. What if Karun awaits inside?

But the room doesn't seem to have been occupied for a while. The next two rooms look the same—curtains drawn, a thin towel folded tidily at the base of each bed. The fourth, though, has books and socks strewn around—the cupboard door hangs open, and a half-filled suitcase rests by it on the floor. "It's not his," Sarita declares, without stepping in for a closer examination.

About to follow her deeper down the corridor, I stop. It can't be, I think, as faint notes of the raga waft in from somewhere. Karun would play this very same composition over and over again while we lived in Delhi—a few times, I actually had to request he turn it off. Sarita recognizes it too, because she spins around. "Do you hear that? It's the *Chandranandan*. It seems to be coming from the other side."

She dashes back towards the stairwell, continuing through the hall to the far rooms. She puts her ear against one of the doors, then another, stopping in front of the third. I come up as she runs a hand over her hair and arranges the edge of the sari over it. She takes a deep breath, then knocks. "Karun?" she says, as I try to position myself in the most visible spot behind her. Nobody answers, so she repeats her knocking more forcefully.

This time, the music cuts off. Metal scrapes against concrete as if someone's risen from a bed. I hear a rustling, like that of curtains being drawn, followed by the sound of nearing footsteps. Panic seizes me—I don't know how I look, I haven't even shaved, while before me, Sarita is blossoming with an incipient glow again. I try to put on a confident face, try to conjure up the magic words that will make Karun mine. But it's too late. The latch turns, the door begins its inward swing, and it's showtime.

SARITA

11

GAURAV. IJAZ. JAZ. JAZMINE. WITHOUT HIM, I CERTAINLY WOULDN'T have made it this far. And yet, how to trust someone when even his name is so hard to pin down?

I know he's hiding something, but what? This much I've decided, he's not on his way to Jogeshwari to see his mother. Even before the suspicious "uncle and auntie" bit, I found it difficult to swallow all the misfortunes he wove around her. And whatever went on between him and Rahim—when I asked him his preference, why didn't he come clean? Did he need to deny his Delhi love interest so vehemently?

Most revealing of all were his fabrications on the ferry. His declaration that we'd just wed, his stories of our romantic travails. Why spin such reckless tales, what did he hope to gain? Perhaps it just comes to him naturally—the shifty wavelengths at which he operates.

Could he be a terrorist? Does that explain his slippery identity, the weapon he carries? Now that we've left the Muslim area, does he plan to infiltrate the Hindus by forcing Karun and me along as cover? Except I've seen his inexperience, his visible discomfort at even holding a gun. Surely the Pakistanis must train their agents better, select jihadis made of sterner stuff.

Since the ferry, I've wondered if he might harbor a more personal motive. Could our paths have crossed in the past, could something unbeknownst to me link us? The possibility sets my mind abuzz, but never for long. The random nature of our hospital encounter always brings my calculations to a halt.

Swooping through the air at Sequeira's, I almost saw the pieces coalesce. The way we met, the reason he followed me, what he wanted, who he was. A flash of awareness so quick, so elusive, it vanished before I could hold on. All that remained was the realization I had trusted him too much. That his protectiveness didn't flow from the pure goodness of his heart. I should have concealed this new insight, not succumbed to the angry laser thrusts that might have tipped him off.

Lying by his side in the Air India seats afterwards, I closed my eyes to shut out his presence. But I kept sensing a seeping curiosity on his part. Not amorous as I may have once feared, but still eerily physical. As if he was appraising me, gauging me, like an outfit hanging on a rack, before trying it on. Or perhaps, given Rahim's revelation, an outfit meant for someone else. At one point, I could have sworn he leaned over to take a deep breath from my neck.

I squeezed together my eyelids even tighter to think of Karun instead. To imagine the two of us flying in our first-class seats to some exotic island in a faraway corner of the world. Except when I awoke, I knew I had dreamt about Jaz. That the plane had launched us on a journey together into a long and complicated future.

Standing in the hotel corridor now, I feel a sense of unease. What inauspicious presence have I brought to Karun's door? Why didn't I try harder this morning to shake Jaz off? I suppose the excitement of nearing the end of my search made me less cautious. The thought that I would soon see Karun, that after we reunited, none of this would matter.

A wave of this same anticipation rises within me as I stand in the dark. "Karun?" I say, and knock harder this time. I hear the stirring inside almost at once. My excitement mixes with nervousness—I still don't know why Karun left, why he didn't return, what could be going on between us. The door will open in an instant. Which of my hundred questions will I ask first?

———

THE MAN PEEPING OUT looks nothing like Karun. His skin is blotchy, his hair graying, and the cloth looping under his chin and around his face is knotted at the top like a cartoon character suffering from a toothache. "What do you want?" he asks.

"I'm sorry. I thought this is where . . . I'm looking for Karun. Karun Anand."

"Who?" he says, even though a startled look comes to his eyes. "There's nobody here."

He begins to shut the door, but I thrust myself forward to block him. "The music you were just playing. Where did you get it?"

"What music? I didn't hear anything."

"And that shirt you're wearing—it's not yours." I push into the room. "That CD player, there—I recognize it. This is his room, isn't it? I'm his wife."

The man's sullenness clears. He hastens to explain he's the manager, alone at the hotel, in Karun's room merely to check up on things. "I thought I'd try out the shirt for fun. Just to compare the size. And the CDs—have to make sure the batteries don't get spoiled in this humidity. All your husband seems to have is ragas. I put one on, even though I don't really like classical music." He looks down guiltily at his shoes. Then realizing they also belong to Karun, he scrambles to take them off.

"Where's my husband?"

"Oh, Dr. Anand? Begging your pardon, but he's gone. He left, along with our other three guests. It's been a week at least, perhaps more. I haven't been too well, so it's hard to keep track." He coughs noisily, then makes slurping noises in his mouth, as if conserving any phlegm he might have hawked up. "Would you happen to have a toffee or something? I'm very hungry."

"He's been gone for a week?"

"He'd have left even earlier if he could. All of them would have. They tried to get to Colaba but the trains stopped running. Once they footed it to the bridge at Mahim, but the Muslims sent them packing. This time, though, they weren't trying to get home. This time, the summons came straight from the Devi."

"The Devi?"

"Well I don't know which one exactly, what she calls herself— Mumbadevi or Kali or maybe even Ooper-devi. But surely you've heard she's supposed to be appearing at Juhu? Right on the beach, twice an evening—showtimes as regular as a movie. What I need is for her to materialize here and conjure up some food for me. That rascal cook disappeared right after the scientists, so there's been nothing to eat." He forces out a pitiful cough, then tightens the knot around his head, as if performing an austerity measure. "Forgive me for rambling— I'm trying to remember the rest about your husband, but the hunger has blanked out my mind."

I stare at him. This has to be the same Devi ma Madhu and Guddi and Anupam were heading to see, the one for whom they dressed and decorated me. But what interest could she possibly have in scientists? How has she wandered into Karun's story?

Jaz opens one of the packets of orange biscuits we stocked up on at Sequeira's and hands over two of them. The manager's fingers tremble as he stuffs them into his mouth. He masticates noisily, ravenously, then closes his eyes. "A van—the Devi sent a white van with a blue stripe—very luxurious, might even have been air-conditioned, I think. Eight days ago, on the eighth—I can see it now—the day before the bombs reduced the streets to rubble. Except they refused to go, can you believe it? 'We have to stamp out superstition, not sell out to this Devi character.' That troublemaker Moorthy, always appointing himself in charge—you know the crusading Madrasi type. He complained from the minute he arrived—sheets not clean enough, too much milk in the tea."

The manager lapses into silence. Jaz feeds him more biscuits, directly into his mouth one by one, as if inserting coins into a jukebox. "I tried warning them this wasn't an invitation to some tea party, that the last thing they wanted to do was annoy the Devi, but they paid me no heed. Moorthy sent the driver back quite grandly, to tell her they would come only if she agreed to a public debate. 'One where we would have an opportunity to unmask any trickery. For the people's sake, because we're scientists.' As if the masses are clamoring to hear what scientists think."

"So they didn't go, then?"

"Not until that night, when the van returned with a bunch of Devi devotees. Except these devotees had not incense, but guns in their hands. They shot out the gate, rounded up all the scientists, and drove them away. Looking back, I curse my stupidity for not trying to slip in with them. If nothing else, I'm sure the Devi must be feeding them well."

I walk around the room. Karun's clothes are strewn on the bed and across the floor—it appears the manager has tried them all out, indulged in quite a fashion show. Even the sock and underwear drawers, usually such a point of order for Karun, appear ransacked. I search the desk for a note or a letter, but the only writing is in a journal full of scientific scribbling.

About to leave the room, I notice Jaz smoothing out the T-shirts in the dresser. When I ask him if he's discovered something, he turns around with a strange expression. "No. I was just looking."

"Your husband," the manager says in the corridor, then breaks into another coughing fit, followed by the same bizarre slurping and swallowing. "Such a good man. So kind, so calm, I liked him best of all. The other scientists—some of them I wouldn't even spit on. I'll pray that you find him." He looks at me with great empathy and compassion, but his gaze can't help straying to the packet, almost empty, in Jaz's hand. We give it to him and leave.

———

THE ONLY LEAD for Karun's whereabouts points towards Juhu. Jaz says walking along the water is safest, so we follow the shoreline. The fissures get even more prominent—the sea's fingers reaching across our path, trying to extend their claim to the buildings on the far side of the road. "I read it's due to rising ocean levels. Something about the drainage ducts laid while reclaiming the land no longer being able to handle the flow." Jaz adds that the material used to pack the connections between the separate land masses might be particularly vulnerable. "Imagine if we revert to the original seven islands—the way the city was discovered by the Portuguese."

I remember Karun repudiating the drainage duct theory, but don't say anything. Instead, I think of him trying to return home to me as the hotel manager said, a fact I turn and twist in my heart for the comfort I'm able to wring out. Why, though, did he leave in the first place? The pretense of the cancelled conference, the first few days he spent in Bandra while the trains might still have been running? If only I'd embarked on my journey earlier, we might have been united by now. Beneath this wistfulness, a sense of alarm creeps in on me. Who has kidnapped Karun? Where has he been for the past week? Could he really be a hostage of this supposed Devi?

The fissures ease off as the shore turns rocky. Thickets of scrubby trees sprout forth from the cracks. Strands of tattered cloth festoon the branches, like decorations intended to give a ghostly look. We stumble onto a grove of sculptures made from trash. One of them consists of gloves hanging from a scaffold. They wave in the wind, empty fingers blowing and twirling, searching for the digits that once filled them. Beyond lies a fishing village at the mouth of a small cove, still reeking of shrimp left to dry in the sun. Two boys playing around a boat pulled up next to a hut quickly disperse as we approach. "Wait up," Jaz calls, but this makes them clamber even faster away over the rocks.

We spot the crows soon after, black specks circling over a break along the shore. Hundreds of them rise and fall in the sky—as we near, we hear their excited calls. Then the stench hits us. The gap in the rocks is actually a vast carpet of bodies, in various states of decomposition— the crows hop and pick and peck among them. Mounds of flowers and vermilion lie strewn about, like the remnants of a slapdash funeral rite. "Stay here," Jaz says, and I am only too glad to turn away.

He returns a moment later. "I know this is creepy, but it has to be done." Between his fingers is a pinch of the vermilion, gathered from around the corpses. "For the Khakis, as you call them. They might think you're Muslim if you don't look more properly Hindu." To my horror, he smears the vermilion down the parting of my hair. "A bindi, too," he says, and presses one onto my forehead with the color remaining on his fingertip.

After that, I insist we walk along the roads. Unfortunately, this does not immunize us from the gore—torsos and limbs lurk in almost every alley and corner. "It's probably the Khakis—their buffer zone, just like the Limbus created," Jaz says. He's right—within a block, we begin to see the familiar pattern of charred buildings and burnt-out storefronts.

Just as I wonder where the Khakis might be all hiding, two of them slide out of a doorway. They spot us at once and stop, blocking our path. "Going for a stroll, all dressed up in red, my *jaaneman*?" the taller one says, wetting a finger with his tongue and slicking his hair back, Bollywood-villain style. I try to look unfazed as he touches me lightly in the abdomen with the tip of his machine gun.

"Is this the way to the Devi?"

"Come with us, we'll personally make sure you get to her," the other one leers.

He's about to grab my wrist when Jaz intervenes. "Actually, we don't need to trouble you. You can just tell me."

"And who do you think you might be?"

"I'm accompanying her—I'm the one responsible for her safety."

I can tell Jaz is thinking of going for his revolver—a terrible match for a machine gun, especially considering the ineptness he's displayed. "Bhim's waiting for us," I blurt out. "I'm one of the Devi's maidens. Can't you see this red sari I'm wearing?" I'm surprised at my own resourcefulness.

Bhim's name gives them pause. I force myself not to wilt as they assess my bedraggled clothes, my hastily smeared-on bindi. Then the taller one spits on the ground. "Keep going until you come to the main road." He spits again. I feel their stares on us as we walk past—I resist the temptation to run.

"I almost pulled out the gun," Jaz says in an awed whisper. "Though I think if I had, we might both be dead."

After that, we slink along in the shadows of buildings wherever possible. We almost run into Khakis on two more occasions, but I manage to spot them and lead us to cover each time. I still haven't been able to figure out Jaz's motives. What is he after? Why does he tag along? Perhaps it's the fact that our positions have reversed—he's the vulnerable one now, dependent on me to shepherd him through this inhospitable Hindu terrain. Should I run and let him fend for himself? Would I feel guilty of leaving him to his fate? Perhaps not a wise strategy—with all the Khakis around, a lone woman, Hindu or not, is probably not very safe.

He seems to pick up on my thoughts. "I hope you don't mind my company. The most direct way north to my mother is through Juhu, and I'd have a hard time crossing alone."

I nod curtly at this return of the phantom mother. "There's safety in numbers for both of us." I try not to think of my own mother, of whether I will ever see my parents or sister again.

Around four-thirty, we duck into an abandoned clothing store for lunch. The show windows have all been smashed, the mannequins stripped of their garments. They lie naked in a tangled orgy on the floor. We sit on stools and divide up a packet of orange biscuits. I've always detested the artificial orange filling, but today I'm glad for the tiny bit of moisture it carries. Jaz, on the other hand, licks it off each side with obvious relish before eating the cookie part.

The unreality of the situation overwhelms me—sitting so tranquilly in the shop, amidst the sexlessly contorted mannequins, dining on this preposterous lunch. Next to this person, a constant fixture at my side for almost a day now, about whom I know little more than the alleged existence of a mother in Jogeshwari. "Will you stay with her once you reach?" I ask.

"No. Too dangerous. Even if they don't wipe out the city this week as promised, Mumbai's too juicy a target—air attacks, another bomb, anything. The sooner one gets away, the *further*, the better. Sequeira's ferry captain friend has the right idea—lay low in a place like Diu, far away from everything. One small enough to be overlooked, one nobody's interested in targeting." Jaz parts open his last biscuit and smears off the lurid cream with his tongue. "You should think of it too—what you're going to do once you find your husband. Come north, and we can be each other's passport—journey through Muslim and Hindu pockets with equal ease."

Except there's no guarantee I'll find Karun. Or rescue him from the clutches of whoever is holding him. I slowly exhale, then turn to gaze at the mannequins.

Jaz breaks the silence. "Don't worry. You'll find him. *We'll* find him. I'll help you get him out, I promise." Instead of comforting me, his offer sets off warning signals in my brain.

THE HUMAN TIDE breaks upon us as precipitately as before. One instant, we gaze at the ramshackle walls of a shantytown from the deserted street outside, the next, we enter to find ourselves engulfed in teeming activity. Jaz spots a boy selling goat milk from a pot and bargains him down to two glasses for a hundred. The liquid tastes riper than I expect, but quenches my thirst and, as importantly, washes away the orange residue lingering in my throat. Farther down, a woman vends long and pungent white radishes from a basket—for an extra five rupees, she gives us each a pinch of salt and chili powder in our palms to dip them in.

Emerging from the slum, we find ourselves on a main road, so crowded with people that I wonder if this is where all the desolate blocks of the city have emptied. Men holding bouquets of incense, women cradling kohl-eyed infants, wizened slum dwellers, bouncy college students—we join their ranks in a procession that slowly wends towards the sea. Hawkers line the edges, selling roots and herbs and shiny crystalline minerals, with pictures of Kali herself promising miraculous cures. Some stand next to contraptions with flashing red arrows that look like games of strength, others vend flowers and pooja ingredients and Devi talismans.

We arrive at the beach at sunset. The scene reminds me of the Kumbh Mela, except one more densely packed. Stalls offer rude-smelling food, bare-chested men spin dwarf Ferris wheels made of rough-hewn wood. Green and blue flames leap up from ceremonial fires to cast an otherworldly effect. Shrines to Devi are everywhere—from small figurines adorned with simple flower offerings to elaborate garland-decked sand sculptures surrounded by jostling worshippers. A few of the HRM's Mumbadevi statues have also found their way down—sentries towering over the festive hordes, their impassive amazon features hued by the sunset. Sadhus and other ascetics weave through the crowd, some with red and white symbols extending up their scalps like elaborately painted skullcaps. In the distance, I think I even see elephants.

As the wonder of the spectacle subsides, Jaz articulates the question that clutches at my heart. "How are we going find your husband among all these people?" The absurdity, the sheer impossibility of this task paralyzes me. Jaz must notice my despair, because he tries to come up with a course of action. "What we need to do is locate this Devi ma—that's where the guesthouse manager said Karun will be."

But although everyone is here for a glimpse of the Devi, nobody really seems to know her whereabouts. *Ahead*, they all gesture with excited smiles, so we follow the general stream up the beach, looking vainly for a stage or other venue where she might appear.

We manage to make our way to the plumes—three tall spouts of water that erupt each time a wave comes in. Smaller ones spring forth randomly all around—people shriek as they get sprayed. The runoff accumulates in a large pond that blocks our path ahead. Skirting it brings us closer to the sea, where a border of devotees squat along the beach's edge. At first I think they are praying, but then realize they are simply relieving themselves. As I watch, a rogue wave churns in to ambush those who have strayed too far off the dry sand.

By the time the Indica Hotel comes into view, our pace has slowed to a near standstill. The dying light burnishes the familiar terraces and turrets, but the Statue of Liberty has vanished from its perch. I strain to make out the faraway windows, to spot the balcony where Karun and I breakfasted the morning after our wedding. Despair clasps at me once more. Will I ever sit with Karun to gaze together at the waves again? Is he even in the vicinity, anywhere on this beach, anywhere near Juhu? Given the way the crowd has swallowed up all the roads, could his van have really made it through?

Jaz tries to bolster me again. "They came several days ago—there must have been a lot fewer people then. I'd say they drove right to wherever this Devi's holding court."

The elephants turn out to be real, not mirages. Young women dressed in red float astride their backs carrying wicker baskets filled with flower petals. Every so often, the women stop the animals, which reach into the baskets with their trunks and scatter petals over the crowd. Bells around the elephants' feet warn of their approach. I find myself jammed against a wall of bodies as one of the animals lumbers through within touching distance.

We barely manage to worm ahead a few paces in the time it takes for dusk to deepen into night. My sari begins to glow again, creating a clot of curiosity around me, which further impedes our progress. At first, people content themselves with pointing or staring, but soon the bolder ones start caressing the fabric, rubbing it to see if it's genuine. I slap and shoo them away, but a girl held in her mother's arms yanks the end off and wraps it around her own head. In an instant, the crowd is pressing in from all sides, hands reaching out to touch me, stroke me, grab at my sari. My flailing and screaming only stimulates their frenzy. Jaz plunges in for a rescue attempt, but is powerless against the onslaught of clawing fingers, thrusting arms.

Just as I feel I will be smothered, the Indica starts to glow as well, in a shade close to a candy version of my sari's. Music wafts from its turrets—the ubiquitous theme from *Superdevi*, reorchestrated this time as a devotional bhajan. The next instant, the entire hotel erupts in fireworks: rockets zoom from its towers, strings of crackers explode on its terraces, flaming waterfalls cascade down its walls. The smoke clears, the hands retract from my sari, and an electric rush sweeps through the crowd. There on the highest turret, from where the Statue of Liberty formerly presided, stands the Devi.

For a moment, I gape with everyone else, my trauma forgotten. Bedecked in gold, the Devi is strikingly visible, yet tiny. I think she holds lotuses in her hand, but it's too far to be sure. What I *can* make out, even at this distance, is that she has four arms—though she engages only the lower pair to wave to her audience. Revolving smoothly like a trinket on a turntable, she bestows benevolence in each direction equally.

"Welcome," she says, and the throngs roar in response. "I'm so gratified you have come to see me." Her face is a bright, shining gold, her voice sweet and reassuring even through the distortion of the loud-speakers. "Do you know the one cure for all the unhappiness in this world, for all the fear and strife you have seen?"

"Devi ma," erupts the reply from the beach, so thunderous, so passionate, I feel like an interloper for not joining in myself. Waiting for the response to subside, the Devi continues to rotate silently.

"What has brought you here today?" she asks, and begins to list the war, the bomb, all the other dangers the audience faces. "Dark forces are at work against your Devi ma, people who do not believe in me." She urges the crowd, in the same honeyed voice, to flush out her enemies and exterminate them without mercy. "Nourish the land with their blood, just like seawater nourishes the beach."

Bursts of acclamation continue to rise from the crowd. She negotiates them perfectly, as if she has premeasured the seconds required for each pause, programmed them into her speech. Her tone never varies too much—she remains equable, immune to the fervor of her admirers' outpourings. "I am your protector, your savior. Once your feet have touched these sands, I will forever keep you safe under my shield."

At the end of her speech, the volume of her voice increases sharply. "To all my charges, to all my beloved children, Devi ma just says, Come to me."

The crowd surges towards the hotel, a few figures even manage to clamber some feet up the tower that bears the turret. The Devi extends her lower arms in benediction and sparks begin to drizzle from her fingertips. Her body rises—almost imperceptibly at first, and then in a more visible corkscrew motion, until she levitates, still rotating, several feet above the turret. The drizzles turn into showers, drops of fire begin cascading from her feet as well. I strain to make out a rope or other support, but can't. She coruscates in the air, like a comet or shooting star, magically pinned mid-flight.

Fireworks burst forth again from the terrace. This time, the night blooms not only with their flashes, but also with the white parachutes released by exploding rockets. Thousands of heads turn up to watch the armada's floating descent—hands point excitedly at the lit Devi idols dangling at each parachute's end. The struggle to snag the figurines gets so frenzied that the airdrop might have been engineered from heaven by god herself. By the time the smoke clears, the Devi has vaporized. The beach roils with excitement for a few more moments, after which the audience settles down to await her next appearance.

"At least we have a destination now," Jaz says, as I stare at the still-smoking terraces, unable to pull my gaze away. Could this be some sort of divine coincidence? The Devi appearing at the very hotel where Karun and I got married? I try to tamp down the irrational optimism billowing up inside. All I need do is make it to our bridal suite, and Karun will be still reclining on our wedding bed, the Buddha looking down benevolently.

My exuberance is short-lived. Sighting the Devi is very different from actually getting to her. The crowd remains as impenetrable as toffee, slurping around to pull us back each time we discover a new foothold. Jaz has an idea: "Perhaps we should try capitalizing on your sari."

He starts announcing I am Devi ma's helper, who needs to reach the Indica urgently. Unfortunately, the enthrallment over my sari has dissipated, people seem quite blasé about my glow after witnessing the Devi's pyrotechnics. A woman stands stoutly in my path, observing me as she might an insect struggling in a web. "Where do you think you're going?"

"Please. I need to get through. To see Devi ma."

"And what do you suppose the rest of us have gathered here for? To enjoy the sea breeze? To eat bhel puri? You're not the only one who wants her blessing."

"You don't understand—"

"I understand perfectly. We're not villagers that you can dazzle us by wearing something bright and shiny. Let's see how you get past." In short order, she's organized a clutch of onlookers, arms crossed, to blockade me.

The night turns darker. "We'll be stuck here forever," I whisper, and Jaz can only offer a ratifying silence. I stare at the Indica in the distance—its turrets now give it the appearance of a fortress, one ensconcing an impregnable bridal suite. The thought that all my effort has been for naught, that Karun may finally be so close, and yet so excruciatingly unreachable, fills me with hopelessness. A pinpoint of light, perhaps the last floating ember from the spent fireworks, hovers hazily in the air. I turn away, unable to bear to see it extinguished.

When I look back, the speck, rather than dying out, has grown, both in brightness and size. I track its path in fascination as it homes in—could it be a firefly attracted to my sari? Except it soon gets too big to be a firefly, looking more like a seated form floating through the darkness—someone on a flying carpet, perhaps. It draws closer, and I begin to hear bells, then feel underfoot vibrations, then discern large auricular outlines that emerge from the dark to flap into life. And finally the recognizable figure, surely an apparition born of my desperation, aglow in a sari similar to mine.

"Didi, up here," the voice calls, as the fat woman screams and her cohorts blocking my path scramble for safety. Astride the giant pachyderm lurching towards us is Guddi.

12

THE ELEPHANT IS BETTER THAN AN AIRBORNE CHARIOT,
an enchanted galleon. As we bob and pitch across the beach, the sea of
humanity parts before us in waves. "It's the only way to get through
such a crowd," Guddi says. "At first I was terrified we'd trample someone. But then I realized people always find the space to squeeze away
somehow. Just like insects. Isn't that right, Shyamu?" She reaches forward and pats the elephant's head. "Except for that one lady this afternoon. Don't feel guilty, Shyamu, it's not your fault. She was quite old,
anyway—how long could she have lived?"

Guddi starts chattering about her adventures since we last saw her,
about the journey on the other side of the tracks that brought her and
Anupam to safety at the Indica the night before. "All thanks to Vivek
bhaiyya. The train driver's helper—did you meet him? He took us
crawling over this big-big pipe—so big we could have probably walked
through, at least Anupam and me. But Bhaiyya said it would be very
dirty inside—all the kaka and susu from the city—*chhi!* And we had
to remain completely silent—otherwise, Bhaiyya said, we'd all end up
like Madhu didi." She stops and bites her lip. "I don't suppose there's
any chance . . . ?" I shake my head, and she starts crying. "I miss her.
And Mura chacha. I wish they were here with us, Didi."

In a few moments, though, she's cheery again. "I couldn't believe it
when I saw that glow—I'd been searching the crowd all evening,
praying to Devi ma with all my might. Did I tell you, Didi, they're
taking me to see her in person tonight? Anyway, Shyamu didn't want

to investigate, but I insisted—I told him the light had to be from a sari just like mine—either yours or Madhu didi's. See, Shyamu? I was right. One has to have faith—even elephants should pray once in a while. To Ganesh, if they like—I'm sure Devi ma wouldn't get jealous if they also asked her blessing on the side.

"You should have seen how amazed the hotel people were when I told them I sat on my first elephant at nine. That we had a whole family in our village, whom we rode all the time. That's why they let me have Shyamu—do you think they would've trusted me otherwise? Sometimes I feel I must have been an elephant myself in a previous life. I knew the instant we locked eyes that we were soul mates—Shyamu, isn't that right?" She strokes his head, but he takes no notice. "Too bad Anupam wasn't as lucky—she'd never even sat on an elephant before, so she's stuck in the hotel kitchen, poor thing. She'll be thrilled to see you, if she ever finishes all the chores they're probably loading her with. But tell me, Didi, how did you escape? You and . . ." She gazes quickly at Jaz, unsure how to address him. "You and *Bhaiyya*."

I begin to call Jaz by his name, then catch myself. "*Gaurav* bhaiyya. Remember, he was the person from the second compartment when the train derailed? He's a friend of Mura chacha. We came through Mahim, not over the pipe like you did. Without him, I never would have made it."

Guddi's eyes widen. "Mahim? Isn't that where all the Muslims live? Don't they do terrible things to virgins?"

"Yes, they *eat* them," Jaz says, and Guddi recoils in horror.

Our ride atop Shyamu isn't the most comfortable. He doesn't have a proper howdah, just a thick blanket that's strapped on, resulting in the constant danger of falling off. Guddi tugs his ears to make him turn right or left, and digs her knuckles into his neck to make him start or halt (her maneuvers succeed only part of the time). "Stop that, Shyamu," she admonishes, upon hearing my startled cry as the tip of his trunk starts rummaging around in my lap. "Don't mind him—he's just looking for the flowers." She pushes forward the basket of petals for him to dip into. At the end of each stop, she loops his trunk around another basket, this one empty, to collect offerings for the Devi. Fruits, garlands, currency notes, even a few wristwatches and necklaces, pour in with each haul. Most of the bananas disappear into Shyamu's mouth, along with the odd piece of jewelry. "Look what someone put in!" Guddi exclaims, holding up a cell phone. "They don't work anymore, so Devi ma has said we can keep these."

Once the petals are all scattered and the large canvas bags hanging from Shyamu's neck filled with booty, Guddi guides him towards the Indica. The ride seems to get less bumpy as soon as the beach gives way to pavement (though Guddi insists Shyamu much prefers walking on the sand). We bob past armies of Khaki guards holding back the throngs of devotees, to the main entry, situated around the corner. Shyamu curls back his trunk and trumpets—on cue, the heavy metal gates swing open. Could Karun's van have passed through this same portal?

Inside, the driveway winds up towards the majestic arch of the entrance, with its golden Mughal domes and alternating baby gopurams. Lights blaze everywhere, profligately so, perhaps to underscore the contrast with the power-starved city outside. The compound is still lush with thickets of Hawaiian shrubs and bushes, though the elephants seem to have chomped off several of their tops. Three of the animals stand in line, like unwieldy planes on a runway, waiting to take off. "The left ramp is too steep—some of them go halfway and get stuck," Guddi explains. "Even with this longer ramp, they can only go up one by one." She starts cooing into Shyamu's ear upon getting the signal to launch. He takes his first tentative steps up the incline, but slows noticeably two-thirds of the way up. By the time we near the top, Shyamu is trumpeting anxiously, pausing between each doddering step. "Come on, you can do it—keep going, don't stop." But Shyamu refuses to go any further. All of a sudden, Guddi jabs her elbows sharply into the sides of his neck. With a startled bellow, Shyamu staggers up the remaining distance and barrels through the entrance.

The lobby still retains a hint of tuberose fragrance, barely discernible under the cloying earthiness of dung. The Anish Kapoor chairs lie jumbled with the front desk in a corner, cleared away to make a path for the elephants. Even the metal detector's two halves have been separated to pachyderm breadth—the machine beeps resentfully as we sail through, indicating it's still plugged in for some reason. The Khakis have been busy redecorating—splashing religious slogans over the panels showing the history of zero, imprinting the Hussain mural with crude likenesses of Hindu gods. A Mumbadevi amazon deployed at a focal point of the central atrium looks curiously stunted by the elephants lumbering past.

Shyamu barges into the Sensex bar, where quotes for long-defunct stocks still whirl around the walls. A huge round metal trough stands on the floor—with a shock I recognize it as the polished torus sculpture that hung over the lobby. Three elephants root through the vegetation mounded in its center, searching with their trunks for rotting cabbages. Guddi tries to steer Shyamu away, but it is the dung-clearing attendants, following us since we entered, who finally coax him back with their brooms and scoops. As we pass through the atrium, he tries to hook onto the plants spiraling down from the cascade of balcony levels above. But their ends are all out of reach—other elephants have already pulled or bitten them off.

Hundreds of people crowd the rear of the atrium, where it widens into the "Stomach of India" restaurant. Some sit listlessly at tables, like diners despairing of ever catching the attention of a waiter, others doze on the floor, curled up under cream-colored tablecloths. "The whole world has come for a glimpse of Devi ma," Guddi says, and I notice the dosa grill converted into a check-in counter of sorts. Apparently, the sight of an elephant tromping through the dining room no longer engages—even the children are too inured to look up.

We ride directly into the garden, through a large opening of dismantled panels in the rear glass wall. The lateral wing of the hotel stretches along our left—somewhere from the third floor, a bridal suite beckons for me to investigate. Except who is to say I might not spot Karun simply walking around? Strolling the hibiscus-planted terrace, ambling by the outdoor Soma Bar, watching a game at the badminton court? I peer at the people we pass, but do not find the face I seek. Cleaning crews, rifle-toting guards, waiters bearing trays—where have all the guests gone?

The floodlit pool offers a smattering of swimmers who do not look like staff. I feel a sharp stab of nostalgia for the morning after our wedding when Karun and I came down here. Our first married dip—could everyone tell this was my husband I swam with? The kiss underwater when I almost lost my nerve, and barely touched his lips.

Shyamu interrupts my reverie, by swinging so sharply that he clips one of the pillars lining the path. "No, Shyamu, no, you can't go in there—the stable's up ahead," Guddi shouts, and I see he is aimed directly for the pool. None of her ear-pulling and elbow-jabbing tricks work, nor do her screams for him to stop. Lounge chairs buckle and pop underfoot as swimmers scramble towards the edges. Nodding his head sagely and curling his trunk up as if to prevent it from getting wet, Shyamu descends a few of the ghat-like steps, then loses his balance and launches us all into the drink.

"I'm still learning how to handle him," Guddi says apologetically afterwards, as we stand dripping at the edge of the pool. Behind us, Shyamu wallows about happily, using his trunk to squirt water over his back and at the attendants trying to coax him out. "Come, Didi, you won't believe where Anupam and I live now. Afterwards, we can dry off."

She takes us up some stairs and through one of the carpeted hotel corridors. I look at each door we pass, wishing I had X-ray vision to check if Karun is behind any of them. "Namaste, Bhaiyya," Guddi says to a gun-toting Khaki outside her room, then throws open the door. "Isn't this amazing? So big—like a whole house, just for the two of us."

Guddi scampers around inside, bouncing on the bed, sliding open the closet door, showing me her comb and her kohl and the five discarded cell phones she's accumulated (six with the new one), all stored in a corner of the nightstand drawer. "Just look at the size of this television, Didi—our own private cinema once we learn how to turn it on." She bows reverentially to the Buddha over the bed, then pulls me into the bathroom. "See this? It looks like a chair, but it's the toilet, believe it or not!" She sits on it to demonstrate, then flushes it excitedly. "All that water—I think it automatically washes your bottom, but I haven't figured out how." She inhales deeply. "Just smell, so clean. Like roses, like chameli. Close your eyes—would you ever guess we're in a latrine?"

Jaz stays behind to use the bathroom while Guddi takes me out on the balcony. "This is where Gaurav bhaiyya can live—that way, we won't have to share the room at night, and he'll have enough space to stretch out. It'll be nice to snuggle with you, Didi—the bed is so huge that last night, Anupam and I felt lost."

I look down at the gardens and pool, at the attendants trying to cajole out Shyamu, who still cavorts in the water. Unlike the bridal suite, where Karun and I could gaze out at the beach, we now face the interior. I think of all the occupants in the hotel, of the hundreds of windows and balconies overlooking the same courtyard—a few lights even illuminate the small buildings by the pool. The odds of locating Karun may have improved tremendously, but it's still going to require a lot of luck.

"Listen, Guddi, I'm trying to find my husband. He came with three friends some days back in a van. They're all scientists—sent for personally by Devi ma. Think, now—have you heard anything of such a group staying in the hotel?"

Guddi scrunches up her forehead in concentration. "What's a scientist, Didi?" she finally asks. I try explaining it to her, but she gets more and more confused, especially after Jaz returns from his inordinately long time in the bathroom and joins the interrogation. "I've only been here since last night," she says, her voice quivering, her chin slumping, her eyes tearing up. Then she brightens. "I know who you can ask. Although we'll have to check with Chitra didi first."

"Chitra didi?"

"She's the supervisor. I'm sure she'll allow you to come along upstairs after we dry off."

"What's upstairs?"

Guddi gives me a startled look. "Why, Devi ma, of course. She knows everything—without her knowledge, not even a leaf can drop."

WITH THE WHISTLE around her neck and white sneakers on her feet, Chitra, the Devi's most senior assistant, looks like an angry coach. "Didn't I say you had an audience with Devi ma this evening?" she scolds Guddi, paying little attention to Jaz or me. "How could you have gotten yourself all wet? As it is we've lost all the Ooper-devi saris in the train wreck—do you know how difficult they were to get?"

"It's not my fault, Didi. Shyamu jumped into the swimming pool."

"And who gave you permission to go outside on him? I told you to practice in the garden, didn't I? Did you think you could just walk off with him on your first day?"

"But in the village I used to—"

"Yes, I'm sure you have a thousand tales from your village—for all I know, the elephants there rocked you to sleep every night. Now take off that sari so we can try to iron it dry. As it is, the first thing Anupam did in the kitchen was splatter herself—her sari looks dyed in a vat of potato curry. So it's going to be just you, which means Devi ma will be furious. We promised to have all of you glowing and ready like Ooper-devi's maidens to accompany her next appearance."

"Why don't we take along Sarita didi? She's wearing the same thing."

Chitra examines my sari. "So you decided to jump in for a dip as well—what is this, an epidemic? Well, don't just stare at me—take it off—we haven't got much time."

While the saris are drying, Chitra supervises our sprucing up—repainting the bridal dots on Guddi's face, but declaring they would be lost on mine. She's surprisingly agreeable to Guddi's suggestion we take "Gaurav bhaiyya" along—Devi ma, apparently, has a preference for male attendants. Jaz, though, balks at trading in his wet garb for the beige and white uniform. Perhaps he fears disrobing will expose him as a Muslim, though I suspect it's his sense of fashion the uniform offends. His one concession, upon Chitra's insistence that nobody bareheaded can be allowed an audience with Devi ma, is the bright red cloth wrapped around his head like a turban. "You look very handsome, Gaurav bhaiyya," Guddi blushingly tells him, as he preens in front of a mirror, adjusting the turban this way and that. I'm beginning to realize there's more than just a trace of peacock in him.

Chitra doesn't recall a van, blue-striped or otherwise, coming to the hotel. "All I've seen on the driveway are elephants, for the past fortnight at least." She's dubious about the whole notion of the scientists being bused in. "People flock here in droves—it's not like Devi ma needs to summon anybody. But you should ask her. All the hundreds of devotees she blesses—only she can keep track, with her supernatural powers."

In the elevator, Chitra swipes a card through an electronic slot to get us moving. "Do you know, we don't have a single generator in the entire hotel? Devi ma is mighty enough to ensure us all the electricity we want—ever since she came, we haven't lost power for a second."

As we approach the third floor, I wonder if by some fantastic coincidence we will be led to my wedding night room. Where Devi ma will be holding court, and Karun assessing the proceedings with a scientific eye, jotting observations in a notebook. But the elevator keeps rising, to the fourth and top floor. Devi ma has taken up quarters in the presidential suite.

Dozens of hopeful faces peer out from behind the Khakis standing guard at the door to the emergency staircase. Some supplicants seem to have escaped into the corridor—they mill around, blocking our way.

Chitra blows her whistle and stamps her foot, as she might to make mice scurry away. "See what I mean about the droves? You have no idea how lucky you are to get an audience." Two separate sets of guards search us—I hold my breath as they pat Jaz down, but neither group finds his gun (he whispers to me that he's hidden it in Guddi's bathroom, behind the flush). The ultimate barrier is a gauntlet of credential-checking clerks, who squint up balefully from their ledgers as we approach. I expect Chitra will help us breeze past, but even she has to grind through the bureaucratic questions they ask.

With all the crowds clamoring hysterically for an audience, my expectations for the Devi have steadily risen. Will she spark and cork-screw in her suite like she did on the beach? Or will she appear in one of those calendar-art renditions, perhaps Laxmi emerging from a lotus with garlands flowing from her arms? Guddi has been rhapsodizing incessantly about enchanted forests and kingdoms of gold, all of which she seems to expect behind the door. She appears nonplussed when Chitra ushers us into a room, enormous and impeccably appointed, but in an ultra-modern, Western style. After the carnival of Mughals and Mauryas and Rajputs and Cholas exploding through the lower floors, the effect is shocking. (Could this represent the pinnacle of Indian culture, its ultimate aspiration?) The only desi embellishment, among the pastel walls and corporate furniture, the abstract paintings so bland that the Khakis haven't even bothered to deface them, is an empty throne—the glitz-painted kind rented out at Hindu weddings to seat the bride and groom. Guddi rushes over to genuflect at it.

"This way," Chitra calls, and leads us out onto the terrace, fortunately redeemed by the return of the Buddhas canopied by Mughal domes, even a gopuram rising above the emergency stairwell. A small plantation of potted palms flanks an infinity pool that seems to flow directly into the Arabian Sea. Attendants scurry around with plates and bottles and pillows, electricians tinker with wiring and panels of audio equipment, a group of devotees in a corner bulges against its cordon of guards. Amidst all this activity, though, the Devi is nowhere to be seen. A second throne, as ornate as the one inside, flanks the pool. But it too is empty.

"Devi ma doesn't like sitting in it, finds it too hard," Chitra explains. She gestures towards a beach chair facing away from us. "Well don't just stand there, touch her feet."

At first, I'm confused by the chair's ordinariness, its utilitarian plastic slats and dull aluminum frame. Then I notice the feet, gleaming with the sheen of real gold, resting on a brocaded red pillow like sacraments presented for worship in a shrine. Guddi immediately throws herself upon them, kissing them with almost fetishistic fervor.

For a moment, I can only stare on. I've always assumed there is some sort of fraudulence to the Devi, but what if she's real, if this is the shimmer of divinity? When I look into her face, though, the illusion lifts—the gold, I realize, comes from a glaze of paint. Tiny creases around her brow and chin give the game away—the pigment is a mask, through which the whites of her eyes float up luminously. Coddled in the chair by a cloud of puffy pillows, her body looks even tinier than it appeared on the turret. How strange that they've used a midget to fill the role, I think. Then she bids us welcome, and I realize she's simply a girl of eight or nine.

"I'm so gratified you've come to see me. Do you know the one cure for all the unhappiness in this world?" The words sound the same as those spoken from the turret, though the voice is different, the delivery clumsy. "For all the fear and danger. For all the fear and danger and . . . the fear and danger and . . ."

"*Strife,*" Chitra whispers, and the Devi girl repeats the word, then the entire sentence a few times.

Guddi finally tears herself away from the Devi's feet, and I bend down for my go at them. Splayed for convenience, raised to be within easy reach of the devotees, they remain perfectly still when I touch them. They are chubby like the rest of her body, even the soles look fleshy. "I am your protector, your savior," the girl says, then again forgets what comes next. She stumbles through a few unsuccessful attempts to continue, then reaches out for a bottle of Coca-Cola on the plastic beach table next to her.

That's when I notice her extra pair of arms. The two appendages emerge from her shoulders, the right longer than the left, but both stunted and elbow-less. At first I think they are prosthetic devices glued on for effect. But then I see the nubbed club of flesh at the end of the left arm, which suggests a birth defect. "Once your feet have touched these sands, I will forever keep you safe under my shield," she suddenly spouts, her memory refreshed by the caffeine.

The perfectly formed hand at the end of her right appendage mesmerizes me. The digits move and bend unconsciously, spider-like, as she concentrates on delivering more of her lines. The arm itself is too short to reach out to grab the Coke bottle, but once she's ready for another sip, the extra fingers adeptly lift the straw out from the neck to her mouth. I want to touch them, squeeze them, trace the bones under the flesh to make sure they're real.

"What are you staring at like that?" she says, stopping mid-sip.

"I'm sorry, Devi ma—I was just lost—lost in your words."

She glares at me, then turns to Chitra. "Where are my maidens? You promised they'd dance on the terrace below me in glowing saris."

"Forgive me, Devi ma, there's been a delay—the enemy attacked our train and stole the saris. Only these two maidens made it out—let me have the lights turned off, so you can at least see what the saris look like."

The demonstration flops. Perhaps the light levels aren't low enough, or the dunking has permanently washed away the fluorescence, but the saris refuse to perform. Guddi's still manages a few weak flashes near the arms and across the chest, but mine hangs as lifelessly around me as a shroud. After screaming for the head of whoever's responsible for the derailment, the Devi turns to me. "Show me what you've brought."

Fortunately, Chitra has warned me of the need to bear a gift, so I take out my last packet of orange biscuits (unharmed within their watertight wrapper) and lay it on the pillow, between the girl's feet.

She rips it open—I try not to gawk as her extra hand rustles around in the packet and brings a biscuit to her mouth. She chews on it, then spits the mush out at my face. "This is horrible. Are you trying to poison me?"

I wipe it off, noticing Chitra's frantic shake of head too late. My action enrages the girl. "How dare you wipe off my blessing? Don't you know everything from me is holy, is prasad?" She rises from her chair to lunge at me when Chitra and Guddi intervene.

"Forgive her, Devi ma, she didn't know. Next time, she'll bring the bonbon biscuits you like." They force my forehead down to scrape it at the girl's feet.

"Get her up," the girl commands, and the two pull me up and hold me between them. For an instant, I think I will be blessed with Devi spit again, but instead, she shakes up the Coke bottle and sprays the froth at me. Seeing me dripping with cola, she bursts out laughing. Then she hurls the bottle at my face. I hear it whiz by my ear and smash on the terrace behind. "What else do you have for me besides biscuits?"

"She's brought a pomegranate, Devi ma," Guddi says, and I turn to her sharply. The fruit fell out when I changed out of my wet sari, but I scooped it back up quickly and didn't think anyone had noticed. "Go on, let Devi ma see how red it is."

I have no intention of squandering it. "It's actually for my husband. I'd be happy to offer it to Devi ma, but first she must help me find him."

The girl flares up instantly. "What do you think, you can bargain with Devi ma? Give it to me, at once, or I'll have you flung off the terrace." She shouts for the guards when I don't move. Guddi starts pleading with me to give it up as two Khakis trot over.

Reluctantly, I hand over the pomegranate. The Devi girl tosses it in a little juggle between her three hands, then presses at it with the nubs of her club to test its ripeness. Before I can stop her, she bites in as if it's an apple. "It's bitter!" she exclaims, spitting out seeds and skin and pith and flinging the fruit away. I almost throw myself after it as the pomegranate bounces across the floor and falls off the edge of the terrace. "I'll have you drowned in the sea for this. I'll have you trampled under the elephants."

Both Guddi and Chitra are begging the girl to show me mercy when Jaz intervenes. "Devi ma, wait. That pomegranate wasn't for you—the actual present my friend brought is with me." He rummages around in his many pockets, then finds what he's looking for and extends it to her in outstretched palms. "For days now, my friend has been saying that this is what the Devi ma craves, this is what she will eat." To my horror, I see he is offering her the Marmite.

The girl looks at the jar suspiciously. "How do I know it's not poison?" The fingers in her extra hand curl warily, like question marks.

I try to think of some way to stop Jaz, impress upon him the lunacy of expecting the girl to find such a foreign taste appealing. But he has already opened the jar to demonstrate it's safe by eating some. "Mmm . . . wait till you taste this chutney. It's so nice and salty."

Her curiosity aroused, the girl sniffs at the jar, then straightens one of her bent fingers to scoop some out. "It's so black." She puts it in her mouth. I wait for her to spit it out, to summon the elephants, but she has a thoughtful expression on her face. "It's like no chutney I've ever had." She takes another fingerful, then grins shyly, toothily, at Jaz. "It tickles my throat. Devi ma is pleased."

JAZ INSTANTLY SEEMS to acquire the status of most favored disciple. The Devi girl allows him to touch not just her feet, but his limb of choice at will (even letting him rub the nubs on her appendage). She undoes her hair and sweeps it playfully over his face, declaring it to be a special blessing she's invented just for him. She insists he feed her pieces of samosa with his own hand—he ingratiates himself further by dipping each bite in Marmite. They take big swallows from a shared bottle of Coke like pals in a TV commercial, giggling as the bubbles come out their noses. As a special gesture of appreciation, she regurgitates some of the samosa and offers it to him in her palm as prasad—Jaz has no choice but to swallow it with love (delight, even) writ all over his face.

When it's time for her next show, Devi girl insists Jaz (who she's christened her horse, her "Gaurav-ghoda") carry her on his shoulders to the turret. An attendant opens a small gate at the end of the terrace beyond which a walkway runs across the top of the building along the crenulated parapet. Jaz, the merry porter, proceeds down this with his joyful load. At the turret, he personally helps the girl into a saucer-shaped stand of sorts, while a cluster of attendants stand by and watch.

"My, aren't we the Devi's pet?" I remark when he returns.

"All to get your husband back," he reminds me.

The fireworks start—rockets whiz by, fire fountains burst into life all around us. With cascades of sparks tumbling from every ledge, I'm surprised the hotel doesn't burn down. Large lotuses blossom from the Devi's extra hands—Chitra has inserted a stem into a cleft in the left. "We're trying to get her to memorize the words so she can address the crowd in her own voice," she tells us, as Devi girl lip-synchs to the prerecorded words piped in through the speaker system.

Chitra gives a signal to the man at the control panel, and the saucer holding the Devi girl begins to rotate. "Watch this," Chitra says as streams of sparks issue from the base of the saucer, which slowly lifts into the air. It occurs to me that this might be the machine from Mehboob Studios that Sequeira said he'd had to give away. I blurt out the obvious question: If Devi ma is real, shouldn't she be able to levitate on her own? Why does she need such aids?

Guddi, shocked, urges me to renounce these blasphemous thoughts before Devi ma strikes me down, but Chitra holds up her hand. "Why, indeed, would a real devi not show off her flying powers?" She looks at me, then Guddi and the rest of the assembly, as a teacher might at a sluggish class to elicit a forgotten lesson. "The answer, remember, is simple: That's the wrong question. Rather, ask yourself why anyone might still doubt Devi ma after she's taken the trouble to grace us in this girl's avatar. What's the true test? Healing the countless invalids who seek her help, or performing tricks like a circus animal? Count again the number of arms she has, then tell me what more evidence you could want."

I stifle the impulse to point out that not all the limbs in question are whole, that their sum doesn't quite total up to four. The attendants all gaze raptly at the spectacle, now certified authentic, but I cannot tell where Chitra stands herself. Was her speech merely for her minions' sake, does she truly believe in Devi ma or not?

The show ends differently than the one we witnessed from the beach. As the girl reaches her zenith, an enormous buffalo effigy, hoisted from the ground at the end of a cable, swings into view. I've seen these as part of the City of Devi celebrations—an enactment of the Devi myth where the goddess slays the buffalo demon. "I am the demon Mahisha, who neither Vishnu nor Shiva has been able to vanquish," a voice intones over the speakers. "I am the lord of the three worlds, and you will marry me." A series of threats from both sides follows, with the Devi promising to cut off the demon's head and drink its blood. Finally, a trident appears in her hand, one that shoots laser-like rays of light through the air to ignite the buffalo. Strings of firecrackers go off in its belly, red and green flares emerge from its mouth and tail. A tremendous cheer rises from the crowd as fire engulfs the animal.

"What's that?" Inside the metal ribcage of the buffalo, I think I make out a shadowy form, one that writhes and shivers in the flames. I point it out to Jaz, but clouds of smoke come in the way before he can see it.

"It's the spirit of the buffalo demon," Chitra says. "Being purified at the hands of Devi ma."

"It looked like something trapped inside. Or *someone*."

"Just a spirit. And Devi ma has liberated it." Her face is serene in the light from the flames.

After the show, Gaurav-ghoda fetches Devi girl back on his shoulders and deposits her on the throne. It's time for the blessing of the pilgrims, at least the wealthiest ones. Chitra points out the matinee idol Roop Kumar, who reluctantly leaves behind his entourage and bows down alone at the throne. A round and suited gentleman, who Chitra says is the owner of the Mumbai Cricket League, follows, after which the president of Mody Industries himself (instantly recognizable from the newspapers) touches the girl's feet. By the time the nightly slot to receive less exalted devotees rolls around, the Devi is quite cranky. Most have some ailment or other that needs curing—she sends them on their way after a perfunctory laying of hands on the affected part. "Only one disease per person," she snaps at a woman who has cancer as well as diabetes. A man who refuses to leave without a handwritten note for his crippled son at home irritates her so much that she stabs him with his own fountain pen through the arm.

"I think it's time to end the session," Chitra whispers. "We don't want her to start putting people to death like she did last night."

On Chitra's behest Jaz hitches the Devi on his shoulders again and carries her around the terrace to restore her mood. She pulls off his turban and perches it on her own head, guffawing when it droops down to her nose. "Will Devi ma grant one more boon tonight—for her loyal horse this time?" Gaurav-ghoda asks. "Help me find the person we're looking for, the one my friend was talking about."

"You mean her husband—that woman who tried to poison me?"

"She brought you that chutney you liked so much, remember? Her husband is closer to me than any brother could be." The statement sounds so heartfelt, it alarms me.

Devi girl gives me a nasty look as Jaz explains about the bus that's picked up Karun and his colleagues. "I know Devi ma gives her blessing to so many people that it's not possible to remember them all these days later. But with her permission, my friend and I would like to look through the hotel."

The girl thinks for a moment, then agrees. "But first take Devi ma around the pool and the palm trees." Jaz gasps as she grips his freshly unturbaned hair, like she might the mane of a horse, and pulls sharply. "Faster this time."

JAZ

13

WE'VE ALMOST MADE IT TO THE DOOR WHEN THE WICKED LITTLE witch of the east calls me back. "Another ride for my Devi ma?" I say, and she nods her fat little head. I remember to brace myself as she clambers on this time—the Jazter has learnt that Devi flesh weighs more per unit volume than the heaviest element known to man. "Once more?" I ask after we've galloped all the way to the turret and back, and to my dismay, my divine porcinity nods yes.

The Jazter has never understood religion, but if this is what the citizens believe will save them, then maybe they deserve to be dead.

Perhaps I'm being too harsh on her Marmite-ship. Lying at her feet all night, I have listened to her tale of pauperdom to popehood, destitution to devi-nity. It behooves me as even-handed raconteur to present the sympathetic side of even the most trying characters I encounter. Who would fail to be moved by the deep scar on her left appendage? The gash where her mother tried to simply hack off the extra arm, failing only because her slum dweller's knife was too blunt to cut through bone? Not to mention the other marks of abuse—the scars on her back, the lacerations on her neck, the cigarette burns on her legs—all of which she displays to me as proudly as stigmata. "To think I might still have been begging outside the Sion post office," she says, choking up a little at the poignancy of her own discovery. Her tears dry quickly, though, vaporized in the heat of the rancor she has stored up inside. "All the people who spat at me, the dogs who laughed at my extra arms, not realizing these were the signs of Devi."

Now that these limbs have attained the status of sacred relics, only the chosen few dare touch them without risking severe bodily harm. The Jazter, most favored member of this club, has discovered the right sequence of knuckle-nubs to press (like finger buttons on a trumpet) to make her coo softly. Thus lulled, into a stupor almost, she discloses her debt to Baby Rinky. "They tried to get her first, even though she was only a make-believe screen devi. Had her mother not insisted on leaving Mumbai when the war worsened, they might never have discovered me. I was so thin then—they had to fatten me with laddoos for a week."

She breaks off, looking up at the sky dreamily. "What I want to do someday is star in my own movie. Would they like me, do you suppose? After all I *am* the true Devi."

"They'd love you, Devi ma. You'd be a much bigger hit than Baby Rinky."

She laughs, and reaches with her toes to affectionately stroke my cheek. "Don't worry—I wouldn't leave you out—we'd find a role for you to play as well. Vishnu's horse, in fact—wouldn't that be the perfect part? Always running and moving and jumping—tell me, my Gaurav-ghoda, what do you think?"

Somewhere in the midst of a long list of things we'll do together (ride through the sky in a magical chariot, eat the same flavors of ice cream on the moon as Baby Rinky, kill lots of bad people with big big guns) she dozes off. The Jazter would have never believed it, but she actually looks innocent—her breath emerges rhythmically through her lips, her cheeks bulge as cherubically as a baby's. Disengaging the curls of my hair clutched so lovingly (if painfully) in her fingers, I stretch out on the floor next to her lounge chair and fall asleep. In the morning, she greets me with a glass of nectar. "Amrit. I made it for you myself."

Except it's not nectar, but urine—still steaming a bit. I tell her I can't possibly accept when the long-suffering devotees behind their chain of guards have been waiting so patiently for prasad. "Devi amrit," they cry, and take a joyous sip each. The Jazter doesn't quite get it—*chacun à son goût*, must be a Hindu thing.

Fortunately, before my personal prasad factory can manufacture something more solid from all the samosas it has processed overnight, a summons arrives from downstairs. Pooja is at nine and Devi ma must preside as idol-in-residence to be worshipped. Between bites of laddoo, she gives me her blessing to go sniff for scientists. I am to be extended every privilege, all through the hotel, with Chitra and Guddi and Sarita to accompany me. At farewell time she wavers—wouldn't it be fun if she came along for the ride? She means this literally—Gauravghoda carrying her around from room to room—after all, she's never much explored the hotel, really. But vermilion and incense and clamoring devotees call from downstairs—not to mention, good God, the promise of more sweets. "Come back quickly," she warns, and for the time being, I am free.

NOW THAT I'VE secured my *Laddoovielfraß*'s permission to look for Karun, how do I actually find him? I can't dial the front desk or switchboard operator and simply furnish his name. Chitra is dismissive when I ask where they store their occupancy information. "Devi knows where even the tiniest ant in the hotel lives. She doesn't need to consult a list."

"Yes, but *you* do. When she demands to see someone, for instance—how do you know which room it is?"

"We ask the clerks. They write down the room number of everyone who comes to visit her."

So we go to the desks outside the suite. The clerks are ferociously protective of their ledgers, and make resentful grinding noises in their throats when Chitra invokes Devi ma's authority to examine the pages. Karun's name doesn't appear anywhere. "Could you have made a mistake?" I ask the clerks, and their grinding turns into outright vituperation. Chitra quickly shepherds us away.

Why is Karun not listed? Doubts, as sharp-eyed as hawks, instantly begin to swoop in: Karun never made it to the hotel, the van took him to some other destination, who knows if he's even in the city still? I dispel these thoughts with one inescapable notion: Karun *has* to be here, since it's the only way we will ever meet again.

Might they record names at the restaurant counters where incoming devotees queue to check in? Chitra believes they did at one point, so we go down to investigate. The lobby hall is as busy as a bus terminal, with elephants arriving and departing in regular succession and attendants trailing after to scoop up their extruded bounty. The restaurant's coffee bar now serves as a canteen for Khakis, dozens of whom mill around, dipping rusks of bread into tea. A mass of supplicants clamors at the counters—seeing the chaos, I realize no useful records can possibly surface, even if we manage to wade in.

Which means the hotel is one giant labyrinth we must scour inch by inch. The lobby and its surrounding arcades spilling with people, the guestrooms of which there are three hundred (though perhaps it's four, Chitra thinks), the teeming grounds and corridors—a wall-to-wall dormitory has even mushroomed in the disco downstairs. Chitra asks if we want to start by checking out the audience gathered for Devi pooja outside. Her offer sounds wan, halfhearted—she already seems eager to call the search off, looking at her watch, muttering how busy she is.

I listen to the sounds of rapture stream in through the doors to the garden, imagine the congregation rollicking in worship. Somehow, I can't imagine Karun in its midst. Nor do the rooms beckon with any special promise. I need time to mull through the sweep of search possibilities to see if anything activates my shikari instincts.

Sarita, though, has a determined plan—she wants to check out Room 318, which three years ago served as their bridal suite. "I know it sounds crazy, but I can still picture him lying in that very same bed." For no better reason than to humor her along, we go upstairs. I feel a rush of misgiving as Chitra swipes open the door—after all, Karun's wedding night marks when I unequivocally lost him (the suite practically qualifies as a crime scene for me). But I needn't have worried. The interior is bloodless, untroubled by ghostly evidence—the linens, hospital-crisp, have not been slept in for weeks. Sarita hugs a pillow to her chest as if squeezing out nostalgia from it, then stands silently on the balcony to stare at the sea.

Now that we're here, the third floor is as good as any to start with, so we check out the neighboring rooms as well. Chitra raps smartly at each door, waits for a scant half-minute (hardly enough for a response, it seems), then unlocks it with her magic swipe card. A plump middle-aged couple looks up startled from a plate of parathas in the first, an enraged film producer (one of the VIPs granted an audience with the Devi last night) chases us out of the second, while the third is empty, save, inexplicably, for a small goat tethered in the bathroom. "Can't I take it to my room?" Guddi asks, and we have to tear her away from it. I can discern no order to the accommodations—next to the goat is a room crammed with workers squatting on mats, engrossed in a card game. Seeing us, they hasten to douse their cigarettes and squirrel their bottles of hooch away.

A few doors down, we enter a room piled ceiling-high with coconuts. Guddi has to run down the corridor to retrieve several that roll out. "Who authorized this?" Chitra fumes. "Somebody's going to have to do some explaining." She strides into the corners of the room and yanks off the sheets covering mounds of trinkets, pyramids of fabric, boxes of molding sweets. Even the bathtub is filled with fruit, much of it brown and rotting. "All the gifts people bring Devi ma—those lazy attendants stuff them into any room that's free."

As we prepare to leave, Sarita emerges elatedly from the bathroom. "Look what I found! To replace the one Devi ma tossed off the terrace." She triumphantly holds up a pomegranate. "It's still perfectly good—not even a mark on its skin." I nod my felicitations at her, though in truth, I'm mystified by this karmic cycle of adopting and losing pomegranates she seems to be embroiled in. (And why pomegranates, why this obsession with them in particular? Why not apples or pears or better still cherries, which would be so much easier to tote along?) Chitra raises an eyebrow at this pilferage from Devi ma's wares, but remains silent as Sarita ties the fruit into her sari.

Somewhere between the college *Superdevi* groupies colonizing Room 332 and the chanteuse singing a hymn to Mumbadevi for the cement tycoon in Room 334, it strikes me I'm not going about this search in the most intelligent way. What if we do come upon Karun? With Sarita at my side, how might I expect him to behave? If history is any indicator, he'll keep his true desires firmly bridled, allow spousal loyalty to canter to an easy victory again. I need to ditch Sarita, in the hope I'll discover Karun while searching alone—the only way to give myself a fighting chance with him.

Not that I expect to find Karun in these rooms. The occupants are too carefree, the atmosphere too festive, the smattering of Khakis don't even pretend to be guarding anything. If someone forced Karun here at gunpoint, wouldn't they keep him more tightly under lock and key? Otherwise, why wouldn't he simply sneak out and try once more to return to the south part of the city? Surveillance at the gates of people leaving seems pretty lax—after all, didn't Guddi decamp with an entire elephant?

What I therefore need to hunt around for (without Sarita) are areas of enhanced security. "I think we should split up. Devi ma might call us back at any time—we need to get through the rooms much more quickly." Chitra rises in opposition to this idea but I hold firm, invoking the authority granted me by the Devi. She then tries to pair up with me—perhaps to keep me subtly off track, as I suspect she's been doing. "Oh, but you and Sarita form such a great team," I say. "Let Guddi accompany me." Chitra's eyes narrow when I ask for her swipe card— she silently fishes another one out from her pocket and hands it to me.

About to part, Sarita stops me. "How will you recognize Karun when you've never even met him?"

I look at her stupefied. How, indeed? How could the Jazter have missed something so obvious? "I guess I'll just have to ask," I reply weakly. Sarita's mouth tightens—she has noted my blunder, added it to the tally.

Before anything else can crop up to scuttle my escape, I promise to regroup later in Devi ma's suite, and cut out with Guddi.

AS A FIRST STEP, we visit the remaining floors in the wing to verify they are equally unguarded. I have to keep shushing Guddi, for whom stealth and unobtrusiveness seem like entirely alien concepts. "We're looking for his friend," she announces to everyone we encounter: cleaning staff, guests, Khakis. "We have permission from Devi ma herself." She frisks through the hotel as if it were a giant amusement park—swinging down corridors, bouncing on the landing sofas, darting into every nook and corner on her eternal quest for cell phones. The escalator to the ground level fascinates her, though she's unnerved by the floor swallowing its endless diet of steps.

By the time we've finished with the wing, Guddi is bored—she suggests we go pay Shyamu a visit. "I'm afraid he might have caught a cold from that dip in the swimming pool." When I inform her that elephant stables are not on our list, she gets downcast. "Can we at least catch the last part of the Devi pooja then?"

I block out her voice and concentrate on Karun. Ensconced in this hotel somewhere. The premise I must keep reinforcing in my mind, since without it (as any shikari knows) there can be no game. As far as this wing goes, though, Karun's trail feels completely dead. The clerks took justified umbrage when I questioned their ledgers—the Devi and he seem to have never met.

Who ordered his kidnapping then? Clearly the same person who runs the show here: this sprawling temple to the Devi, the fireworks, the electricity, the elephants. With such a vast enterprise, it has to be Bhim. The great white Hindu hope, as deft at multitasking as Vishnu himself—whether it's Muslims in need of massacring or the nation in need of saving. Though what he might want with a vanful of physicists, I can't guess.

Why haven't I discerned more evidence of Bhim's presence at the hotel? Does he maintain a low profile to keep the limelight focused solely on the Devi? Is he holed up in a secret section along with his armory and his men? Wouldn't locating him lead me to Karun as well?

I make a mental inventory of the parts of the hotel I haven't explored: the guestroom floors in the towering front wing, the arcade of onetime salons and boutiques next to the lobby, the disco dormitory in the basement. Then there's the half-complete annex behind the garden enclosure, which Chitra says has remained unoccupied ever since one of the shoddily built floors collapsed inside. A small conference center stands near the badminton courts, along with a shorter building, perhaps a gym, by its side. More structures under construction loom hazily in the rear—to check everything, my parole would have to last well into the night.

But perhaps I needn't go down my list. Perhaps Bhim's Khakis can lead me to him. They're sprinkled rather sparsely throughout the hotel, with the exception of the restaurant coffee bar, where they swarm around the food like insects. Like *ants*, more precisely, I think—why not track them to get to their anthill?

A little reconnaissance reveals a good number of them peeling off towards the annex. So I take Guddi past the garden for a little stroll in that direction as well. The building is drab, almost ascetically plain, as if to atone for the Indica's over-the-top excesses. Dark windows with stingy panes of glass more befitting an office complex stare out from between concrete strips. Even the side facing the sea has no balconies. The project, announced in the first few flush days of the hotel opening, looks like it stalled even before the war started. Spikes of metal pierce through the unfinished top—after all this time, only three and a half floors stand completed. Belying Chitra's claims of tottering construction, these floors look quite sturdy, well-fortified.

The entrance actually lies on the other side of the wall enclosing the pool and garden courtyard, which further perks my interest. The barrier means that annex occupants can be kept quarantined, away from hotel residents. The locked metal grille built into this wall is unguarded—a swipe with Chitra's card opens it. Ahead, though, two Khakis slouch against the building doorway, engaged in casual conversation. As we near, they briskly pick up their rifles. "Where are you going?" they demand in unison, clearly annoyed we have caught them chatting.

Neither my "open sesame" card nor my Devi-level security clearance impresses them. "You need special authorization to enter this building." When I ask them from whom, they simply glare, as if this will clarify what they've said.

Guddi steps in with such a spirited try that I feel ashamed at underestimating her. "If you think Devi ma is going to forgive you two pups for disobeying her command, you have another thought coming. Just yesterday, she had an attendant's ears cut off—he didn't hear her order, that's all." She snips at a guard with scissor-like fingers, so close to his ear, he backs away.

"I'm sorry, sister. What to do? Nobody is allowed in without permission—the order comes from Bhim kaka himself."

"So if Devi ma herself came, you wouldn't let her in either? What if I fetch her now and see what your Bhim kaka says?"

The guards look down sheepishly. Although they hold their ground, Bhim's name confirms this is his den. "Devi ma would burn you to ashes if we reported you for this," Guddi calls out as I pull her away.

GUDDI WANTS TO GO complain to Devi ma and return with reinforcements, but I nix this idea, since it would alert Sarita about my lead. "Devi ma's already been so generous, let's not trouble her anymore. Let's try to get in ourselves."

So instead of returning through the metal gate, we duck behind a hedge and circle back to the annex. The entire ground floor is wrapped in concrete, with the occasional window, sealed and brooding, embedded as an afterthought. I'm struck by the bunker-like look of the building—hardly a design to appeal to tourists. A recessed side entryway leads to a door which, in addition to a card reader, bears a sturdy, old-fashioned padlock. We discover two more doors in the rear, similarly secured.

I'm wondering how we can create a diversion and slip in past the guards when I realize there has to be another entrance: the doors we've seen are all much too narrow to get beds and other large furniture through. Could there be another level beneath us? I draw Guddi back to the rear of the building and pull myself up chin-high to peer over the wall that runs past. Sure enough, we're at an elevation—a driveway down below cuts toward us through a small compound. Unfortunately, I don't see any steps—jumping seems the only way down.

What to do about Guddi? Certainly, I don't want her by my side when I find Karun. But leaving her behind presents its own danger, since she might go back and report my whereabouts. The wall decides for us: raised on a diet of village parathas since birth, Guddi is unable to hoist her four-foot-ten body to the top. "Stay here until I return," I tell her, hoping she'll obey for at least an hour. I jack myself up all the way on my arms, then swing a leg over to straddle the wall.

"Gaurav bhaiyya," Guddi yells, just as I lower myself on the other side and hang by my fingertips. "Gaurav bhaiyya, Gaurav bhaiyya, we should have brought Shyamu along. Then he could have lifted me up in his trunk and sat me on the wall." She pauses for a second. "Would you mind if I go check how he's doing? I promise to return by two."

What an excellent idea to keep her out of trouble! I assure her there's no need to hurry back, she can spend as much time with Shyamu as she wants. "In fact, why don't you try to sneak him out to the beach again?—I'm sure he'd like that." As Guddi squeals in appreciation, I yell goodbye and release my grip on the wall.

14

I ONCE READ A BOOK CONSISTING SOLELY OF A CHARACTER'S thoughts as he fell from a cliff. Apparently, in the time it takes to hit the ground, an entire lifetime can be relived. Being airborne reminds me of my own unlaunched memoir—what a perfect interlude to dissect my childhood this would have been! I could lay bare the vulnerability of the Jazter soul, recap my great and poignant love for Karun. The last primarily for my own benefit—to remember again why I'm so witlessly hurtling down to my doom.

So here I am, moonstruck lover turned action hero—Superman plunging through the air, Jaz Bond dropping into the villain's lair. (Perhaps I could write my Jazternama as a comic strip, ensure the first bestseller after the apocalypse.) For a moment, I lie stunned on the ground. Not from the fall, but from the sight of the two vans parked in a bay under the wall. The first has its back door open—a stack of boxes lies beside it on a pallet. It's the second one, though, that leaves me agape: white and compact, a blue stripe runs across its side, as sharp as a laser ray.

Ever since Colaba, I've had to keep my doubts tightly bottled, accept the notion of finding Karun as an article of faith. I allow myself a moment of jubilation at this evidence I'm closing in. More good fortune: wooden crates prop open the large metal doors of the loading bay. I slip inside—almost immediately, another door blocks my way. This one isn't padlocked, it just bears the familiar electronic locking mechanism. Will the Devi's powers work so far from her domain?

I swipe the card through the slot. Not much happens. The lock makes an anemic whirring noise, which quickly fades.

I try again, with a silent prayer to my Laddoo Queen, showering her with all the sweets in the world. This time, the lock whirs more enthusiastically and opens with a click.

A bare bulb illuminates the passage. Boxes of supplies line the walls—I tear a few open, and find bottles of water, tins of baked beans, tomato soup, fruit cocktail. There's no can opener, so I take some deep swigs of water to try to cure my sudden hunger pangs. (All I've been offered since morning is the glass of "nectar" I turned down.) A large chamber ahead houses even more boxes, containing not only foodstuff, but also such essentials as blankets and medical kits. I count at least a dozen small doors, all identical, built into the walls—metal-forged and tightly sealed, they resemble the hatches in a ship. The one I try opens when I pull down and twist the lever handle, which is fortunate, since just then, the sound of someone wheeling a cart comes from the corridor ahead. I barely have enough time to scoot through the door and squeeze it shut.

Groping around the wall, I find a light switch, which turns another naked bulb on. The room around me, little more than an alcove, is crammed with so many boxes that I almost don't notice the steps leading down. The level below turns out to be much more rugged, like a cave shoveled out of the ground. Chunks of rock protrude right through the roughly slapped-on plaster in spots. A central opening leads to a multitude of peripheral pods, ones in which any attempt at finish or décor has been abandoned, and a burrowing animal might feel quite at home. Most contain cots, complete with mattresses and pillows, a few the odd table or chair. In one, I even spot a television set sitting unplugged on the ground.

Could this be a post-apocalyptic colony, for survivors to wait out the nuclear winter? A fine crush of dirt drizzles down on me as I walk around. I try not to make too much noise, lest I bring the whole place (and with it mankind's future) crumbling down.

I retreat to the safety of the upper alcove. There's no way to tell if the person I heard still lurks outside the heavy steel door. I turn the lever, count to three, and cautiously poke my head out. The chamber is deserted. I hop out, then continue along the passageway, until it ends a short way down at the double doors of an elevator. I blow on my card and rub it between my palms, hoping the Devi's magic hasn't been all used up. I'm in luck—a single swipe, and the doors part, as if the elevator has been waiting patiently for me on this floor all along.

Judging by the buttons numbered all the way up to twenty, the construction has an ambitious way to go. The "G" level surely swarms with Khakis, so the choice is between the numbered floors. I decide to start at the top and push four (will the elevator pop out of its sleeve since the building ends at three and a half floors?). The doors close and we begin to rise—how ironic that I was *falling* into danger just a few minutes ago. I try to channel the steeliness of Superman, the *sangfroid* of Bond. If only I'd made some excuse to stop by Guddi's room and retrieve my gun.

The doors open without warning on "1." To reveal not a battery of leering trigger-happy Khakis, but a waiter manning the entrance to a banquet hall. The strums of a sitar invite me out, lulling away any notions of danger lurking around. After the concrete and bare earth in the basement, I'm surprised by the feel of carpet under my feet, the sight of green and gold birds (peacocks, I think) taking flight on tapestries. The lushly planted garden visible through the large picture window seems particularly incongruous, given the building's fortress-like exterior. It takes me a moment to realize I'm gazing at a blown-up photograph.

"You're just in time, sahib," the waiter says with a bow. His turban tilts towards me, as flamboyantly plumed as a cockatoo's comb. "We were wondering if anyone else would make it for lunch." He unhooks a metal-detecting wand from the wall. "I hope you don't mind, but we have to check anyone new." He scans my body—I guess I wouldn't have gotten away with the gun after all.

Inside, more peacocks adorn the walls. I half expect a posse of Khakis to leap out from behind them and surround me with weapons drawn. Instead, I notice some of the diners are women—even a few children run around. However, I can't spot Karun—at least not in my quick visual sweep of the room. "This way, sir," the waiter says, and ushers me to an empty place at a round table. "They've already cleared the buffet, but I can bring your food here if you tell me what you'd prefer."

"Dosas," the man seated next to me recommends, pointing at the remnants on his plate. "The chutney's fresh and spicy today—Devi ma must have decided to donate some of the coconuts she gets." I nod to the waiter, who closes his eyes to convey the astuteness of my choice, then gracefully withdraws.

"You're new here," my neighbor remarks. "I didn't realize the van was still bringing people in." He introduces himself as Professor Das, from the microbiology department at Kalina. "I've been here almost since the beginning, so I can answer any questions you might have. For instance, in case you're wondering, the food here is great, as you'll discover in a minute."

The dosa *is* very good, the potatoes redolent with tamarind and curry leaf, the wrapping crisp enough to shatter into pieces as I dig in. So good, in fact, that I wonder if this could all be a meticulously arranged setup—the Khakis masquerading as diners, the potatoes drugged to knock me out. Will I wake up in Bhim's lair, my body stretched on a rack, my digits clamped in thumbscrews? There's little recourse if that's to be my fate, except to eat up.

Professor Das introduces the others. "That's Dr. Jayant from Lohan Chemicals beside you, and next to him, Dr. Sethi, one of Mumbai University's premier mathematicians." I realize, as he goes around the table, that I've hit the Noah's Ark of techies—surely this has to be where Karun is housed. Behind Dr. Deepender, the mechanical engineer from IIT whose hand I reach out to shake, are the rows of banquet tables. Is Karun at one of them, his back towards me, his face obscured?

The thought fills me with an urgency to scan the room more thoroughly for him. I interrupt Das mid-sentence, saying I need to make a quick trip to the bathroom. Even though he clearly points it out, I wind through all the tables on the way there, as if confused about the location. But my search disappoints—I don't find Karun.

"You must try this lassi, Dr. Pradhan," Das says upon my return, and pours me a glass from a jug. More drugs? I wonder, but it's so refreshingly cold that I take several gulps. "So tell me, did they pick you up, or did you heed the call?" I'm not sure what I should answer, so I reply I was picked up. Das nods understandingly. "Just like most of us. Some complain about it, but I tell them to see it as an honor, that we've been chosen as the cream of the crop." He looks pointedly around as he says this, as if aiming his words at the table at large. "Safe and well-fed in the middle of a war—what more could one want?" As if on cue, the waiter delicately lays another dosa in front of me with a pair of tongs.

So far, the other diners have stared down impassively at their plates, but now Dr. Sethi breaks their silence by asking what I do. Obviously, I must be a scientist if picked up by the van, but with so many fields represented at the table, I have to answer carefully, to avoid being exposed. I finally settle on geologist, giving my institution as the University of Lucknow, which I hope will be obscure enough. "I didn't think they even had a geology department," Sethi says, frowning at me. Das quickly interjects to say he's heard they just started one. I nod in vigorous agreement—who knew?

The large monitor suspended above the buffet table blinks on before Sethi can pepper me with more questions. "It's Bhim," Das whispers. "He likes to address us whenever he comes to the hotel." The face that fills the screen looks nothing like the blood-spattered visage I remember from the grainy video of the Haji Ali massacre, or the one spouting rabid exhortations to violence on the nationwide rath yatra. Rather, it is calm and clean-cut, the eyebrows neatly trimmed, the hair carefully coiffed. Could he be tripping on his Emperor Ashoka persona again?

"My friends, I hope you're having a nice afternoon." His manner is congenial, his voice so soothing, it's almost mellifluous. He announces that the refurbished gym has opened on the second floor, that more laptops will arrive shortly, though the internet remains down. "Don't forget the roof garden—there's no better way to start your morning than a walk there. And afterwards, you can come have a dosa—we'll start serving them for breakfast as well since you like them so much."

He continues in this hotel-manager vein for a while, as if explaining the guest facilities at a resort. Just when I'm expecting him to announce the Jacuzzi and shuffleboard hours, he starts describing the finishing touches being put on the "paradise" at the subterranean level. "Your own television, your own private bedroom, not to mention pantries bursting with delicious food and drink. We'll finally open it up tomorrow, so you'll be able to see for yourself."

Surely he couldn't be referring to the crumbling bunkers I stumbled upon in the basement? Apparently so, because he quickly mentions a "trial run" on the nineteenth, "just in case there's any problem." "It's more for your own peace of mind—all these empty threats and rumors floating around. You're the most brilliant intellects in all of Mumbai—my responsibility is to keep you happy and sound."

He pledges to reunite the assembled diners with their loved ones. "Some we've already brought together, others will have to wait a bit. We've found many of your spouses, your children—gathered them up in special units. Be assured they're getting five-star treatment—I promise we'll keep them safe."

Bhim concludes with a burst of declarations, claiming that he only believes in freedom, that he only asks for a commitment to the country, that despite what people may have heard, he doesn't insist on any particular religion or philosophy. "One day this war will end, my friends, and we will begin to rebuild. Let's all look together towards that day and in a united voice shout Jai Hind."

"Jai Hind," the crowd replies, and I can't help sensing something forced in the response, even though it is accompanied by a ripple of applause.

Bhim's soft-spoken manner leaves me a tad disoriented. Would it have been too much to expect at least a little fanaticism, a bit of anti-Muslim rhetoric? Perhaps my image of a betel-chewing heavy was over-the-top, but surely Bhim's résumé of exploits warrants someone more flamboyantly unhinged?

"A true visionary," Das declares. People nod in agreement around the table, and again, I get that Stepford Wife impression—perhaps they *do* drug the dosas after all. "Tell me, are you married, Dr. Pradhan? Do you have a family? If so, you can rest assured Bhim will do his best to arrange a reunification."

Sethi snorts. "Perhaps Dr. Pradhan should look around and count the number of women and children he sees."

"I'm sorry, Dr. Sethi—are you trying to ask our new guest something?"

"Yes, I'm asking him to count the number of reunited families. It's more a threat, isn't it, this promise of reunification? To let us know he has them in his clutches, just like he has us."

Das looks taken aback. "Dr. Sethi, what are you saying? You know Bhim is doing the best anyone could. Would you like to try yourself, find someone without his help?"

"That would hardly be possible, would it? I'm stuck here, like the rest of us, whether I like it or not. Whatever happens tomorrow or the day after, whether or not the bomb falls."

"You know that's not true. We all stay voluntarily." Das turns to me. "Everyone here is free to leave. Bhim just requests you let him know in advance."

"Yes, in advance. Like Moorthy, like Sinha. Is that what happened to them? They were complaining so much, so Bhim stamped their passports and set them free?"

"Surely you're not suggesting that Bhim—?"

"What if I am? Will I be next? Is that what you're going to threaten me with? Another knock in the middle of the night, and nobody will see me again?" Sethi gets up so abruptly that his chair topples over backwards. "Well I don't care anymore. I've had it with this." A waiter hastens to set the chair back upright as Sethi flings down his napkin and strides off.

The other scientists seem to freeze in their seats. Das smiles at me reassuringly. "Don't mind our banter. Some of our colleagues haven't been well lately, so they're staying in their rooms. Like the ones Dr. Sethi mentioned. Others just come for the earlier shift, so we miss them. It's really nothing. Now about your family members—are they still in Lucknow?"

I cook up suitable answers for the questions that follow, but something about Sethi's words keeps looping through my mind. In a flash it comes to me—the name Moorthy. He was the scientist mentioned by the guesthouse keeper in Bandra, the one kidnapped along with Karun. "I'm sorry, but did I hear correctly that you have someone here by the name of Moorthy? Doesn't he work at the Institute for Nuclear Physics?"

Das seems instantly wary. "Perhaps. Why? Do you know him?"

"Not him, but a colleague of his—Karun Anand—we've been friends for years. I was half expecting he might be here as well, but of course he's not."

"Dr. Anand?" Das adjusts his glasses to peer at me as if I'm a biological specimen, finally come into focus. "As a matter of fact—"

STANDING IN FRONT of Karun's room, I'm struck by how doors have played such a pivotal role through our relationship. The ones Karun has closed in my face, or tried to escape through, or entered when he wasn't expected. What will I discover behind this one? Where will it lead us? Das has assured me Karun simply prefers to eat in his room, but what if he's been mistreated, lying inside hurt? I knock, standing aside from the peephole so he can't see who it is. When there is no reply, I knock again. Then I remember my magic swipe card—it smoothly unlocks the door, and I step in.

The curtains are drawn, but I recognize Karun at once on the bed from his familiar sleeping position. One hand folded at his side, the other resting on his pillow, above his head. I stand over him, checking for bruises or trauma—he looks unharmed, angelic. A sheet drapes his waist, revealing the luxurious swathe of hair on his chest—a pillow on which I want to rest my head, a carpet on which I would fly anywhere. The corridor outside recedes, the war wages in another city somewhere. "Karun," I whisper, and when he doesn't awaken, bend down and kiss him lightly on the lips.

His eyes open, and focus sleepily for an instant. Then, with a strangled sound, he scrabbles away, falling to the floor in the process. "Who are you? Stay away," he cries out, kicking off the blanket entangling his legs. He's on his feet and heading for the door (how tiringly predictable) when I manage to find the light switch.

"Karun. Stop. It's me, Jaz." I position myself under the ceiling fixture so he can get a good look.

"Jaz?" He lets me draw close enough to embrace him. Through his chest, I feel the thump of blood, the tautness of muscles primed for escape. I'm careful not to squeeze as tight as I want to, lest he feel I'm trying to restrain him. Just as I think my time's running out and he'll surely pull away, he slumps into my arms as if he's decided not to resist. "I thought it was the guards. They came for Moorthy next door—I heard them."

"Shhh, I just startled you. You were asleep—are you OK? They haven't hurt you in any way, have they?"

"No, I'm fine. Sometimes I feel I just nap all day. That and my yoga—there's little else to do." He squeezes closer, buries his head in my shoulder.

A part of me knows we have to leave at once, to tarry is perilous, the Khakis may already be on their way. But I've waited all this time, persevered so long, with just a craving, a hope, an image. I allow my body to melt into his, between the bed and the door, under the ceiling light that blesses our embrace. For a moment I wish would stretch out forever, we are tranquil.

Then the inevitable questions unloosen within him. "What are you doing here, Jaz? How could you have found me? I can't believe it—there's no logical way."

This is the juncture I've dreaded. I cannot relate the true saga of my odyssey without revealing that Sarita, ensconced within the hotel walls, waits for him with long-suffering wifely devotion. Lying, on the other hand, could lead to a minefield that might blow my account at any step. "I'll tell you when we're less pressed—it's too fantastic a tale."

I pull Karun towards the door, but he unhooks his arm. "You followed me somehow, didn't you? You must have, right from the first day. Step by step, though I left at dawn—that's how you're here today." He shakes his head in wonder. "All the times I begged you to stop harassing me. Even when you saw I had my own life to live."

I try steering him out once more, promising to discuss everything later, but he draws back a step. "Why hunt me down like this? When you know I'm just trying to get away?" His voice becomes angry, plaintive.

By now I can see he won't accompany me unless I refresh the map of the past for him. "Get away from what, exactly, Karun? I'm hardly so formidable a force that you had to make such a dramatic break for it. All you needed to do was look me in the eye and say you didn't feel anything. It's not me you're trying to escape, Karun—it's yourself. Just be honest for once—you're scared you'll give in, that your true feelings will prevail."

"We've been through all this before," he says wearily. "There's no need to—"

"Do you know how much danger I've put myself through to get to you? Bombed and shot at and almost executed? Perhaps you should ask yourself *why* I'd do this. Why I'd come here, into the lair of Bhim himself, even though he'd kill me in an instant for being Muslim." My voice breaks, my eyes tear up with frustration.

Karun doesn't say anything. We stand in the room, the ceiling light getting harsher by the instant. An overwhelming sense of exhaustion overcomes me. How much of my life have I spent pursuing Karun? How much more must I spend before he relents? I feel my Jazter persona cracking, my Bond incarnation slipping away. This is what I have been reduced to, and I'm not really sure how to rescue myself. "I suppose there's no point asking you to come with me if you can't find it in your heart to give voice to what's there." It's finally my turn to head towards the door, alone.

"Jaz, wait."

Had I written the scene, he'd have run and hurled himself at the door before I could reach it. But I suppose that would be out of character—his words are enough of a departure as it is. I stride over and kiss him. He holds back only for a second or two before allowing himself to fully join in. We close our eyes and the next instant, are young and brash once more. Racing through parks, playing with toy trains, lying in each other's arms on balconies and barsatis again.

The threat of danger recedes to the sidelines as we fall into bed, still kissing. I realize how much I have craved his body, how much I have missed it. The way my mouth fits the hollow of his throat, the press of my belly against his waist—a scent, a taste, returning from the mists of nostalgia, my very own madeleine. I take off my shirt and rub my chest against his in that familiar long-ago way, smile to myself when curls of our hair snag again. We divest ourselves of the rest of our clothes and lie there, savoring the contact between even our mundane parts—toes, knees, clavicles, shins. Already, I look greedily beyond his body—I want another shot at an entire lifetime with him.

And then Sarita's shadow wafts in. I see it first in his eyes—her memory flickers across his face. She's not so assertive a presence that I couldn't divert attention with a good roll in the hay. But I hesitate, handicapped by a sudden affliction of guilt. Wouldn't Karun want to know about her waiting just a few buildings away? Am I taking advantage not only of Sarita, but also of him? Is withholding information (lying, some might label it) the best way to rekindle a relationship? The nape of my neck tingles—Sarita might as well be peering down at us like a mural from the ceiling. "Perhaps this isn't such a good idea," I say, hardly believing the words as they emerge from my mouth. "We need to get going, figure out our escape."

Karun seems relieved to agree. "There may be a way out through the basement." He starts looking for his clothes and covering up his body with distressing alacrity—socks, undershirt, shirt. "The bomb shelters there are the one area they keep off-limits, stupidly enough—we're free to roam the building everywhere else." He's rummaging for his briefs, describing Bhim's crazy utopia project, when I pull him back into bed—despite the advancing danger, the Jazter needs to fortify himself with at least another nip of physical contact. I love you, I want to declare, but only if I can be sure of hearing him say it as well. Instead, I squeeze my thighs around him and kiss the back of his head.

He reciprocates with a quick half-kiss before spotting his pants and slipping off the bed. I gather my own clothes—it's time to cover the ol' Jazter as well. "So tell me, how *did* you get into the hotel?" Karun asks, still searching for his underwear, as he holds his trousers by the belt.

"I rode in on an elephant."

He laughs. "The ones collecting money from the crowds, that Bhim funds his operations with? And how much did you have to pay the elephant to find what room I was in?"

"Actually, the elephant only told me how to get to the dining room. It was lunchtime, he said, so you'd surely be there."

Karun shakes his head. "I've stopped going. It's safest that way. You never know who might be spying on you—too many of Bhim's men. That's the mistake Moorthy made—spouting off against everything, never could stop being a firebrand. After he vanished, I just started getting the food delivered to my room—thankfully, they're willing to do that. I hope you left once you couldn't find me, didn't stick around to chat."

"Well, I *had* to chat a little, to find you. But only with science and engineering types, all of them. Let's see—there was Sethi and Jayant and Deepender and Das. He's the one who gave me your room number— seemed to know you quite well."

Karun stares at me. "Das? The stubby one with the mustache? He's the most snake-like of them all—has his fingers in everything, from top to bottom. I wouldn't be surprised if he personally engineered Moorthy's disappearance." He frantically throws off the pillows from the bed, finally uncovering his underwear. "We should have left right away as you said—quick, get dressed."

I'm fishing my own underwear out from the pile of clothes I've assembled when the door lock makes its familiar whirring sound. It opens, and two guards burst in, followed by Das. All three stop and gawk at us, flustered by our state of undress. Finally, Das speaks. "Really, Dr. Anand. I never would have guessed." His eyes focus directly on what I'm trying to hide. "With a Muslim, no less."

THROUGH HIS YEARS of forays across beaches and parks, through his entire illustrious career as a shikari, one unsung achievement sets the Jazter apart. Except for that single time with Harjeet, he's never been caught with his pants down. Which is why Das and company's appearance is such a shock. I scramble to enrobe myself, even though the secret, so to speak, is already out. Perhaps I should have flaunted things, stared the villains down. Surely Bond would have acted nonchalant, proud.

Despite his attempt at wryness, Das is visibly relieved once we are dressed. He glares at the guards to arrest their smirking comments, then gets very chatty, trying to smooth over the situation, perhaps. "We'd been expecting your friend," he tells Karun, as if talking about an extra dinner guest. "The guards at the front entrance alerted us, and we saw him looking around through the garden cameras as well." He turns to me and inquires whether the journey to the dining room went smoothly enough. "We had to figure out your intentions, find out whom you came to see, where you went. Sorry to barge in like that, but the microphone in the room wasn't working very well."

He leads us to Bhim's suite on the third floor with a profusion of "This way's" and "Mind your step's," his manner so collegial that he might be accompanying us to a university colloquium. "You're lucky Bhim's here today—he has so many other centers to tend." The outer room is set up as an office, complete with computers and file cabinets—a secretary informs us we'll have to wait awhile, Bhim is busy with someone else. "Always a problem when you come to see him," Das laments.

So we sit there, like in a doctor's waiting room—one sorely lacking in magazines, but with guards at the ready to ensure we keep our appointment. Das gabs on, about the weather, the city, even the physics Karun researches—interspersed with his babble, I notice crafty attempts to tease out information of more consequence. He's very interested in our relationship—whether we know each other in a professional, or only the biblical sense. He tries to ferret out who the maiden accompanying me to the annex was, where she might be now, how I got into the hotel. He asks such keen questions about my purported geological expertise that I'm forced to confess my true field is finance. "Why didn't you say so?" he exclaims. "I could have introduced you to our economists sitting at the very next table. We have other fields here too—Bhim's been collecting the brightest and best in all of them."

We wait almost forty minutes. I keep glancing at Karun, wanting to sit closer, to hold him in my arms for comfort, for reassurance. The Jazter has paid no heed to danger all this time, but now that he's found his love, fear has also found him. With it, an emerging wistfulness about the future, a seeping dread that we may not make it. Karun's face displays neither the anxiety nor the yearning I feel—I can tell he is meditating to quiet himself.

The door to the inner chamber bursts open, and a pair of Khakis emerge, propping up a man between them. Blood trickles down his brow and around both sides of his nose from a cut on his forehead. "That's Sarahan, Bhim's chief commander," Das whispers. "He looks after practically everything, so much so that I've been lending him a hand. I wonder if——" He calls out as the guards go past. "What happened, Sarahan kaka? Are you all right?"

The inquiry revives the bleeding man, who pulls himself free and lunges for the door. But the guards tackle him almost at once. They punch him till he's quiet, then drag him across the doorstep into the corridor outside.

A buzzer goes off on the secretary's table. She presses a red button and the sound stops. "Bhim kaka will see you now," she announces.

BHIM STANDS AT A DESK with his back towards us——the great leader himself, absorbed in the contemplation of his own greatness. Despite myself, I feel a slight frisson——a bit like catching a glimpse of a film star or president. Except one who looks less imposing in person, shorter than expected. Could this be worthy enough a villain for a Jaz Bond script? The room around him is disappointingly bereft of props——no tigers a-growling or skinned on the floor, no map on the wall charting world control. A few more guards, yes, but where are the thumbscrews, the torture rack, the electrodes? "Come in," he says, and turns around. I look into his eyes: They seem to reveal only affability as windows to his soul.

Then I notice the red on his cuff, the blood on the floor, the baton on the table splintered in two. Das takes it all in as well, and his curiosity spills out. "We saw Sarahan leaving. Did something happen with him?"

Bhim ignores the question. "So you're the gentlemen they spied snooping around. I suppose I should be honored——people normally try to leave, not get in. Were you hoping to assassinate me? Is that how I can be of assistance?" He turns to Das. "Have you found who sent them? I thought there was only one, not two of them."

"There *is* only one, the one on the left. Apparently, he came by himself. Not for you but Dr. Anand, next to him."

"He came to kill one of our scientists?"

"No, not kill. Just to be with him." Das shifts uncomfortably. "They seem to be *together*. Like boyfriend-girlfriend."

It's the perfect opportunity for Bhim to display his mettle as a villain. He could laugh derisively, he could rage and froth, he could ham his way through a flamboyant bigotry pageant. Instead, he lapses deep into thought (so cinematically listless), as if sifting through his memory banks for a past frame of reference. "No, I don't believe it," he says at last, shaking his head. "It's too preposterous, they're up to something else. You surprised them, and this is the first story they could think of to dupe you with."

"We, uh, found them naked. Both Dr. Anand and his friend. Gaurav Pradhan, that's what he calls himself, even though he's really Muslim."

Bhim's frown deepens, but eases the next second—a smile begins to play thinly at his lips. "I suppose it could be true, then. The vice of the Pathans—not to mention the Turks, the Arabs and the rest of their tangled sects. Though I have to say I'm startled. Startled and disappointed. You, Dr. Anand—a Hindu, a scientist no less. Do you know how much we've spent bringing you here, feeding you, keeping you safe? Is this how you repay our investment?"

"Your investment?" Karun bursts out. "You call kidnapping someone an investment?"

Before he can proceed with his rant, I smoothly cut in. "He's not to blame. I'm the one after him, forcing myself time and again. He didn't even notice me, all the days I followed him. He couldn't have had the slightest inkling I was coming."

Bhim waves my words away. "It doesn't matter—all will become clear once we investigate. Das, make preparations for these two gentlemen. They're probably telling the truth, but we'll need to make sure, the usual way. I know, I know—I'm doing it to another one of your scientists, you're sure to protest again."

I can guess what comes next, Bhim's instruction doesn't bode well. Karun shouts at him, but words will hardly help. The Jazter is to blame for this predicament, it's up to him to get his beloved out of this mess. Otherwise, lavender love the world over must hang its head in shame.

So I fling down the get-out-of-jail-free card I've been holding so tight to my chest. "Let him go. He's married. You want me, not him."

My revelation doesn't quite have the desired bombshell effect. Bhim seems to find it amusing more than anything else. "Is that true, Dr. Anand? Do you really go both ways?" He signals to the guards as Karun angrily responds it's nobody's business. "Please, show the way to the good doctor and his *companion*."

Which leaves a final disclosure that might help, one extremely painful to make. Something that's been turning inside me, charring slowly, like on a rotisserie within. I look at Karun longingly, aware his eyes will forever fill with contempt upon hearing what I am about to say. "There's something else you should know, before you lead him anywhere. His wife is the one who brought me here—she's in the main hotel, waiting for him."

Karun looks stunned. "What? Sarita's here? And you didn't tell me? Are you crazy? Is she OK?"

"I'm sorry," I say, unable to raise my head to his stare. "She's the one I tailed, not you—she's fine, don't worry. I knew you'd want to rush to her, so I couldn't bring myself to tell you right away."

"Where is she, Jaz?—my God, I can't believe it. How low can you sink, trying to hide something like this? Each time I think I've seen your last betrayal, you find a way to do it again. What story did you feed her?—all your old lying tricks."

As I stammer to explain myself, to assure Karun I haven't revealed anything, to deflect the rancor emanating from him, Bhim laughs grandly, theatrically, in the manner finally befitting a villain. "A lovers' spat. Well, well. Perhaps we *will* have to separate you two after all. Das, it looks like we'll only need a single spot, to host our Muslim friend. Though we should check out the story first, make sure Dr. Anand's wife really is in the hotel. Why don't you take him over and see if you can get them happily together again? We'll present them at breakfast tomorrow as one of the success stories of our family reunification program."

Perhaps it dawns on Karun what fate Bhim might have in store for me, because the anger drains from his face. He begins to appeal on my behalf, plead that I be allowed to accompany him back to the hotel. I am buoyed by the desperation in his voice, cheered by the knowledge he still cares. "Why not let him go when you know he's completely harmless? It's not like you have to kill everyone from the wrong religion."

Bhim's smile disappears. He stares at Karun, then replies in a quiet voice. "Is that what you take me as, a murderer, a bigot? Do you really think that's my goal, to clear the country of every Muslim?" Even Das gapes, momentarily confounded by the question.

"I merely meant—"

"Yes, I know what you meant, what you call me, you and everyone else. Bhim the butcher, Bhim the fanatic, Bhim, who's so bloodthirsty that he slaughters innocent women and children. But does anyone ever bother to ask why? Does anyone understand the dharma I must fulfill? Look at the world around us, torn to bits. Do people realize I'm the only one balancing our fate?"

Bhim starts holding forth about how the country has to "stem the tide" as he puts it, how the Hindus are the only remaining hope, the sole standing bulwark, against the terrorist religion (not mentioned by name, but with a meaningful look at me) sweeping the entire planet. He claims to have the backing of not only the CIA, but also Russia, Israel, and the "Asian Secret Service." He invokes his favorite king Ashoka, but in an unexpected nod, the Muslim emperor Akbar as well (what a lovely gift my parents' opus would make for him), pointing out that both rulers had to go through similar crusades of violence before achieving enough stability to renounce bloodshed. "People look at my campaigns and tell me I'm too cruel, too merciless. But the enemy rears up every time I lower my guard, spreads its mayhem at the slightest show of lenience. Then the same people go around complaining Bhim has softened too much, that he can no longer muster the required ruthlessness."

I'm about to give his performance a B-plus in terms of Bond-worthiness, when he adds just the right touch of looniness to take it over the top. Still chafing, apparently, from the charge of annihilating Muslims, he defends himself by underscoring how many *Hindus* he kills. "Just yesterday, I had to give the order to wipe out a whole gathering of them at Chowpatty," he says with a sad and remorseful pride, and I wonder if he's talking of the beach carnage I witnessed while following Sarita. "Do people ever take *that* into account in their calculations?"

After that, Bhim launches into a litany of wrongs—how quickly people assume the worst of him, how slow they are to show appreciation. "They still believe I'm the one who spread the Pakistani bomb rumors— just because no other leader could be that computer-savvy, they say. Then they turn around and blame me for just the opposite: cutting off their web and phone service. Forgetting that without TwitterSpeak, I can no longer summon the multitudes that used to be just a message away." He seems particularly chagrined about his elite guests, who clamor "like spoiled and greedy children" for laptops and internet access, while taking for granted such luxuries as the uninterrupted electric supply. "Do you know how difficult it was to seize the grid? I had to lead the charge on the Khopoli power station myself." He's tired of questions about the nuclear shelter delays, exhausted by the ambitions of his subordinates, whom he must keep constantly in check, fed up with catering to Devi ma's antics, who's much more of a handful than he anticipated. "All the backers I have to juggle on top of this, all the contacts I have to maintain. Nobody can conceive what a thankless job I have."

I'm wondering whether he's angling for our sympathy, and more bizarrely, why I actually feel a smidgen of it, when his tone shifts. "But there I go again. You must be thinking, look at Bhim with all his complaints—a sure lack of will, a sure sign of weakness. Forgetting what I read somewhere—that all great leaders experience such internal conflict."

Karun seizes upon his words to renew his rescue attempt, complimenting Bhim on his wisdom, reassuring him about his image, suggesting that to free me would be a sign of strength, not weakness. But Bhim sadly shakes his head. "I have to do what Ashoka might in such a situation, there's very little choice I have. When it came to what's best for his kingdom, he never hesitated, never took a chance." He glances at me for support, as if his logic is so implacable that I will happily sacrifice myself.

When Karun persists, Bhim flares up. "Haven't you been listening to anything I said? Here I am trying to save the world, and all you can do is prattle on about this one degenerate." He reaches for his baton, picking up the bloody halves and trying to fit them together. "Perhaps I was wrong about you—perhaps I need to knock some sense into your head and send you along with your Muslim friend."

It's time for the Jazter to step in for another save. "There's no need for that. His wife is waiting at the hotel. I'm ready to be taken away."

"It really is for the best," Bhim says, calm and smiling again. Karun lunges at Bhim, but a guard seizes him. "Don't worry, I promise—I won't lay a hand on your friend." Karum struggles to free himself, his cries getting increasingly desperate as I'm led away. Bhim gives me a little bow, then folds his hands in namaste, like a very karmic diner acknowledging the selflessness of a steak.

IT LOOKS LIKE THE worst has transpired, even if it's a tad clichéd. The Jazter seems set to follow a long list of ancestors who've willingly laid down their lives in stories and films. The homosexual who must swallow the big enchilada in the finale to pay for his sins.

But has the Jazter really sinned? He's enjoyed himself, to be sure, even been a bit of a cad as far as Karun and Sarita go (though don't they excuse this in love and war?). No matter, this gesture should more than suffice to compensate. The Jazter nobly offering himself up so they can live out the rest of their hetero fairy tale. Somehow, the picture leaves me less than fulfilled. The joys of martyrdom are definitely overrated.

The guards bring me down to the basement. Clearly, I lack Guddi's talent at instilling fear, since they ignore my demands to notify Devi ma, and actually titter when I threaten to sic her on them. To add to this insult, they find my Open Sesame card and confiscate it. They leave me locked in a nuclear survival pod, where I contemplate my future, soon to be abbreviated. The past also engages: I count all the crossroads in my life at which I could have averted my coming fate.

I'm up to juncture nine or ten at least when I hear a rustle from the shadows behind. "I see they've sent me some company," a voice says. I make out a figure seated on a cot in the anterior of the space. "I'm Sarahan. Bhim's deputy. Until this afternoon, that is."

I begin to introduce myself as Gaurav, then pause. It hardly matters now, does it? "I'm Jaz," I tell him. "Ijaz Hassan, that's the full name."

"A Muslim!" Sarahan exclaims, and peers at me, undoubtedly to check out what member of my tribe would be stupid enough to blunder into this place. *Love-struck*, not *stupid*, I feel like correcting him. Although I guess the two are one and the same.

I examine him as well, especially the wound on his forehead, which by now is dry and caked. He appears recovered enough—in fact, my presence in the pod seems to energize him. He's dying to know how I ended up in Bhim's lair, so I say I came to save a friend, reveal some select highlights from the meeting upstairs. "Too bad you didn't have a gun," he tells me. "How fitting were Bhim to be killed by a Muslim!"

Sarahan relates how he used to be an engineer, how he rose through the ranks after the HRM recruited him at one of their rallies. Apparently, the train I hitched a ride on is to blame for his downfall today. "I was bringing in another cache from our depot near Churchgate—all the right palms greased as usual to ensure safe passage. Someone must have tipped off the Limbus about the cargo—I don't know who, but they ambushed the train in Mahim, ran it right off the rails. Needless to say, we lost everything, which is what got Bhim so enraged."

He starts complaining about Bhim ignoring advice, how if they'd cleaned up Mahim as Sarahan had lobbied for weeks, they'd have never lost the train. "Always the same reasons for holding off—that we need a nearby enemy region to fire up our own ranks, that it's insurance against any nuclear attack. As if the Pakistanis would care—they'd happily martyr half the Muslims in India and deliver their bombs just the same."

I try to focus Sarahan's attention on our predicament, on suggesting a way out, but he's on a roll with his gripes against his boss. "Do you know he sabotaged a prayer ceremony yesterday? Just because a rival temple dared organize it? Killed hundreds in the rampage, every one a Hindu we could have recruited. How can he have forgotten what got him this far? Which—and please don't take this the wrong way—was to massacre a lot of *Muslims*."

No offense taken, I assure him. "Now about this nuclear shelter we're in, how do we—"

"Shelter, ha! To save the city's brains, he claims. He should have just bought everyone a helmet instead, rather than this joke he's built. Do you know, if the power goes, the ventilation goes with it?" Sarahan kicks the wall and gravel falls from the ceiling like rain.

I ask if we can dig our way out, but Sarahan says it's too dangerous, the whole place might collapse and bury us. "As it is, such a miracle that the hotel still stands, that the Pakistanis haven't destroyed it. There would be bombs falling on us in an instant if our patron friends ever walked away from the protection they've promised. And what does Bhim do? He simply ignores them—it's been weeks since he's bothered to communicate. All he can do is talk about Ashoka, and now even Akbar—this obsession with how history will judge him. Our men can't help but notice his distraction—that's why they're executing things so shoddily, becoming just as erratic as him."

I'm piqued by these patrons Sarahan mentions—does he mean the CIA? He informs me I'm behind the times, that in this day and age, the CIA is passé. "It hardly matters who—the important thing is for Bhim to go—my run-in with him today has left me even more convinced. The future of the entire organization is at stake."

Which is all very well, with the Jazter delighted that the HRM has such deep thinkers looking out for it. But could we return to more immediate concerns? To repeat: Does Professor Sarahan have any ideas for escape?

"Oh, that. Well, someone's bound to come, aren't they? You can't just lock me up and think nobody will notice." He lies back on his cot, and studies the ceiling, as if the Big Picture is inscribed on it.

An hour elapses, and then another two, during which Sarahan plots out a scenario where *I* will actually be the one to assassinate Bhim. "It's perfect—we won't even alienate anyone that way—blame it all on the Muslims." I point out that nobody's come to our rescue yet, but Sarahan assures me the loyalty of his cadre is beyond question. "They'll come as soon as they figure out a strategy. It's not like Bhim will finish us off today."

Except Bhim seems determined to do precisely that, perhaps having recognized the danger Sarahan poses. The door opens to reveal a trio of guards, not the rescue team I've been promised. They want to put on handcuffs, to which Sarahan objects at first, but then agrees sportingly, as if it's all a big charade. He smiles as we're led out of the cell, even giving me a conspiratorial wink.

As we walk through the subterranean tunnel, it strikes me that Sarahan might be overly optimistic, even deluded. I can't rely on him—I need to plan my own escape. My best hope is that someone will spot me on the way and inform Devi ma of my handcuffed state. Unfortunately, we're sequestered from view in the tunnel, from which we emerge into a shed that's equally secluded. A tall animal figure with an outlandishly swollen belly looms in front of me—looking around, I notice a whole herd of them.

At first I think they are decorative sculptures, examples of folksy local craftsmanship. The statues stand perfectly still, their heads slightly cocked, as if interrupted by an unfamiliar sound in the midst of their graze. Then I notice the horn-shaped protuberances, the short stump-like limbs, the hooks on their backs attached to sturdy hooped braces. One of the animals is legless and rests on the ground like a giant egg, another is all skeleton—a woman works rolled-up newspaper into the crevices of its blackened metal frame. "The buffaloes," Sarahan says, pointing at them with his chin. "I had an inkling that's how they'd do it."

I'm not sure what he means, not immediately, not beyond the fact that they've brought us to see the buffalo-demon effigies the Devi sacrifices. The woman comes over to introduce herself as Mansi, offering us a sheet of canvas-like material spread over her outstretched arms. Noticing our cuffed hands, she holds it up for us to examine, telling us this is what they use for the buffalo exterior. "After we've squeezed as much paper and pulp as we can into the frame, we stretch this tight over the surface like a skin. It lights on fire instantly because of the ghee we smear over it." She leads us on a tour of the buffaloes, stroking their backs as if they're alive, informing us about the individual names she's given them. There's even a Shyamu—no relation, presumably, to Guddi's elephant.

I keep getting the impression, as Mansi points to the special features of each buffalo—the roominess of the belly cavity, the colors and designs painted on the sides, that she's trying to sell us something. "So?" she asks, after touting a particularly festive model with green good-luck swastikas imprinted on its forehead. "Will Birbal be the lucky one tonight?" Sarahan defers to me, and with no particular animus against Birbal, I shrug yes. Mansi beams. "Let me show you the fireworks then."

She leads us to a corner of the shed, where she removes the lids from

a row of large bins. Inside, I see tangles of rockets, strings of red crackers, atom bombs neatly packed in boxes, fire whistles glistening like
foil-covered chocolates. "Don't be shy, fill them with as many as you
like," she says, handing us each an empty bucket. I load mine as
instructed, getting a bit greedy with the spinners and fountains at the
end. Mansi nods in approval. "Those burn spectacularly—Devi ma
just loves them."

After we've set the buckets down by Birbal, Mansi tops each off
with several white bricks of camphor, whose astringent aroma reminds
me of Vicks. "For that nice sizzling effect." I must be dense, because I
don't get it even when she tells us they clean the frames thoroughly
each morning. "All very hygienic—you won't smell any trace from the
previous burning." It's only when she starts reassuring me about how
comfortable it is within that I wonder if she could possibly mean what
I think. I look at Sarahan, and he nods, as if he's been watching the
awareness flower with such aching slowness on my face.

"Don't worry," he tells me. "Remember what I said in the basement
about my men." Turning to Mansi, he compliments her on how splen-
did she's made the buffalo look. "I'm sure they're just as nice inside—I
didn't realize I'd actually get to try one myself."

Mansi blushes in delight. "I still have a pair of fire wheels left. We're
not really supposed to use them in the buffaloes, but Devi ma likes
them even more than the rockets. I'll let you have them as well."

Our actual insertion into the effigy is a decidedly unceremonious
affair. The guards lift Birbal onto a dolly, then lean a ladder against his
side, then nudge us up at gunpoint with our hands still cuffed behind
our backs. One of them flips open a trapdoor on the top and pushes
Sarahan in—I hear a groan as his body hits the base of wooden planks.
He cries out even louder when I land on top of him. As I try to wriggle
myself off his belly, a cascade of firecrackers pelts us—first one bucket,
then the other. More material comes raining down—wood shavings
and pulp this time, and I realize the guards are emptying the wastebas-
kets of burnable scrap.

The patch of sky visible through the trapdoor opening is already purple by the time we are wheeled out of the shed. I manage to flip myself over so that I lie squeezed next to Sarahan, feet to head (giving me my first true appreciation of the term "packed like sardines"). After rolling along for several minutes, during which I distinctly hear us serenaded by devotional music, our bovine chariot comes to a halt. A tackle hangs in the hole above, suspended by wires that disappear towards the looming Indica turret beyond.

At least they've left the trapdoor open for us to get some air, I think, just seconds before someone slams it closed. Bolts are drawn, fasteners snap shut, the buffalo rocks and shudders as footsteps sound on the flat of its back above. Will this be it? I wonder, as the blackness begins to stifle. I strain against my cuffs, struggle to shake the crevices of my body free of nestling fireworks (the rocket with its cone pointed at my groin proves particularly stubborn). My empty stomach churns with acid—shouldn't someone at least offer us a last mutton fry or masala chop?

"It's OK," Sarahan intones. "They'll come, don't you worry." He tries to keep his voice encouraging, but I can detect the first flurries of unease from him swirl in the dark. He starts singing (though it sounds a bit like praying) as if unencumbered by a care in the world.

We're in there for an hour at least, or perhaps it just seems that long, having to listen to Sarahan's labored vocal efforts at affecting nonchalance. I try to get my mind off my situation by thinking of Karun, but that's even worse. He lolls with Sarita by the pool sharing something frosty in a glass (the Jazter's sacrifice, already forgotten, bleaches in the past). Just when I'm all good and claustrophobic, ready to scream for the barbecue to start, I hear the bolts on the trapdoor being drawn. "See?" Sarahan says, his relief audible. "I told you they'd come."

Except it's not the much-ballyhooed rescue brigade peering down at us, but Das. "Sarahan? Everything going well down there, my friend? I know it must be a bit uncomfortable, but it's not for very long."

"Das? What are you doing here?"

"Bhim told me what happened. The train hijacked, the weapons lost, even Mura killed—what a terrible shame. I came to say how much I'm personally going to miss you—without your presence, things simply won't be the same. You may not realize this, but ever since I arrived here, I've looked up to you as a role model."

"That's very nice to hear. Now could you pull me out?"

"I want to, Sarahan, believe me, there's nothing I'd like more. But with you leaving so abruptly, and nobody else around to take your place, Bhim just appointed me of all people, put me in charge. All very spur-of-the-moment—I guess he'd heard about me helping you out—I can't very well now betray his trust. In fact, I actually came here to seek your blessing. I'm nowhere near as worthy, I know—just pray I can succeed even half as well as you did."

I hear a sharp intake of breath from Sarahan. "So it was you, then," he says, slowly. "All this time I've been racking my brain. The one who tattled to the Limbus, the one who told them to derail the train. You must have been planning this all along."

"No, of course not. How could you ever think I—?"

"Bastard. Dogfucker. And now you have the audacity to come seek my blessing? If I were free—" Sarahan heaves and thrusts next to me, raising and lowering sections of his body like an earthworm.

Das steps back a bit. When he speaks again, his voice has an injured tone. "Here I am, come to seek your blessing, and instead you heap me with such abuse? Do you know, I actually brought something for you, something to thank you for everything you've done?" He holds up a can of some sort. "Here. I'm going to leave it for you, whether you appreciate it or not." He lowers it through the hole, at the end of a rope tied around its girth.

The container alights on our bodies, straddling my thigh and Sarahan's stomach. As I adjust my leg, I feel liquid slosh within. "It's to make the transition easier," Das says. "As you've seen, Devi ma's fire can be slow and arduous."

Sarahan hears the sloshing too, and begins to curse louder. Das shakes his head. "This is gratitude? Do you know how hard it was to find, how I had to smuggle it out? Don't tell anyone, but it's a whole can of petrol, enough to explode a bus. You'll be vaporized in an instant, not burn bit by bit, not have your skin peel off."

As Sarahan's shouts fill the buffalo interior, Das shakes his head sadly. "Such anger. Such conflict. At least feel happy you're celebrating the glory of Devi ma." He gives a short wave, then seals the trapdoor shut.

IT'S TIME TO FACE the tragic truth. The Jazter will never pen his memoir. Too bad these meditations will die with him, how sad he couldn't even Twitter them out.

What, in any case, should be my concluding thoughts? What paeans should I compose, what advice dispense, what legacy of wisdom bestow? What insights will stand the test of time—a much more plausible task, now that time itself seems poised to wind down? I find myself at a loss. The sparkle has deserted me, now that the fun and games have stopped. I can summon neither wit nor pithiness, not even use my experiences to extrude a trite epitaph.

And yet the brown and cloying aroma of ghee reminds me to hurry up. It seeps through the lining of Birbal's stomach, mixing with the sulfur of firecrackers and the sourness of wood pulp. The maidens have begun to smear on our flammable coating, I can hear them titter and laugh. Where does all this ghee come from? The cows that give the milk—don't they know there's a war going on? Sarahan understands the fragrance as well, because his prayers, nominally disguised as singing, turn into frantic chants.

I realize I'm not immune from fear myself. For all this time, I've kept it at bay, my cockiness surrounding me like a wall. The panic floods in, now that this defense has fallen. The Jazter was not born to play the role of Bond. Or, for that matter, Joan of Arc. He's always yelped at the tiniest burn. He can't imagine the prospect of immolation, much less face it with aplomb.

With fear so palpable, the air inside the chamber dwindles fast. I lie in the dark, my breathing labored, my throat burnt by fumes, my mouth gritty with dust. This is how I will die—bound and gasping, pressed against the jelly mold of Sarahan's quivering body, here in this buffalo's stomach. The realization shocks me. I never thought my search would end so sordidly, always imagining my existence charmed.

What does one do in these last few minutes? What tips do gurus dispense to calm oneself before the death blast? I try to conjure up pleasant memories. Meals enjoyed, concerts attended, the first qawalli disco cut I mixed, a long-ago vacation with my parents in the Swiss Alps. The timeless cycle of search, battle, and victory on the epic fields of shikar. And then, of course, Karun—the montage softer, more lyrical, tinted in a rainbow of luminous colors. Perhaps the imminent heat of conflagration makes the memory of cooling barsati snow tales stand out in particular.

But none of these recollections, not even Karun, can keep me anchored strongly enough. I must liftoff to distance myself from what I face, I can no longer remain earthbound. Like the stages of a rocket, the different components of my identity begin to drop away: Jazter, Ijaz, Jaz—the shikari, the son, the holy lover. I rise higher, faster, freer, as I jettison every façade, every persona.

What will I discover about myself in these final instants? What awaits me as I break through these clouds? I've never ventured so high, confronted my own unvarnished being, gazed so directly into the self's blinding sun. I know I cannot look for more than a second, but that glimpse will be enough.

And then it comes. The flash, the insight, the explanation, the awareness that sums me up. To my surprise, I find it's tragedy that defines me—no matter how carefree a gloss I put on it, no matter how I try to bury it in fun. The tragedy of a spirit not quite formed, a character not yet done. I need more time to realize myself, to grow up fully, to assume my place in the world.

Except there is no more time left—the vision already begins to fade off. The clouds fold over me again, I find myself plummeting back into the dark. The layers I have shed cling back on, sodden and suffocating, weighing me down. Sarahan has started screaming, now that the sound of the maidens outside has died out.

All of a sudden, he stops. Noises waft down from above—metal clinks, footsteps scrape. It sounds like the tackle being attached to hooks, they must be preparing to winch us up. I close my eyes and take a deep breath, not caring that my lungs fill with gunpowder. Only one thing remains now—to wait for the buffalo to deliver us.

SARITA

15

AT FIRST, I FEEL FAINT AT THE THOUGHT THAT THE NEWS HAS
been a cruel hoax. Abandoning my fruitless search of yet another hotel
floor, I've raced back to Guddi's room and burst through the gaggle of
guards outside. But I only see Anupam. "Where is he?" I gasp, my
knees threatening to buckle, my breath squeezing through in spurts.

Anupam points towards the balcony. "Over there, Didi. He's your
husband, isn't he?" She smiles shyly and covers her head with the edge
of her sari. "I'll be outside, in case you need anything."

I venture deeper into the room and stop. Through the balcony doors,
framed by the billowing curtains, I behold the familiar silhouette. Light
swirls around Karun's body, splashing over his shoulders, dappling his
hair. I feel myself transported to all those years ago at the beach picnic,
watching him emerge once more from the incandescent waves. Or the
mornings that we practiced yoga, lit by the sunshine streaming in from
outside. For an instant I want to just stand there and drink him in incre-
mentally, savoring every feature as I focus on it. But then he moves closer
and calls out my name, and I rush up to bury my face greedily into him.

"Karun," I repeat like a mantra over and over again, trying to lose
myself in his feel, his scent, the line between his lips. No matter how
hard I hug his body or press my mouth against his, though, I can't seem
to squeeze out enough reassurance, can't seem to make up the deficit.
Perhaps all the agonizing days of separation are to blame, the hours
and minutes and seconds that have played out, drip by drip. Even once
I've sated myself, I think, I might never let go of him again.

Although his embrace is tight, even frantic, I cannot feel any joy communicated by him. In fact, his entire body seems strangely wound and unresponsive. Drawing back, I'm shocked to see how miserable he looks, how agitated. He squeezes his eyes shut when I ask what's wrong. "Jaz. They have Jaz. And I wasn't able to do anything about it."

His words tumble out faster than I can keep up. Something about the hotel annex, something about Bhim, something about a colleague never heard from again. "At first I was furious when I learnt you were here and Jaz hadn't even told me about it. But now I realize he offered himself up just so we could be safe." My confusion must show, because Karun stops and holds me at the shoulders with both arms extended. "You do know who I'm talking about? The Jaz who found me, the one who followed you, the one you came with. They'll kill him if we don't find some way to save him."

Although I'm still blurry, the expression on Karun's face is beginning to fill me with dismay. "Do you——?" A multitude of questions throng my mind and I can't think of which one to choose. "Do you know him—Jaz—from before, then?"

I have to repeat my question a few times before it gets through, before Karun's train of words slows, then comes to a halt. He drops his hands to his sides and stands in silence, or perhaps contrition. "It happened a long time before I met you," he finally says. "He and I—we were—we were together."

Together. Is that it, then? All that needs be stated? The way it's announced these days? Together. How should I respond? What emotion should I bring to my face? Of all the reactions that flood my mind, none seems entirely appropriate to display. It's not as if I haven't brooded about this possibility, as if I didn't have any warning, any time to prepare. Perhaps my defense is I've never encountered a Mills & Boon heroine confronting this situation, I don't have a template to follow from Bollywood films. Shock or disappointment or horror or hurt—I wait for the spin to stop, for the arrow to point the way. "I'm sorry," Karun mumbles.

And then the wheel bearings lock—in a surprise photo finish, anger wins. It no longer matters whether I saw this coming or not—my fury sweeps all such irrelevancies away. The rigors of my journey, the strain of the past weeks, the insecurities of our entire marriage perhaps, fill me with a desire to exact vengeance, to punish Karun for the pain he has inflicted. Sorry is not enough. *Together* is not enough. Vast reservoirs of indignation rage inside me, they must be tamed.

I make him start at the very beginning, tolerating no omissions, brooking no euphemisms. Each time he tries to finesse over something private, I insist he reveal every embarrassing detail. How exactly did Jaz initiate him that first time? What did he do to reciprocate? What is the physical sensation like, lying on his stomach and being penetrated? Is that it then—my spouse's preference? What my pati-dev, my husband-god, specializes in?

At some point, Karun begins to cry, but his tears are insufficient to slake my need to humiliate. I show no expression, no vulnerability, even though my insides churn at the things I force him to relate. How many times did they do it on the library balcony? Where did they dispose of the soiled newspapers afterwards? Could they smell the bird shit as they fornicated amidst it? I ask each question as clinically, methodically, as if administering a lie detector test. This is surgery that must be performed, I tell myself, an exorcism that must be completed. Perhaps cruelty also plays a part in it.

"Stop, we have to save Jaz, don't you understand?" Karun cries out. He has pleaded with me that he didn't bring it up before marriage because it was all in the past, that he has never been unfaithful since, never given in to Jaz's demands. But I remain unmoved. Why did he run away to Bandra? I ask yet again, even though he's already explained the harassment (but really, wasn't it temptation?) he was trying to escape. This time he simply sobs and doesn't reply. I soldier on, trying to formulate more questions to torture him with.

Eventually, my wrath is spent, my vitriol voided. The churning in my stomach has given rise to nausea—I'm revolted by the sordidness of what I've wrung out of Karun, appalled at myself. I step outside, leaving him slumped on the sofa. "I'm going for a walk while Sahib sleeps," I tell the guards.

One of them insists on tagging behind—an order he's received. I take the steps down to the garden and sit in a beach chair by the pool. The tiles have been baking in the sun since morning, but I take off my sandals to let the heat sear the soles of my feet. The only people I see are in the distance on the stage, preparing for the devotional songs later this evening. An elephant labors amidst them, ferrying poles in its rolled-up trunk. I turn my face up to the sky—I want the sun to sublimate the anger from my body.

Perhaps the sunrays do have healing properties, because through my torrent of emotions, I am able to latch onto a single steadying thought. For the first time, I can begin to unravel the years of questions jamming my mind. All the attempts that failed in bed, all the times I blamed myself. Here, in the middle of this war, in this hotel where we wed, I start to see my marriage with Karun in a revealing new light.

What I keep returning to is whether I want to continue with Karun, whether this is something I even *can* do. The Jantar Mantar, the snatches of intimacy, the stars and statistics—will they still be enough? The prospect seems uncertain, now that the mystery is gone, replaced by a raw openness. How will I forgive Karun, recalibrate the delicate balance of our alliance?

On the other hand, what is the alternative? What chance do I have to start again, with the war and all its looming threats? Surely with some work I can salvage enough of my earlier contentment. Screen off what happened, since it occurred before our marriage—not let it drive us off the track.

I'm pondering the question of trust, about how I can be certain Karun won't go trawling after other men in the future, when my line of thought leads me down a less than noble path. Karun's been faithful all these years, somehow keeping his cravings in check. Perhaps it's a consequence of his low sex drive, but he's never gone burrowing through the muck for anything else. The only reason he acted this time was that Jaz reappeared. I feel my indignation spike towards Jaz—not only for the blatant invasion of our marriage, but also for the way he hood-winked me into leading him here. Should I be that devastated if he gets his just deserts? Wouldn't we be safe if this stimulus never returned? Surely it's in my interest—*our* interest—for the temptation of Jaz to vanish, once and for all?

Instantly, I feel mortified, ashamed of myself. I mean no ill, I rush to reassure the life forces of the universe, to clarify for any hovering spirits. Without Jaz's help I wouldn't even be here—it isn't in my nature to wish harm on him or anyone else. I think of Karun's despera-tion, of his anguished pleas to save Jaz, who's apparently ready to sac-rifice himself for our sake. Despite any lingering resentment, of course I will try everything I can to rescue him.

And yet, a corner of my mind can't help make the guilty calcula-tion: What chance do Karun and I have against the whole of Bhim's apparatus? No matter what our tack, the odds of prevailing look grim—I try not to let this realization run wild in my brain. It's not my fault Jaz decided to follow me, I remind myself—I should have noth-ing on my conscience if we don't find him. Which wouldn't necessarily signify something morbid—for all I know, Bhim could have secretly released him.

Returning to the room, I find Karun hasn't moved from the sofa. I do not reveal my decision to stay with our marriage. Instead, I go to the bathroom and wash my face, then bring out a wet towel and hand it to him. "We have to see the Devi. She's taken quite a shine to Jaz. If anyone can save him, she will."

THE GUARDS EXPLAIN their orders apologetically. We're allowed to descend chaperoned to the garden, but cannot converse with any-one. An audience with Devi ma is out of the question. They'll let me talk to Anupam, but technically, even she should be off-limits.

Before they can change their minds, I hurriedly give Anupam my message. "Tell Devi ma my husband saw her beloved Gaurav taken prisoner in the hotel annex. She has to find him and free him at once or Bhim will have him killed."

Anupam gets very nervous—she won't remember the message, she has to report to the kitchen for work, do I really expect anyone will allow her up to see Devi ma? I tell her she can convey it to Chitra in that case, make her repeat the lines a few times, and send her on her way.

There's little to do now but wait. The prospect of lingering in the room with the claustrophobia of what's passed is too grim, so Karun and I sit on a bench near the base of the steps. He will not look at me— holding his head in his hands, he rocks his body to and fro silently. Every few minutes, he gets up to pace, like an anxious relative keeping vigil outside an operation theater. I try to summon up sympathy for him, but my own self-pity keeps getting in the way.

I expect the Devi to send for us, for Chitra to appear, or even Anupam to return and tell us what happened. But nobody comes. The hotel turrets turn gold, then crimson in the setting sun, their shadows lengthen over the pool and badminton courts. An attendant brings us tea, then a plate of biscuits and samosas. The sounds of dholak and musical tongs waft across the gardens—I notice an audience has clumped around the stage. Through the darkening twilight, a large white buffalo shape glides surreally past the backdrop of the farther-most hotel wall.

Just when Karun seems to have rocked himself into a trance, and I'm despairing that everyone's forgotten about us, the guards approach. "They've called you upstairs. To Devi ma's floor."

THE CLERKS OUTSIDE the suite are as stubborn and nitpicking as before. They want to know who Karun is, where he has appeared from, why they weren't apprised of his visit in advance. Our escort of guards fails to impress them—only when Chitra appears and answers all their questions, do they grudgingly allow us to proceed.

"I'm glad Gaurav was able to find your husband," Chitra says, her tone sounding anything but pleased. "Though letting him go off with Guddi has created a big headache for us. Devi ma is very upset. She keeps asking for her Gaurav-ghoda. Without him, she refuses to eat or even talk to anyone."

"But I sent you a message. Through Anupam. Didn't you get it?"

"Yes, yes, the girl from the kitchen who ruined her sari. She came up to say that Gaurav's been captured—somewhere in the annex, apparently. Despite all my warnings to keep away—now you see what happens to those who don't do as I say."

"But haven't you informed Devi ma? All she needs is to give the order. To have Gaurav freed, no matter where he might be."

Chitra makes a scoffing sound. "If only it were that easy. We're talking about Bhim's annex—despite what you might imagine, Devi ma doesn't control everything. If that's where Gaurav is, we can't just blunder in—why do you think I kept pretending it was unoccupied? Guddi seems to have vanished as well, or I'd ask her what happened, exactly."

"You mean you haven't done a thing to look for him?" Karun cuts in. "All this time my friend might be getting killed and you've kept us waiting around uselessly? I've already told you what happened, what more do you need?"

Chitra stiffens. "I have bigger problems to worry about, whoever you think you might be. If your friend had listened to me and not gone in there, he'd be safe. Instead of endangering not only himself, but also poor Guddi—"

"If he had listened to you, he'd have never found me—"

"What my husband means," I interject with a conciliatory note, "is that perhaps you could at least try telling Devi ma, to see if something might come of it."

"Tell Devi ma?" Chitra laughs. "Do you hear that racket outside?" I pause to listen—muffled crashes issue from the terrace, interspersed with yells and screams. "That's her, breaking every bottle and plate because Gaurav's missing. Any minute now she's going to decide to escalate into her Kali mode—demand a drink of human blood or try to set fire to the place. My job is to protect her, prevent her from getting to that stage. Goading her on about Bhim, when she can't really do anything about him, will only get her more inflamed."

Chitra shakes her head. "Besides, Bhim is the only one who can calm her down from this state. He'll be here any moment now—in fact, he's the one who ordered you brought up to wait for him."

"Well, I've waited enough," Karun says. "If you won't tell Devi ma, I will." Sidestepping Chitra, he strides towards the terrace. He dodges the guards and bursts out through the door, as Chitra, shouting for him to stop, gives chase. I follow as well, narrowly escaping the grasp of a Khaki who lunges my way.

The air outside smells of burning plastic—by the edge of the infinity pool lie the smoking remains of a beach chair. One of the potted trees is also on fire, which the attendants try to douse with water scooped out from the pool in a saucepan. Biscuits and pakodas and colorful orange laddoos float in the water, along with wooden trays, a plastic table, even an upturned throne bobbing amidst a swirl of red fabric. The terrace is littered with such a profusion of broken china that I wonder who could have supplied the Devi so many plates. At first I can't locate her amidst the pandemonium of all the people running around. Then, behind a ring of devotees broken free from their guards, I spot the flash of a neck painted gold, the glimpse of a stunted arm.

We all run up to this human barricade, where Chitra tries to cajole the Devi out. The devotees chant and raise fists in response—the plates must be spent, because only a few odd pieces of cutlery come sailing out. A cry of pain shudders up from behind the cordon—through the shifting thicket of legs, I catch a glimpse of an attendant lying ashen-faced on the ground. Red stains the collar of his beige uniform. The Devi lies stretched atop him, her face buried deep into his neck, as if engaged in something carnal. The legs shift again, and now she looks up. Blood drips from her mouth, like from a feeding animal's snout.

"Get them away," Chitra shouts, and the guards get busy using their rifle butts to knock devotees down. But each time one falls, two more surge in, their passion so strong that first one, then another Khaki gets swallowed by the crowd. Somewhere in the melee, the supine attendant manages to crawl away, his neck awash in blood, as if punctured repeatedly by a fledgling vampire just learning to suck. I catch a glimpse of a woman disciple eagerly take his place—she unbuttons her blouse to bare her neck, a look of beatific anticipation on her face.

Eventually, though, the rifle butts prevail—the gauntlet is penetrated, the Devi exposed. Startled, she springs off her new and freshly bitten donor, landing cat-like, on her hands and feet, in a crouch. She hisses at the advancing guards, then rises to her full height and growls. "Careful," Chitra cautions. "Remember that touching Devi ma is not allowed."

"Yes, remember touching me is not allowed," the girl mocks, lunging at the guards, forcing them to back away. She raises her good arms above her head, then flaps them up and down, as if chasing after birds or pretending to be a plane taking off. It's a move I remember from *Superdevi*, used by the heroine each time she wanted to change herself into a particularly fearsome avatar. Nothing happens—the Devi girl remains untransformed. "Kneel down and touch your foreheads to the ground," she commands, apparently undaunted by this deficiency in her transmogrification powers.

One by one, the guards and attendants obediently prostrate themselves, with the devotees (those not already knocked down) enthusiastically joining in as well. Chitra looks on tight-lipped as Devi ma steps on the nearest Khaki, mashing his face into the floor with her foot. She zigzags across the arrangement of backs as if playing a sprawling game of hopscotch. "Why are you still standing?" she demands, coming to a stop before us. She beats her arms vigorously—perhaps a last-ditch effort to give her metamorphosis a kick-start.

Chitra draws back a bit but Karun stands his ground. "Because I have something to tell you. I know where your Gaurav is."

"Who are you?"

"His friend. The one he came to find. We were together when Bhim captured him."

No sooner has Karun pointed the finger when Bhim himself walks through the terrace doors.

I'VE SEEN BHIM in photographs and videos, but never in person, nor in full regalia. Locks cascade from under warrior headgear, gold breastplate and armguards gild him as splendidly as Devi ma, the fringe of his tunic billows in a brocaded swirl. He strides across the floor, decked out like an emperor of yore. Despite quibbles about appropriate heft and height for one so powerful, the awe he commands is palpable. Khakis and devotees alike jump back guiltily to their feet, as if caught playing games in class by a roving principal. And yet his manner, as he bends down level with the Devi's face, is gentle. "Is something the matter?" he asks.

I expect her to curse or stomp or whir her arms, but instead, she calms right down. "Gaurav-ghoda. You took my Gaurav-ghoda. I want him back." She bursts into sobs.

"Gaurav-ghoda? Who's Gaurav-ghoda? Bhim kaka doesn't have any Gaurav-ghoda." He turns to Chitra. "What's she talking about? Didn't I tell you to keep her in a good mood at all costs?"

Chitra starts to apologize, to explain about Jaz, when Karun cuts in. "Don't believe what he says, Devi ma—ask where he's hidden Gaurav."

"Ah, so you're the one filling her head with this. The wife no longer quite satisfies your urges, I see—still pining for your *friend*." He leans down again to the girl and holds out his open arms. "The man's right,

Dev ma, forgive Bhim kaka for having forgotten. I do have Gaurav-ghoda, all safe and sound, more special to me than any guest. We'll go see him at once, right after your show is done."

"He's lying, Devi ma, listen to me—he'll have your Gaurav-ghoda killed, he told me so himself. Go right now and save your friend, or you may never see him again."

But the Devi girl has already allowed herself to be picked up in Bhim's arms. She snuggles against his chest, her stunted right hand playing with his locks, the nubs on the left stroking his neck. "He gave me a present," she says, producing the empty Marmite jar from a pocket and forlornly turning it over for Bhim to see. "The chutney inside was so tasty, I licked it clean."

"And you didn't save any for Bhim kaka? We'll get some more, don't worry." He kisses her forehead. "As for your Gaurav, I promise not to touch a hair on his head."

"Don't trust him!" In desperation, Karun tries to clutch at the girl's shoulder to get her attention. She screams as his fingers slip past and wrap around her malformed appendage instead.

"How dare you touch Devi ma! I'll have you put to death. Guards, you heard what I said. Right now, this instant, in front of me. Slice off his head."

The guards look at each other and I nervously draw closer to Karun. Bhim starts laughing. "Now, now, Devi ma—that's quite a drastic punishment. Perhaps you can show some mercy, because I need him and his wife tomorrow, at breakfast." He lifts her up on his shoulders so that she sits straddling his neck. "Bhim kaka has never seen you summon Kali quite like that before—he's very impressed."

The praise pleases the girl. She waves away the Khakis from atop her perch and makes a big show of granting Karun a pardon. "It's almost time for your appearance," Bhim reminds her, patting her leg. "Today's the big night, isn't it, to speak your lines yourself? Bhim kaka hasn't forgotten—let's go get the gold on your face touched up and fit a microphone around your neck."

He carries her away, walking at first, and then, as the girl says "Bhim-ghoda," breaking into a gallop.

THE CROWD ERUPTS in euphoria the instant Bhim appears on the walkway with Devi ma. I now understand the ostentation in Bhim's outfit—it connects him to the girl, echoing her golden splendor, conferring upon him the same supernatural aura: if she's the anointed daughter, he must be the divine father. He deposits her atop the *Superdevi* machine and raises his arms high in the air to elicit even more roars from the beach. Then, taking off his helmet, he bows with folded hands for her formal endorsement. By now, the stand has risen just enough for her feet to be conveniently within reach without him having to stoop too inelegantly to touch them. The Devi bestows her blessing on his head, the transaction smooth and choreographed, except that as she straightens back up, the lotus in her right appendage pops out from its slot. The crowd doesn't care—its cheering grows twice as loud, its exultation swells. Bhim basks in the adulation as long as he can, until behind him, the Devi starts levitating in earnest. As the spotlight leaves him, he hesitates, then makes his way back to where we stand.

"Welcome. I'm so gratified you have come to see me."

The girl's voice sounds a bit thin at first, her words shaky, but she quickly seems to gain confidence. Bhim nods in approval. "I knew, the moment I saw her in her slum at Dharavi, that she would be the one." He shushes Karun, who's now switched to earnest appeals to save Jaz. "Not now. I want to see if she delivers this part properly—it's about the bomb."

Like an anxious parent tracking a school play debut, Bhim mouths the words along. But his youngster doesn't quite pull it off. "Come to me, and I will save you from the fire," she says, then gets stuck. The seconds tick by, and Bhim gets increasingly fraught. He's about to give the signal to switch to the canned version when she sputters back to life. "I will save you from the destruction of our city, I will save you from the bomb."

Bhim claps at the end of the recitation, causing his entire entourage to burst into applause. Seizing the opportunity of Bhim's genial mood, Karun pleads again on Jaz's behalf. "Ah yes, your friend. Don't worry, I hadn't forgotten. But first, let me ask—this lady by your side—are you his lovely missus?" He bids me namaste and I instinctively fold my hands to respond. "Such an honor to meet you, so wonderful to unite you with your husband. But tell me, has he informed you about the secret Muslim hobby he's developed?"

There's nothing to do but look away, which prompts Bhim to emit a horrid little laugh. "So you know already. And what do you think? Should I release this Gaurav so you can be one happy family from now on? Or would you rather remain a twosome, prefer I remove this impediment once and for all?"

"If you think I want anyone killed, you're crazy. Release him at once."

"Bravo! Putting your husband's interests over your own—spoken like Sita herself. The ground should part open any moment now to acknowledge such a noble sacrifice. But why do I feel our Sita's not quite ready to be welcomed back into the earth's fold just yet? That she wouldn't mind if instead of her, the Muslim got swallowed instead?"

"That's such a lie. I would never want—"

"No, of course not. You'd never want it on your conscience, I understand. How could you even face your husband afterwards if he's so sad and hobby-less? But fear not. We won't let your hands get dirty—we'll leave that to Devi ma instead. Look, here comes her magic buffalo, in fact. I had them move it to the earlier show so we could all enjoy its sacrifice."

I turn around to behold the airborne buffalo, bobbing just inside the parapet. The body looks plumper than yesterday, as if it's been gorging all night to fatten itself. A line of green swastikas runs along its brow like dots adorning a bride's forehead. "I am the demon Manisha," it bellows through the speakers, and the Devi stands defiant against its threats.

"This part's still prerecorded," Bhim apologizes. "Devi ma hasn't been able to memorize the lines yet." He seems to know all the words— so well that I wonder if he's composed the script himself. *"Repent, or I will cut your buffalo head and incinerate your sinful flesh,"* he booms at Karun, mimicking the metallic voice that blusters across the terrace. "But yes, as for your request. Watch carefully, because here comes the good part, the one that concerns your friend."

Bhim grins impishly and I start to feel chilled. "I promised not to lay a finger on him," he says, winking, as a trident appears in the girl's hand. "This way I get to keep my word, and bestow a bit of happiness on Sita as well."

"It couldn't be," I whisper, almost to myself. Last night's image, of the spirit, as Chitra called it, flailing inside the buffalo frame, fills my mind. "He couldn't be inside."

"Excellent," Bhim exclaims, his head eagerly cocked to catch everything I've said. "Even though you've spoiled my surprise, even though I was going to save it for after the show." He beams as if we can't help but be delighted at this twist he's engineered for our entertainment. "Of course, with all the fireworks shooting off, you'll barely catch a glimpse of your friend."

"He's inside," I shout, clutching at Karun, who hasn't quite understood. "Jaz is inside the buffalo—they'll light it and set him aflame as well." From her stand, the Devi waves her trident, hurling more threats at the buffalo, which floats in bloated obliviousness. "I saw it yesterday— someone burning alive—we only have a few seconds left."

My words galvanize Karun. "Stop," he shouts, waving his arms to catch the Devi's attention. "Stop, Devi ma, stop, your Gaurav-ghoda is inside." He charges off, sprinting halfway down the length of the pool before the guards catch up with him. "Stop," he screams, struggling to break free from their grip.

Bhim shakes his head. "Tell your husband to relax and enjoy the show—there's nothing he can do to help. Devi ma just imagines she's doing the igniting—we light it by remote from up here." As he speaks, a burst of laser-like rays sparks from the girl's trident.

Karun is still screaming when a small flame pops alive on the buffalo's skin. It climbs up the face and leaps onto the neck, burning along the nape like a fiery mane. Smoke wafts out of the nostrils, buds of orange sprout along the legs. As they burgeon and flower, people start cheering from the beach below.

With a luxurious whoosh, a cloak of flame enwraps the buffalo. Strings of firecrackers burst forth from the eyes, a volley of rockets zooms out of the mouth. Responding to the crowd's acclamation, the Devi holds her trident victoriously aloft. The fire burns right through the posterior from tail to haunches, leaving the underlying frame exposed. I try to make out the grisly sight I know the interior imprisons, but already there is too much smoke.

A tremendous explosion rips the belly apart, generating a fireball large enough to swallow the entire animal. Bits of debris flame through the sky like meteor remnants, a shower of cinders drops sizzling into the infinity pool. The heat is so intense that the cable holding the frame melts right through, the remnants crash out of view below. Attendants rush down the terrace to douse the fronds of a palm set ablaze in its pot.

"Good show," Bhim says. He inhales deeply, as if pleased to be breathing in smoke from the air. "See, that wasn't too traumatic. Stop looking so horrified—don't you realize this means you're free? One day you'll thank me—competing with such a hobby is not so easy."

The guards try to lead Karun back, but his legs give way under him. I rush over as they prop him up against a ledge by the pool. I cradle him in my arms, tell him neither he nor I could have done anything. But my efforts barely penetrate. "So little time. We had so little time together," he keeps repeating.

Holding his stricken face between my hands, I see what he has managed to hide so well even this afternoon (or is it simply something I have refused to acknowledge?). The bond I ascribed to sexual attraction is deeper, more threatening. Despite the horror of what has passed, I want to ask: What if it had been me in the fire instead? Would his expression be as tortured, his devastation as complete? Or would his grief be more sculpted, staid—a bereaved spouse's dutiful mourning? "So little time," he says again. Hasn't he spent even fewer years with me?

But then his suffering overwhelms me. I find myself dissolve in his anguish, cry for the love he has felt and lost, for the love I have for him, and for the love, even if not as strong, I know he has for me. I hold him close to my body, kiss his face repeatedly, tell him I'm there to comfort him, I will always be by his side. Somehow, I think, we will put Jaz behind us, find a way, no matter how painful, to focus again on the two of us.

I'm wondering where we go from here, what tentative steps we take into our future, when the first shots ring out. The Devi screams, as Das, accompanying her back from the turret, slaps his neck as though bitten by a gnat, and crumples.

JAZ

16

THE FIRST THING I DO WHEN SARAHAN'S MEN PULL ME OUT IS retch. My tongue feels coated with gunpowder, my throat with fear—I double up on the ground, trying to expel the taste, the smell. Sarahan, meanwhile, gets busy smacking the person who unties his hands. "What were you waiting for? A few more minutes and I'd be a tandoori chicken, roasting in the air."

"Forgive us, sahib—the guards we managed to bribe, but they told us Das usually stops by just before the end." The man looks down morosely at his feet, trying not to flinch as Sarahan rains down more slaps.

Although the small courtyard in which Sarahan delivers his whispered upbraiding (right next to Birbal the buffalo) is, indeed, unguarded, there's no point tempting fate. "Couldn't we continue this somewhere else?" I suggest.

We repair to the nearby emergency stairwell, where Sarahan unveils the grand plans for the revolution. "Kill Bhim. It's not terribly complicated." He seems to have recovered enough from the near-death ordeal to affect his earlier nonchalance. "Have you handled a gun before?" he asks, and I nod vigorously—a technical truth, given the way the question is phrased. "Good. I want you to be the one to do it."

"You want me to—?"

"Don't worry, we'll back you up, shoot from our hiding places as well. I've thought things over and it really makes the most sense. We can simply blame it on a Muslim infiltration this way—we won't have any problem afterwards rallying Bhim's men." He hands me a revolver weighing twice as much as the pistol I've stashed in Guddi's bathroom. "Of course, they'll probably want to kill you, tear you apart and chop up your limbs. But you have my word, I'll personally make sure you escape with your friend."

Sarahan flicks his eyes between the revolver and my face, as if aware of the risk he's taking with the firearm, of the calculations spooling in my brain. Except he's wrong—I don't have the slightest intention of trying out my marksmanship on him. I stuff the gun into my waistband—with the most macho swagger I can muster, I tell him to lead the way.

We take the steps up to the Devi's level. A single follower awaits us on the landing, instead of the army I expect. I'm no expert at coups, but surely four people (five with the newly recruited Jazter) is a bit skimpy. Sarahan brushes this number off. "They'll join us in swarms. Once you've slain Bhim."

We slip in during Devi ma's show, right as Karun races along the pool to save me (the Jazter's insides wrench with emotion). Our deployment leaves much to be desired—all five of us clump around the entrance to the stairs. The plan seems so rickety, so harebrained, that I almost make a break for it, dive back into the stairwell. But Sarahan and his men are too jumpy for me to take the chance. They gesture at me to advance, and when I don't, one uses his gun to prod me along.

Das drops as soon as the shots start flying. Sadly, I fail to discharge my gun yet again, ducking behind a storage tank as soon as a volley of fire comes our way. When I emerge, one of Sarahan's men is dead, and the rest (including Sarahan himself) have fled. "Don't shoot," I say, and raise my hands into the air.

They bring me to Bhim, for whose unscathed condition the Jazter head must surely hang in shame. At least we got Das, I think, but his wound turns out to be no more than a skin graze. Both of them express astonishment—not only at my escape from the buffalo pyre, but also at my apparent intrepidity at masterminding this coup (a failure, but still).

Then they remember Sarahan. "He's the one behind this, not you, isn't it?" Bhim asks, and I'm only too glad to relinquish credit.

Which doesn't quite save me, since they start discussing the relative merits of immediate execution versus torturing me for information first. Das wants to investigate whether I'm part of some larger Muslim conspiracy, but Bhim deems it a waste of time. "We already talked to him, didn't we?—at the annex with his friend. Just do away with the gandu—he didn't seem to know anything back then."

By now, Karun has realized I'm still alive—I see him run up, Sarita in tow, and struggle to get through the encirclement of guards. Bhim notices too, pointing him out to Das with a tilt of his head. "See—a gandu, nothing more, just like I said. Surely if it were a plot, they'd send a proper man." He inquires if they have more buffaloes ready. "Go find Sarahan—I like them stuffed in as a pair. Two sacrifices in one night—the crowd will be thrilled."

Since I've just escaped the hospitality of Hotel Birbal, these new preparations make me very uncomfortable. As the dread seeps back in, I catch my name called out in a voice I never thought I'd take such delight in hearing again. "Gaurav-ghoda? Where were you? I've missed you so much." Devi ma squeezes through the human cordon surrounding us and attaches herself to my leg. "You promised we'd spend the day together, but I waited and waited after pooja and you never came."

Her thick girl-neck has never felt so welcome as I lift her up against my body. The laddoo-fed kilos seem to simply evaporate. I nuzzle my nose against her belly, kiss every digital nub, every cherubic append-age. She smiles at me happily. "What were you talking about with Bhim kaka? What's happening?"

"Your Bhim kaka wants to kill me," I announce, and make a sad face. "I escaped from the buffalo you just sacrificed, so now he wants to stick me in another and have you also set that one aflame."

"Why would he want to do that?"

"I don't know. Ask him."

"He's lying," Bhim tries to scoop the girl out of my arms, but she evades his grasp. "Tell me, would you rather trust Bhim kaka, whom you've known all this time, or him?"

Perhaps it's because I'm holding her—the reassurance of my arms, the sincerity transmitted with every thump of the Jazter heart, that she picks me. "Gaurav-ghoda is my friend. Don't anyone dare touch him."

Seeing Bhim bow, I decide to press my advantage. "Also, if it pleases Dev ma, could she tell him to release my friend?" Grudgingly, Bhim nods, and both Karun and Sarita break free through the ring of guards.

"And my gun. He took my gun. I need it back to protect you, Devi ma."

As expected, Bhim balks, which causes the girl to flare up. "Do as Gaurav-ghoda says," she commands. Bhim pretends not to hear, which excites her so much that she scrambles out of my arms onto the ledge I'm standing next to. "Didn't you hear me?" she shouts, stomping her foot. "Return his gun at once."

Bhim bows again, even deeper this time, then straightens. "Forgive me, Devi ma. But this has gone far enough." With a quick swoop, he picks her up by her shortest arm.

The girl screams as he swings her at the end of her stub. She tries to claw at him, but Bhim holds her further away from his body, then walks to the infinity pool and dangles her over the water. "Does Devi ma know how to swim? It would be such a pity if she drowned." He dips her feet in, then dunks her up to the waist. She kicks and thrashes and tries to wrap all her appendages, like a panicked squid, around his arm. "Will you behave yourself if I set you down?"

Her eyes streaming tears, she nods. But she spits in his face the instant he deposits her on the ground. Then she kicks him in the shins and runs. "Guards! Attendants! Quick, get him, someone." The maidens all look stricken, but none of them makes a move to respond. "Didn't you see how he treated me? Kill him at once." Anupam steps forward to help, but freezes under Chitra's disapproving glance. "It's my order. From your Devi ma." Still shrieking her commands, she trips and falls.

Bhim takes his time lumbering up to her. "Did you really think you run the show here? Go ahead, shout all you want." He stands over her, smiling indulgently at her cries, then bends down and slaps her hard. She screams throatily as he lifts her by the hair, then tries to crawl away whimpering, after he punches her in the mouth and lets her drop. "Do you understand now? Most *respected* Devi ma?"

He's about to hit her once more when the rumble from the devotees distracts him. They're milling around, riled at their devi's treatment, their outrage barely contained by the guards. Bhim lets off several shots in the air to calm them down. "Look, she's fine," he says, lifting the girl to her feet and trying to wipe away the blood. "They'll have her fixed in no time." He thrusts her into the weeping maidens' arms.

Unfortunately, the gun he's fired seems to jog his memory. "Ah yes, the Muslim. We were about to do away with you, weren't we, before the interruption?" He checks to see if the gun still has bullets, then waves the guards closest to me away from my body.

Suddenly, I feel very exposed. The wind blows in from the sea to swirl around my frame, highlighting its vulnerability, its isolation. "Ordinarily, I'd prefer something with a little more flair, but packing you back in a buffalo would take much too long." He points the gun at my chest, and I feel my stomach contract, my breath stop. It seems too soon, too abrupt—I can think of nothing to say to give myself even another few seconds, nothing to do except stare paralyzed into the point-blank muzzle.

"Jaz!" Karun runs up and pushes away Bhim's hand just as the gun discharges.

The bullet goes off into space. Karun falls against me, and I hold him in my arms and look into his face—in that one instant, I witness something I've never known, never even believed existed. The love I see there, the lips mouthing my name—this is what people live and die for, what they spend their entire existence seeking. It is the most intimate moment we've shared, conveyed entirely through touch and gaze, with nothing left to articulate. What good deeds did the Jazter perform to deserve such a moment?

Then I hear Bhim shout to get Karun off me, as Sarita, screaming, flings her body at us. Das tries to pull her away, the guards join in to separate the tangle, and at the edge of this drama, I notice the Devi creeping up on Bhim. This time, she carries her trident—with a yell, she plunges it with all her might into his thigh.

Bhim bellows in pain—so loudly, that for a moment, we all stop. The girl steps back to gaze regally at him—a devi staring down at her vanquished demon in triumph. But then he pulls the trident out, and she retreats a few paces. He raises the weapon and aims it at her—she gives a yelp and scurries away. The crowd parts to let Bhim through as he limps after her. A guard comes to his assistance, but he waves him away. "Come back. Bhim kaka has a lesson to teach you." He hurls the trident after the girl, but it clatters harmlessly across the terrace.

"Help," Devi ma screams, trying to get to the clamoring devotees sequestered near the audio shed. But the guards have learnt Bhim's trick—they fire their weapons into the air to tamp down the group's fervor. The shots drive the girl away—she veers instead towards the path leading to the turret. Her cries trail off as Bhim chases her past the potted palms, through the gate, down the walkway next to the parapet.

Abruptly, the speakers come alive—the transmitters are still on, and the Devi's microphone has drawn into range. "Help," she says. "Help me, he's trying to kill me." Her words roll across the terrace, sweep over the plants and the pool, reverberate from end to end. The devotees shout and strain in rage, but can't break free of their cordon. By now, despite his injury, Bhim has closed in—used to being toted to and fro, the girl keeps tripping, her puffed cherub legs unused to maintaining this pace. "Help. Help me, I'm being killed." With Bhim almost upon her, she clambers onto the parapet to try to get away.

He latches onto her foot—the microphone is sensitive enough to pick up his words. "So this is why I brought you here? This is why I saved you from your slum, you witch, you chudail?" He tries to pull her down, but she kicks him in the head with her other foot and scrambles away. Her screams echo across the entire beach, broadcast through the crowd below by the speakers stationed everywhere.

He catches her again and tries to throttle her. Her limbs thrash around, her head hangs backwards over the parapet between a pair of crenellations. The amplifiers blazon every sob she emits, every wheeze, every terrified grunt. Her choking pleas roil the assembly below. A stream of debris starts raining down on the parapet—stones, shoes, coconut shells—anything people can lay their hands on. One of the projectiles strikes Bhim and he lets go, pressing both hands to his forehead.

Devi ma stumbles away screaming. The crenellations impede her—she almost falls off several times negotiating their treacherous topography. Reaching the turret, she realizes she has nowhere further to flee. She flaps her arms uselessly, then spots the levitation machine. She squeezes into it, pulling at its supports, wrapping its straps around her neck and torso, as if hoping it will magically transport her. But she remains earthbound. "Help me please, help your Devi ma," she pleads to the mob below. Thousands of hands rise towards her, some with garments stretched like nets to catch her should she jump. She peers over, looking for a balcony or ledge to break her fall, but the turret has none. With Bhim only steps away, she inches up to the very edge and mewls.

She waits too long. Bhim nabs her before she can jump, hoisting her into the air like a puppet at the end of his arm. By now he has seen the turmoil below, picked up on the wrath of the crowd. "Look, she's just an ordinary girl, that too from the slums. She's not a real devi, so no need to work yourselves up this much."

His words are faint, and the girl's screams almost drown them out. He sets her down to rip off her microphone—she seizes the opportunity to squirm out of his grasp. But she's not fast enough—he catches her by the arm and spins her around, then slams her headfirst into the parapet stone. The microphone captures the sound of impact impeccably, amplifying it for the benefit of the crowd.

I can feel the outrage from the beach rumble under my feet even where we stand. Bhim's response is to forge on. "I'm the one who found her, installed her here for you to worship. The miracles, the fireworks, it's all a show—I even write the lines she mouths." He holds her aloft again, her head lolling like that of a freshly slaughtered calf. "A true devi wouldn't be so helpless, would hardly allow me to smack her around. If she's real, where is her holy power, why doesn't she strike me down?"

Perhaps Bhim doesn't see what we can from our vantage point— the angry sweep of humanity below him curling along its edge like a carpet to climb up the turret wall. "Follow me, not her. I'm the one, not she, who will save you from the enemy bomb." Each time he shakes her rag-doll body in the air to underscore the Devi's helplessness, the crowd presses forward, more of its members scrambling atop or trampled under the rising surge. The edifice, however, proves too tall to scale—halfway up, the embankment of bodies comes toppling down.

But the mob has also discovered the balconies forming a grid up the wall closest to the terrace. As Bhim booms on about uniting against the enemy colony in Mahim, the first devotees shinny up carved poles and swing over Rajput railings to clamber onto the walkway ledge. Khakis around us promptly shoot them down. This, however, galvanizes the long-cordoned terrace disciples, who finally manage to overpower their guards. They stream down the walkway, hauling their beach compatriots up over the parapet. "Shoot them," Bhim commands, but even with weapons dutifully fired, the surge is already too thick to staunch.

His escape cut off, Bhim backs away to the edge of the turret. He threatens to toss the girl over, waving her body in the air. Perhaps it's the breeze from this motion that revives the Devi. "Welcome," she says to her army of followers, then twists around to claw at Bhim's face.

The next moment is a blur, with Bhim shouting, devotees charging, and the Devi woozily spurring them on with snatches of her speech ("Show them no mercy," "Nourish the land with their blood"). Seconds later, both she and Bhim hurtle down towards a mosaic of shirts and saris held aloft (together with the odd devotee pulled along). The loudspeakers continue to chronicle Bhim's fate even after his body is swallowed from view—his screams mingling with the frenzied cries of the hordes, followed by a subtle series of pops quite distinct from the static, like knuckles cracking or a stale baguette snapped in two. It takes me an instant to realize this might be the sound a body makes when pulled apart. I look at the eddies of activity swirling in the floodlights, and although I can't be sure, I think I spot Bhim's head bobbing away like a coconut.

The Devi, on the other hand, seems none too worse for her tumble. Dazed but intact, she rides the adulatory swells resting on her back for a while, then sits up to test-wave each of her three hands in turn. In short order, she is presiding over a group of people pulling up loudspeaker poles and lashing them together to cant against the hotel as climbing ramps. The last glimpse I have is of her leading the charge to reclaim her abode, the arms supporting her invisibly tucked under. An airborne presence, like Superdevi herself, gliding magically over the sea of her followers.

Now that the danger from Bhim has dissipated, Sarahan and his companions finally emerge from the emergency stairwell. I shout to Karun and Sarita to follow me—the last thing we want is to get caught in crossfire between competing factions. We swim against the tide of devotees, pouring in steadily now up the various flights of stairs. As we struggle down to the second-floor landing, Sarita comes to a stop. "Would you mind waiting here? I've left something in Guddi's room I need to get."

"You can't be serious. Not again."

"It will just take a second."

In the end, we all go. While Sarita rummages around the cupboard for her pomegranate, I slip into the bathroom to retrieve the gun, with which I seem to be playing my own karmic game of lost and found.

Even the detour's five extra minutes exact a price. By the time we get to the ground floor, the entire beach seems to have crushed its way into the hotel. As we watch, the wall behind the stage ruptures open, and more devotees burst in. "The elephants," I shout to Sarita, and we push our way towards their stables.

Where, bless her little Bride of Ganesh heart, we find Guddi, who has somehow managed to install herself in the role of chief mahout. "Their supervisor was ill, so with all my experience in the village, it seemed only natural to help them through this fix. That's why I couldn't return to the annex, Bhaiyya—I hope you're not too mad for leaving you like that."

I assure Guddi all is forgiven, but we need Shyamu and her now to convey us to safety over the throngs. She frowns at the suggestion. "But I'm in charge here. I can't just take off—it's much too important a job. Just look how the noise has agitated the elephants. What if I leave and something goes wrong?" On cue, one of the animals trumpets, pulling with such force at his chain that he almost yanks the peg out.

But then another wall collapses and more people gush in. The mahouts inform Guddi that the only way to protect the animals is to ride them away to safety somewhere. They start mounting their charges and leaving, despite Guddi running around protesting that nobody should go until she decides what's best. She gets very angry when I ask some of them if they will carry us along. "Didn't you just say you wanted Shyamu and me to take you? Are we suddenly not good enough?"

Once I've soothed her feelings, she lines Shyamu up at the mounting stand so we can all get on. Clambering onto his head, she aims him towards a breach in the hotel wall through which the silvery sea is visible. She feeds him a small laddoo produced from somewhere under her sari. Then, unmindful of the screams of panicked devotees underfoot, Guddi steers us out towards the freedom of the sands.

SO IN THE END, fate gives the Jazter a last-minute reprieve, another shot at the Karun sweepstakes. I would have preferred just the two of us on the elephant (or, since we're fantasizing, on a boat to some safe and secluded island), but still. One thing that's changed: Karun has told Sarita about us—I can tell from their silence, see it in their faces. Which is excellent news—best to have everything out in the open, should Sarita claim the moral high ground because they're married, or Karun be tempted to choose duty over love again. The Jazter has outgrown his Mahatma phase—no longer will he cede or sacrifice, watch his love wrested away. Now that it's down to the home stretch, he's going to make sure this journey ends the way he wants it.

SARITA

17

AFTER THE EUPHORIA OF ESCAPE HAS SUBSIDED AND THE CLAMOR of the crowds abated, after the moonlit beach has turned pristine and unpeopled again, I experience the strange sensation of being transported to another time, another place. Perhaps it is the rhythm of the elephant, the rocking cadence that pushes me back and forth against Karun, the soothing comfort I derive from the shoulder against which I brace myself. The stars shine down fondly on us, the breeze blows in coolly from the sea, and I feel secure, protected. Then I realize Karun is holding on to Jaz's body just as I am holding on to his. Instantly, I find myself in the present again.

Too many thoughts flare up in my head, thoughts I haven't been able to utter in Jaz's presence. After the roller coaster of events, I no longer know where I'm headed, where I stand. With Jaz glomming onto us so resolutely, what odds of victory can I reasonably expect? Hasn't Karun already tipped his hand by fleeing precisely such a situation in the past? The feelings he has let slip, the artless craving in his face I've glimpsed since. I watch the long white strands of waves ripple in silently, curl in on themselves with barely a splash. The brooding buildings that line the beach, the shuttered bungalows that sightlessly contemplate me back. The choice will be made tonight, there seems no way to avoid the contest. Already I can see the approaching showdown, its inky clouds billowing with portent.

The elephant lurches and the pomegranate, round and firm, presses against my thigh. Urging me to have faith in myself, reminding me I have not played the game yet. I think of all the times I've lost and recovered it—surely there must be a reason providence has intervened so often. What magic will the fruit work tonight, how will it showcase my strengths? The memories it conjures: the elixirs before bed, the flavors and scents, the lips tinted red—will Karun simply succumb to them? I close my hand over the fruit to charge me with energy, bolster my confidence. My secret weapon, my enchanted orb—if nothing else, it will reveal my standing in the contest.

Guddi interrupts my reverie. "Where exactly were you expecting me to take you?" she asks us. "This boat you said you're trying to catch? Shyamu's not used to carrying so much weight."

"Madh Island. Where the ferry from Mahim stops—it's up ahead." Which is technically true, since it's north along the beach, though hardly close as Jaz's words suggest.

After that, Guddi starts muttering a stream of complaints. Shyamu doesn't like walking in the dark, there's nothing for him to eat or drink, he misses the other elephants. Although she's happy we found my husband, this means Shyamu now has the three of us to carry, which as anyone knows, can ruin an elephant's back. "What will I say if he's crippled when we return? Devi ma will be very upset."

Things come to a head when we reach the creek that cuts across the sand to mark the start of Versova Beach. The tide is low enough to safely wade across—however, the sluggish current renders the water stagnant, giving it the reek of a drainage channel. Guddi puts up a fuss about both the smell and the supposed danger involved. "Chhee! I'm not letting Shyamu wade into *that*. What if he gets stuck? What if he sinks?" No amount of cajoling seems to move her. Finally, Karun remembers the cell phone he's carried, uselessly, through all his misadventures. "So many buttons!" Guddi exclaims, punching at the keys and pressing at the display, trying to coax it to light up. "Does it take pictures? I hope it's not dead, like the rest of them."

She's dubious about Jaz's explanation that she only needs to charge it with electricity at the hotel. But she's already formed an attachment to the phone in the few minutes she's held it in her palm. She ferries us across.

"Say goodbye, Shyamu. To Sarita didi and Gaurav bhaiyya and Mobile bhaiyya." She waves, the phone in her hand glinting in the moonlight. Shyamu flaps his ears back, trumpets twice, then turns around and disappears splashing into the night.

The moon has climbed high enough to light our path, so we walk on. The sea forms a constant presence on our left, a vast and endless plain, the waves so muted they seem to stand still, like barely visible furrows. No signs of life break the horizon—no ferries or fleeing ships, no dhows with picturesque white sails. The sands are equally deserted—even the crabs seem to be in hiding.

It occurs to me that this is the first time Karun, Jaz, and I have been alone. So alone, in fact, that we could be the last three people on the planet. Didn't Karun always maintain three was the basic configuration of the universe? That triples governed everything from space to quarks? The geometry we lived in, the primary colors we saw, the particles pulsing around in our atoms, the stars in their celestial triads above. Except not all trinities are as natural or sustainable as he claimed. For instance, this triangle in which we find ourselves unwillingly conjoined.

We try the doors of a series of bungalows along a lane branching off from the beach, but none are unlocked. Jaz even smashes open a few windowpanes, but the jagged shards in the frames prove too difficult to pull out. In truth, I'm glad we don't find a place to stop. My chest contracts at the prospect of the reckoning to come. We have scrupulously refrained from all but the blandest of interactions. No talk about shared futures, no expressions of affection. Not even a touch, for fear of setting off simmering jealousies. The longer we continue walking, the further we postpone a face-off.

Just past a thicket of coconut palms, we come across a shed with a bamboo door that swings open readily when tried. Most of the shed's roof is missing, making the shelter it offers over camping out on the sand rather illusory. But Jaz points out that the beach has been shrinking steadily, and narrows even more drastically up ahead, making it too treacherous to negotiate in the dark. Karun also wants to spend the night there, so I go along with the idea. "At least the inside is well-lit," I say, pointing to the patterns on the wooden slats formed by moon rays slanting in. In one corner, we even find some rolled-up reed mats, as if someone anticipated our sleep-in.

Jaz starts dusting the mats out and announcing how tired he feels. I'm instantly on high alert—is this all a strategy? Getting us to spend the night, controlling how the mats are laid out, pulling some physical ploy with Karun once we turn in? I need to have some time alone first, play my trump card of the pomegranate. "Could I talk to you alone for a few minutes?" I ask Karun.

Before he can answer, Jaz cuts in. "There's nothing you can't say in front of me. I think we're all adults, we all know what the situation is."

"I was talking to my husband. It doesn't concern you."

"I find that hard to believe."

Karun intervenes, whisking Jaz away. I can hear their voices outside, talking in excited whispers. Finally, Karun returns. "I'm sorry. Jaz apologizes as well. He's promised to wait by the palm trees until I come get him."

I'm at a loss on how to respond. The naked competition, the open hostility, has unnerved me. I pick up the mat Jaz was dusting and unroll it with a snap in the air. But then I can't decide where to set it down. How should our bodies be aligned? What would be acceptable, what would be *fair*, what would avert the accusation of wresting too much advantage for myself? The question feels outrageous. Aren't Karun and I married? Do I need to get permission now, haggle for special dispensation just to arrange our beds?

"Are you all right?" Karun comes over to where I stand immobilized and takes the mat unfurling limply from my hands.

"I'm not sure. I'm not sure where we go from here."

"What do you mean?"

"I can't tell what's on your mind. All this guardedness, all this tension, ever since we left the hotel. I don't want to be a third wheel."

"You're not a third wheel. You're my wife."

He says and does all the right things—telling me how much he loves me, how much he treasures me, stroking my hair, kissing my forehead and my lips. His palms press tenderly on my back, until I feel that familiar melting, that incipient helplessness, that makes me long for him, long for his body, long for a return to our bed, our marriage, our life. And yet, he makes no mention of all that lurks unsaid, all the questions the night brings, the figure skulking alone in the shadows of the trees. I am afraid to look into his face—will I see love in his eyes, or mere understanding? Or worse, evasion. Even worse, pity?

But then I remember my advantage. The secret that bulges at my side. Music and candles would accompany the ideal unveiling—I lead him instead to where the moonlight is most intense. "You won't believe the trouble I took to get this for you." I cup my palm around the pomegranate and extend it to him, giving it a quick rub first with the edge of my sari. A part of me shrinks as usual at investing in such a flimsy chance, but I remind myself I have little to lose, little alternative.

He picks it from my hand and holds it up—the skin is lustrous in the lunar rays, the crown sharply etched. I look for signs of nostalgia or entrancement, but he appears curious more than anything else. "A pomegranate. Where did you find it? I haven't had one in such a long time."

"This one's from the hotel. Someone brought it for the Devi, I think. You'll have to use your hands—I don't have a knife."

He works a thumb into the crown to pry it open. The skin makes a tearing sound as he splits it apart. A few of the arils spill onto his palm as he holds out the halves. I push his hand towards him, saying he must consume it all. But he swings it back. "Not without sharing, I won't."

The fruit is a bit overripe, but very fleshy and sweet. Its heady aroma envelops us. Even in the limited illumination, I can see the juice darken his teeth. Perhaps he notices my gaze, because he closes his mouth self-consciously. More light glances off his upper lip than his lower, bringing the familiar line into focus. I watch it part in anticipation, ever so slightly—when we kiss, it tastes, unsurprisingly, of pomegranate.

Standing in that hut with the moon spilling in, I feel the future fill with possibility again. Surely it's the fruit working its magic, focusing Karun's attention on me, making the distractions loitering outside fade. I pull back to look at his face, am heartened by the encouragement I see in it. Would it be too forward to roll out the mat? Lie there and let the night waft us away?

My gaze falls to his hand, to the quarter of the fruit he still cradles. The white of the pith gleams in the moonlight, stark against the fleshy darkness of the arils. "Would you like me to take the seeds out for you?" I'm ready to crush them between my fingers for juice if he wants, ready to indulge any whim.

"You don't have to do that." Although it's too dark to see, I can tell he blushes when he says it. Perhaps the same sultry memories have welled up in his mind, the same desire to reenact past nights, and he doesn't quite know why. Perhaps I should confess the connection, spill out all the cures prescribed by Uma, the love potions, the aphrodisiacs, the Kama Sutra myths. As we scoff and giggle at the fantastic claims together, I can coyly point to their validation, at least in our case. What refutation will his scientist mind come up with? How will he feel about my long-drawn-out campaign to mesmerize him?

"Actually," he says, continuing in his shy tone, and I lean over to kiss him again. It's worth it, I want to assure him, all the losing and recovery, all the hunting and games, whether or not Uma and her coven of old wives are correct in their tales. All I need is for him to forget what lies outside the shed even for a moment, and I will feel vindicated, relief will pour in. The pomegranate will have delivered its answer, fulfilled its long-heralded promise, reassured me about where

I stand with him. I wait for the words that will bind just the two of us, wait as they emerge even now from his lips.

"Actually, Jaz might like some, too. I thought I'd save this piece for him."

WE ARRANGE THE mats side by side to form one big rectangle. I feel uncomfortable sleeping together with Jaz like this, but it's the only way to defend my interests—lying apart would leave Karun completely exposed to his wiles. Karun has already parried my hints that Jaz remain outside—claiming it's too open, too sandy, too unsafe. "All I can think of is how amazing it is that we're all alive, that we all escaped. Let's just concentrate on sleep tonight, celebrate that way. Leave any problems for tomorrow—we've endured enough for one day."

The mats are very thin, each reed presses separately into my skin. Jaz finds pieces of gunnysack in a corner to fold into pillows for our heads. Neither he nor I say much—we repose on either side of Karun, the status quo configuration inherited from the elephant. I want to be close to Karun, feel my body tingle against his. But I refrain even from putting my arms around, for fear of touching Jaz, or worse, provoking more aggressive maneuvers by him.

Even with the sea so close and the roof so compromised, the air inside the shed feels hot and still. I lie on my back and try to make out the mosquitoes I can hear swarming above my head. Karun curls his hand around mine and rubs it, more in reassurance, I believe, than anything else. Is he also rubbing Jaz's hand the same way?

I must doze off, because I have the sudden sensation of waking. The moon is lower now, its rays so oblique they now form a patch on the wall. The mosquitoes circle and hum as before. Perhaps the heat has roused me—sweat drips down my neck, soaks through the layers of my sari. I notice Karun has removed his shirt, so I unwrap the fold of material covering my blouse. This doesn't cool me much, so I decide to rid myself of the entire sari. Slowly, quietly, I ease out the pleats tucked into the waistband of my petticoat.

Despite my efforts at soundlessness, Karun stirs. He reaches out to squeeze my fingertips, then draws closer to snuggle against my chest. Perhaps my blouse is too moist with perspiration, because almost immediately, he lifts his head off. I stiffen as he starts undoing the hooks—after all, Jaz reposes only inches beyond. Karun kisses the space between my breasts once he frees them from the cloth. "Your petticoat is damp too," he whispers.

We both end up naked. I feel too exposed with Jaz in the same room, so I draw back my divested sari to spread like a sheet over us. Every rustle and scrape gets amplified in the confines of the shed, and I keep worrying we will awaken Jaz. But he dozes through it all—the kisses and nestling and exploration as Karun and I reacquaint ourselves with each other's person. "So long since I slept next to you," Karun says, and I wonder how I could have mistaken his earlier dispassion, misread the pomegranate's call. As his excitement reaches its usual modest plateau, I realize I can't sustain it. We don't have enough room for free movement, for gymnastics like Jantar Mantar. My body ignites just as his fades. He embraces me in a cuddle that promises only affection, unaware of the chemicals that surge through my blood ways.

Karun nuzzles against my body. I caress his neck as he drifts away. It takes me a while before I can calm myself enough to follow him.

Neither the night nor the heat has lifted when my eyes next open, but something has changed. Karun's breath comes in rasps—he still holds me, but his body seems further away. Abruptly, he arches back his neck, and I feel the fullness of his manhood press into me. I think he's in the midst of a dream, but through the darkness, I glimpse his eyes are open. He subsides, then pushes forward again, his whole body arching this time, his legs and torso meeting at the focal point of his groin. Seeing me awake, he buries his face in my neck and covers it with kisses. As he presses forth, he pulls me to him, so that my body bends against his in the same arc, like in the yoga asanas we once practiced. I feel his penis climb up my thigh.

His hands caress my breasts, his lips work down the hollow of my throat to my chest. Thrown off by his movements, my body nevertheless responds to his touch. He groans as I take him in my hand. I'm unsure what drives him, but I want him to continue, I will help any way I can.

That's when I glance beyond. At first I think it's just an aberration, the darkness massing together into a shadow more substantial. As my eyes adjust, I realize it's Jaz. Naked and awake, engaging Karun in what way, I can't exactly tell. Instantly, I retract. Karun tries to hold on to me. "Wait," he gasps.

Jaz wraps an arm around Karun's chest and draws him away towards his own body. "Wait," Karun says again. "No, not yet." His eyes close and his words trail off as he leans his head back. Jaz twists around as if preparing to devour him—clamping his mouth over Karun's, silencing him before he can utter anything else.

For an instant, I watch as Karun lolls helplessly in Jaz's control. Limbs flash, chests strain, muscles flex. This is the image I never had: what it looks like between the two of them. Not content to be just a spectator, I latch onto Karun's waist. As their conjoined bodies thrust towards me, I grasp Karun again and guide him into myself. He cries out my name, his pelvis pushing forward, his shoulders tilting back.

Matching their rhythm proves elusive. I lose Karun, have to repeatedly tuck him back in. To my amazement, he neither wilts nor fades, unlike any of our previous attempts.

Perhaps Jaz decides my lack of synchronization hampers his efforts as well. He positions Karun prone over me, caging him against my person, splaying his hands on the floor as if he might escape. Lying under Karun, I now feel the sensations reach deep inside me—every time he presses in, every thrust that drives into his body. I try not to think of these thrusts, try to ignore the sounds from Jaz's heaving frame. Instead, I concentrate on the rising throb of pleasure and pain within me, the same interplay I see mirrored on Karun's face. The realization that he feels every stimulus when I do, endures a version of every sensation he inflicts, fuses my experience with his. As the tides gather and the wave begins to build, I have a flash of intuition. I suddenly know what it feels to be Karun—the passivity at the core of his being, his need to be a conduit, the passion he can experience only when thus initiated. I want to share this insight with him, assure him that I empathize, that I accept and forgive. But the wave is already too close, its waters too high—before we can slow down, its obliterating form thunders in. Karun's features dissolve, my insides turn liquid, and as Jaz labors on, the two of us are simultaneously swept away.

Surely supernovas explode that instant, somewhere, in some galaxy. The hut vanishes, and with it the sea and the sands—only Karun's body, locked with mine, remains. We streak like superheroes past suns and solar systems, we dive through shoals of quarks and atomic nuclei. In celebration of our breakthrough fourth star, statisticians the world over rejoice.

Afterwards, I lie on the mats as before, with Karun at my side. I savor the familiar smoothness of his ankle, the steady sound of his breathing, the reassurance of his fingers clasped with mine. A bubble of optimism buoys me. We will complete our journey to safety, set up a house in another city, live once again in normal times. Even the dream of realizing our family trinity seems within reach now—the door has opened to this opportunity, to finally trying for a child.

Then an alarming thought occurs to me. What if our trinity is already complete, with Jaz forming the third element? Surely he doesn't plan on leaving—Karun would be unprepared to let him go anyway. More critically, wouldn't the union we just experienced have been impossible without Jaz? Wasn't he the catalyst, the very engine, without whom Karun and I would have never made it past the foothills of the slope we climbed?

I feel chilled, even though the air around remains as oppressive. I imagine a lifetime of sharing, of deference, of compromise, the role of a less privileged wife. What allowance would I get of Karun's day, what part of his attention, his love, his life? Given Karun's hopeless passiveness, wouldn't I have to struggle with Jaz over every day, every minute? And sex—would it play out like tonight, Jaz calling the shots each time? The indispensable savior, the proud conqueror, riding in on his own wave a few seconds after mine?

The sky slowly lightens in the hole above us. I watch the dawn advance, swallowing the stars most weakened from their vigil through the night.

A TERRIBLE THIRST, much worse than the accompanying hunger, afflicts us all in the morning. We look longingly at the coconuts sprouting from the unreachable tops of the nearby palms, fantasizing more of their sweet juice than their meat. Jaz breaks into a cluster of shuttered stalls just off the beach, finding the first three completely stripped of their wares. In the fourth, he gets lucky while feeling around under the counter, discovering both a one-liter Pepsi bottle filled with water and loose Marie biscuits in a plastic bag—someone's personal stash, perhaps. "Not quite Gluco," he tells Karun as we eat the biscuits, and they both smile. I feel left out at the private joke, but nothing like the shock I experience when Jaz leans forward and plants a kiss on Karun's lips.

"You shouldn't mind him," Karun says, while Jaz is off trying to break into another stall. "The Gluco biscuits—when we first lived in Delhi, we shared a packet for breakfast every day."

I look at the sea, at the resurgent tide, at the frothing waves. Perhaps I need to take solace from their exuberance. Perhaps I need to tell him I can't do this, he has to choose, pick a side. "He's actually very nice. You'll see when you get to better know him."

As if to prove Karun's point, Jaz returns with some salted gram he has found, which he divides between us, scrupulously to the last grain. "There's a bit of water left, too," he tells me, "if you want it."

Jaz's prediction of the beach narrowing quickly comes true—in fact, the sea sweeps right across our path along several stretches. The waves force us to clamber over the rocks stacked as reinforcement against the water. Behind the rocks rise walls, some topped with spikes and barbed wire, which enclose towering skyscrapers—or their bombed-out hulks. The barbed wire continues across the mouths of several of the lanes running perpendicular to the shore—a post-war addition, no doubt, to keep out beach riffraff like us.

The trio of fighter planes appears as we make our way over a particularly challenging tract of rock. They pass harmlessly overhead as we try to scramble up and flatten ourselves against the wall. "The enemy's," Jaz says. "I used to think that could only be Pakistan—now I'm not so sure. But we should be safe from them—they must be looking for something bigger to bomb." Before I can offer a correction based on my personal experience, we hear a fourth jet—one with a lower-pitched drone (could it be the same one that shot at me on Marine Drive?). Fortunately, the wall has an overhang of sorts under which we can all squeeze in, so the pilot probably doesn't see us. My unease is well-founded—seconds later, we hear him farther down the beach, strafing the rocks.

We sight more jets. None fly directly overhead, but their presence reminds us that the war continues in full force. Surely this increased activity is ominous, considering that the nineteenth is tomorrow. Jaz feels just the opposite, given the sounds of bombardment we hear. "If they were planning on dropping the Big One in twenty-four hours, why would they bother with this small stuff right now?" Minutes later, a volley of explosions sounds from the direction of Juhu, as if the Devi might be putting on a special morning edition of her show. A black column of smoke rises in the distance—Karun wonders if it's the hotel.

"Might very well be. Bhim apparently had a special thing going with the CIA or some other such protector—who exactly, I didn't find out. With him gone, the Pakistanis—" Jaz breaks off, as a fresh series of explosions send an enormous tree-shaped cloud of smoke into the sky. "Such a glaring target, what with the Devi and all. I'm amazed they held back for so long."

As more smoke billows up, I have a vision of Devi ma bursting through the cloud. Darting after the jets that bombed the hotel to shoot lasers at them with all four extended arms. One after another, the planes succumb, disappearing in loud and spectacular fireballs. Even as the wreckage falls towards the water, Devi ma lets loose some extra rays to dispatch the parachuting pilots—she's never been known for mercy, one cannot expect impunity messing with her. Then she heads back to land, towards her cheering droves, another morning's errand done.

BY TEN, WE STAND at the northwest edge of Versova, where Malad Creek cuts off the land. Madh Island lies directly across the water, barely a few hundred meters away, the ruins of its fort visible on a knoll to the left. The rickety landing wharf is gone, probably the victim of a bombing attack. Craters line our side as well, which is puzzling, since the shore had little worth bombing to begin with. No terminus, no docks, not even an elevated landing platform—the place has always been notorious for forcing ferry passengers to disembark directly into the mud. Further down the creek, the mast of a capsized boat sticks up through the water, its exposed lines still supporting tattered pieces of sailcloth. Two small fishing vessels float next to it like dead fish, their hulls overturned.

The bombs have not spared the fishing village next to the shore either. Even though most of the shantytown lies in ruins, a fair number of people mill around. A man walks ant-like along the water's edge with an enormous bundle on his back, while in the shade of a small tree, a woman sits next to a pile of belongings nursing an infant. Jaz goes looking for hawkers selling food, and returns with four plastic bottles of water and a stack of chappatis, stale to the point of crispness.

"I think I saw some Khakis in there. Best to stay hunkered down, in case Das and his men have made it here from the hotel."

We realize we don't know where the ferry will stop—on this side, or across the water. Jaz goes back into the village to ask around, but nobody seems sure which ferry he's talking about. "All they know is that one of the boats taking people to the opposite bank was bombed, after which the other two took off. Since then, people have been forced to swim across. Some of them drown."

Since we can't take the chance of the ferry missing us, the only sure way is to have someone stationed on either side of the creek. "Why don't I swim there?" Karun suggests. With no boat available, and both Jaz and I possessing only rudimentary aquatic skills, we have little choice but to go along with this idea. However, I'm filled with apprehension. What if something happens? If Karun gets caught in debris lurking under the surface, or falls victim to the current? Who knows what dangers lie on the other side, where he'll wait alone and unprotected? "Don't worry," he tells me, as he strips off his clothes and piles them neatly next to the provisions Jaz has assembled. "There's no controlling fate." At the last minute, he decides to take his pants tied around his waist, because he doesn't want to wait on the other side just in his underwear.

As he wades into the water, some sort of premonition makes me shout after him. "Don't go. We'll be fine waiting here—the ferry's bound to see us if we wave."

He turns around. "Stop worrying, or I'll have to take you with me." For a moment, I wish he would, that we were back at the pool and it was time for a lesson again. Then he lunges forward to embrace the water, and swims away with sharp, precise strokes. I stand on the shore with Jaz, watching the third vertex in our triangle recede further and further away.

"He's always been very good in the water," Jaz says, after Karun's made it to the other side, after I've finally stopped looking for the shark or tidal wave that will claim him, finally exhaled. "I remember, once we went to a beach at Marve and——" He stops, perhaps sensing my unresponsiveness. For a minute, we both watch Karun wring his trousers to squeeze the water out—he puts them on and waves.

"I want to apologize for following you the way I did."

I suppose I could answer that I would have done the same. But I don't—I'm not quite ready to play the make-up game. And yet, the fact that Karun is far away from the two of us brings me closer to Jaz in a way I can't quite understand. Perhaps it's the act of looking across the water, the bond of both being in love with the same person. Is this what wives feel in a harem?

"I know it's going to take some adjusting," Jaz says. "Certainly for me it will. But I think we can work things out, wherever we end up. Once we accept that all our interests lie in this."

I feel a sense of unreality hearing this from him—the idea of starting life anew, in another place, in such an altered relationship. Could he really have thought much about it? Not just about the grand issues, the ones dealing with body and emotion, but the hundreds of mundane decisions we'd have to make—cooking food, doing laundry, choosing toothpaste? Again, I don't answer, and the conversation stops there.

The ferry arrives early—saving me from the panic I might have felt if it were even slightly delayed. We needn't have worried about the two different banks—Sequeira, on the boat, spots us right away. "My favorite married couple! How's your honeymoon going? You've decided to get away?"

"As you seem to have, Uncle."

"Yes, although it breaks my heart. It's not so much to escape the bomb, as to escape Bombay." He's dressed spiffily in a cream-colored safari suit, together with an ancient pith helmet—the kind an Englishman venturing into the jungle a century ago might wear.

During the short ride to the other side to pick up the "brother" I was looking for, Sequeira tells us about the attack on Bandra—how the Limbus have hijacked a train filled with arms and are using the cache to try to expand north. "I didn't dare open the club last night, even for the final dance—too dangerous, with all the marauding gangs about. Thankfully, Afsan still came by to make the ferry run as he'd promised." The explosions we heard were, indeed, at the Indica, though Sequeira isn't sure whether Limbus or enemy jets engineered the strike. "Rumors have it Bhim's been killed—can you imagine how long people have waited to hear this? With everyone getting so wild and ugly now, Mumbai's the last place to be. Before Pakistan can destroy the city, its citizens will."

But I have stopped listening. Because there stands Karun on the shore towards which we close in. Chest still glistening from the creek, pants wrinkled against his skin, he extends his arms. I know the gesture is not just for me, but the only emotion I can hold on to after even such a short separation is relief. As soon as the landing plank has been lowered, I run across the marshy land to embrace him.

WE STAND WITH our elbows on the railing of the ferry and watch Bombay ebb. The creek, the sandbar, the fort on the knoll, all blend in, until only a crust of land rises above the waves. Sequeira explains we'll follow the coastline to Daman, before turning west towards the southernmost tip of the lobster-claw landmass of Gujarat, where our destination of Diu is located. "Have you ever been there? Such a sleepy and peaceful place. So few people, especially after Bombay."

"Wouldn't it be better to cut across the sea and go straight there?" Jaz asks. "That way, you'd be less likely to encounter any roving fighter planes."

Sequeira laughs. "See that green and blue flag Afsan's raised? It's to warn the pilots off. Part of the protection package for which I pay the gangsters controlling the coast."

It's difficult to think of enemy jets while gliding over the waves. The sea frolics around, spattering us playfully with spray, as if it's pegged us as weekenders out on a sail. The land in the distance has turned green, the city tones replaced by the coastal lushness of Gorai and Bassein. Nothing ominous flies past above—only seagulls swoop down from the sky.

"This is it," Karun says, to Jaz or me or both, I can't say. "The great escape." I'm learning not to wonder too much to whom exactly his words are directed—Jaz or me. The important thing, I tell myself, is to find the joy in them and celebrate. He leans over the railing and opens his mouth to breathe the breeze in. "I feel so lucky."

It occurs to me that I've never seen him this carefree, this uninhibited. The fact that he's losing his house and livelihood, the possibility that his city will cease to exist, the unknown nautical and nuclear dangers ahead, not to mention the pitfalls in relationships—none of these dampen his spirit. Has he even given any thought to how he proposes to appease Jaz and me, standing side by side, looking at him in shared amusement? "The wind," Karun says, his eyes tearing with the force of it. "Can you feel it?"

I do feel it. More than the wind, his unspoken belief that we will work it out, this trinity he has assembled. I look from Jaz to him. Perhaps there is room for optimism. I can't see it now, can't imagine how, but given his energy, perhaps it will be okay.

Maybe I can blame it on the wind that Karun keeps drawing our attention to—combined with the sea and the waves and the spray. Or maybe it's the roar of the boat that drowns out everything else, though I know these are but excuses. I can't shake the feeling that I'm the real culprit, for letting my vigil down, for letting Karun's buoyancy so carry me away. It's true that the arrow of jets doesn't fly overhead first in a warning pass, that by the time I see the rogue plane it's already too late. The same plane that's set to weave its deadly loop in future nightmares—to ensure, no matter how I defend myself, that the guilt remains.

One instant, Karun gestures towards us, to come join him at the railing, together breathe in the fresh and free coastal air. The next, he flies forward, the force of the bullets lifting him off his feet. Somewhere behind me the deck bursts into flame, with Sequeira calling all hands to battle the blaze. Jaz runs across the planks, pulling out a gun, firing uselessly at the sky.

But Karun. I turn him over, unmindful of the explosions rocking the boat, the smell of smoke and burning wood, the rasping drone of the jet as it nonchalantly flies away. He moves his lips but the sounds don't emerge—the line I love gets smudged and thick. Jaz comes over and rips open his shirt to try to staunch the blood—joining hands and laps, together we cradle him. Karun looks at the two of us and tries to grasp our fingers, he tries to speak or smile or reassure but the effort is beyond him. A bubble of red forms between his lips, and he turns to look at the sky as if the stars are beckoning him.

I lose track of the boat—whether we drift, or head back, or prepare to sink. Perhaps I hear Sequeira shouting, perhaps I even feel the heat from the flames. Jaz and I sit there, with Karun between us, as if we have just put him to sleep with a relay of fairy tales. We hunch over a little so that our shadows combine to block out the sun, to form a protective veil over his face.

My mind is capable of a single task—trying to rewind the reel. The plane recedes into a malignant dot, one I can forever rub off the film. Karun stands once more at the railing, gesturing us to join him. His request seems audacious, but only because it's so innocent—he's asking for something, he doesn't want to be greedy, it's only if we can accommodate him. Neither Jaz nor I can resist his schoolboy earnestness, the dash of guileless charm mixed in.

He's awkward at first, holding us stiffly on each arm as we sidle up. The pose is new, he was only half expecting to succeed, he hasn't quite learnt this language. But then he relaxes and draws us closer—so close that we could all three kiss if we wanted. His arms around our necks, he hugs us closer yet, as if this is a group shot and he wants to make sure he squeezes us entirely into the frame.

This is the still I will carry with me, the image by which I will remember him. His eyes glistening with gratefulness, his smile joyfully lit, as if he can't believe his luck, the fortune he's hit. The unsureness that's always lingered like an underlying shadow replaced by the new radiance of belonging on his face.

The sea spreads out as carefree as before, smoke from the smoldering deck tinges the spray. We rise and fall under the empty sky, borne back towards the land by the frisking waves.

JAZ

18

WHO KNEW THE JAZTER WOULD BE CONDEMNED TO COMPOSE THESE thoughts? That his story would be led so astray? This, then, is the harsh lesson he must learn. Endings need to be lived, they cannot be ordained.

Afsan manages to steer us into Arnala, a small port just north of Bombay. While Sequeira uses his mafia connections to wrangle another boat, Sarita and I search the brush above the shore for wood. Some of the pieces are too green, others too thick—many of the branches are little more than twigs. I try not to think of what they're for, try to focus on the task at hand through my shock.

We set up the pyre on the beach itself, well above the tide line. Sarita says she will light it alone, but relents at the last minute, inviting me to assist. Together, we hold a burning branch to the stack on which Karun reposes—it seems to take forever to catch. As the flames leap up, singeing the body I've cradled and caressed and loved, I have to hold on to Sarita to be able to watch. She clutches me as well. Neither of us wants to leave before the embers cool, but Sequeira eases us away. He arranges for one of the fishermen to sort through the ashes in our absence and immerse the remains.

Back at sea, my grief gives way to rage. Rage against the enemy, rage against the war, rage against everything that's conspired to snatch Karun away. How arbitrary, how wasteful and unfair, after the impossible gauntlet of hurdles we overcame. I scour the sky like King Kong, ready to reach up and pluck off Pakistani planes. Bring on your worst,

I silently rail—bullets, bombs, nuclear explosions—I'm ready to confront them all.

But the horizon remains untroubled by jets or mushroom clouds. The sky doesn't rend, no seaquake announced the arrival of the scheduled doomsday. We journey through the night, reaching Diu on the nineteenth around eleven a.m.

The town is in a panic, even though Ahmedabad, the nearest target on the list of eight, lies three hundred kilometers north. People crowd the dock waiting for long-departed boats to convey them to safe havens (where these might be located, nobody can probably pinpoint). Some hunker down in their houses, hoping their bolted doors and shuttered windows will persuade any impending malignancy to move on; others roam the streets with clubs and pellet guns and old muskets, searching, perhaps, for the leader seasoned enough to mobilize them. "Why did you leave Mumbai?" an acquaintance asks upon spotting Sequeira. "Hasn't the Devi appeared there in person to keep away the bomb?"

Sequeira takes us to his family mansion off Fort Road, where his siblings Vincent, Paul, and Mildred live in a large joint household. He tells them about our recent bereavement, but enthralled by the approaching cataclysm, they barely register our grief. Vincent and his son take turns cranking a hand-generated emergency radio, only to get static no matter where they set the dial. Sarita and I crowd around as well—perhaps the future will distract us from our own mourning. But our attention quickly veers back—nothing can feel as real or compelling as Karun's loss. The drama of Diu's survival (or for that matter our own) is like a television show in comparison, one we find only moderately engaging.

The sun emerges as brightly the next morning. The heavens look clean and radiant. Relief washes through the streets and the docks, now that the nineteenth has passed, now that Diu has survived the date without any harm, any nuclear shockwaves. Sequeira's sister Mildred complains of a smokiness in her throat, a greenish tinge to the air. But by the time the magnificent sunset lights up the seafront, with its golden rays reaching towards the old Portuguese church on the hill like the fingers of God, she agrees it has to be her imagination. The next evening, when the sun makes an even more spectacular exit, with eloquent streaks of orange and red and magenta, she's ready to proclaim the end of the war. The local Jain community floats little earthenware oil lamps into the sea to give thanks—a ritual that soon encompasses Hindus and Muslims and Christians as well.

Sequeira drags us to the celebration by the water's edge to cheer us up. I watch as people launch bits of candles on rafts, diyas made of wicks and tin cans. All I can think of, as the points of twinkling gratefulness carpet the bay, is Karun. Could we have remained safe in Bombay, did we lose him for naught? What if he'd survived just one more day?—would that have conducted him past the end of the war?

Mildred interrupts my rumination to tell me about Diu's charmed existence. Except for a stray air raid on some old office buildings in the center, the town has remained unscathed. Moreover, religious rancor has not been a problem—not like nearby Veraval, with its brutal massacres of Muslims. "Yes, our electricity's gone, and our lifeblood of trade choked off—we can no longer find flour in the market, and half our workers have wandered away. But show me one place in the world that doesn't have these problems now. Diu's escaped the worst of it, thanks to the lord."

More people turn out the next evening, drawn by the sunset, which now scintillates with an extended palette from yellow to purple. Even I'm amazed by the unusual striations of green, ribbing the sky like a sprawling celestial skeleton. Revelers throng the terraces of the old houses overlooking the harbor to watch the show below, the diya lamps now replaced by triumphant bonfires blazing from victory floats. Something about this escalating drama makes me uneasy. We have yet to receive any news from the outside, even from Ahmedabad (Vincent can still only crank static from his radio). I try to recall what I've read about particulates in the atmosphere, about dazzling sunsets after volcano eruptions. But caught up in the town's festive mood, I decide I'm fretting for no good reason.

The fish start washing up at dawn. By midmorning, the shore is so thick with them that the water no longer flows in waves, sloshing instead against a solid rim of carcasses. Although most of the fish have decomposed or been partially eaten, several still have intact heads, their eyes clear and wide open, as if witness to a sight so shocking it has caused instant death. Given the scarcity of food supplies, some of the townsfolk go up with baskets to salvage the more edible-looking chunks.

The sea soon turns black, putting an end to the foraging. At first, it looks like a vast expanse of shadow, the kind that rolls in under approaching clouds. But the sky is clear, and the shadow turns out to have great density and substance—clumps of ash and filament and debris, as if a giant cremation urn has been emptied into the sea. Larger pieces float in as the tide intensifies—charred lumber and furniture, blackened corpses that joust with the fish for space on the beach, even an enormous banyan, its leafless branches as tarry as its roots, hurled onto shore by the increasingly angry waves. At some point, it starts looking like a tsunami, and residents gather at the fort, abandoning their low-lying houses. But although the sea advances all the way past the waterfront stalls and across Fort Road, it eventually subsides, leaving behind a profusion of listlessly floating objects. A mass one could almost walk across, like ice floes in an Arctic waterway.

Is the debris radioactive? The local government surveyor examines the depth of the char marks and declares it likely. Parents start shrieking at children to get away from the banyan, whose roots have somehow become irresistible playthings to swing from. A woman hysterically tries to vomit up the fish she's ingested for lunch. A gang of urchins continues sorting through the wreckage for valuables, unmindful of the commotion.

Assuming the soundness of the surveyor's diagnosis, a city has been hit. The question is which one? The only possibility can be Bombay—

none of the other seven places on the list lie on the Arabian Sea. Except it's October, when the monsoon currents are in the process of reversing. The debris could equally well have floated in from the other direction, down from Pakistan—in which case the city destroyed would be Karachi. Or even some place further, like Muscat, in Oman.

The panic, which bubbled off into euphoria just a few mornings ago, surges back. Nuclear bombs are like potato chips, nobody can stop at just one. Every scenario predicts that a country under attack will launch all its weapons at once to avoid losing them. Does this mean all eight targets on the list have been struck? What about the remaining two hundred or so warheads in the combined possession of India and Pakistan? With even a single missile fired, wouldn't the two enemies have responded by launching this entire arsenal?

Continuing this line of thought, once such attacks started, wouldn't other countries be unavoidably drawn in? Could they have set off enough devices to obliterate life on the entire planet?

The true horror of the bodies in the harbor starts sinking in: this just represents a speck of the hundreds of thousands already killed. How many untold more are set to perish?—does Diu have any chance of escape? All eyes turn to the sky, to keep watch for the legendary death clouds. The toxic masses which must now rove the globe like giant dinosaurs, devouring anything that moves in their path. Depending on how many bombs have detonated, the clouds will either dissipate over time or merge together to wipe us all out. Sure enough, the first smudge appears a day later, clotting the air from sea to sky in a sweater-like knit of grey. As some flee and others shutter themselves, the wind intervenes to blow the mass off to the north. A second cloud the next week blusters right into town. But it brings nothing more baneful than rain—perhaps a holdover from the long-expended monsoon.

Reports stream in about towns that have not fared as well—over which lingering palls have triggered ballooning tumors and instant blindness. Babies vomiting blood, cattle driven mad and chewing on their own limbs, well water so toxic it leaks right through people's throats when they try to drink it. However, no actual refugees fleeing such stricken spots accompany these accounts.

One day, a couple does arrive, announcing they've trekked all the way from Ahmedabad. The woman's face is black and oozing, the man has a stump for his left hand. But they seem in remarkably good spirits. At least two nuclear bombs went off in the air on the nineteenth, they say, describing horrific funnels of death through which bodies melted like wax and fireballs gusted like wind. They've walked to Diu to offer a coconut to their family shrine in thanks. They'll go to Junagadh next to climb to the temple atop the ten-thousand-step hill.

People marvel at their pluck, offer them chappatis and milk. But after their departure, there's puzzlement about how they could have escaped, drinking tea on their verandah, when everything around them vaporized. Perhaps they've embellished things—at the very least, the bombs they saw explode couldn't have been atomic.

By now, rumors swell unchecked by the day—pouring forth from neighboring villages, alleged radio broadcasts (even some miraculous ones on television), and most prolifically of all, people's imaginations. Delhi lies in ruins, as does the entire belt of north and northeastern states. The Ganges has evaporated, the Deccan plateau collapsed, the heat has melted the entire Himalayan range. The center of the country has been so mercilessly bombed that seawater now erupts through a hole in the land. Only the southernmost states have been saved, the ones out of Pakistani range. Which means that for the generations to come, darkies will reign.

Vincent tries boosting his radio's reception with an assortment of improvised antennas. The most successful of these involves a long length of downed power cable strung just so between the papaya trees in the garden. One night, he tunes in to a ham operator warning people to stay away from Delhi, which has been wiped out by at least six warheads. The next day, he chances upon a conversation between two hams in the Delhi suburbs, discussing where one might still be able to buy fresh milk. Over the next few weeks, he collects similar snippets from Calcutta, Bangalore, Hyderabad, and Chennai, pointing to contradictory fates. He even believes he "copies" England in the wee hours one morning, but the signal is so weak he can make out little beyond the British accent. Only the sign-off streams in loud and distinct. "Cheerio, old man. G6AQR clear."

COCOONED IN OUR private loss, Sarita and I remain insulated from the prevailing disquiet. We listen to the Sequeiras argue about the radio broadcasts: despite the frequent claims of destruction, could their rising number imply the country (and by extension, the planet) has been spared? What is the significance of the clouds petering out? How harmful are the growing bouts of diffuse haze? Given that so many had already fled the cities based on the warnings, how high will the death toll rise? Questions that in our benumbed state, seem to pertain to some abstract alternative universe.

I don't own up to my deception—Sequeira still believes I'm Sarita's husband, Karun her brother. "Ijaz and Sarita," he introduces us to everyone. "Getting married against religious norms at a time like this. Truly an inspiring example, a couple whose bravery will lead the way." He has championed us so passionately to his family (direct descendants of the original Portuguese duke who set up the colony, he claims) that they have embraced us as their own.

Living with them, we must maintain our charade. At night, we sleep on thin mattresses on the floor, easy enough to separate. The little touches of intimacy that come naturally to married couples prove more challenging to simulate. Each time our hands accidentally touch at dinner, I have to remember not to pull away. We rehearse some stories together so that we can occasionally complete each other's tales. We try to give the impression that we depend on each other to survive these distressing times, that we are true soul mates.

In fact, grief does bind us together. At first, it seems like a competition—who feels more devastated over Karun, who deserves the title of most bereft? But then our individual pools of sorrow merge to form a common lake. We each swim in this lake, see each other bathe in its melancholy chill. Our grieving body of two, though small, offers us community, nevertheless. We silently stare at each other from our mattresses, reliving memories of Karun too personal to share.

After a while, though, this bond starts to become oppressive. Night after night, we return to the same crushing fact—Karun is no longer in our midst. Like our own personal cloud of gloom, the memory of that last shared encounter on the beach hovers and clings. I wonder how much time I have left on this planet. Will I squander it all pining like this?

So I resolve to leave. Armageddon or not, I want to live again, rediscover my Jazterness, revel in it. Especially since it's begun to appear that the world's end might not be nigh. The doom-laden signals Vincent receives seem much too robust to originate from the midst of the devastation they detail. I could journey along the coast, avoiding hot spots along the way—surely Gujarat is a wonderful place to explore, the *goût de terroir* is great. Perhaps it's safe to even paddle myself back to Bombay. Anything would be better than the stifling hours spent next to Sarita, the memories that slowly tighten around us day by day.

I tell her one morning. She almost seems to expect my announcement. "I'm pregnant," she says.

SURELY IF THE JAZTER took a poll on what he should do next, the advice would be overwhelmingly Hallmark. Let your heart melt, O hoary old scallywag! The cannoli in the belly, the tadpole of joy all curled up—take those tiny fingers as soon as they emerge grasping for love. Pledge to stay by the mother's side, to welcome this gurgling blessing with an open heart.

Except the Jazter has never willingly abided infants. They always look too larval, too raw, like protoplasm not cooked enough. Besides, wouldn't it be the end of everything he stood for? The end of exploration, of discovery, of experience? All those unscaled heights, those unmapped pavilions, were he to succumb to paternity's crew-cut call?

Sarita is astounded when I say I still plan to go. "Go? What do you mean?"

"I mean Sequeira can look after you. You know he'll be thrilled—it's not like you'd be having the baby all alone."

"But you're the one responsible."

"What?"

"You know. That night. It never would've have happened. You're the father, too, as much as Karun. If nothing else, think of what he would have wanted."

She throws herself into the campaign to make me stay, urging me to feel her stomach, shamelessly trotting out the "Can you hear it kicking?" shtick, even though it's months too soon to detect anything. She then claims it was Karun's directive in his dying whisper, that he grasped for our hands at the end only because he wanted to put them together. "He saw the three of us forming a family after he was gone. He always believed in trinities, as you remember—said they represented perfection in the universe." I tell her I *don't* remember—in fact, I'm quite certain he mentioned no such notion to me. That in any case, he could have had no inkling of her pregnancy. She shakes her head sadly. "He could see. He always could. You'd do as he wanted if you truly cared about him."

Such statements enrage me. Not only is she invoking a love she's never even properly acknowledged, she's trying to manipulate me with what she decrees are its responsibilities. With Karun, it had always been just him and me—we didn't get far enough to consider something as unconventional as taking in a baby. I know she's doing it for her child, a mother trying to ensure her blood more protection. But how dare she horn in so transparently? The more she prods, the more I want to leave.

I start looking more seriously into possible destinations. By now, Vincent has pronounced both Delhi and Hyderabad radiation-free, but getting there on foot is best left to hardened ascetics. Ahmedabad, the closest big city, also gets a safety certificate—unfortunately, it doesn't hold any particular allure for me. My thoughts keep returning to Bombay: the land of new beginnings, of opportunity; compared to overland routes, a sea voyage might be easier. Vincent still urges extreme caution, because of the many conflicting signals received. However, the most tangible evidence of nuclear annihilation to wash up on our shores no longer incriminates Mumbai. A small, recently discovered plaque attached to the tree trunk still sprawled across the harbor playground announces (in both Urdu and English) that this is the third oldest banyan in Karachi.

There's another reason I want to make the trip: it's the only way to definitively break away from Karun. I feel I should walk the streets I strolled with him, frequent the same beaches, the same restaurants and coffee places—most of all, revisit the shikar grounds where we first met. This is the catharsis I need, the pilgrimage that will set me free.

The more I think about it, the more the idea appeals to me. I seek out Afsan, still stranded in Diu for lack of fuel. He's spent his time refurbishing the ferry as a sailboat—as expected, he's itching to get back on the sea. He's not too keen on Bombay, though—not without more evidence of its safety. Yes, he knows the debris the sea carried in turned out to come from Karachi, that Vincent hasn't heard any convincing reports of a Mumbai strike despite two elapsed months already. "But the risk is still too great without firsthand testimony—we should wait to hear it from the mouth of a refugee." He finally agrees to venture as far as Daman, where we could stop to reevaluate the situation.

Leaving Sarita proves harder than I think. She cuts off her pleas, stops talking to me. I expect her to enlist Sequeira to exert pressure on me, but she keeps scrupulously mum about her pregnancy. At night, she lies on her back and stares at the ceiling—sometimes, I notice her gently rub her belly. I rush to assist when she falls between the tables one afternoon, but she picks herself up, refusing my hand expressionlessly. Her silence makes me feel so guilty that I start spending my days away, stealing away from the house before she awakes.

Early one morning, I head down to the waterfront to check on Afsan's progress with his ferry. I'm surprised to see a small crowd already gathered at the beach along the way, pointing out at sea. An enormous rectangular box-like object tosses in the waves—some cry out it's a truck, others a shipping container. The edges rise high above the water, then crash back with great bursts of spray. For a while I think it will just lurch off, perhaps to heave up on another shore somewhere. But then, as if tired of playing with this toy, the waves lift it one final time and send it hurtling shoreward.

It comes to rest on the beach—a compartment from an electric train, as can be seen from the pantographs still attached to the roof. My heart lurches when I see the "Western Railway" logo on the peeling brown and yellow paint—indisputable evidence that it's from Bombay's suburban rails. For a while, I peer through the broken windows, at the metal floors and empty seats. I feel vaguely dissatisfied, as if a bottle has been delivered, but without the requisite message inside. Then I realize the message is the car itself, telling me I will not be returning, the city has not escaped. Curiously, the paint hasn't scorched so much, so perhaps there's hope that Mumbai has fared better than Karachi.

I walk along the water for much of the morning, thinking of Karun, seeing our story play out against the Mumbai vistas again. Then I go home and tell Sarita I will stay.

IN SHORT ORDER, the Jazter molts his curmudgeonly crust and gets more intrigued by the coming baby. Perhaps not as excited as Sequeira, who goes around touting it as the miracle child, the new seed for Hindu-Muslim unity, a symbol of religious tolerance to set us free. He somehow manages to procure all sorts of fruit—bananas and guavas and yes, even her obsessively coveted pomegranates, which I peel and de-seed and sometimes juice for Sarita. Her teeth turn crimson, her eyes tear a little each time.

On nights when the dusty haze rolls in to fill the air, I cover Sarita with a dentist's X-ray apron Sequeira has found, to protect the unborn baby from any lurking radiation. She lies under it, sweating in the dark, and I fan her with an old newspaper to cool her off. Sometimes, she gets so warm that I have to sponge her forehead with a wet towel. It's probably overkill, we both realize—we simply don't want to take a chance. The heat is good, I tell her—she'll hatch her egg more quickly, like a chicken. She must be developing a sense of humor (Allah be praised), because she laughs.

For the first time, I get a sense of her physical self. The sense that eluded me when I lay next to her on our "suhaag raat" at Sequeira's club (even sniffed her, as I embarrassedly recall). I feel the familiarity in her touch as she holds on to me for support, the intimacy in her gaze as she waits for me to lay the apron over her. Her expression expectant, her body compliant, like someone being packed in sand at the beach for a play burial.

Sometimes, while she sits up to read in bed, I can glimpse what Karun might have seen in her. Her brow smooth as she gazes at the page, her skin lustrous in the window light. The curve of her neck leading like a fluid brushstroke to the roundness of her breast, the rise in her belly. A certain shy voluptuousness she may not even be aware of, which I can envision Karun may have found appealing. Of course, in the rosy bloom of her pregnancy these days, she simply radiates beauty. The Jazter blushes at his former ungenerous assessments— made, he sheepishly admits, in the heat of jealousy.

Every so often I imagine hugging Sarita as we lie together at night. Not in a sexual way or as an erotic experiment, but just because I think her softness would feel nice. I remain on my carefully separated mat, however—I suspect it would confuse her otherwise. As it is, Sequeira hints that given the country's probable need for repopulating, we should already start thinking of having more children (an entire litter of mixed-breed pups, why not?). I stay on the lookout for opportunities to convey my lack of romantic intentions to Sarita. Fortunately, the Hindus have endless brother-sister festivals like Rakhi, perhaps to express precisely such sentiments.

Tonight, I squeeze her hand and pat the apron over her belly. She's been pining not only for Karun, but also her parents and sister and infant nephew in the south somewhere. I reassure her they should be fine, that she will see them soon enough one day. Perhaps it's the surging hormones, but she keeps latching onto thoughts that bring her down. "All that haze outside. Won't it reduce our life spans?"

"Perhaps. But it's a lot better than being dead. Besides, if everyone's going to live a month or two shorter, what of it? Aren't statisticians supposed to look at the average?"

On the contrary, she informs me somewhat severely, it's the standard deviation that's needed, to figure out what percentage might get shortchanged at the left end of the curve. "*If*, that is, the distribution is Gaussian," she adds in warning, as if I'm raring to go out and commit a statistical crime.

I tell her it doesn't matter. "We're six hundred kilometers away from Karachi, three hundred from Mumbai. Where we still don't know what happened, incidentally. If anything, you'll be at the favorable end of the curve, with all the care Sequeira's expending."

This also makes her morose. "All the fruit he brings, this shelter, this safety. When so many are dead—I feel so guilty."

I point out that the only alternative to survivor's guilt is eternal serenity: the clear and happy-go-lucky conscience of a corpse. "Besides, why don't you think instead of all the people saved? Lahore to Calcutta, Chennai to Rawalpindi—Vincent's determined that every single one of the remaining cities came through all right. Remember, by then even Mumbai and Karachi had almost emptied. The Pakistanis got a warning too, just like we did—think of the ninety percent or more who fled in that fortnight."

I do a quick calculation for her: the loss cannot be more than 0.4 percent of the combined population of the two countries, 0.08 percent of the world count. "It might sound callous, but one has to think of percentages at a time like this."

She stares at my numbers. "It's actually 0.3 and 0.06 percent. You made an arithmetic mistake." She starts to show me all the people she's saved, then puts the paper down. We both know there's no way around the sickening magnitudes still represented by these decimals; the horror of all those burnt and twisted bodies cannot be juggled away.

ON HAZE-FREE NIGHTS when Sarita doesn't need my ministrations, I descend to Vincent's candlelit communications center in the basement. He has cannibalized the hand-cranked radio, along with various other pieces of equipment (some "borrowed" from the Diu airport) to construct a transceiver set. "Almost as good as the ham radio I had, before the power surges blew it out." Wires leading outside can be connected to different antenna configurations laid out in the garden (his "aerial farm," he calls it)—for nighttime hours, he finds the swastika shape works best. The family has dedicated the diesel generator, with its precious remaining supply of fuel, to his communications experiments.

With his enhanced setup, Vincent manages to put together a much clearer picture of what lies beyond Diu's shores. The two-way communication allows him to quiz operators to test their genuineness. "What numbers do you see on the large sign at the end of the runway?" he grills someone claiming to be at Delhi airport, and they promptly go off the air. "From where did you say you viewed the bomb fall on Hyderabad, old man?" he asks VU2ARF, who confesses he only heard it thirdhand.

He succeeds in contacting not one, but two hams in Lahore, and they both talk about recently returning from the countryside. "Not just here and Rawalpindi, but also the other cities. People are still trickling back, after fleeing the Indian nuclear threat." The modus operandi of the warnings sounds exactly the same—swamping of the internet, followed by a deluge of calls on mobiles. "But what your savages did to Karachi—who imagined anyone would actually go through with it?"

Mumbai remains resistant to revealing its fate. Vincent still hasn't been able to find anyone transmitting while physically in the city. The most persistent rumors claim a warhead was indeed launched by the Pakistanis, but hampered by some sort of malfunction—the device detonated either too high in the atmosphere, or several kilometers off course. If so, the most severe destruction may have occurred within a smaller radius, the fallout leaving Mumbai virtually uncontaminated. Some of the airwave chatter sounds clearly wishful: the Devi has saved her city, the missile has fallen harmlessly into the sea, the Hindus have reconciled with the Muslims, even the cracks along the shoreline have begun to heal. More apocalyptic assertions, of shockwaves liquefying reclaimed land to plunge large sections of the city into the sea, appear just as spurious. Nobody can provide a plausible explanation as to why India and Pakistan each stopped at exactly one target instead of throwing their all into the melee.

Except, that is, for G6AQR—"Mr. Cheerio," as Vincent calls him. "He must have an encyclopedia just on Diu right next to him. Dozens of questions—about street intersections, museum idols, even the number of cannons at the fort, to check on me. I've never seen a ham so suspicious—all to confirm I wasn't some other nationality."

To Vincent's chagrin, Mr. Cheerio refuses to reciprocate. "He claims to be a former BBC broadcaster, says it's too dangerous to announce where he's located. For all I know, he could be a jihadi hatching a terrorist plot from somewhere in Iran or Yemen."

What Mr. Cheerio does share is news about the rest of the world. The most serious loss of life, wide swathes of it, has resulted from nuclear plant explosions. "Two confirmed reactors in each of Canada and France—a near-affirmative on at least a dozen more." The cyber viruses have ravaged the more computerized countries of the globe, incinerating power lines, transformers, anything plugged in, down to kitchen blenders and laptops. "They say the plague was bad, but this epidemic is worse. Enormous electric surges in alternating directions—that's how the basic strains work. No easy way to repair the grid—things will continue like this for months."

Mr. Cheerio does have some cheerier news, however. "Don't believe all those lids babbling about EMPs—or for that matter, tsunamis or earthquakes or locusts. As for the terrorism, it's pretty much faded. Dirty bombs have become superfluous, the jihadis retreated to their caves."

He's philosophical about the India-Pakistan exchange. "It was time. Too much tension had built up. Not just in your corner, but the world over. For quite long, the mere prospect was deterrence enough. But eventually the memory fades, there arises the need to see and smell and taste blood." He points out that the bombings immediately cut off combat not only between the two countries, but across the globe. "It stopped World War III in its tracks—hopefully, for at least a few decades to come. Even the civil war insurgents in Pakistan have forgotten what they were fighting for."

So far, although we can't verify any of his claims, Mr. Cheerio has spoken in the measured, authoritative voice of a seer, an oracle. But now he starts spouting a mess of allegations, for which he freely admits he has little or no evidence. "It all comes down to the Chinese—not just the computer viruses but also the scare of October nineteenth. Operations meant to blow off steam, kick up the sand, take their rivals down a few notches." He believes it had to be the Youth Democratic League. "They recently executed all the group's hothead leaders according to my Hong Kong old man. It might be a while before they go the liberalization route again—democracy isn't for the fainthearted."

Like a conspiracy theory buff, Mr. Cheerio has an answer for everything, even for the facts that don't quite fit comfortably. Since jihadis appear to have been involved, the young Chinese renegades had doubtlessly forged links with Islamic terrorists. The September 11 anniversary date must have been chosen, quite plainly, to draw suspicion away. He believes the Chinese had been funneling in support to both the HRM and the Limbus to keep India in a state of ferment. "Maybe even with their government's blessing. At least until things spun out of control, until the nukes got wheeled out and the viruses went crazy."

At first, my inclination is to dismiss everything—Mr. Cheerio seems to suffer from a particularly virulent case of Yellow Peril Fever. But then I start wondering. Ascribing sophisticated cyber sabotage techniques to jihadi organizations like Al Qaeda always seemed a stretch. And the communiqués that contained such accurate information of attacks coordinated with Pakistan—who else but the Chinese could supply such details? Come to think of it, didn't Rahim mention something about Chinese guests visiting his guesthouse? And weren't there reports that when the Indica faced bankruptcy, a Chinese company had saved it? Could they be the puppeteers who forbade its bombing, the protectors Sarahan refused to name?

"Let me tell you how I think the nuclear exchange played out. The Chinese must have owned up when they realized how far their pit bulls' juvenile scare had gone. Egg on their face, it's true, but they hardly would want to actually blow up either India or Pakistan. Unfortunately, even a warning issued well in advance would have trouble trickling down through all the communication breakdowns. Who knows what Pakistani general, blinded by the fog of war, triggered that one errant bomb?

"Of course the missile partially malfunctioned—I'm still trying to verify what happened and how. But could the Indians believe it inadvertent, even if the Pakistanis themselves sent an apology before it came down? There was good proof it was an accident: instead of the multiple warheads trained on Mumbai, Islamabad had made only a single launch. The Indians retaliated, as they must—they bombarded Karachi with four to Pakistan's one. Not just to ensure against malfunction, but to warn against further escalation, to punish for the insult.

"You might think me cold-blooded, but this is one of the best possible outcomes in terms of human cost. Only one or two cities struck, that too almost empty—can you imagine the minuscule probability? There was bound to be an exchange, either now or in the future—things had gone too far. Every war-game simulation I've ever seen predicted results more final, more unthinkable, than how this seems to have played out."

SARITA TALKS A LOT about Karun's triangle—the trinity the three of us formed, the one the baby will restore. In fact, she gets a bit obsessed with the idea, seeing triads everywhere she goes: sea, land, air; earth, sun, moon; even India, Pakistan, and China. It's as if she can only deal with the universe now by breaking it down into these triangular building components. "We're going to have a son," she announces so often that she might be trying to browbeat her belly into this outcome. The choice of "we" instead of "I," so alarming to the Jazter sensibility of yore, now gives him a feeling of reassurance. Sarita even claims to have the perfect name: "Karun"—a prospect that completely weirds me out. Too Freudian, I finally get across, and she reluctantly agrees to think of another.

A jag appears in our triangle. Now that life returns to normal, isn't it time to enrich it once more with the venerable custom of shikar? The Jazter finds Rohil on the dunes of Nagoa Beach one afternoon. Rohil of the long hair, Rohil of the green eyes, Rohil of the olive ancestry that shows in his skin. He's very young, only twenty or so—but oh, such a promising student.

We start meeting every afternoon in one of the crumbling barracks of the fort. There are no tourists these days, so the guards have gone, the gates never close. The Jazter teaches his eager disciple everything he knows. We mostly just lie in each other's arms—it's not really shikar, those days have grown too old. Afterwards, perhaps as a substitute, we play hide-and-seek (though sometimes soldier and sergeant) through the nooks and crannies of the fort.

Perhaps the experience with Karun has sharpened her instincts, because all of a sudden, Sarita knows. "About your friend," she says one night as I arrange the apron over her. I begin to ask whom she means, but she simply breathes in deeply. "Whoever it is, I just want to tell you it's OK. I've been through this before, and I'm not going to make the same mistake again. I know you have your needs—it's actually good for us all if someone ties you to this place." Her forehead creases, but neither anger nor jealousy colors her face.

"Ordinarily, I wouldn't impose. But these times are hardly normal. The baby's chances will be so much better with two parents behind him instead of one. If you ever think of leaving, you have to let me know. With Sequeira expecting so much from us, we'll have to think of what to say."

I try to assure her of my intention to stay, but can't quite clear the worry from her eyes. She lies there like a doll with her arms tucked close to her sides under the apron. "I know I might not have much you want. I only have the baby to give."

The night is much cooler than any so far, and Sarita soon relaxes into slumber beside me. But I cannot sleep. I toss and turn. I stare at the ceiling. Perhaps doing so intently enough will allow my gaze to penetrate through to the sky beyond.

At dawn, I finally get up. I'll go to the water, I think. The haze swirls around in the incipient light, lifting like mist from the sea. Although a few pieces of wreckage still bob against the dock, by now the tides have swept the bay clean. I look for Afsan's boat with its mismatched sails and newly fitted mast, before remembering he left last week. I told him he was lucky to have such an adventure ahead. A pioneer embarking into the unknown, like Vasco da Gama, like one of the original Portuguese. "Why don't you come along?" he replied, glancing at me slyly.

I make my way east, to the jetty below the fort. Steps lead down on either side of the strip, a lone cannon rolls on its side at the end. Across the water floats the old prison island, the sun bubbles on my right under the sea.

I think of Afsan in his boat. Waiting to see the same sunrise. What if I'd taken him up on his offer? What would I have found, how far would I have reached? Sailing along the coast with him, the explorer within me set free?

But there are discoveries waiting here as well. The future is just as uncharted, as unrevealed. The step I have committed to, the role I'll assume—becoming a father, taking on responsibility. Isn't it precisely the newness of this experience that attracted me?—the rung towards adulthood, towards filling the gap I sense inside? Had Karun recognized this need, tried to communicate it to me from the beginning? Could he have seen into the future as Sarita claimed, set up this opening as a gift to me?

Or did he, as seems more likely, envision it for himself? The three elements he was drawn to—wife, lover, and child, counterbalanced around him as evenly as the particles in an atom? Perhaps not a calculated configuration, one that he constructed consciously, but when he saw it, he recognized it as exactly where he wanted to be. And then, like one of those same particles knocked out in a collision to make room for another, he relinquished it all, allowed me to step into his destiny.

The sun has not appeared yet, but its light is already reflected by celestial streaks. They remind me of vapor trails from a jet airplane, which I know they cannot be. Are they cloud wisps, meteor paths, some other heavenly body's cosmic tracks? Believers might point to them as godly evidence, the Devi's ethereal scribblings.

Perhaps Karun would have some esoteric explanation for them. Ions colliding, atoms disintegrating, quarks cascading—all the other tricks performed by his exotic menagerie. The luminous arcs of motes as they flare through time and space. I think of all the bodies in motion, creating their own trajectories. Afsan sailing through the water, leaving a wake across the surface of the sea. Sarita and I adapting our paths so that we can continue as a family. Even the life inside her making the tiniest of adjustments to ensure it stays alive. The particles that were once Karun, now streaming free in the universe, at liberty to recombine.

Perhaps this is the place to stop. And acknowledge these myriad paths along which we strive. The sun peeps out and begins to shine on the Jazter's face. The bruised earth hurtles along, hoping to survive.

ACKNOWLEDGMENTS

TOP KUDOS GOES TO AGENT ARAGI (DOUBLE-OH-ONE), FOR HER undercover work in getting this book completed: her cunning refusal to believe me, each time I declared I'd given up on the manuscript, ensured I kept slogging at it. An enormous thank-you to my editor, Jill Bialosky, for her unwavering support through this entire triptych of novels—like its predecessors, *Devi* has acquired much polish and definition under her generous attention. My family and friends have kept this project (and its author!) going over the years with their interest and encouragement—particular thanks to Sunilla and Satinder Mody, Rosemary Zurlo-Cuva, Viji Venkatesh, Christie Hauser, and especially Nancy and Frank Pfenning, for their valuable feedback on this manuscript.

I am grateful to several people for technical assistance and background details: Dr. Sunil Mukhi of the Tata Institute of Fundamental Research for his expertise on quantum physics, W3TDH (Thomas Horne of the Montgomery Amateur Radio Club) for information on ham radio and emergency communication, Dr. John Bersia of the University of Central Florida for an illuminating discussion about China, Dr. Sumit Ganguly of Indiana University, Bloomington, for his valuable insights on Indo-Pakistan arms proliferation, and Hans Kristensen of the Federation of American Scientists for the chilling details he shared on the potential use of nuclear weapons. Ashok Row Kavi was a wonderful resource in helping me imagine gay life in Delhi, as was Parmesh Shahani, through his informative book on Gay Bombay.

Thanks to Devdutt Pattanaik who first introduced me to the alternative Vishnu-Shiva-Devi interpretation of the Hindu trinity, many years ago.

I would like to acknowledge wonderfully productive residencies at the MacDowell Colony and the Ucross Foundation. Thanks also to my university, UMBC, and in particular, President Freeman Hrabowski, for nurturing not only the mathematician and writer but also the Bollywood dancer in me.

Finally, thanks to my partner Larry Cole for too many things to list here, none as important as the tremendous joy he brings to every day of my life.

THE CITY OF DEVI

Manil Suri

A NOTE FROM THE AUTHOR

What would happen if the world around us drastically changed, if the comfort of an assured future vanished and we saw the possibility of Armageddon heading our way? What would remain important to us in such an altered universe, where wealth and long-term goals ceased to matter and everything nonessential was stripped away? I've always been fascinated by this scenario: what would keep us going?—what hope, what aspiration would be strong enough to pull us from day to day?

The only answer that makes sense is love—blinding, compelling love, the kind that demands to be fulfilled, even if it is the last goal we ever attain. To what lengths would we go to be united with the one we love; what battles would we wage, what dangers would we be willing to face?

Sarita, my heroine, embarks on just such a journey to find her missing husband. Once I cast her, though, I quickly realized I needed another ingredient to subvert any expectations the reader (and the writer!) might have. Something to blast us all out of our comfort zones, to make this novel completely different from the ones I'd written before. Thus was Jaz born—Jaz of the snarky aphorisms, Jaz of the irrepressible optimism, who lives for physical pleasure and roves around every city looking for hidden adventure—truly an author's dream character. With him aboard, nothing was off-limits anymore—together, we barreled through the ravaged streets of Mumbai, having a rip-roaring time, taking potshots at every sacrosanct target. The novel acquired an exuberance, a freedom, a roller-coaster feel I never could have imagined—guns, quarks, elephants, even a Bollywood incarnation of the mother goddess Devi materialized in its pages. In taking some of these elements over the top, I was also able to slip in a tongue-in-cheek commentary on the expectation of "exoticism" in Indian fiction.

While this put an entertaining spin to the end of the world, how to make such a scenario believable? For this, my inspiration came from the near–nuclear confrontation between India and Pakistan in May 2002. I was in Mumbai at the time, and was amazed by how unconcerned everyone was—life went on completely normally even as various foreign embassies were ordering their personnel to evacuate. It is this sense of the surreal that I observed, the absurd, that I have tried to bring out in this novel. Perhaps this is the flip side of how we cope with the unthinkable—concentrate on the here and now, cling to the quotidian. Go to the market, as Sarita does in the first scene, and haggle for pomegranates.

DISCUSSION QUESTIONS

1. *The City of Devi* has three major characters. Hinduism has three central deities. Sarita ends up with a different kind of family of three than she once imagined. Describe the role that trinities play in the novel.

2. The novel is narrated by Sarita and Jaz. How would our experience of the novel be different if Karun were a narrator as well?

3. Compare and contrast the two romantic relationships in the novel.

4. *The City of Devi* is set in the future, but in some ways it eerily resembles the present: nuclear war is a familiar threat and *Superdevi* is described as a combination of contemporary hit movies *Superman* and *Slumdog Millionaire*. Describe the ways in which the author uses this future world to reveal something to us about our present one.

5. The Devi ma who appears to save her city is both a religious figure and a figure from popular culture. What draws the citizens of Mumbai toward her? Describe the role that religion, mythol-

ogy, and pop culture play in the city as it teeters on the brink of destruction.

6. How does each of the three major characters experience physical intimacy? How does each character's relationship with love and sex transform over the course of the novel?

7. From the dead fish at the aquarium to the girl transformed into Devi ma, *The City of Devi* is full of striking, surreal, and darkly funny scenes and images. What other images from the novel will stay with you?

8. Sarita is a statistician. Karun is a physicist. How would you characterize the role that math and science play in both characters' minds, in apocalyptic Mumbai, and in the novel overall?

9. Both Sarita and Jaz are forced to disguise their identities at various points throughout the novel. The Devi ma who appears in the city is also in disguise. In a less literal way, Karun, too, has to hide who he really is. Describe the ways in which characters assume false identities. What is the significance of the theme of disguise in the novel?

10. In the end, all three major characters understand love and family in a new way. Were you surprised by the ending of the novel? Did the ending expand your understanding of what love and family can mean?

SELECTED NORTON BOOKS WITH READING GROUP GUIDES AVAILABLE

For a complete list of Norton's works with reading group guides, please go to www.wwnorton.com/books/reading-guides.

Diana Abu-Jaber	*Birds of Paradise*
Diane Ackerman	*One Hundred Names for Love*
Alice Albinia	*Leela's Book*
Andrea Barrett	*Ship Fever*
Bonnie Jo Campbell	*Once Upon a River*
Lan Samantha Chang	*Inheritance*
Anne Cherian	*A Good Indian Wife*
Amanda Coe	*What They Do in the Dark*
Michael Cox	*The Meaning of Night*
Suzanne Desrochers	*Bride of New France**
Jared Diamond	*Guns, Germs, and Steel*
Andre Dubus III	*Townie*
John Dufresne	*Requiem, Mass.*
Anne Enright	*The Forgotten Waltz*
Jennifer Cody Epstein	*The Painter from Shanghai*
Betty Friedan	*The Feminine Mystique*
Stephen Greenblatt	*The Swerve*
Lawrence Hill	*Someone Knows My Name*
Ann Hood	*The Red Thread*
Dara Horn	*All Other Nights*
Pam Houston	*Contents May Have Shifted*
Mette Jakobsen	*The Vanishing Act*
N. M. Kelby	*White Truffles in Winter*
Nicole Krauss	*The History of Love**
Scott Lasser	*Say Nice Things About Detroit*
Don Lee	*The Collective**
Maaza Mengiste	*Beneath the Lion's Gaze*
Daniyal Mueenuddin	*In Other Rooms, Other Wonders*
Liz Moore	*Heft*
Jean Rhys	*Wide Sargasso Sea*
Mary Roach	*Packing for Mars*
Johanna Skibsrud	*The Sentimentalists*
Jessica Shattuck	*Perfect Life*
Joan Silber	*The Size of the World*